PRINCE & PRINCESS

INTO THE SHADOWS

— VOLUME 1 —

HENRY R. LOVELADY

VALOR PUBLICATIONS CO.

Constructicons: May you continually construct.

And to *You*, you know who you are: thank you for all of
your support throughout it all.

⚔ Contents

PRINCE & PRINCESS

Into the Shadows

— Volume 1 —

CHAPTER I

LOSSES & LOST

I believe this will be a good clearing," Bandor says, leading a his wife to the edge of a meadow.

He smiles and steps into the bright morning sun, heaving an ax on his shoulder. He nods to the woman, who continues to hug the shadows of the forest. Bandor's wife, Maggie, wears a white cotton dress and brown burlap apron. Her brunette locks rise and fall in the gentle breeze as she cautiously slips out of the dense shrubbery. Bandor raises his axe high above his head and drops the blade onto fallen logs.

Thump, thump, thump.

He smiles wider with each thud.

"What do ya think, Maggie?"

His wife remains silent, eyeing the meadow with skepticism.

The wedded couple are honest and happy wanderers, free to roam and dwell where they please. Bandor finds dignity in being a vagabond, proudly scoffing at peasants that find security in the service of a king.

Although Bandor hates to admit it, his wandering days are over. He fears that another harsh winter in a drafty, coastal cave would be the end of his beloved wife and daughter. Pushed continually by the wailing fears of his wife, the faint whimpers of his daughter, and the memory of the burning fever that nearly claimed the wee lass during the winter, the noble father realizes that it is either shelter in the woods or death in the caves.

"With all this timber, I will make me family a nice cottage," he bellows, but what he is really thinking is that his family will survive, even though his traveling days will not. He glances over at Maggie for approval. Happiness beams in his green eyes, but worry clouds hers.

"I know you leveled the ground a fortnight ago, but had you considered that there is no safety in this vast opening?"

"Ahh," Bandor groans, waving off his worried wife. He spits in his hands and wipes the muddy matter on his patched trousers.

"I think we would be safer along the edge of the woods," Maggie continues.

"Maggie, you know the edge of the forest is no safer than this field."

"Then why build here? Can't we move away from the terrors of the forest and closer to the Kingdom of Forth?"

"You would have me subject to a year of service in the king's guard, bound by tax, and chained by the routines of man?"

"Kingdoms are safer than cottages."

"Tyrants are worse than the terrors."

Maggie sighs in defeat. "Have it your way, Bandor, but we do not dwell here at night until that cottage is completely finished!"

"We will be back in the caves before the sun sets," Bandor grunts.

Distracted by a frenzied buzzing, Maggie brushes a wisp of hazelnut hair out of her face. Her blue eyes search the sky while she waves her hands around her head, dismissing legions of mosquitoes.

"Is it safe for our little one?" she inquires.

Bandor raises his eyebrows.

"I am *not* a fear monger!" Maggie preemptively refutes, wringing her hands.

Bandor chuckles. He had affectionately nicknamed his wife "Fuss-Bucket Maggie" for her tendency to blurt out the worst scenario possible, verbalizing her nagging worries to the world.

"Can't build a home on fear," Bandor reminds her between booming strikes.

"Will the cabin even offer protection at night?"

"Relax, 'tis a beautiful day, love. This solid oak will protect us just as well as the caves." Bandor inhales deeply, drawing in the musky scent of the forest.

"The caves were not very safe to begin with," Maggie fires back, shaking her head before turning to the forest. "Come, child. All is well," she calls out to apatch of ferns.

Her daughter Princess hesitantly peeks around the base of a thick tree trunk and leans into the clearing. "I'm scared," the child squeaks before retracting into hiding again.

Her mother sighs, takes a seat on a mossy log, and pats the spongy spot next to her. "Come sit by Ma; Da will protect us."

Reluctantly, the child steps out of the dreary forest and into the warm rays. Gaining confidence, Princess skips toward her mother but abruptly trips over a root and plummets face-first into the soft soil. Her doting mother jumps to action. "You must be more careful, darling. Beasts from above and below are not the only dangers that threaten us," Maggie counsels, helping her clumsy child to her feet.

Princess snivels and wipes her eyes, smearing the soft soot on her wet cheeks.

"Oh Princess, you surely are the most helpless creature in the forest. Come to mommy." Maggie tenderly wipes dirt stains from Princess' pretty face. Tears continue to well in Princess' striking blue eyes.

"Oh, there, there, child, you are restored to whole, now shed not one more tear of remorse," Maggie comforts, pressing her daughter to her chest.

Princess sniffles. "*Tinksel*, Ma." The child wraps her arms around her mother's tiny waist.

Princess looks up and observes her father. Inspired, she hops to her feet and begins jumping from one exposed root to another.

"Look Ma," she giggles. "Am I like father?"

Maggie absent-mindedly nods and looks up at the forest. A gentle breeze sways the leafy oaks and alders. Rustling leaves scratch against each other, mimicking the sound of a rushing stream.

"He never listens to me," Maggie sighs. She walks over and takes her daughter in her arms.

"Mommy, how'd you get the sky in your eyes?" Princess asks, pinching a strand of hair and twirling it around her finger. Scattered spots of sunlight dance across her mother's face.

Maggie cups her daughter's cheek in her warm palm. "That's what you and I have in common, daughter: our eyes, our hearts, and our wits."

Always curious, always interested in everything going on around her, Princess is the type to ask questions, not the type to stare into another's eyes for long. Distractions like floating butterflies, dragonflies, buzzing bumble bees, and long-stem daises attract her attention.

"Daughter, do you understand what I'm saying?" Maggie asks gently. Her daughter's attention snaps back to her.

Princess nods. "What have I in common with Father?"

Maggie looks up at Bandor, who works without a care in the world. "At times, courage," she winks at her daughter. "When you're not hiding in the shadows like a scared little rabbit, that is." She wrinkles her nose and pretends to sniff like a bunny.

"Mommy, you're *ridic … eewwwrous!*"

"Come rest on Ma's lap. We'll watch Da build us a home."

Princess nestles into her mother's lap and watches her father work. Slowly, the girl nods off to sleep. Maggie yawns and her eyes droop.

No ... Bandor's Way. Unsatisfied, he tries again: *Princess' Knoll.* A warm smile crosses his face. He confidently grins and raises the axe high above his head, lost in his labor.

✷✷✷

Maggie slowly opens her eyes. She feels Princess' warm face and rapid breath against her chest. She moves slowly, not wanting to disturb her daughter. For the last few weeks, Princess has not slept well, disturbed by frequent night terrors. As Maggie carefully sets Princess on the ground, she feels a cool breeze on her face. She looks up and sees that the shadows are lengthening and the light is receding.

"BANDOR!" Maggie yells, standing to her feet. "You let us rest too long!"

Bandor keeps working, stacking one log on top of the other.

"I'm almost finished putting up the wall."

"'Tis growing dark fast!" Maggie panics.

Bandor looks up with a start and glances around at the dwindling daylight. His hands begin to imperceptibly shake when he realizes that the sun is fading fast. He swallows and reassures his wife, "We'll get back just—"

An enormous brown flash smashes down on Bandor's muscular frame, cutting him off midsentence. Like a twig under a foot, Bandor's body snaps. The sudden impact whites out Bandor's vision and knocks the wind out of his lungs. A sharp, intense pain radiates down his legs. He tries to move his feet, but his legs won't respond. A clenching tremor courses up his abdomen and offsets his equilibrium.

Nausea washes over him and his arms flail uncontrollably.

Nothing makes sense. Bandor vividly remembers stacking wood, then feels the cool grass pressed against his face. He smells the strong earthy scent against his scruff.

Pain jerks him back to reality. Finally, he realizes he's been attacked.

Maggie shrieks, "*Bandor!*"

Princess jolts awake. Her eyes widen and her bottom lip pokes out. She wails and runs to her screaming mother. She buries her face in her mother's skirt.

Maggie's ear-piercing cry echoes in the forest and attracts the attention of a monstrous griffin, whose white eagle head hovers over her husband. The bird's burning red eyes flash as its beak opens.

The massive beast pushes its curved, black talons deeper into Bandor's abdomen. With its hefty beak, it clamps down on the meaty portion of his shoulder.

"Auurrgh…," Bandor gurgles. With his good arm, Bandor tries to block the incessant biting. The sharp pains in the center of his back, weakening him further. His despondent struggle is no match for the massive griffin that presses its full weight down on his frame.

Terrified, Princess peers past her mother's skirt and finds the creature looming over her father. Its long lion's tail twitches, moving back and forth behind hindquarters covered in golden fur. When the beast shifts its weight, its gigantic muscles bulge. Farther up its torso, chestnut-colored feathers protrude around its neck. The griffin's powerful wings rise, presenting its fierce wrath. Its giant eagle head cocks to the side. Princess catches a gruesome glimpse of a bloodstained beak. She clings to her mother's leg and clenches her eyes shut.

"Nooo…," Maggie bewails. The griffin looks at her and blinks a leathery lid. It turns and gulps down a severed arm. She stands awestruck and terrified as the eagle's gullet bulges. Trapped between terror and distress, Maggie watches the vile creature dismember her husband.

This isn't happening! This isn't real! her thoughts scream.

Feverishly, she steps back, ushering her petrified daughter toward the forest. She turns to Princess. "Run, child! We must find refuge!" Her eyes dart around the dimly lit forest. A single beam of sunlight rests on a hollowed-out log, its narrow opening partially covered by moss. Maggie scurries over to the shelter, pulling her daughter by the arm. Behind her, Bandor's tortured screams abruptly stop.

Maggie hastens to tuck away her precious daughter so that she can rush to her dear husband's rescue. She sweeps debris away from the entry and thrusts Princess into the dark, scratchy hole. Princess slides into the shelter, just small enough to fit snugly.

Feeling her mother's warm hand releasing her, Princess grasps her mother's fingers. "Don't leave, Ma! There's room for you!" she pleads.

Maggie shakes her head in protest. "No, your father—I can't leave your—"

Time stops for Princess then proceeds in slow-motion. Though she doesn't blink, she sees a series of frozen images. Maggie's hands go limp. Then her face turns white. Princess sees the infinite source of her mother's love—her blue eyes— widen and then dim. As their eyes lock, Princess witnesses her windows glaze over. Maggie's bottom lip quivers and—Princess isn't sure—but she thinks she hears her mother laugh.

All at once, Maggie is ripped from Princess' outstretched fingers.

Hearing the fluttering of wings, Princess hides her face in her hands.

The griffin snips violently with its razor-sharp beak. Maggie doesn't scream or cry out; she simply dies, inches from her daughter's touch.

Inside the log, Princess begins to cry as the last images of her mother burn into her memory. The sound of cracking bones causes the girl to cover her ears with her hands.

"Mommy will be okay—" she reassures herself. "She's not crying!" She shuffles backward into the dark cavity, terrified of the monster outside her shelter.

From outside Princess' hiding place, the terrifying griffin raises its head and swallows the last remains of Princess' parents in a few swift gulps.

Looking down from high in the treetops, no one would know that two people even stood in the woods a few moments ago, had it not been for the disturbed ground and blood soaked grass.

Inside the tight space, Princess peeks through her tightly pressed lids only to discover a large red eye filling the circumference of the hollow log. The probing pupil narrows when it spots Princess in the dark.

"Aauughh!" the child screams. With no time to mourn, Princess scampers back, shoving herself yet deeper into the damp refuge. Horrified, she realizes that it is her turn to die.

Her sudden movements attract the griffin's predatory instincts. It pecks at the timber, tearing away small pieces. The griffin strategically tests the log, using the point of its hooked beak to search for weak points. Frustrated that its prey eludes its grasp, it flaps its mammoth wings and stomps, crushing larger chunks of the bark. The ravenous monster then sifts through the dense wood with its beak, hoping to find its prize.

The jostling impacts overwhelm Princess and she screams. Pressing her palms into the wood, she wedges herself into the narrowest part of the fallen tree until she can retreat no farther.

The griffin releases thunderous lion's roar that trails off into an eagle screech. From behind the small child, the griffin's talons punch through the thick wall of oak and puncture the bottom of Princess' foot. She yelps and realizes that her tight shelter is no longer safe. Preparing to meet a terrible end, she screams until it burns her lungs and strains her throat. The death cry sends the griffin into a frenzied attack. It seizes the log with its claws.

At breakneck speed, it spreads its gigantic wings and lifts the log off the ground and above the trees. The hollow entry whooshes with rushing wind that presses against Princess' face. Lodged in the tight place, the little girl covers her face and hyperventilates in terror. The mighty griffin releases the log. The sudden freefall instantly lifts Princess' stomach into her throat. She wants to scream, but instead gags and coughs. Her timber haven falls through the air, crashing against flimsy pine branches that slow her imminent doom. Smashing against each tree jostles her with an earth-quaking force, rattling her body against the wood.

With a bang, the torn log hits the ground and begins rolling down a grassy knoll, folding the green blades and kicking up clods of dirt. Princess is tossed and banged around, but the narrow cavity holds her.

Earthy grit grinds against her teeth. Through the entry of her hiding place, converging images of green and blue circle so fast that her mind cannot separate the sky from the ground.

Farther down the hill, the earth begins to change from thick vegetation to loose stony ground. The log grinds against the solid earth, gaining momentum until it launches off a steep cliff. Smashing against a jagged rock wall, the shelter breaks in two. The halves free-fall into a dark canyon.

Soaring through the air, the griffin dives down on the descending log pieces. It snatches at one them and misses. The creature narrows its wings and dives ever faster, closing the slight gap. It successfully seizes its target with gripping claws and screeches in victory.

It turns out of its dive and soars upward, leaving massive brown feathers floating down in its wake.

The shorter section of wood continues to fall and narrowly passes between jagged cliffs. It slips through a shoreline mountain crevice, plunging into chilly water below. Sucked in by the tide, the log floats into a dimly-lit cavern. Water droplets fall from the rocky ceiling.

Drip, drip.

High in the fading sky, the fierce griffin clutches its prize, ripping it apart splinter by splinter. In vain, the beast frantically searches the falling brown pieces for its prey. When it discovers its loss, it releases a deafening screech of defeat. The massive monster flaps its powerful wings and searches for the other part of the log, but cannot locate it.

Its efforts frustrated, the griffin abandons the hunt.

Inside the dark cave, Princess slowly regains her balance. She faintly realizes that the log is no longer falling, but can process nothing more. She takes big gulps of air, her eyes wide and her pupils dilated. Her stomach reels from the fall.

"Ohhhh," she moans, threatening to throw up in the remains of her formerly protective space. She grabs her stomach, closing her eyes in pain.

"Ma…?" she calls. The echo from her small voice rebounds off the cavern walls, scaring the girl further.

"Da!" she yelps from inside the bobbing log. Isolation swirls around her. Princess' body tingles from fright and her muscles spasm. Everything seems to go numb, except an overpowering nausea in her aching belly.

Finally, the full realization of what has happened crashes down on her. She screams again and again—heart-wrenching screams that rise from her diaphragm and into her throat without control. When her throat goes raw, she breaks down and sobs, shaking in the floating log.

When Princess stops sobbing, her instincts kick in. She crawls forward, anxious to see her surroundings. Her movements upset the balance of the log and it begins to roll in the water. Princess cries out and frantically claws at the splintered sides to stabilize it. She gulps and moves forward with caution. When she reaches the edge of the log, she peers out into a dark cavern filled with water.

The girl rubs her stinging eyes. "I'm all alone," she whimpers. She pulls the collar of her dress over her nose and begins to draw quick breathes. Her hot breath traps a bit of warmth while her shelter rocks back and forth with each panting breath.

"What will become of me now?"

CHAPTER II

FOUND & FINDING

Princess feels her fingers and toes going numb. Though her wooden shelter floats, it is filled with a layer of freezing water. She moves backward and hits her injured foot against the side of the log.

"Ouch!" she cries. Warm blood leaks from the open wound. The girl tries to survey the injury but is inhibited by the narrowness of the log and the thick darkness of the cavern. She reaches back and uses her finger to feel along her heel. When she presses on the base of it, she yelps and pulls back from the pain. Her hand hovers helplessly over the wound.

The coldness in her hands begins creeping up her arms, turning her skin blotchy.

The empty cavern that conceals her from the griffin now introduces a far more menacing foe: the emerging threat of freezing. At first, the apparition presents itself to the wailing girl with determined silence, then the physical presence of a chill distils upon her. She responds to the unwelcome guest with clattering teeth that rattle her jaw. A deadly dance ensues with a predator that has no fang, no claw, and no appetite, only fatal patience.

Princess tries to lift her arms out of the water and wrap them around her stomach for warmth, but loses her balance and pitches face-first into the layer of water in the log. The girl moans and puts her frigid hands back into the water to support herself.

The tide takes the log into deeper into the dark tunnel. Princess' damp dress and distressed eyes fade into the darkness with each tug of the swelling tide. Her pale face looms in the shadows until the current pulls her into the deep unknown.

As she is sucked into the tunnel, Princess' lips begin to turn blue. Dark circles form under her eyes and she shakes uncontrollably from the cold.

"Be still," she whimpers. "Be so very still."

Though Princess' mind is immature, her instincts kick in, subconsciously gleaning facts that will improve her self-preservation. In her current predicament, the mind signals the body to safeguard itself by unraveling a mortal truth: death is never very far from life.

"Our eyes, our hearts, and our wits." Princess recites her mother's last lesson. "That's what we have in common, Ma."

The cold lulls Princess into a deadly comatose state. Princess dismisses her last flickering moments of mortality and prepares to be reunited with her mother in the unknown beyond.

The dance with the cold progresses, the cadence now set in motion by the dull thud of waves.

The vessel smashes against the cave wall. "Ahh!" Princess screams. Her nerves pull tight, snapping her back into the fight for survival.

"Our eyes, our hearts, and our wits," she repeats, as she shifts her weight, trying to stabilize the log.

A howling breeze blows through the cavern and nips at her cheeks. She feels herself going faster and faster, the wind and the darkness brushing against her face.

"Our eyes, our hea—ahhhh!" she screams as the rushing current speeds her along the dark depth. "Wits! Our wits, that's what we have, Ma, our wits!"

The rushing water suddenly spropels the child into the open ocean. Drifting a short distance off the coast, the bobbing log defies the gray ocean the satisfaction of filling her little lungs.

She keeps her eyes shut in dread and expects to see the glowing white spirit of her mother at any moment.

"You're wrong, Ma. I've no wits or courage. I'm a little *coward*."

A seagull's cawing emboldens Princess and she tentatively opens her eyes.

Through the log opening, Princess glimpses a vast body of water and spies a distant coastline rising up from the rippling gray horizon. The sun has nearly disappeared behind faraway jagged peaks. She sniffs and rubs a red blotchy cheek with her numb hand.

On the distant horizon, two dragon silhouettes emerge into the descending darkness.

One by one, tiny stars pop out of the dusky heavens. Their numbers increase with the darkness and offer a sliver of hope.

Trapped between the two infinite planes of water and sky, Princess gazes helplessly at the darkening shoreline.

Slowly, a full moon rises and illuminates the distant shore, as she drifts through the water.

Beneath the child, a pair of large, glowing eyes circles her makeshift craft.

Unaware of what lurks in the water, the child rests her chin on her right palm, raises two fingers, and waves a weak goodbye to the fading land. Her fingers are now so numb that she can barely move them with any degree of control.

The grumbling ache of hunger reminds Princess that her body needs sustenance. "Oh…," she moans and slides her hand to her tummy. "No honey, no bread."

A hard thump at the base of the log propels it out of the water.

Startled, Princess instinctively reacts by putting her hands on either side of the log to maintain her balance. She cautiously crawls forward to the edge and peers out into the dark waves. A pair of glowing eyes surface in front of the log. Terrified, the little girl yelps. Flashes of blue energy pulsate over the creature's body, revealing a pug nose, two large manta ray wings, and a long, narrow tail.

Princess ducks back into her safe hollow. Seconds later, her curiosity piques and she lifts her head back up. She sees a ball of the crackling energy gather at the manta ray's tail and discharge into the water behind it. The blue sphere of energy continues to sparkle as it sinks into the dark ocean.

The manta ray continues to discharge energy, creating a pearly string of lights that disappear into the depths.

Princess watches the beautiful display and feels a wave of enchantment, but continues to cling to her refuge.

The giant manta ray presses its soft snout against the log and flaps its powerful wings, propelling Princess backward. Bulbs of energy with hints of red, green, and yellow trail behind the giant manta.

"Stop that!" Princess exclaims through chattering teeth. Suddenly, the log jerks to a halt. Princess looks over her shoulder to see what she hit. She discovers a pale hand resting against the back of the log and feels a thrill of joy rush over her.

"Ma?" she whispers. The hand disappears and Princess scrambles within the narrow space. The log begins to rotate, forcing Princess to stop and stabilize her vessel. Shaking with anticipation, she tries to look under her arms and legs to the opening behind her. Disappointment sets in when she finds nothing there. She looks up in frustration and finds a woman's face staring at her through the log's front opening.

The girl starts. "You're not Ma!" she squeaks.

A slender, wet arm slides into the opening, glistening in the moonlight. Princess' eyes bulge as the woman rises further into view, her pale torso partially covered in sparkling silver scales. Wet, golden hair spills into the log opening.

Hesitantly, Princess stares into the stranger's alluring face. "Found or finding?" the lovely woman asks.

A strange tone like a wind chime tickles Princess' ears. "Uhm … I'm Princess," the child responds.

"I am Setchra of Esseria."

"Is your voice made of music?"

The strange woman laughs and tilts her head to the side. The harp-like sound of her voice soothes Princess and subdues her fears.

"The manta summoned me to you," Setchra continues, waving to the large ray and clicking her tongue.

The manta's wings break the surface and rise into the air. It pauses, slaps its wings against the ocean's surface and then disappears back into the depths of the sea.

Princess peeks over the edge of the log, but misses the disappearance. The woman puts her hand on the child's.

"Would you like to go back to shore?" the woman asks soothingly. Her white teeth gleam in the starlight.

Princess nods and averts her eyes. Even in dire circumstances, she cannot restrain her bashfulness.

"How did you get out here?" the child asks, suddenly wondering how the lady can stand the freezing water.

"With this, my dear," the woman laughs, raising her silvery mermaid's tail out of the water.

"Are you a fish?" the girl asks in confusion.

The mermaid laughs. "Would you like to get out of that cold log?"

Princess nods.

"Very well, then." The mermaid grabs the log's opening and flicks her tail in the water, pulling the shelter forward.

Swimming against a strong current, she pulls Princess toward a wide, shallow bay. The little girl watches the mermaid swim like a dolphin, submerging and then surfacing. Princess scoots forward, hoping to catch another glimpse of the mermaid's tail. She moves too close to the log's edge, tilting the shelter forward and falling into the water. Instinctively, the mermaid grabs the flailing girl. She flips over onto her back and fins her way to shore, cradling the child on her scaly lap. Princess' little face tilts down but her sad eyes turn up. She shivers uncontrollably.

"Are you planning to eat me?" Princess asks somberly, nestling into the mermaid's arms.

The mermaid taps the child's nose. "You? Never," she promises in an angelic voice.

The mermaid jettisons the child to the shore, walls of water parting around her slender shoulders. A thrusting wave beaches them on the rocky shore where a number of round stones litter the coast. The mermaid gently sets Princess down, the seawater lapping at the child's bare ankles.

Princess gasps when a foamy wave recedes, revealing the woman's lower torso. Shimmering silver scales cover the woman's waist and travel down her magnificent tail. Strange, ribbon-like flesh hangs in aquamarine streams from both sides of the tail.

Princess yearns to touch the shimmering tail, as she does all things intriguing. She breathlessly reaches out to make contact. The flipper slaps against the wet ground as if to say, *Don't touch.*

Princess pulls her hand back. Unsure of what to do, she bows.

"*Tinksel*, Ma'am," the girl sheepishly murmurs.

"*Tinksel?*" The mermaid raises an eyebrow.

"Ma says to say *tinks.*"

The mermaid smiles, realizing the little girl is saying thanks. She bows her head in reply.

Princess turns to look at the shore and wobbles on some loose rocks. The mermaid grabs the child's arm and stabilizes her.

"Careful," the mermaid counsels. She looks at Princess curiously. "How is it you are out here with no protectors?"

Princess face crumbles. "I fell...." she begins to whimper.

"You fell? From whence?"

"From the forest."

Setchra gives the girl a perplexed look but continues. "Where are your guardians?"

"They – " Princess stops and clears her throat. The horror of the day's events crashes down on her. She awakens to a realization. "They – they *dieddddd*." Princess sobs. Her legs weaken and she begins to teeter.

The half-woman, half-fish wraps her arms around the little girl and pulls her onto her lap, protectively warding off danger.

Princess fully succumbs to her emotions and crumbles into an exhausted heap. Seeing nothing, hearing nothing, she is lulled by the mermaid's rocking arms.

"There, there, child," the mermaid soothes, running her cool hand over Princess' frazzled hair.

"You are safe with me." The mermaid moves her hand in circles on Princess' back. "All will be well."

The overwrought girl drifts off to sleep, relying on Setchra's care. Through her silver irises, the mermaid searches her surroundings. Her metallic vision pierces every shadow and reveals only contrasting shades of silver.

Time passes, unbeknownst to Princess. Finally, she cracks open her eyes and finds a world that appears to be a shimmering, glowing gold. With the mermaid leaning over her, Princess is veiled in golden hair. The moonlight shimmers through the strands, lighting up the space around Princess in a golden hue. Princess smiles and instinctively reaches up, tempted by a single strand of pearls growing from the mermaid's scalp and braided into her locks.

Without restraint or forethought, she grabs the pearls, unintentionally tinkering with the gateway to a mermaid's heart. Little did Princess know that touching a mermaid's pearl forms intense, eternal relationships, pledging the mermaid to the individual who dared to touch.

Gasping, Setchra feels fiery warmth ignite inside her veins, instantly bonding her to Princess. Feelings of love, connectedness, and attachment flood in, creating a connection even more potent than a human mother's. Had Princess been a mermaid, she would have been able to reciprocate the intensity.

When Princess bonded to Setchra, an internal fire as strong as the rising sun overtook the mermaid and cascaded down every scale, causing her tail to flutter in gentle flaps. These symbiotic bonds are experienced only by merpeople and unite bound to bonded in a circle of fire that literally warms their core for an eternity.

That physical warmth felt by Setchra is a manifestation of love shared through the connection of pearls. As the epitome of beauty, every merperson has one grand purpose: to fall in love, build love, enhance love, and progress in love. They thrive on those powerful emotions, using them to form familial pods and build underwater empires.

Setchra closes her eyes and takes in the emotions that wash over her. A warmth flows into her heart, causing Setchra's pale face to glow. Her perfect, pointed nose tickles against Princess' cool cheek, causing Princess to giggle.

Setchra is able to see the person she has bonded to in full color, rather than the usual shades of silver.

The crown of Princess' head changes from shimmering silver strands to rich walnut brown. The shifting color cascades down the child's long hair. Her pale cheeks flush with fleshy tones and glow with a round hint of rose. Princess' dark silver lips slowly turn pink. Setchra watches the little girl's silver irises turn bright blue. The mermaid smiles at the beauty she can now observe the child. "If I had a daughter," Setchra sighs, "I would want her to look exactly like you."

The mermaid glances out to the silvery horizon and then back at Princess. She can now see the girl in full color, but for everything else, her vision remains silver.

"Are you going to leave me here?" Princess interrupts Setchra's glorious emotional surge.

Setchra shakes her head, tossing her radiant blonde locks around her face. She smiles warmly and her pupils catch the pale moonlight, eerily holding a luminous halo in the center of her silver irises.

"Your eyes are very pretty," Princess giggles, putting her hand on Setchra's cheek, which magnifies the inferno inside the mermaid.

"I will ensure your safety," Setchra whispers softly, gently tapping Princess on the nose.

Unexpectedly, Setchra flips over, arches her back, and cracks her tail against the hard rocks with a violent rigor. Water droplets explode off her iridescent scales and fly through the air as perfect spheres. The droplets then separate into beads and splash on the rocks. With several swift pops of her tail, Setchra's scales seem to peel back.

Princess flinches with each cracking jolt. "You said you wouldn't eat me!" she whimpers, her fear rising.

Scales begin to dislodge and fall off.

CHAPTER III

CHANGES & CHANGING

Setchra smiles. "You will fear me less, when I walk on two legs like you." She snaps her transforming tail.

A pile of translucent scales slides off the mermaid's partially veiled legs and clatter onto the rocks beneath her. Orange crabs scamper over the rocky shore, cantankerously pinching each other as they duel for the mermaid's savory scales.

Setchra grabs a kelp vine and wraps the lengthy wet leaves around her waist, fashioning a dark, glistening skirt. With a few more powerful flips, the fin bones of Setchra's tail abruptly separate into two feet, completing her conversion.

Princess' eyes widen. She pulls her head in like a turtle's and flinches at the popping sound of the scales.

"Does it hurt?"

"A little," Setchra calmly respond. She stands, putting one wobbly foot forward. "Ohh—" she cries, falling to the stony beach.

Princess giggles.

"Must I crawl before I walk?" Setchra bemoans. She reaches for Princess, who provides a small shoulder. Setchra stands and takes one small step forward, then another, until she recovers the balance required for walking.

"Oh my, it *has* been a while." She pats her human-like hipbones, shifting from one leg to the other, feeling the shifting angles beneath her fingertips. Setchra takes wobbly steps toward a mound of seaweed on the shore. She falls to her knees and rakes her delicate fingers over a clump of seaweed.

"What are you searching for?" Princess asks, keeping a safe distance from the water.

"A bulb," Setchra replies, tossing handfuls of seaweed to her left and right. "There we are," she proclaims, triumphantly raising a slimy cord of kelp with a round bulb as big as her fist. Rising up, she returns to Princess. "We shall be on our way soon."

Setchra bites down on the vine holding the bulb in place. Sand fleas leap off the algae and tickle her face.

"Where are we going?" Princess asks.

"Tep-meneble" Setchra replies through a mouthful of seaweed.

Princess gives her a stern look and points her finger authoritatively. "You are not supposed to speak with your mouth full!"

Setchra smiles and spits out pieces of the slimy green bulb, then picks her teeth.

"Truffle Nufflele," she says with her finger in her mouth.

Princess wrinkles her brow in confusion. "Where?"

The lovely mermaid tilts her head to the side and pulls the slender finger from her mouth. "I'm taking you to Tremble Nemble," Setchra repeats clearly. "But first, I have to find a blue ring octopus." The duo moves toward a trickling stream that runs down from shadowy mountains and empties into the ocean.

At the bank, Princess curiously watches while the mermaid flips over flat, round rocks, carefully standing back from the water.

"What happens if your feet get wet?"

Setchra holds her hands up around her mouth like gills and sucks her lips into a fish shape. "I turn back into a fish."

Princess giggles. "I like you!"

Setchra smiles warmly. She tenderly brushes the child underneath her chin. "I like you, too."

Faded driftwood litters the shore, looking more like scattered bones than bleached wood. Bordering the coast, a dark forest of pines, maples, and oaks rises up. Princess glances at the eerie tree line and prays she will not have to enter. Her stomach grumbles. "Pardon me, Miss Mermaid, but I'm real hungry," the girl says, grasping her empty belly.

Setchra wraps seaweed around her swirling wrist, and hands it to Princess. "Eat this, it will satisfy your hunger."

Princess sticks out her tongue. "That smells dreadful."

"It is very good for you," the mermaid coaxes.

The girl takes a bite and makes a face. "Yuck!"

Setchra laughs. "'Tis not all that bad. You will grow used to the taste. Just take another bite."

The girl looks at the seaweed and then down at her grumbling tummy. She sighs and takes another bite. She makes another face but feels better as she swallows.

The mermaid looks back at the fading tide. The moon is completely covered by clouds but provides enough light for her to see through the shadows. She turns a rock over, examining microscopic silver urchin needles, invisible to the human eye, but visible to her mer-vision.

On a rock's surface, she detects a pair of staggered crab tracks. She follows the trail until two green, glowing crab eyes pop over a rock. She looks past the crab and discovers perfect, flashing blue phosphorescent rings. "Where there's crab, there's prey," she murmurs.

Following the flashing blue rings, she closes in on a tiny fleeing octopus. Miniature, stretchy arms bend and cycle through the water as an inky cloud disperses, temporarily concealing the invertebrate. The octopus darts here and there, hoping to escape to deeper waters before the mermaid can snatch it. It manages to tuck itself into a rocky crevice before the mermaid corners it. Cautiously, she pinches the palm-sized octopus by the top of its head. Instantly, the octopus' slimy skin flashes gray as the creature wiggles and writhes.

"Why are you doing that?" Princess asks.

Setchra thrusts the octopus into the green kelp bulb and presses a small spiral seashell into the hole, sealing the opening. She smiles triumphantly, holding up her handcrafted nautical lantern.

"Why are you doing that?" Princess repeats, unable to subdue her curiosity.

"For light on our journey," Setchra instructs, tapping her prisoner's bulbous cage.

Princess squints, searching for any sign of light. The girl sees only faint rings of blue pulsing within the bulb. "'Tis not very bright," she says.

"While you see only dim circles, my vision perceives powerful beams of light," Setchra clarifies.

Princess wrinkles her nose, trying to process the explanation. She shrugs and reaches for the bulb.

The wise mermaid pulls the lantern back. "This tiny creature has enough venom to kill a dolphin," she sternly warns.

Princess recoils, yet a moment later she cannot resist leaning in for another look at the frightened octopus.

Setchra strokes Princess' hair. "Don't tempt fate," the mermaid smiles. "We have the upper hand, but only as long as the creature is inside this shell." She taps on the thick kelp bulb. The tiny octopus shrinks back from the deafening thuds.

Setchra holds the bulb up to her face, admiring the cascading lights.

"Through my eyes, I can see its beautiful splendor. It shines bright silver, like a twinkling star, except circling instead of pulsing." Setchra inhales and gazes into the light. Her eyes trail up to the dark heavens, which hold thousands of stars perfectly in place.

Princess looks at the faint blue ring, glowing and circling. "But it's blue, not silver."

Setchra chuckles and clicks her tongue. "Mm-hmm. You may hold it, but only if you are careful not to squeeze the bulb."

Princess nods and excitedly takes the lantern, examining the octopus inside.

From inside the bulb, the octopus sees Princess' nose expand and distort through the kelp wall. Huge blue eyes swell and swivel into position as the girl brings the bulb up to her face. The octopus pulls itself back as far as it can, its lightening-blue circles glowing brighter with fear.

"Come child, we must go." Setchra retrieves the lantern and takes Princess' small fingers in her own. Setchra walks straight into the dark forest, stomping down thick thorny bushes so that Princess can follow her path more easily.

Princess steps on a pointy twig with her wounded foot. "Oww!"

Hearing the child cry out, Setchra feels a flash of icy energy avalanche inside her. The shifting emotions cause her heart to flutter in panic. For a brief moment, she feels as though she can't breathe. Setchra whips around, and scoops Princess up, clicking her tongue. "Are you well?"

"My foot hurts."

Setchra lifts Princess' leg and examines her wound. "Be careful, child. We must hurry."

"Why?"

"When the sun rises, I can no longer see."

"What's wrong with your eyes?"

"Nothing is wrong with my eyes. They are just different than yours."

⁂

Back down on the beach, the wind catches Setchra's shimmering scales and scatters them down the coast. Crabs continue to compete for the fishy feast. Down the coastline, a flying streak of glittering gold spontaneously zips in and out of the forest. Like a firework's sparkling trail, the gold haze is followed by pink, green, purple, and red fairy trails that explode out of the dark woods and blast down the rocky beach.

"I told you I could smell a mermaid," the gold fairy shouts over her shoulder.

The fairies zip and zoom toward Setchra's scales, leaving a wake of spectacular, shimmering, rainbow-colored dust. A beautiful blonde fairy with shoulder-length hair and golden eyes creates a shimmering gold dust trail. Clothed in a yellow skirt of lily petals, the sprite greedily snatches up an armload of scales and presses them against her chest.

"Tillie, that's not fair!" shouts her sister, Nillie. "My wings are worn and torn. It's time for a new set and a new shine! The beach is full of wings. Full! Full! Full! Get your own!" Nillie latches onto the scales and tugs.

Tillie pops up and swiftly kicks Nillie in the stomach. She sticks out her tongue and flies away in an explosive burst of golden glitter. Nillie doubles over. She looks up, grits her teeth, and growls. In a burst, she chases after her sister, leaving a pink cloud of glitter beside her sister's gold one.

✷✷✷

Deep in the forest, owls hoot and crickets chirp.

Princess continually strains to peer at the glowing octopus.

Setrcha watches the girl's small face light up from the luminous orb. Princess announces, "We should name it!"

Setchra laughs and shakes her head at the resilient child.

As the two continue to travel through the forest, Princess' head begins to nod from exhaustion and she hobbles along on her injured heel. "How much farther?" Princess asks, her shoulders slumping.

"Traveling isn't without difficulty, child. But be patient, we are near."

"Are we there yet?" Princess yawns.

"Almost."

"Yeah, but are we there *yet?*"

"Almost," Setchra responds in the same moderated tone.

"But when will we be there?" the child persists.

"After."

"After what?"

"After after."

Princess scrunches her brows together and presses her lips to the side of her face. "After after what?"

"After—oh look, we're here," Setchra says, spotting sparkling water through breaks in the trees. She sets Princess down and pushes branches back, creating an opening in the thick foliage for the child. Princess tiredly stumbles through the break, rubbing her eyes. She steps onto a riverbank and looks in awe at a wide river with strong swirling currents.

Stars fade as sunlight peeks over the distant hills.

"I must be in the water before dawn," Setchra says, examining the horizon with trepidation.

"Why?"

"I cannot see in sunlight. I can get along fine in the water, but I'm not very steady on land, even when I can see." The mermaid looks around, deep in thought. "'Twould be best if you remained here and covered your ears." She turns and leaves Princess on the riverbank, re-entering the forest.

Princess watches Setchra briskly tie the kelp bulb to her seaweed skirt before disappearing into the trees. "What could she possibly be doing?" Princess mumbles. Curiously, she walks to the forest's edge and pokes through the foliage. She peers around, trying to locate the merwoman.

A ray of rising sunlight breaks through an opening in the trees. Setchra throws up her hands to shield her eyes. She peeks over her shoulder at the bright, reflective light coming out of the breaks in the vegetation. The blinding reflection is so intense that she is forced to look away. *Only a few more moments*, she thinks, hurrying forward.

Setchra stops and cups both hands around her mouth. She braces herself and releases a high- pitched sonar blast from her sinus cavity.

Images immediately begin to surface in her mind. White sound waves, traveling out like ripples in a pond, give her a full view of her surroundings. She sees a densely populated forest with long-standing elms, bushy oaks, and maple trees packed together in tight formations. Finally, she sees Princess covering her ears and running back to the bank of the kingdom-bound river. Setchra smiles. *I warned her*, she thinks.

Armed with a cursory overview of the landscape around her, the mermaid walks over to a tree and wraps her slender arms around its trunk to measure the width. *That'll do*, she decides.

She raises her right hand and flicks her wrist. In an instant, long black claws erupt from her nail bed. With a violent swipe of her hand, she sinks her claws into the thick fibers of the pine, tearing out the tree's core. The unmistakable sound of splitting timber echoes through the forest. Needles shower down from the devastating blow.

Setchra puts one hand on the towering timber and gives it a small push. The creaking tree sways gently, then begins to fall. It crackles and snaps as it splinters apart. The trunk hits the ground with an earth-shaking thud, sending critters scampering in all directions. Setchra strides to the narrow end of the fallen tree, clicking her tongue as she goes. The clicking ripples off Setchra's surroundings, creating short-range images in her mind.

The mermaid sinks her fingernails into the wooden core and starts to drag the heavy trunk to the riverbank. She heaves the hefty log through the woods, moving through the brush until she meets Princess on the shore. The astonished little girl stands with her mouth open before running up to a flimsy branch and tugging on it.

"I'm strong too!" she chimes.

Setchra drags the log into the water, docking it on the shore as the sun breaches the mountain peaks. Now without sight, the mermaid eagerly slides into the murky brown river.

Steam billows off the water's surface. Setchra unties the kelp skirt, which now encircles her magnificent silver tail. The kelp bulb, still holding the octopus prisoner, drifts away with the current. The creature presses its tentacles against the translucent bulb as if to say, *Release me, I played my part.*

The mermaid swims in a circle, rejoicing in the water that replenishes her scales. She bobs to the surface, gasping and blowing bubbles. Her hair floats around her shoulders in golden sheens.

Delighted, Princess claps her hands. "You're a fish again!"

Setchra nods and grows somber. "The water has brought fins, but the sun has brought blindness."

Princess pinches and tugs on her eyelids. "How?"

"My eyes see in the night," the merwoman replies, motioning for Princess to jump onto the log.

Princess tiptoes to the water's edge then hops backwards.

"Uh, I would rather stay on land," Princess resists.

Setchra laughs and holds out her hand. "I will help you."

Princess hesitates. "What if your singing cuts me in half, like the tree?"

Humored, Setchra grins. "My singing didn't cut the tree in half," she smirks, "It was my claws." Setchra holds up her right hand and stretches her fingers, displaying her long nails.

"Oh," Princess gulps.

The mermaid pats on the log's rough surface. "Come now, we must go. We aren't there yet but we soon will be."

Princess bravely puffs up her chest. "I would much rather walk, *tinksel.* Hiding on a log is hardly courage, and Ma *said* I have courage!"

Setchra sighs. "You will not be hiding on the log, you will sit upon it."

Princess hesitates. "Must I?"

"Unless you would rather live in the ocean with me."

Princess thinks for a moment. "How would I breathe?"

"You wouldn't."

"But I have to breathe."

Setchra nods.

"Okay, I'll get on the log."

Princess takes Setchra's helping hand, moving in and amongst the branches before finding a spot to sit on the wide tree. Careful not to fall in the water, the girl sits down, straddling the coarse bark with her legs. She adjusts her dress while her dangling toes skim the water. She lies back on the trunk, lifting her arms behind her head and locking her fingers.

Princess yawns. "I'm sleepy."

Setchra buries both sets of claws into the log and drags it into the swirling brown water, successfully driving against the current. Startled by the sudden movement, Princess turns over on her tummy and hugs the prickly bark with both arms. Using her tail as a rudder, the blind merwoman uses the current to orient the tip of the pine so that it points downstream. The slow current floats the duo away. "It won't be long 'til we arrive."

Princess doesn't answer. Her shallow breathing indicates that she is fast asleep.

"Rest child," Setchra whispers, reaching up with a claw to tuck Princess' brown hair behind her ear.

Setchra faces the log and, with a powerful thrust of her wide tail, lifts her body farther out of the water. She folds her arms on the buoyant timber and rests her chin on them.

What will become of this child? she ponders. I know I should let her go, yet, perhaps I could keep her as my own? She wracks her mind, considering the options. Oh dear, this is complicated, she sighs.

"I think 'tis best you be with your own," she lovingly whispers to the child.

Birds sing morning praises and welcome the day. The flowing river makes a relaxing trickling sound. Setchra sighs as she guides the makeshift raft down the river.

The two peacefully journey until late afternoon when Setchra hears the sound of shuffling grass. She turns toward the riverbank, but cannot see the white-bearded man fishing for his supper. The man sits on a tree stump without a shirt, curly white hair cascading down his wrinkled chest. Upon spotting the odd pair floating down the river, he leaps from his stump.

"You there! Ya be well?" he bellows.

Setchra tenses at the sound of his voice, unable to see what manner of creature hails her from the shore. She begins clicking her tongue and waits for a report, but is only able to see a blurry image. She debates using her more powerful sonar blast in order to determine the size and location of the threat.

"May I be of assistance, mum?" he yells.

Detecting the genuine concern in his voice, she decides not to use the blast, but remains guarded.

"Afternoon," she replies, blindly looking past him. She clutches the log, staying close to Princess.

The old man leans forward eagerly. "Looks like ya caught a bit more than I," he chuckles, putting a wood pipe in his mouth.

Setchra and Princess slowly drift past him.

"I'd offer you aid, but I've no rope long enough to reach ya."

Although wary, Setchra decides to inquire directions of the stranger. She arches her back, pushes out her chest, and flicks her powerful tail, holding the massive tree stationary in the middle of the strong current. Swelling swirls spin around the log and spill over Setchra's slender shoulders.

"Not that you'd be needin' a towline to drag ya in," the man says in astonishment, noting her strength.

"How far to Tremble Nemble?"

The old man lifts a stick from a smoldering fire and lights his pipe. Smoke clouds billow out of his mouth. "Oh, closer than ya might think." He points downriver with a wrinkled hand. "'Tis just around that bend."

"Thank you," Setchra waves goodbye.

When she raises her arm out of the water, the man catches a glimpse of her silver top. He stares and puffs rapidly. "By Poseidon's beard! Was that lady a mermaid?"

He watches the log drift around the bend and looks down at his pipe. "What manner of herbs burn in me pipe?" He turns his pipe over, knocking the red embers out. "'Tis me 'magination," he assures himself, shaking his head.

The current moves Setchra around a bend. She clicks her tongue and catches a faint image of a wooden dock with two small fishing vessels tied to it. Carefully, the mermaid moves closer, clicking her tongue continually to keep her bearings. She maneuvers the log until it pushes onto the shore next to the pier. Once it's settled along the bank, she gently pats Princess on the arm. "Wake up, child. We've arrived."

Princess smacks her lips sleepily, pushes herself up, and moans, "Ma?"

The mermaid helps her sit up.

"I had terrible dreams, Ma," the girl mumbles, leaning forward she slips off the log. The mermaid catches her and holds her against her chest. She sighs and tenderly rubs Princess' back. Bark imprints on Princess' face turn pink as the blood flows back into her cheeks.

"There, there, child," Setchra soothes.

Instinctively, the little girl wraps her arms around Setchra's neck and breathes deeply. The mermaid leans back and rests against the soft muddy embankment. She cradles the little girl in her arms and lets her rest a little longer.

As time slips by a family of swans enters the small cove. Setchra hears the mother enter the pool first, then her chirping cygnet, followed by the much larger father. He spreads his wings and flaps before he shakes his beak, body, and tail.

Princess' closed eyelids rapidly shift back and forth. She moans once and her leg jerks.

Inside her dream, her mother eerily whispers, "Courage," before she is again torn from Princess' outstretched hand. Still asleep, Princess feels her mother's fingers slip through hers.

She gasps sharply and wakes herself. "Ma!" she wails.

Setchra presses the child's head against her chest and rocks her. "Shhh, it will be alright, child." Setchra's soothing words eventually calm Princess.

The crisp air changes, welcoming the cool evening. She continues comforting the distraught child and reluctantly sets Princess on the dry, dusty pier. Setchra props herself against the side of the pier. Scales around her waist reveal her true form. She feels the child's warmth leave her arms. The intense and sudden withdrawal sends immediate stabbing pangs to her heart. *Am I doing what's best?* she wonders. The mermaid fights back what feels like an ocean of tears. *The child simply cannot live with me in the sea.*

Princess stands alone on the dock, her dress rumpled and dark circles beneath her young eyes. She stares blankly and toys with Setchra's hair.

"Follow the path beyond the dock," the mermaid directs. "It will take you to the kingdom of Tremble Nemble. There are people like you."

Setchra longs to reach for the child and reignite the blaze, but manages to refrain. "Be *sure* to stay on the path," she repeats.

"Will the people be kind like you?" Princess asks.

Setchra nods, trying to hold back tears.

"Even better than I," she replies, blindly looking past the child.

Princess leans over the water's edge and hugs Setchra for the last time. The mermaid feels a surge of warmth overwhelm her and knows that if she doesn't leave now, she never will.

"Will I ever see you again?" Princess asks.

Setchra nods.

"But I don't want you to go," Princess protests, her bottom lip trembling.

"I don't want to go either," Setchra responds, lowering herself into the water.

"How will I find you?"

Setchra reaches up and pinches a pearl in her hair. She twists it back and forth. Princess hears a noise like breaking glass and watches Setchra wince in pain. A little blood seeps down a perfect blonde lock. The mermaid dips her pearl in the water, rinsing it clean.

"When you want me, bring this to the shore," she explains, placing the rare jewel in Princess' palm. "Cast it into the ocean, but remember that I can see it best on a full moon."

Setchra pushes away from the pier.

"What if you don't see it?" Princess calls in alarm.

"When I sing, like in the forest, it has a certain tone that draws me near it, and to you."

Princess, enraptured by the smooth white pearl between her fingers, gratefully whispers, "*Tinksel.*"

Setchra gently moves farther into the fast current. Her heart nearly breaks as she waves and swims away.

"Wait!" Princess shouts, tears welling in her eyes. "I'm all alone!"

With a heavy heart, Setchra exercises every ounce of willpower to push herself farther and farther away.

"No! Stop! Where are you going? Don't leave me here!" Princess yells, tears now streaming down her cheeks.

Setchra feels the current sweep against her side and accepts the invitation to reunite with the cold darkness. Like the child, tears flow down her cheeks.

"I will never be far!" she shouts, then sinks into the glistening river and exposes her magnificent tail for the last time. A swirl of murky current disturbs the water's surface and the mermaid is gone.

Princess draws a deep breath and wails as another guardian disappears.

CHAPTER IV

FRIENDS & FOES

Princess grips the pearl tightly and hobbles up the trail, her chest heaving from the emotional loss. The child passes a wooden sign that declares the waterfront to be "King Henry's Port."

Chirping crickets announce the cool spring twilight. Their classic song calms the girl's tortured nerves.

"When crickets chirp, danger is...," she pauses, reflecting on the saying her father taught her. "Danger...," She waits for a moment, thinking back on his face and voice: *When crickets chirp, danger diverts,* she hears him say. In her mind, Princess sees her father run his fingers through his hair, his stern eyes locking on hers: *When crickets be still, danger is near.*

Although struck by a pang of grief at the memory of her father, Princess is grateful for his guiding counsel, even in his absence.

She walks along a narrow path lined with tall willows and wild grass. A light breeze sways the cattails and blows apart their puffy tops. Floating seeds sail away until their brown bodies are reduced to skeletal stumps. Buzzing mosquitoes hum in her ears and pester her with stinging bites. She runs down the path to escape their wrath. Soon, she hears frogs ribbitting all around her.

Princess watches a frog slowly roll out its sticky pink tongue and catch a dragonfly. With two harsh snaps, the winged insect disappears into the frog's gullet.

"Yuck!" Princess exclaims. She hurries forward and looks for a new diversion.

She holds up her gleaming pearl. "What 'tis your name?"

She lowers her voice to respond: "Setchra."

"I know a Setchra! She's a mermaid," she responds to herself excitedly. "Don't worry, I won't let anything happen to you."

She looks up at the fading sky. "I'm tired," she yawns.

The girl steps off the path and looks for a place to lie down. Cool, squishy grass covers the ground and pines sporadically dot the valley. Princess finds a thin tree only a few steps from the road. The lowest branches are near the ground and bow downwards, creating an evergreen skirt.

Princess lifts a branch and crawls underneath. Pine needles stick to the bottom of her wet feet and irritate the dark scab on her foot. Once inside, she leans against the scratchy bark and pulls her knees up to her chin.

"Oh no," she whispers, pinching her thumb to her forefinger. "'Tis sticky." She attempts to wipe the pinesap on her dress. "'Tis very sticky," she grumbles.

With a sigh, she looks around for a place to safely tuck her pearl as she prepares to sleep.

Her eyes light up. "You can sleep with me," she tells the pearl, sliding it between her sticky fingers. She opens her hand and shakes it, but the pearl remains stuck fast to her fingers.

"See," she smiles. "I told you I would keep you safe." The cool evening air descends on the countryside, but the evergreen haven remains warm and dry. Princess rests her arms on her knees and her chin on her hands, and breathes in the soothing pine. She blinks once, then twice, and falls fast asleep.

Before sunrise, the familiar sound of sparrows and morning doves awakens the orphaned child. A morning mist makes her shiver.

The young girl stretches her hand out, holding the pearl out from underneath the pine skirt. "'Tis safe!" Princess croaks in a dismal replication of Setchra's silky voice.

"Are you sure?" Princess whispers. "'Tis awful scary." The surfacing memories of her parents cause her to hesitate.

She answers herself with a low grumbling voice. "I know, but I'm very hungry."

"Me too," Princess confides to her pearl.

She moves the pearly surrogate eye high and low.

"No danger, come on out!" Princess creaks in a low voice.

"Alright then."

Lying on her stomach, Princess scoots along the foggy ground, "Ouch!" she cries out. She emerges from the pokey tree and brushes her dress to knock off the dried pine needles. "That's not nice," she scolds the prickly offenders.

Once Princess removes the painful pine needles, she skips back to the dirt path and notices her heel isn't burning as badly. Though the throbbing is duller, the wound reminds her of her shattered, painful past.

She folds her arms and promises herself that she will be mindful of her deceased parents. She marches her legs high with her arms folded squarely, honoring her parents' loss with a respectful, one-person parade. After several pounding steps, she leaves the willows behind and enters a grassy valley, with a dense cluster of trees a great distance away. Her empty tummy grumbles. "Ahhh!" Princess moans, her dry throat cracking as she rubs her stomach.

Princess surveys her surroundings: she finds no food, no homes, no farms, and no people. She presses her hand to her stomach and whimpers, "I think Setchra's a liar!"

"No she isn't," Princess grumbles in a raspy voice. "Carry on."

"Where are the kind people?" Princess demands, furrowing her brow. "You don't understand, Setchra, 'cause you don't have a tummy."

Princess picks up a stick at the path's edge and holds Setchra's pearl on the tip, pretending her pearl is a head of a stick figure.

"Now you understand what an empty tummy feels like!"

She looks at the pearl with satisfaction, but then feels guilty for making her pearl hurt.

"You are my new baby." She cradles the stick. "It will be okay, baby. I will protect you." She holds the stick closer to her chest, trying to keep the pearl on the tip of the stick.

"Do you walk like me or swim like Setchra?"

"I can swim," her low, creaking, pretend voice answers.

"Really? Show me."

Princess holds the stick up high and pretends to hover her imagined baby over the distant trees. With one eye closed, she moves the stick up and down like a dolphin diving into the green treetop ocean. As her hands move, she makes a splashing sound. "Whoosh! Spoosh!"

Far off in the distance, a blue sky reflects a shiny object that catches her attention. Clutching her pearl in one hand, she drops the stick and shields her eyes with her other hand.

"What is it?" she asks her pearl.

"We should go see," her raspy voice answers.

At the pearl's urging, Princess sets off eagerly.

The early morning light graciously releases yellow beams through puffy white clouds. Princess hobbles along until she feels a sudden chill under her feet. She looks down and finds that she is standing atop a cobblestone road with piles of dried horse manure on it. Princess squats down and pokes at a flat yellow stone, noticing gray cement between the stones.

"A very unusual path," she observes.

She stands back up and moves faster toward the shiny object, sparkling above the treetops. The child energetically skips a few paces until the memory of her parents brings her to a guilty halt. Her shoulders slump and she hops backwards once, rebuking herself for feeling joy.

"I know, I miss them, too," she sniffles to her pearl.

Princess decides to reverently fold her arms and walk down the road holding the pearl in her fist.

The dark blue sky lightens as the morning progresses, but Princess' eyes remain fixed upon the glistening object in the sky.

After a short distance, the tree line reveals a dark blue cone pointing directly into the bright morning horizon. A golden needle protrudes from the top of the cone, reflecting the early morning light. Beneath bushy trees, gray mist covers the valley like a sea of vapor.

Still unsure of what she's seeing, Princess throws Setchra up in the air so that the pearl can get a better look. Momentarily blinded by the rising sun, she fails to catch her prize. Frantically, she scampers around for a moment, then finds the white sphere on the cobblestones.

"I was so worried," she professes, cupping both her hands around it.

"You swore you would protect me," Setchra whines in a raspy voice.

"What was it you saw?" Princess demands.

Setchra whispers, "'Tis a blue cone that *sparkles* on top."

She giggles then hurries down the road.

Her scratchy burlap dress shuffles back and forth while her little feet travel along the hard road. Soon, the horizon reveals a radiant white tower beneath a blue cone top. As she continues along the path, two smaller towers capped with matching cone tops comes into view on either side of the largest pillar.

"'Tis many towers," Princess tells her pearl.

As she continues on the path, a giant white wall comes into focus, towering over the forest.

"'Tis a castle," Princess rumbles in Setchra's voice.

"A CASTLE!" she shouts, breaking into an uneven run. In just a few moments, she tires and feels a cramp piercing her side. She pinches her abdomen for relief.

"Why do you pinch your side?" her pearl asks.

"Because Ma says it feels better!" Princess answers herself in gasps.

"Does it help?"

"No," Princess whimpers.

Princess continues her journey as the massive castle continues to rise into view. White birds fly over the forest and pass in front of the blue slate cones.

Princess watches the morning scene with wonder until her stomach growls. "My tummy hurts," she mumbles. She looks at the pearl and licks her lips. "No," she decides, "I couldn't. I eat what you eat."

She continues walking toward the township, nibbling on her bottom lip. Tall grass turns into open green fields. From where she is now, the castle is still a half-day journey by foot.

"We're never going to get there, Setchra!" Princess whines, her excitement fading.

She stops abruptly in the middle of the road and looks around, now gripping her aching tummy with both hands. Out in the center of a long green field, spots of red catch her eye.

She instantly sprints out into the rectangular clearing. The red objects multiply before her eyes.

"Please be food!" Princess prays.

Pinching her side and holding her pearl, she bounds into a thick, leafy strawberry patch.

"Do you see it, Setchra?" she enthusiastically asks the pearl.

Without hesitation, she shoves fist after fist of strawberries into her gaping mouth.

"You there! HALT!" a woman with fiery red hair shouts. The woman hikes up her blue apron and storms into the field, charging toward Princess.

Princess, caught with a red berry ring around her mouth, looks up at the woman with a startled expression. She snatches a few more strawberries, stands up, and tries to flee.

"Don't you run away from Auntie!" the woman yells, pointing her crooked finger. She charges toward the child, her cheeks turning bright red.

Princess crams the last few strawberries in her mouth. In her haste, she bites down on the pearl. She inhales sharply, lodging the half-chewed strawberries and pearl firmly in her throat. Panicked, she tries to run back to the road. Her throat constricts and she starts to choke. The girl grasps at her neck and begins to cough and gag.

"I've got ya now, you thieving little bugger!" With one hand, Auntie reaches for Princess. She raises her hand, prepared to swat the perceived criminal.

Princess tries to run away but can't move with the pearl blocking her airway.

Auntie seizes Princess by her elbow and whips her around, ready to slap the teeth out of her head.

She softens when she sees the little girl's face turning blue.

"See what thievery gets you?"

Princess tries to inhale, but cannot. Her vision fades and stars begin to cluster.

Auntie takes a knee, whips Princess around and bends the little girl over her lap. She slaps the child on the back, dislodging the pearl with a powerful blow. Princess coughs up pieces of red fruit. Her once pure pearl is now mingled with strawberry chunks on the ground. She regains her sight and immediately reaches for the pearl. Before Auntie manages to spin her around, Princess snatches the slimy jewel from the ground.

"BREATHE, CHILD!"

Princess gratefully obeys. As swiftly as she can, she replenishes her aching lungs.

"Trying to get y'self killed over a handful of berries, are ya?"

Princess tries to respond, but her throat is too sore. She presses one hand to the base of her throbbing neck. With a sulking glance she attempts to beg Auntie's pardon.

"Oh no, you shan't!" Auntie counters, resisting Princess' pucker. Without mercy, she seizes the little girl by the arm and hauls her across the field.

"Of all the things, thievery is the worst, if I dare say so m'self." She shakes a finger in Princess' face. "'Cept, for lyin'. Lyin', I dare say, is worse than thievery! Well, what have you to say for y'self?"

Princess opens her mouth and tries to speak, but the woman cuts her off.

"Nothing, you've nothin' to say for y'self, now do ya?" the middle-aged woman huffs. "Even if ya did, it'd all be lies. Lies, lies, lies!" Auntie rests her hands on her plump hips. "Next, it'll be murder. Of course, murder is the worst of them all, and I do dare say so m'self!"

Auntie drags the child across the field toward a small cottage in the distance, barely letting her feet touch the ground.

"Let me get a good look at ya." She examines the terrified child from head to toe. Her eyes soften even more. "Beautiful, aren't ya?"

She squishes Princess' cheeks together, inspecting her teeth. Princess squirms, trying to turn away from Auntie's rancid breath and crooked yellow teeth.

"Well then, are you going to tell me your list of woes or aren't ya?"

Princess takes a deep breath and looks down.

"My parents," she clears her throat, "were killed by a monster. My log rolled into the water where Setchra—" she holds up her pearl, her eyes still on the ground, "saved me."

"Setchra saved you?"

Princess uses her low voice, pretending to be the pearl. "Yes, she did."

"What's this?"

"Setchra...."

"You were saved by a pearl?"

"No ... I was saved by the mermaid Setchra. She gave me this pearl. I named it Setchra."

"Oh, I see." Auntie's temper evaporates. "Well, alright then," she taps her finger to her cheek, deep in thought.

After a moment, Auntie takes the pearl, wipes it down, and holds it out, giving it a good look over.

"If I were a dirty little thief," the middle-aged woman says, raising a scrutinizing brow, "I would keep this for m'self."

Princess shuffles her tiny feet, her heart sinking. *Please don't let her keep it*, she prays. She sniffles. "I'll never get Setchra back now."

Auntie inspects Princess' pathetic state. Her tone softens. "But I'm not a dirty thief, so I'm not going to steal." Auntie hands the precious jewel back to its rightful owner. Princess gratefully smiles.

"Tinksel."

"Bless you," Auntie says, mistaking Princess' misspoken gratitude for a sneeze. "Have ya learned your lesson?"

Princess nods emphatically.

"Will ya tell me the truth?"

Princess nods faster.

"Were your parents really slaughtered?"

Princess nods slowly, her bottom lip protrudes. Tears well in her big blue eyes, eviscerating any remnants of Auntie's wrath.

A shaggy shepherd dog bounds toward them, barking.

"Shut your blasted mouth!" Auntie shouts at the hound.

Princess' expression shifts from sorrow to a slight smile.

"My folks was killed too, ya know. 'Tis dangerous times, no doubt about it, 'tis dangerous times indeed." The fiery woman clucks her tongue and takes Princess' hand, forcing her to look away from the dog. "C'mon then, let's get ya cleaned up a bit."

The fierce garden warrior disappears, her fiery rage now replaced by unfathomable kindness.

CHAPTER V

SOWING & REAPING

The cock crows at the crack of dawn. He perches on top of a wood stack, proudly announcing the new day.

Princess sluggishly sits up in bed and takes a moment to piece together where she is. The sorrow of her loss sweeps over her. She shakes the tears from her eyes and pushes the pain away. "Oh, I hope that wonderful doggy is still here, 'tis happiness if he is," she says, grabbing a plain white dress by the bed and slipping it over her head, "and more sorrow if he's not."

Princess bites her lip and runs over to the window to see if the dog is still in the yard. She unlatches the metal hinge and pulls the window back, breathing in the crisp, spring air. She presses her hands on the window sill and jumps up and down, catching glimpses of a wagging tail.

"Hello, there!"

She flips around and searches for Setchra. When she finds her pearl, she snatches it and runs out of the room, carrying her leather shoes. She hops and tries to slip them on one at a time as she heads for the kitchen.

Light streams through the rectangular window and rests on the impeccably clean wooden countertops. Scents of lavender, thyme, and rosemary flood Princess' nose. Herb sprigs hang near the window. A copper pot on an iron stove billows steam. Auntie heaves the heavy oven lid open and tosses a log in.

"That should keep the pot warm!"

On the opposite side of the room, the fireplace stands empty, flanked by a pile of stacked wood and a tin basin that holds an old washboard.

Princess skips for the door.

"Where are you heading this early, dearie? Come and eat some breakfast."

Princess debates whether she should sprint out the door or sit down.

Auntie folds her arms and purses her lips together. "Don't test me child, I've little patience for disobedience."

Princess surrenders with a sigh and slips onto one of the wooden chairs. The little girl hurriedly shovels pottage into her mouth.

"My! You're an eager eater." Auntie shakes her head, her red-and gray-streaked hair shifting in a large bun.

Princess shoves the last spoonful of mush into her mouth and chews. "Done!" she proclaims with a smile.

Auntie looks in the bowl. "Yes, well, I'm not as eager as you."

"Can I go play with the dog?"

"I suppose, so long as you do your dishes."

Before Auntie can finish, Princess' long brown hair flashes out the door. Auntie chuckles to herself.

After finishing her breakfast, Auntie stands. "Oh!" she cries out, as a fierce pain freezes her knee in place. She puts her other hand on the table to support her weight and breathes deeply. "I don't need to be made whole, Lord. I just need to be manageable." Auntie puts pressure on her foot, testing the tenderness of her joint. A few moments pass before the pain subsides. "That'll do. Thank you, blessed Lord." She hobbles out of her cottage, carrying her bowl.

Princess runs up to the fluffy dog and throws her arms around its neck. Clouds of dust poof from its fur. Princess hacks. "You taste like dirt!"

"Arthur, you mangy mutt, get down!" Auntie grumbles, coming out the front door.

Arthur pants and licks Princess' face.

"He likes me!" the little girl shouts.

Arthur looks at Auntie as if to beg, *Can we keep her?*

"Have you met the rest of the bunch?" Auntie asks.

"You have more dogs?"

"No, no. Arthur is me only dog. Though the neighbor's dogs sometimes come over and try to lick me bowls." Auntie slowly kneels down and pets the happy dog. "The cock is Lancelot, the cat is Guinevere, and this," she proclaims as she picks up a shovel, "is Excalibur."

"I like Arthur! He's my second-best friend."

"Who's your first?" Auntie asks, hoping it is her.

"My pearl."

Auntie frowns. "Yes. Well, say goodbye to Arthur, who doesn't feed you or clothe you or save your life." Auntie thrusts Excalibur at Princess. "We've a field to till."

Princess stands up and brushes Arthur's fur from her hands. "Goodbye, Arthur, I'm going with my *bestest* friend, Auntie, who feeds me and clothes me and saves my life. We'll be back later, if you're still here."

Auntie smiles, her hurt feelings mollified. "Well, perhaps he can come with us, so long as you pledge to do all your work."

"Oh, I pledge. Wait, what is a pledge?"

Auntie smiles and kneels down so that she is eye level with Princess. "A pledge is when you vow to do something with your word."

"Then I pledge."

"Do you know what it means to keep your pledge?"

Princess presses her lips together and raises her head. "It's when a big eagle-lion is about to eat you but you stay in the log anyway, 'cause that's what your mum told you to do?"

Shocked, Auntie blinks rapidly. "Yes, well, 'tis that as well...." She shakes her head, clearing her thoughts. "Keeping your pledge is when you do what you say you are going to do."

Princess nods.

"But sometimes, it's not so easy, is it?"

"Then why do it?" Princess asks.

Auntie folds her arms. "Well, without pledges and labors to back them, no one would trust anyone, now would they?" Auntie pinches Princess' cheek. "And trust is what makes the moat go round."

"The moat goes ... round?"

Auntie extends her hand. "Come, follow me. I'll show you. But remember, you pledged to do your work first, before you play with Arthur."

"I remember."

Auntie leads Princess to the strawberry field she had found the girl in the day before. She takes the rusty shovel and pounds on the untilled portion.

"Farming requires constant labor," Auntie teaches. Gripping the handle, Auntie shoves the tool into the earth. She tries to pull back on it, but it won't break free.

"What's wrong?"

"Stuck," Auntie grumbles. "Worthless merchant metal!"

Princess looks back at the dog longingly and then reluctantly yields her attention to Auntie.

"This is not how we are supposed to use Excalibur." With great effort, the middle-aged woman frees the shovel. She lifts it up and thrusts it back into the ground. This time, she stands on it with both feet, pushing it farther into the earth. She pulls back on the handle and removes a chunk of grass. It makes a ripping noise as the roots tear from the soil. Princess smells the rich earth and smiles.

"Flip the grass over like this—" Auntie turns over the chunk of grass, then hacks at the clinging roots.

Princess focuses on the earthworms writhing as the blade cuts them in half. Her eyes widen and her mouth drops.

"Eeewwww!" she shrieks.

"It's good for the soil," Auntie responds.

Princess removes rocks while Auntie spends the rest of the day carving out a small clearing and dividing the earth into rows. Sweat drips down Princess' back and saturates the neck of her dress.

"'Tis a hot day!" Auntie says, fanning herself in the late afternoon heat. She removes a handkerchief and pats down her face. Feeling faint, she sits down on a rock for a moment.

"Once we divide the earth into rows—oh my, let me catch me breath," Auntie gasps. Her pupils narrow, and her face flushes white.

Princess sees the opening and runs over to Arthur. As she is about to pet him, she stops and asks, "Is it alright if I play with Arthur now?"

"Oh, there's much more work to be done, dearie."

"What about the pledge? You said if I did my work that I could play with Arthur."

"Fine then, go pet the dog!" Auntie waves Princess off, dismissing the child.

Mostly recovered, Auntie unties a cloth pouch from her rope belt.

"We must sow—" she pokes her finger in the moist soil and pushes a single seed deep into the earth, "so that we can reap."

She plants a few seeds, then calls Princess over to plant the rest.

With his tail wagging and tongue panting, Arthur watches Princess push the seeds into the soil. He tips his head left and right each time she stabs the earth. Suddenly, his ears perk up and he barks loudly.

Princess jumps up to see what Arthur is barking at. She hears the sound of clacking metal and stomping horse hooves clattering on cobblestone. Off in the distance, the sun's rays reflect off polished armor and blind her. She shields her eyes with her cupped hand, squinting to catch a glimpse of the approaching envoy.

Arthur sprints across the fresh clearing, his feet stomping down the wild grass as he runs past Auntie's house toward the road.

Instinctively, Princess runs over to Auntie and wraps her arms around the woman's round waist. Auntie pats the girl's head. "'Tis alright," she comforts.

As the procession nears, Princess sees a black knight with a silver dragon emblem on his chest. He rides a dark stallion at the head of the brigade. Behind him, a silver knight carries a crimson flag depicting a green dragon. Following the flag-bearer, men holding lances in one hand and broad shields in the other march at a steady pace. The shields vary in shape and size, each one displaying the family crest of its owner. Armor-plated Clydesdales lumber forward with thundering hoofs. They snort and neigh, their ears twitching. Around their necks and bulging chests, the warhorses carry heavy protective breastplates.

Princess feels the earth shaking beneath her and wonders how Arthur has the courage to bark.

"See that flag there, out in front?" Auntie points to the lead flag.

Princess nods.

"'Tis Sir Harmon's Dragon Brigade. Someone must've spotted a wretched beast."

A shiver goes down Princess' spine at the thought of a dragon. She grips Auntie's leg. "Will we all perish?" she squeaks.

"No, no, child. The Dragon Brigade will protect us."

Behind the knights, a group of peasants push a wheeled platform housing a large catapult shaped like a crossbow. Their caterpillar-like legs roll the wooden wheels forward with agonizing grunts and growls. An arrow, as long as a tree, is mounted on the enormous crossbow. Eight unarmed clydesdale horses pull the ballista while the men press against huge wooden posts to keep the weapon oriented.

"The test of a maiden is in her ability to catch a knight's eye," Auntie explains, batting her eyes and curtsying. The flag-bearer acknowledges Auntie by lowering the crimson flag. The brigade behind him uniformly renders a salute.

"You see?" Auntie boasts, continuing to bat her lashes.

Princess mimics the master and curtsies. A few of the knights wave, but fail to render her a salute.

"You have to be the first to curtsy, dearie. That's how a true lady attracts a knight's tender affections." She pulls out her handkerchief and waves it at the last knight. "Yoo-hoo!"

Buffeting her advances, the inexperienced knight snaps his helmet back to attention.

Mimicking Auntie, Princess pinches her pearl and waves it at the knights. "Yoo-hoo!" she squeals.

Princess persists until the entourage marches out of sight. A trail of dust looms in their wake.

Auntie sighs. "In my younger days, I attended many a ball," she reminisces. She sways back and forth and pretends to dance with Excalibur. "One day, you shall as well."

She hands Princess her handkerchief and returns to the task at hand. "But until then, we have to teach you about profit. Back to work!"

Princess looks at the handkerchief, then up at the castle. "First to curtsy gets the knight. So, what do I do with the handkerchief?"

Auntie dismisses the question with a wave of her hand. "In only a few weeks, we have crops."

"How much food does one person need?"

"Oh, this isn't all for me. We take the excess to the market."

"Where's the market?"

"In town, a short distance from the castle."

Princess' face lights up. "Can we see the castle from the market?"

"I should hope so, dearie! That's where we go to get our crop certified and weighed."

Princess jumps up and down, shouting, "I'm going to the castle!"

Arthur gets excited and jumps up with his front paws on Princess' shoulders.

"I'm the luckiest girl, Arthur!"

Arthur licks her on her mouth.

Princess turns in disgust. "Yuck!"

CHAPTER VI

BIDDING & BUYING

Weeks later, Princess has fallen into a normal routine. She hurtles out of bed, swiftly throws on her dress, and perches at the table. Auntie has already adjusted to the young girl's enthusiastic schedule, getting up the moment Lancelot crows.

For breakfast, Princess gobbles the last bit of leftover pottage and opens her mouth to speak.

"You may go and play with Arthur before washing the dishes," Auntie permits.

Arthur stands with the warm morning sun on his back, panting in the doorway as he waits for Princess.

Princess scoots out of her wooden chair and scampers over to kiss Arthur on the nose. She wraps her little arms around his neck and squeezes tightly. "I love you, Arthur!"

Giggling, she jumps on his back and whistles. Arthur whirls around and darts outside with Princess on his back.

"Press on, Arthur!" Princess shouts. She grits her teeth when Arthur speeds to a trot. "Wait, not so fast!" she squeals, pulling on fistfuls of fur.

Auntie smiles. Looking through a window, her eyes light up with delight as she observes Princess and Arthur playing. Warmth fills her heart. She places her hand on her chest. "Thank you Lord. Laughter is truly one of many things that was missing in my home."

A short time later, Auntie comes outside in a maroon dress, adorned with a hat that resembles an upside-down flowerpot. A white lace ribbon tied beneath her chin secures the absurdity to her head.

"Princess, 'tis time to go to market," Auntie calls out.

Princess totters out of the barn toting fresh milk in a tin pail with both hands. She huffs with each weighted step. "I'm coming, Auntie!" she shouts back.

Arthur runs close behind her, stopping to lick up the delicious cream that spills over.

When Princess covers the short distance to the house, Auntie lifts the pail out of her hands. "Such a big helper you are, dearie," Auntie notes, raising an eyebrow at the now half-empty bucket.

"I've laid a dress out for you, a bit nicer than what you normally wear." Auntie lowers her tone. "Try not to dirty it, tangle it, or destroy it." Her tone rises. "We must look our best at the market or no one will purchase our goods."

Princess nods and scampers into the cottage.

She hops through the narrow hall unlacing her work boots. She pulls her work dress over her head and momentarily gets stuck. Flailing her arms, she wiggles her way out.

Once freed, her attention is immediately drawn to a beautiful white cotton dress on the bed. A single light blue ribbon is tied around the waist with the initials T.S. embroidered on the corner. Princess' eyes dart around, examining every detail of the floral lace collar, the tiny holes in the needlepoint, and the soft, thin fabric that forms the body of the dress.

Placing one of the ribbons between her fingers, she feels the smooth fabric. *'Tis what the sky feels like*, she thinks. Gently, she lifts the dress by the shoulders and looks it up and down.

Auntie appears at the doorway. "Would you like a little help?" she kindly offers.

Princess nods and hands Auntie the ensemble. "I've never worn anything so beautiful!"

Delicately, Auntie pinches the dress by the shoulders and lifts the beautiful dress high above Princess' head. "Well, you've also never been to market. Now, put your arms up," Auntie instructs.

Princess stretches her arms high and wiggles her fingers as the dress slides over her head. One slender arm pushes through a thin sleeve and then the other.

"Simply beautiful," Auntie coos, watching Princess spin.

Princess giggles and adjusts the waistband. "What is this?" she asks, pointing to the monogram.

"Those are letters. Can't you read them?"

Princess shakes her head.

"I was hoping you had some learning." Auntie pats Princess on the back. "When chores slow down, we shall plant the seeds of knowledge, just as we planted the seeds of crop."

"So what does this mean?" Princess contorts her head to look at the letters on the ribbon.

Auntie laughs. "Those are my given initials, Tabatha Shepherd."

"I thought your name was Auntie."

"My nickname is Auntie. My given name is Tabatha Shepherd."

Princess pushes her lips together and looks up inquisitively. "Do I have a nickname?"

"No, not yet," Auntie responds.

"You could call me Setchra," she proposes.

"That's the name of your pearl."

"I know."

"Well you can't name everything the same as your pearl, or we won't be able to sort you out."

"How about…," Princess taps her finger to her chin, "White Furry Petal."

Auntie stares, bewildered. "That's a terrible nickname. You can't force a nickname, dearie. It just comes along." She buttons up the back of Princess' dress. "Look at you! So pretty."

Princess follows Auntie out of the room. In the hallway, she pats her pockets and gasps. "I'm such a bad ma! I've left Setchra all alone!"

She whips around, runs to her room, and snatches the pearl from beneath her pillow. She turns back around and quickly catches up to Auntie at the door.

Seeing Princess, Auntie rubs her hands together and declares, "Now let's get to market! Me mouth is watering for profit."

The two depart the house holding hands and head toward the barn. Inside, Auntie places a metal bit in her horse's mouth. She fastens leather belts around the horse's ears and face, reining in the towering Clydesdale. The horse's blonde mane shakes back and forth as he adjusts the mouthpiece.

"That's a good boy, Merlin."

Auntie holds an apple in front of the horse's nose and keeps it just below his chin. With her other hand, she backs the horse out of the stall, keeping one hand flat on the top of his snout so he doesn't rear up.

Arthur circles Princess a few times and barks. Eventually, he positions himself between the girl and the horse, shielding Princess with his shaggy body.

"I know, Arthur, Merlin sees you!" shouts Auntie.

Once the massive horse is free from the stable, Auntie saddles him. She then steers Merlin to a cart with two wooden handles and secures them in place with a ring and pinion.

Princess looks inside the cart and sees that it is packed with radishes, lettuce, beets, cheese, potatoes, sweet potatoes, carrots, cabbage, and tobacco. Princess eyes widen. "Will we buy our own castle with our profit?"

Auntie laughs and shakes her head, her flowerpot hat shifting loosely.

"'Fraid not dearie, 'twould take many more carts than we have here."

"How many carts?"

Auntie helps the child into the back of the cart. "I said I would plant the seeds of knowledge, I didn't say I could teach you how to count. I hardly know m'self."

Auntie escorts Merlin and the trailing cart over to a set of log steps. She makes her way to the top and takes a moment to rest her knee. With both hands on the Clydesdale, she springs onto the muscular horse, slinging half of her torso over the saddle. "Ouugghhffff!" she exhales. She pushes herself upright and sits sidesaddle on the great Merlin.

"Why don't you drape your foot over the other side?" Princess asks.

Auntie, never missing an opportunity to instruct, gives the child a stern look. "Because, my dear, we are ladies and ladies musn't straddle!"

Merlin whinnies in affirmation.

With a jerk of the reins and cluck of her tongue, Auntie starts the group off toward the castle. Princess' feet fly up in the air from the sudden jolt. She tumbles backwards over the produce, landing in a white ruffled heap.

The little girl crawls over the burlap sacks of potatoes, carrots, and radishes, hurrying back to her place before Auntie can scold her for wrecking the dress. Princess stands up and fixes her dress, using all the powers of subtlety she can summon.

"I can hardly contain my excitement," Princess whispers to Setchra.

With a flip of the reins, Auntie leads the horse onto the cobblestone path to the castle. The cart rattles as the wheels roll over the densely packed stones, jostling Princess. With a vibrating voice, the girl asks, "Can I walk with Arthur?"

Auntie shakes her head and waves for the little girl to sit down in the cart. "First part's the worst part!" she shouts.

Princess sighs but obeys Auntie's orders. She leans over the right side of the cart and focuses on the pointy peaks of the castle to distract herself from the aching ride.

Auntie slows Merlin's pace with a pull of the reins, making the ride less painful.

"Middle part's not the worst part, but 'tis almost as bad as the start," she informs Princess.

Arthur trots behind the cart, keeping a faithful eye on Princess.

Princess reaches in her pocket and removes her pearl. "We're going to the castle, Setchra. Are you terribly excited?"

"Yes," Princess creaks.

"Do you want a closer look?" Princess asks, as though the pearl were a curious person.

"Yes," Setchra's voice answers.

Princess lifts the pearl up as though it were an eye. "Alright, but you must be careful. I don't want to drop you, like you made me drop you last time," Princess warns. A worried look flashes across her face and she presses the pearl to her cheek. "You are far too precious to be lost!"

She smothers the pearl, then carefully holds it up over her head again. She moves the pearl all around, making sure it gets a long glimpse of the three towers before bringing it back down.

"I want to see more," Setchra's voice croaks.

A dip in the stone road bumps the girl hard enough that she drops the pearl.

"HALT! HALT! HALT!" Princess shouts. She jumps up and looks around.

Auntie pulls back on the reins, bringing the carriage to a sudden stop.

The momentum smashes Princess against the box plank.

"What is it? Did you drop your pearl?" the wise woman inquires.

Princess leaps to her feet and nods.

"Well, what did you think would happen if you held it up like that?"

"You could see me?" Princess asks sheepishly.

Auntie folds her arms. "I may have been born long ago child, but I wasn't born so long ago that I couldn't anticipate your—" Auntie spots the pearl on a pile of green peas. "Oh look, 'tis right there in the peas."

Princess looks down, scanning everywhere. "Where?"

"Haven't you eyes girl? You are practically standing on top of it."

"Where?" Princess whimpers.

"There child, right there!" Auntie says, pointing directly at it.

Princess gasps when she spots her precious pearl. "I've found it," she cries.

Auntie raises a brow. "Oh, *you* found it, have you?"

Princess sits down and pinches the pearl between her fingers.

"We've a good distance to the castle and we have no time for your meanderings. Now as much as I hate to say it, sit still, put the pearl away, and secure yourself." Without warning, Auntie turns back around and flips the reins. As before, the cart proceeds.

"I could have lost you!" Princess mumbles, squeezing Setchra as tight as she can.

"Ouch, you are hurting me," Setchra rasps.

"I don't care," Princess sulks, punishing her pearl for misbehaving. After scolding Setchra, Princess releases her grip. "Now you behave!"

Awhile later, Princess leans on the side of the carriage and begins to hum a soft, vibrant tune. She is mesmerized by the tall swaying grass and wild white lilies popping out of the ground. Along the towering cluster of trees, a raven zips in and out of the woods.

"Come," she says, beckoning it to follow her. The bird flies in the opposite direction and Princess huffs in frustration. She rests her elbows on her knees and her chin on her hands. She looks down the bumpy path and sees a bend in the road.

"Have we arrived yet?" she asks, but Auntie ignores her. "I can't even see it," she sighs.

As they approach the bend in the road, Princess sees beams of light through an opening in the foliage. The abnormal luster piques her interest. As the carriage clears the foliage, the ivory columns to the castle come into full view.

"'Tis heavenly," Princess murmurs in awe. "How much farther?"

"Half a league. Be patient child, you're grating on me," Auntie warns.

At the top of the tallest tower, Princess thinks she sees an arched window. As Merlin pulls the cart forward, she sees the morning light reflect off paned glass. She puts her hand in her pocket and clasps her pearl.

"Can you see her, Setchra?"

"I can't see anything," Setchra rasps.

"I see a beautiful, angelic woman with brunette hair and blue eyes brushing her daughter's hair."

"What's her daughter's name?" Setchra asks.

"Probably Princess."

She imagines several doting maidservants faithfully laboring to beautify the royal daughter. Princess pictures herself surrounded by piles of meat pies, fruit pies, and towering sweet cakes. Her taste buds tingle. She can only imagine what heavenly treasures lie in the top of the Queen's tower. She sighs heavily and pretends to listen to the wondrous melody of a harp. Her mother had described the instrument once, but Princess herself has never seen one.

At the top of the royal castle, three white flags with red crosses in their centers rise and fall with the gentle breeze. High on the castle's wall, it looks as though every other block has been removed.

"Why are there spaces on the roof?"

"Eh?" Auntie asks.

"Up on the roof of the castle, they forgot several spots."

"Where?"

Princess points to the roof of the castle and notices a man pacing between the missing blocks. "Who's that?" She stands up in the carriage and waves wildly at the marching archer, who doesn't appear to notice her distant greeting.

"Probably just a guard trolling past an archer's break," Auntie answers, keeping her eyes on the road.

From on top of the castle, a tall man named Bort peers through the archer's break. The expert marksman scans a grassy plain and sleepy rolling hills just beyond. A large, wide forest spans over the horizon as far as the eyes can see. Bort scans for any potential disturbances in the dense vegetation.

"Spot any smoke trails?" lead officer Cremwell asks.

Bort shakes his head. Cremwell sighs and falls into step next to Bort.

Behind Bort and Cremwell, a stout archer named Rudy smashes a mosquito against his cheek. After inspecting his hand, he covers his mouth and yawns. Rudy clucks his tongue at an ancient archer named Withers. "What'll ya bet?" Rudy prods.

"Eh?" Withers cups his ear.

Rudy rubs two fingers together, signaling money, and mouths the word, "BET."

"Two sticks," Withers responds.

"Two pence," Rudy sets the terms. "One for each stick."

"One pence." Withers replies. "Two sticks."

Rudy shakes his head no.

"Ah, go on then!" Withers caves.

"Done," Rudy solidifies the deal.

Rudy reaches in his pocket and removes a fist full of twigs. Withers turns about, then begins marching a few feet in front him. Rudy rubs his hands together and blows on the twigs for luck. Withers excitedly wiggles his fingers and anticipates the toss. With a quick motion, Rudy tosses the twigs over his shoulder. Withers bites his bottom lip, then eagerly cups his hands together. The old archer proves nimble, catching four twigs with unexpected swiftness.

"Four pence!" Withers proudly proclaims, holding his wrinkled palms open to show Rudy that he caught more than two twigs.

"Those were not the terms!" Rudy rebuttals.

"One pence per twig!" Withers shouts, nudging Rudy with the four twigs.

"Two pence, those were the terms, ya deaf lug!"

"You filthy cheat! Your reputation'll be sullied if ya refuse to pay. No one will play catcher with a scoundrel the likes of you."

�֎֎֎

Traveling along the cobblestone road, Princess gazes at the massive castle. *How can it be so large?* Princess puzzles.

When the cart comes to a complete stop, Princess lowers her gaze and discovers a wall directly in front of the cart, stretching both directions without end.

"How are we going to get over that?" Princess asks.

"Hush, child, let Auntie tend to business."

Princess shrinks back into the cart.

"What do you see?" Princess croaks in Setchra's voice.

"Hush, Setchra, let me tend to business," Princess scolds.

Auntie cups her hands around her mouth and shouts, "HELLO UP THERE!"

Princess peeks over her guardian's shoulder and spots two tall oak doors with a giant gold eagle etched onto them. Princess cringes at the sight of the eagle's talons. Rising above the gate, two gray watchtowers stand erect.

A slender man with a thin black beard appears on top of the wall. The man leans forward, exposing a chrome helmet with a wide circular rim. Six armored men holding spears appear next to the other guard. They glare at the red-headed woman and child.

"State your business!" shouts the gatekeeper.

"Bidding and buying," Auntie shouts.

The gatekeeper grabs a scroll and unravels it. "Name?"

Auntie squints up at the gatekeeper and shouts, "Tabatha Shepherd!"

The man glances through the scroll. "Ah, yes. Inventory?"

"Produce."

"Produce? The scroll lists you under 'livestock.' Unless you are selling livestock, you cannot enter," the gatekeeper sneers.

Auntie purses her lips. "I can't feed me flocks without grain. Grain requires pence. So I sell produce to buy grain."

The gatekeeper shakes his head and looks at the line of merchants that have begun to noisily gather in line behind Auntie, "Wait your turn!" he shouts. He glances back at Auntie. "I can't let you in with produce. You'll have to trade or grow your own grain."

Auntie shouts, "Charles!"

"Beg your pardon?"

Auntie shouts louder, "CHARLES!"

"Ma'am, my name is Winston, not Charles," the guard responds.

A heavy hand falls down on Winston's shoulder, jolting him. He turns to see a towering, seven-foot man with an enormous belly and muscular arms.

Charles leans down until his scarred face is nearly touching Winston's nose. The giant pokes Winston in the chest with a sausage-like finger. "I'm Charles, ya lug."

Winston gulps, frozen in place by the goliath.

"And that there is Auntie," Charles explains. "She's my friend." The giant's cool blue eyes firmly fix on Winston's.

"Yes, sir," Winston mutters.

Charles leans in and whispers in Winston's ear, "That means she's your friend, too!"

"I-I-I didn't know your first name was Charles," Winston stammers.

"Well, now ya do," Charles places his hefty hand on Winston's shoulder. "Tell ya what, since you're new to the gate and you think inventory is within the scope of your power, how's about you escort that sweet, dear friend of mine to the market and help her set up shop."

Trembling, Winston gulps. "Aye, Sir."

"And since ya need to be working on your keeping, how 'bout you stand post by her lot and make sure no thieves get the better of her."

Winston nods. "Aye, Sir!"

Charles pops his head over the tower. "Mornin to ya, Auntie! Still the first merchant to market, I see," Charles bellows.

"'Tis the only way to find a suitable lot. I take it I'll be selling me goods?"

Charles smiles, revealing tinted yellow teeth. "Aye, and it looks like you'll be gettin' some help."

From behind the gate, Winston scurries down the narrow catwalk. He holds his helmet on with one hand while he orders two men to remove a large beam locking the towering doors in place.

The massive oak doors swing open.

"I'm Sergeant Winston. I'll be escorting you to market today, Ma'am." Winston grabs the leather reins from Auntie and begins directing Merlin.

"Excellent," Auntie smirks.

As the cart passes through the gate, Princess looks up and sees a spiked portcullis secured above her head. She shudders at the thought of it crashing down on her. Winston leads Merlin toward a towering wooden fence that runs parallel to the outer stone wall. The wooden wall is made out of stripped pine trees that have been whittled to a point at the top.

Princess furrows her brow and decides to risk showing Setchra her surroundings. She pretends to hold her pearl above the sharply pointed fence spikes and impale the innocent friend over and over again.

"Ouch! That hurts, huh, Setchra?" Princess whimpers.

"Yes, it does," she says in Setchra's gravelly voice.

"Oh, that's not nice. I'm sorry." Princess repents and presses the smooth gem to her cheek.

Winston glances over his shoulder and shoots Princess a scowling glance.

Princess draws her pressed lips to the side of her mouth and scrutinizes Winston. "I don't like you," Princess blurts out.

"Princess! You musn't say such things," Auntie interjects. "Sergeant Winston must not be ridiculed, even if he is deserving." Auntie places her hand on her heart and looks toward the heavens. "'Tis unbecoming of ladies such as ourselves to criticize."

Princess mimics Auntie, placing her hand over her heart and pointing her nose to the sky. "Indeed!"

Winston, now utterly humiliated, hangs his head and accepts his lot. "Where to, Ma'am?" he grumbles.

"Corner lot three, if you please," Auntie responds.

Winston pulls tight on the reins and guides Merlin through a set of pine doors with a red dragon painted in the center.

Princess bubbles with excitement. She crouches down and rests her chin on her fingers, ready to see this new place called "market." She leans out of the cart and shouts, "Hurry! I want to see the castle!"

"Princess, sit back this instant!" Auntie scolds.

Princess holds her pearl up. "It wasn't me. It was Setchra."

Auntie gives her a firm glare over her shoulder.

Princess lowers the pearl.

"Alright, it *was* me." She retreats down into the cart as they pass through the red dragon gate. Princess' mouth drops open in awe as the full splendor of the glorious castle overwhelms her.

CHAPTER VII

SQUIRES & SIRES

"Oh my," Princess says, finally seeing the castle up close. Her eyes climb the tallest glistening tower, which seems to touch the heavens. White triangular flags with red crosses are posted at the top of each castle spire, the wind causes them to flutter.

"'Tis divine," Princess declares. She cranes her neck straining to take in the length of the castle. "'Tis as long as our farm, Auntie!" Princess shouts.

Auntie glances at the castle. "'Tis a magnificent sight," she admits.

Winston continues to lead Merlin down the cobblestone road. Princess finally tears her eyes away from the castle to discover she is in the middle of a town.

8White plaster houses with slate roofs line the narrow road through town. Wavy glass windows allow Princess a look inside the homes. As she passes by, Princess glimpses decorative desks, chairs, tables, couches, and furnishings of exquisite taste. For the first time, she realizes her poverty. She slowly sinks down into the cart. Overwhelmed by the abundant presence of civilization, Princess begins to feel small and alone. She clutches Setchra in her sweaty palm, trying to draw solace from her pearl.

The journey through the center of town seems to take forever. A woman dressed in a navy velvet gown steps out of her brick home. Her long brown hair is tied in a loose, braided chignon. The flowing gown covers her feet, making it seem as though she were floating along the ground.

Princess holds Setchra up and makes the pearl glide through the air like the woman does. "Do you like that, Setchra?"

"Yes, it makes me feel pretty."

The woman greets another woman dressed in a violet gown with a beaming smile. The two ladies exchange high-pitched pleasantries. Princess smiles and waves, but the lovely ladies ignore her. She sees a little girl run up to the fancy woman in violet and take her hand. Memories of her parents stir and Princess sees her mother's loving eyes. The little girl feels sadness and then a crushing jealousy when the mother and daughter unite. Fighting back tears, Princess waves at the raven-haired daughter, whose dress matches her mother's.

Rather than returning the pleasantry, the girl cocks her head to the side and sneers at Princess. Princess lowers her hand in shame.

The cart enters a grassy field. Winston brings it to a sudden halt a short distance from the castle. Princess tumbles over, falling into a pile of carrots. She hits her head on the side of the cart with a *thunk*.

Princess whimpers and rubs her head.

With Winston's help, Auntie dismounts Merlin. She curtsies, forcing Winston to salute. "Thank you, kind Sir," she simpers. Behind her, she hears Princess starting to whimper.

"Why, whatever is the matter, darling?" Auntie asks, more motherly than usual.

"He hit my head on the cart," Princess snivels.

Arthur claws at the cart wheel, concerned for Princess.

"Oh she'll be all right, Arthur," Auntie reassures him.

Merchants begin to cluster in the market, setting up their wares. Princess watches as men in brown tunics and green stockings hammer wooden stakes and strap down canvas tent flaps with rope.

"Now listen here, dearie. When the orders start coming in, I'll take the money and you distribute the produce. Auntie loves profit!"

"How much do I give them? I don't know how to count."

"Most of them don't know how to count past their fingers or toes, but if they ask you for more, just give them more."

Princess presses her eyebrows together in confusion. She looks at her wiggling fingers and down at her toes.

Several ladies step out of their homes at the same time, holding various baskets. Some have their hair gathered above their ears supported by gold or silk nets. Many are adorned with long, flowing veils of varying widths and lengths, some secured with jeweled headbands across their foreheads. The sleeves of their dresses vary in width and decoration. Their elaborate velvet dresses range in colors from dark blue to pastel pink, separating the reputable consumers from the plainly dressed commoners.

Ladies hustle about from merchant to merchant, asking, "How much for this?" or "How much for that?"

Auntie wisely selected the best spot nearest the road. She doesn't waste time setting up a tent or table.

"Fresh celery! Crisp carrots! Ripe radishes! Best prices and best produce!" Auntie hollers, waving for customers.

The women of Tremble Nemble swarm her cart. Several small, womanly hands bypass Princess to handle the produce themselves.

"Stop!" Princess rises to her feet inside the cart and shouts at the clamoring women. "That's my duty!"

Auntie circles the clustering woman, collecting coins of different weights and metals. "Pay as you go! Your word is good! Pay as you go!"

"Half price on all produce!" shouts a thin man, wearing a brown, hooded cape. He points to his tent just down the row from Auntie. A few women break away from the pack and head toward his produce.

"I'll have half a dozen turnips, one dozen eggs, and a pound of potatoes," shouts an old woman, dressed in a dark gray cook's uniform.

Princess feels like her head is swimming. A mix of the ladies' perfumes engulfs her and their shouting inundates her. Their roaring voices and sweaty faces multiply. Princess struggles to hear her own thoughts, feeling smaller and smaller.

"I'll be needing two dozen strawberries, a half-pound of cheese, and a bushel of carrots!" yells a striking young woman in a golden dress. Princess eyes her wedding band as she unknowingly hands her more than she's ordered.

"Thank you!" The woman says, dropping a silver shilling in the cart.

Winston leans against the cart, watching Princess. He reaches forward and stops a greedy woman's hand. "Mind if I aid you with that?" he asks Princess. She obligingly nods, her big blue eyes filling with relief. Winston takes the goods out of the cart, counts them, and then collects the money from the woman who attempted to take more than she paid for. Winston begins taking multiple orders, exchanging the proper number of goods for the exact price. He dumps the coins in Auntie's moneybag and continues taking orders. Oblivious to Winston's assistance, Auntie continues to gather as much money as she can.

"Last time you gave me twice as much!" shouts a woman at Auntie.

"Times are hard on all of us," Auntie counters.

"I'll take my business elsewhere."

Auntie flips her hair. "I'll give you the same as before, minus the eggs."

The woman glares at Auntie defiantly. Auntie squares her shoulders.

"Very well!" the woman caves, handing Auntie her coins.

Terrified of the market commotion, Arthur hides beneath the cart.

"Settle down, ladies, settle down! All orders go through me!" Winston shouts.

"Is that so?" Auntie folds her arms and looks sternly at Winston.

"Well, ah...." Winston stutters, his face turning bright red as he hands her a fistful of collected coins. "I yield to your iron will, my lady." The gate guard bows.

Ladies descend on Auntie. She wipes streams of sweat from her brow.

Princess holds up her pearl. "*Tinksel* for coming to Setchra's Market."

✕✕✕

High in the west castle tower, two barons stand before an open window looking down on the marketplace. One baron thoughtfully strokes his short, black beard. Sir Harmon, leader of the fierce Dragon Brigade, is the most senior, battle-hardened knight of Tremble Nemble. He folds his arms, flexing his chest muscles beneath a long velvet tunic with an embroidered silver dragon.

"I wonder," Sir Harmon speculates, turning to Sir Cynric, "if the boys aren't ready to become squires?"

Sir Cynric runs his fingers along his brown beard. "We weren't much older than they when we earned our royal emblems." His gray eyes flash with excitement.

"Do you think the king will approve of two barons, such as ourselves, wasting time thrashing fledgling squires?" Sir Harmon asks, fidgeting with his golden rope belt, from which hangs a silver-handled dagger in a black sheath.

"I daresay, he will only be upset if we fail to include him in the plot," Sir Cynric replies. The two men exchange a knowing smirk and nod in agreement. Sir Cynric puts his arm around his good friend's shoulder.

"As fathers, and as men, I've been counting the days until our sons would take this journey," Sir Cynric proudly proclaims. The seasoned warriors both grin.

"Shall I fetch the lads or would you rather?" Sir Harmon asks.

"You are the king's Master of Arms. I assume His Majesty would prefer to be briefed by you as his second in command. I will go for the boys."

The barons bow as they part company.

Sir Cynric strides toward the exit of the circular stone room. A golden lion painted across his chest reflects the patterned light shining through one of the stained-glass windows. At the thick oak door he grabs the iron door pull and twists, pushing open the creaking door.

Sir Cynric clanks down the spiral staircase, a long, sheathed blade thudding against his thigh. A golden eagle is embroidered on his left shoulder. The mighty bird grasps crossing swords, signifying his rank as Baron of the Home Guard, a rank lower than Sir Harmon's. He and Sir Harmon hold the Baron title along with eight other senior knights.

A draft sweeps through the stairway, causing the pigeons to rustle. Cynric hardly notices. He reminisces of his boyhood excitement when he earned his Royal Emblem long ago. He remembers his father guiding him and Sir Harmon up these very stairs to the Barons' Tower for the first time. Cynric smiles.

He knew then that Sir Harmon would one day be Master of Arms, but he had had far less confidence in himself, not realizing that he would one day be serving beside his brother-in-arms.

Small arched windows light a course for Cynric and illuminate the stone floors and plaster walls. He stops, realizing he has lost track of which floor he is on. He looks out the closest east-facing window toward the tower directly across from him. Using his thumb as a place marker, he counts the number of windows to the ground. *One, two, three, four, five.* He determines that he is on the fifth floor. "Perfect," he murmurs.

Cynric progresses down the stairwell onto a small stone landing. Turning the door's ring, he walks through the entry and moves into a tall candlelit foyer. "Prince!" he calls. His voice echoes off the dim hallway. Turning to his left, he walks over scarlet-carpeted floor and draws back a velvet curtain, securing it with a gold clamp.

Daylight floods the hall, revealing its vast depth and richly decorated interior. Marble columns are positioned near the walls of the room. Decorative golden rings wrap around each column's capital and base. Each ring is inscribed with a knightly principle. Cynric passes one and silently mouths, *Strength and Honor.* Tracing his fingers across the next golden band, Cynric reads, *Falter Not.* He moves on to the next, *Press On.*

Coming out of his reverie, Cynric shouts, "Prince, come forth!" He walks down the opulent hallway, his leather boots moving soundlessly on the hand-woven rugs. Finely-carved furniture decorates the corridor and immense oil paintings with gold frames hang on the walls between richly-covered windows. A pair of eerie green eyes seems to follow Sir Cynric as he moves through the wide passage. Passing the pale lady in the portrait, Cynric shivers involuntarily and quickens his pace.

Muffled voices attract the baron's attention. Moving beneath a row of crystal chandeliers, he slows his pace. The baron stops in front of a wide doorway with a Latin inscription etched in the stone archway, reading "Bibliotheca." He opens one of the thick doors and enters the expansive room.

"Father!" shouts a sandy-haired boy.

"Prince," Cynric spreads his arms. The child scrambles to his feet. The other royal children remain seated with open books on their laps. They sit circled around a priest dressed in a brown robe. Bright light flows in through the glass-paned windows, illuminating the domed ceiling above their heads. Picturesque tales depicting Tremble Nemble's history are painted within each sunken panel. A portrait of a woman holding a basket is silhouetted by a yellow painted sun. Her eyes are a powder blue and she wears a white peasant's dress with a navy apron. Neighboring the woman's portrait is a knight in shining armor with his helmet removed. He battles a menacing green dragon with his flashing sword.

The priest, Father Hayden, nods his head to acknowledge Sir Cynric.

Prince's eyes widen with excitement as he sprints toward Cynric. The boy wears an outfit similar to his father's, but with only a twine belt and no rank or title marked on his clothing.

Wrapping him in a fatherly embrace, Cynric lifts Prince off the ground. "Today is your day, my boy."

Prince glances upward. His eye catches one of the ceiling's many paintings. He notices a painting of a young boy, not unlike himself. He is viewed from behind and appears to be loading a stone into a sling. A muscular bearded giant towers over him with his massive sword raised.

Cynric releases Prince and claps him heartily on the back. Looking past Prince he calls out, "Leon, you are needed as well!"

A bright, chubby boy with blond hair stands and bows to Father Hayden.

The priest nods, acknowledging the request, and waves him on. Dressed in a plain black tunic like his father, Sir Harmon, Leon walks toward Cynric. He slams his leather-bound book on a flat carving of the Earth. On the map are the British Islands in an exaggerated scale and a single land mass representing the rest of the world. In the southeast rim of the island, a white castle indicates the capital's location.

A head taller than Prince, Leon stands in front of Sir Cynric and bellows, "Reporting for duty, Sir!" Leon raises his closed fist straight up into the air and then out toward Cynric. "FOR GOD AND KING!" he shouts.

"Excellent salute! I see you've been working on it," Cynric remarks proudly.

"I've been working on my salute as well, Father," Prince says. Instead of measured breaks between each phase, Prince does it all at once and whistles, "STRENGTH AND HONOR!" He smiles, missing his two front teeth.

"Hmm, shall we be getting along?" Cynric asks, dismissing his son's unpracticed display. Prince sighs and hangs his head.

Cynric leads the boys back up the spiral staircase to the Barons' Tower. Prince tries to keep up with his father.

Leon gasps for air and manages to huff, "Sir Cynric, pray tell, what is this… good and noble task… the king…would have of us?" He puffs and groans miserably.

Cynric pauses and frowns. "Battle plans are never discussed without the king."

"Battle plans?" Leon huffs.

Prince turns to Leon and mouths, *Battle plans!*

Cynric turns and continues up to the Barons' Chambers. At the pinnacle of the tower, the trio enters a modestly-furnished round room. It contains a round white oak table that is empty except for a finely-carved penholder housing nine white-feathered pens. An inkbottle rests next to them.

"The Round Table," Prince whispers, his voice filled with awe. He extends his hand to touch it, feeling a reverence for the honored space.

An entourage of footsteps echoes through the corridor. The king's booming laugh fills the room as he enters the chamber. Stocky, the king wears a fine white shirt, black pants, and a belt of interconnected gold squares. The buckle on his belt is shaped like the royal emblem of the golden eagle. His rotund girth nearly envelopes it. A red satin cloak conceals his shoulders and drapes down his back.

Both boys immediately kneel.

"Sire, I've retrieved both youth as we've discussed," Sir Cynric reports.

King Henry nods. A modest golden crown rests on his head.

"Rise," King Henry commands.

From the corner of his eye, Prince catches a glimpse of the king's young daughter, Faye, waving at him from beneath the round table. He stares in surprise but obeys the king's command. When he stands up, the table conceals her perfectly.

"Are you each prepared to take the sacred oath of squire?" the king's deep voice rumbles.

"Yes, Sire!" the boys shout in unison.

"Excellent. Be seated."

Harmon and Cynric pull out tall mahogany chairs from under the round table for their boys and then for themselves.

"Are you boys familiar with arms?" King Henry asks, taking his seat at the round table.

"LANCES ARE METAL-TIPPED SPEARS, WEIGH SEVEN POUNDS AND CAN PENETRATE—" shouts Leon. His father leans over and speedily covers his son's mouth, while King Henry recovers from the boisterous outburst.

"Sire, perhaps some specifics for the eager boys," Sir Harmon pleads, while muffling Leon's shouts with his palm.

"Very well. Are either of you familiar with catapults?" King Henry inquires.

Both boys nod eagerly.

"Can you navigate to the War Chambers?" he asks, his maple brown eyes twinkling mischievously.

"Of course, Sire," Prince replies.

"Very well. This is your task: acquire as many eggs as you can from the kitchen, retrieve the miniature catapult on the map table, and meet us on the top floor of the Barons' Tower as quickly as your little feet can carry you."

Both boys nod with excitement.

"Oh, and tell Priest that the king requires his assistance at the center of the marketplace, by the fountain," King Henry adds.

Sir Cynric covers a smile with his hand.

"Anything else, Sire?" Leon asks.

"That'll do. Now if you are somehow discovered in your task, you must show loyalty to the king by not mentioning this meeting to *anyone*."

"Especially the queen," interrupts Sir Harmon.

"Yes, *especially* the queen! But if you *are* discovered, you will not receive your royal emblem or squire title," King Henry warns.

The boys exchange worried glances. King Henry stands and the others follow suit. The king and his knights move toward the arched doorway to leave when a tiny voice squeaks from beneath the table.

"But what's *my* task, Father?"

Shocked, the group looks beneath the table and discovers Faye poking her head out. King Henry returns to the table, kneels down, and extends his hand. "*You* can join us on the roof."

"But I want to go steal eggs from the kitchen!"

King Henry holds his finger up to his mouth and shushes her.

"Nobody is *stealing* anything," he corrects his daughter.

"Are the eggs theirs?" she asks.

King Henry's face grows serious. "Let us avoid the debate and get to the point. What is it you want?"

"I want to go with Prince to the kitchen!"

"Will you keep this a secret?"

"I won't tell Mother, if you let me go." She smiles mischievously and holds her pinky finger up.

King Henry extends his jeweled pinky and her tiny finger wraps around his. Locked in the most sacred of shakes, their hands move up and down as their heads nod.

"I have your word." King Henry seals the deal and helps the child out from beneath the table. The light spilling in from the window illuminates her radiant blonde hair.

Faye's green eyes flash. "You have my word." She curtsies.

"You have your tasks; now let us get to it!" King Henry orders.

Cynric and Harmon follow King Henry out, leaving the children alone. Faye walks over to the boys.

"Prince, soon you shall be a squire and then—" Faye clasps her hands together, "a sire."

CHAPTER VIII

TASKS & TALES

Prince, Leon, and Faye go back to the library to summon Father Hayden.

"The king requires your presence in the market by the fountain," Leon informs Priest. Dimples form in his chubby cheeks as he speaks.

Priest's face grows long. "Did he say why?"

Leon shrugs.

Father Hayden looks at his small circle of royal students. He blinks and tries to comprehend why his daily lectures must be interrupted. Sighing, he rubs the bald spot on top of his head.

"Alright. Matthew, continue the lesson in Latin," he instructs a young squire.

Priest slowly closes his oversized Latin Bible, stands and stretches. His arching back cracks from the base of his spine all the way up his neck. "Oh," he moans, then straightens his robe and reluctantly exits the library.

Confirming that Priest is out of earshot, Faye directs her attention to the small group of students. "We're going to need your help," she says with a gleam in her eyes.

Matthew shoots up, adjusting his shirt. "Who put you in charge? I'm the oldest and I'm a squire! I should be in charge."

Faye's face turns frosty cold. She marches over to Matthew, her eyes narrowing. Without warning, Faye lifts her little leg and stomps on Matthew's foot.

Surprised, Matthew's jaw drops. As he registers the pain, he screams, hopping up and down.

"I'm the king's daughter! You'll do as I say!"

Her quick and violent retaliation gains the full attention of the class. With ladylike composure, Faye fixes her hair and restores her face to calm. "Gregor, Hamish, and Kenzie, fetch the helmet from that suit of armor."

The two boys, dressed in yellow and red, respectively, snap to attention. They promptly rush to the side of the armored statue. Kenzie's pink dress rustles as she hurries across the room to join Gregor and Hamish.

Faye turns and faces Prince and Leon, motioning for them to move closer. "Here's the plan…," she starts, lowering her voice.

Faye's whispering captures the attention of the children, but none dare spy on her furtive plan.

Behind Faye, Matthew winces and tests his injury. He removes his shoe and sees a purple bruise forming in the shape of a circle on top of his foot. He glares at Faye.

"You must know better than to cross her," says a young boy named Rex, his big brown eyes full of sympathy for Matthew.

"Mind your business," Matthew snaps.

Several minutes later in the whitewashed kitchen, Gregor's yellow shirt flashes as he scrambles up onto a wooden butcher's table. Fresh bloodstains from the butcher's kill sully the surface of the scarred wood. Gregor reaches above his head and grabs a silver spatula hanging from a brass hook. Hamish throws the knight's helmet on the butcher's table, then quickly mounts the flat surface, where he momentarily recoils from the dark blood stains.

When Hamish lifts up the helmet, Gregor bangs on it with the spatula, chanting, "I'm the king of the castle, you're a dirty rascal!"

Hamish then places the helmet on his head and closes the face shield.

Kenzie looks through the doorway and laughs at the duo.

Suddenly, a streak of white flour flies from the pantry and hits Gregor in the face, engulfing him in a powdery cloud. He stops singing as he goes into a coughing fit.

From the pantry, a portly middle-aged woman named Sue shouts, "After me eggs, are ya? Well, you'll have to do better than that—ha!" She hurls an egg at Hamish, who ducks in the nick of time.

One egg smacks Gregor in the mouth, another splatters in his eye. He begins to cry and jumps down from the counter. He runs away, leaving a powdery trail down the hall.

His white footprints on the carpet make Kenzie laugh. "Oh, they'll tan your backside for that!" she shouts after him, laughing. She, Prince, Leon, and Faye wait against the wall in the hallway adjacent to the kitchen's doorway. Faye abruptly cuts Kenzie's laughter short when she nudges her forward into the kitchen.

"I'm not going in there," Kenzie resists. "I am a lady. Ladies aren't supposed to behave in such a manner."

Faye, holding a bottle of brandy, presses her lips together and squints. "Don't cross me," Faye warns, then pushes the jug into Kenzie's hands.

The flustered little girl stumbles into the kitchen. Eggs, flour, and salt come flying out of the walk-in pantry. Hamish darts around the projectiles, barely missing each one. He pushes himself off of the table and ducks behind it for cover. Kenzie hesitates at the entrance and looks back at Faye with trepidation.

"Do it!" Faye hisses.

Kenzie bites down on the cork and pulls it out of the bottleneck. She tips the purple bottle upside down as she runs into the kitchen, spilling repugnant liquor all over the stone floor. When she passes the pantry door, the concealed kitchen crew blanket her in an assault of flour, salt, and eggs. In seconds, the young girl is smothered. Her mouth falls open and she drops the brandy bottle. It clatters when it hits the marble floor. When Kenzie inhales, flour dust fills her mouth, and, like Gregor, a coughing fit ensues. She grabs her throat and follows Gregor's white footprints in retreat.

Awaiting their turn, Prince and Leon nervously shift in the hallway outside the kitchen. Faye turns to the two remaining boys and says,

"Okay, now I'll light the brandy while you fetch the eggs. Ready?"

Leon's thick eyebrows press together and his mouth alls agape. "You're going to light the kitchen on fire?"

"Don't be silly. I'm just going to light the floor. It'll flush them out of the pantry and Prince can run through the flames and get the eggs."

Prince's eyebrows shoot up. "Why would I run through the flames?"

"Do you want to be a knight?"

Prince and Leon both nod.

"Then you have to run through fire."

Not giving the boys time to respond, Faye turns, takes hold of a candle from a nearby desk, and runs into the kitchen.

Inside the pantry, the servants wait for another assault. Sue holds an egg in her hand, ready to launch it at the next child who comes into view. Without warning, a stream of fire erupts in front of the pantry doorway.

"Ahh!" she screams, dropping the egg. "Fire! They've lit me kitchen on fire!" She lifts her skirt and gallops into the kitchen. The rest of the servants clear out of the pantry and run outside toward the castle moat. Sue runs after them, barking orders.

Leon sprints into the kitchen and grabs a huge pot off the counter. He watches in disbelief as Prince jumps over the flames. "Wow!"

Faye smiles as Prince springs through the flames, his heroic image burning into her mind.

While the flames flicker and die out, Leon runs into the pantry and holds a pot for Prince to fill with eggs. "If you would've waited a moment, the flames would have burned out," Leon says to Prince.

Prince looks up, shaking from the adrenaline. The two make eye contact for a moment. Leon takes notice of the relief in Prince's eyes, nods, and turns to stomp out what few scant flames remain.

Outside, the servants form a line and begin handing each other buckets of water. Last in line, Sue grabs her pail and rushes up the stairs. Before she can reach the door, it slams shut in her face. Her body collides with the unyielding wooden barrier, making a loud *thunk*. She staggers backward and falls down the stairway, landing in a heap at the bottom.

Through the window, Faye watches the servants scamper about. She slides a wooden lock in the door handle and giggles.

"Grab another pot," Faye orders Leon and Hamish. She then dashes into the pantry, where she discovers that Prince has already filled his pot. Impressed, she smiles and feigns a lady-like manner again. "I told you it would work."

"Yes, but how did you know they would be waiting for us?" Prince inquires.

"I was hiding under The Round Table when I heard Father and Sir Harmon hatching a wretched plot to embarrass you. "Twould have been a pity if they'd succeeded."

"We are forever in your debt, Petals" Leon thanks Faye.

Prince grabs more eggs. "Get another pot, Leon," he orders.

Leon and Hamish return with another pot and the three boys quickly fill it. Grabbing the pots by their handles, the boys scurry toward the hallway.

"What about the catapult?" Leon asks.

Faye thinks for a moment. "We'll hide the eggs in the passage and make the subjects carry them to the roof while you two fetch the catapult."

"Subjects?" Prince asks, confused.

"Students, subjects, 'tis all the same," Faye answers, grabbing the other handle of Prince's pot and helping him carry the eggs to the hall. Leon grabs his side of the pot and scurries out of the kitchen, his belly wiggling as he struggles with Hamish to keep up with Prince and Faye.

The children set their heavy loads down on the thick Persian rug in front of a large portrait. Faye uses both hands to push on the picture frame. With a creak, the whole painting springs from the wall, revealing a hidden servants' passageway.

Leon and Hamish lean their heads inside to inspect the dark tunnel. Determining it to be free of trickery, they take the heaping pot by the handles and scurry into the darkness. Faye moves toward the tunnel, stops, and turns to Prince.

"After today, you're going to be a squire," she says with a knowing smile.

Prince takes a hand off the handle and runs his fingers through his sandy blonde hair. "And?"

"And, it is only because of *my* help. Don't you think my labor is worthy of a kiss?" She closes her eyes and leans forward with puckered lips.

Prince's eyes dart left and right, looking for an escape. After a long pause, he reluctantly leans in and pecks her on the cheek. "The wedding edict prevents me from kissing your lips," the boy mutters, avoiding her reaction. He steps past her, snatches the pot's other handle from her grasp, and slips into the shadows.

Faye opens her eyes and gasps, pressing her hand to her cheek. Her heart flutters from Prince's soft, warm lips. "Wretched marriage law!" she sighs, scurrying quickly after the boy.

�֍✷✖

On the castle rooftop, Sir Harmon, Sir Cynric, and King Henry wait for Prince and Leon to return from their noble task.

"Where are those fledglings?" King Henry asks.

Sir Harmon scans patrons at the market, looking through a spyglass. He searches for Priest. "I see him!" He hands King Henry the glass.

"I trust the task was difficult, but not impossible for our budding squires," King Henry grabs the spyglass from the wrong end and looks at the crowd through the wide circle.

"Sire, the task was no more difficult than ours was at that age," Sir Harmon replies.

"Are my people really so tiny?" King Henry asks, straining one eye.

Sir Harmon takes the spyglass from him, spins it around, and lays it before the king. "Perhaps His Majesty can see better from this end."

King Henry scans the crowd through the scope. His eyebrows lift in surprise. "They're so close I could touch them." He extends his hand, reaching for the crowd. "What is this magical wonder?"

"A new device delivered from Persia, My King," Sir Harmon answers.

"There's that *holy critic* right there," King Henry growls when he spots Father Hayden.

The trio duck behind the stone, their backs pressed against the thick, cool wall.

❊❊❊

Inside the War Room, flickering torches illuminate two tall statues. The statues face each other with firm gazes, fixed for eternity. The figurine on the north tilts his head nobly to the left, his hand on a sheathed sword. At the base of the sculpture is etched the Latin phrase, *Si pacem vis bellum para*: "If you want peace, prepare for war." On the south side of the room, the matching statue's sword is drawn. He grits his teeth and leans forward, ready to engage. At the base of his sandal, the gold Latin letters read, *Bellum immineat est*, or "War is imminent."

Leon and Prince creep into the room from the hidden entry behind the legs of the stone warrior at the north end. Prince peeks around the muscular stone calf. He puts his hand on it and squeezes.

Looking at his own calf, he wonders if his soft, boyish muscles will ever be that firm.

Prince scans the room looking for a threat. He sees four torches silently glowing on each side of the room. Several decorative suits of armor stand erect against the far wall. Each one reflects the torches' glowing flames. Each suit of armor holds a different weapon – a sword, an axe, a mace, and a shield.

"I think it's clear," Prince whispers to Leon.

Leon bites his bottom lip, contemplating. "I'm older than you, I should go first."

Prince gratefully steps aside. Leon takes two deep breaths and runs out into the room. Completely exposed, his eyes frantically scour the room for the catapult, his hands poised to attack anything that moves. When he realizes that the room is empty, he moves toward the mahogany table in the center of the room. On the table, several carved characters stand on a map featuring the entire outlay of Tremble Nemble.

"I don't see it. 'Tis not here," he whispers to Prince.

"What?" Prince responds in a low tone.

"'Tis *not* here." Leon strains in a low, harsh voice.

"I can't hear you," Prince says with his hand against his ear.

"Oh, come off it; there's no one here," Leon says, now speaking normally. He waves for Prince to come over.

Prince slowly steps out from behind the statue's leg. "What about over there?" he whispers, pointing to a dresser the length of the room.

Leon runs over to the drawers and begins searching. Prince joins him and the two begin hurriedly opening and closing drawers. "You're too close to me!" Leon complains, pushing Prince away. "Start farther down."

Prince hurries down the room to the opposite side of the dresser.

"Never mind!" shouts Leon. "I've found it!"

Both boys loom over the contraption. Its frame is crisscrossed with thick wooden boards, tightly fitted together with dark metal rivets at the joints. A metallic handle and ladle-shaped holder rest on a metal crossbeam affixed to the catapult's center.

A circular wheel with a small handle is attached to an outer beam.

"Looks heavy," says Leon, wiping sweat from his brow.

"You take that end," Prince orders.

The two boys grab opposite ends and carefully lift the awkward, heavy catapult. They grunt and groan as it bumps against the open drawer.

"Rest it down," Leon grumbles, lowering his end before Prince does. Their huffs and puffs echo in the empty room. Once they set the apparatus down, Prince begins cranking the wheel while Leon makes a fist and places it in the spoon-shaped launcher.

"How do you think it works?" Prince inquires.

Leon looks up and shrugs.

The boys kneel down to examine the small catapult. Suddenly, a large chain hurtles through the air between them. Prince immediately looks left toward the direction of a thunderous *thwack* of metal on wood. He sees the end of a mace firmly embedded in the now-splintered drawer. Simultaneously, Leon looks up and to the right, perplexed as he witnesses the decorative knight suit standing next to him come to life before his eyes. The boys' faces drain of color.

CHAPTER IX

DODGING & MOBBING

Ahhh!" Prince and Leon scream in unison.

The now-animated knight twists and backhands Leon across the face. Blood spurts out of his mouth as his head jerks sharply to the right. He tumbles across the floor. The knight then seizes Prince by the back of his shirt and throws him across the room.

"Wha—" shouts Prince just before his little body lands on the war table. The impact knocks the wind out of him and sends him tumbling over the table's end. He crashes heavily onto the floor.

The suited knight puts his metal foot on a drawer and pulls the mace free. He turns to face Leon and Prince, lifting his face shield. "Take nothing!" shouts Sir Maverick from inside the helmet, swinging the swirling spike above his head with ease. "Earn everything!" he roars, his Scottish accent echoing off the stone walls. Tufts of curly red hair protrude from the helmet.

Prince struggles to get up. He looks around the room for Leon. Already on his feet, Leon wipes the blood from his mouth and leaps for the catapult. The knight swings the ball inches from the boy's face and smashes it into a wooden chair. Leon hops back, staying out of the knight's reach. Realizing he doesn't stand a chance, he darts under the table and crawls to the other side.

Prince examines his surroundings for some kind of leverage to use against his attacker. He notices a suit of armor holding a shield a few feet away from him. He squints and sees the words, *Cerebro ercutere induro*, engraved on the shield, or "Brains beat Brawn."

Prince get up and run toward the suit of armor. "What if someone's in there?" Leon shouts after Prince. Prince ignores his warning as he struggles to remove the shield from the knight's glove.

Leon scans the room spots a sword in another suit of armor's grip across the room. He dashes toward it and comes to its side. The copper writing on the blade that reads, *Brawns pulsu cerebrum*, which means "Brawn beats Brains." With a wry smile, he yanks the sword free.

The weight of the weapon is more than Leon had anticipated and it clanks against the hard stone floor. He desperately tries to lift it, but after a couple of failed attempts, he gives up and lets the sword clatter to the ground.

Sir Maverick swings the spiked ball above his head. The chain clanks and the sphere whooshes through the air. "Yeh want to be squires, 'eh?" his voice echoes. "Yer hardly pages. I think yer better mothers than squires! Ha!"

Sweat drips down Leon's flushed face as he fights for breath. His heart races and he briefly thinks, *Do I really wants to be a knight?* Shaking doubt from his mind, he glances over at Prince, hoping that he has had more success. To his dismay, Prince is still attempting to wrench the shield free. Hoping the shield is lighter than the sword, Leon sprints over to Prince. The boys try to lift the massive shield to no avail. "It's no use," Prince gulps, trying to pry the frozen metal fingers apart. "'Tis firmly fixed."

"What's to be done?" Leon asks between deep breaths.

Prince shakes his head. "Quit?"

"That's it boys, quit! Neither page passes the task. You are nay squires and never will be knights! Ahaha!" he mocks from the other side of the table.

Prince's face flushes in anger. Leon glares at Sir Maverick, catching his breath. "If it's the last thing we do, we've got to shut that filthy mouth of his!" Leon pledges.

"Worthy to clean my stable is all you're going to be!"

"This metal weighs us down. It has to weigh him down, too," Prince thinks out loud. He looks above Sir Maverick's head and notices a sizeable iron chandelier hovering over the knight.

"Let's go get the sword. I've got an idea," Prince proposes to Leon, who follows him back to the weapon.

"Still got a little fight in yeh, eh, boys?" Sir Maverick antagonizes, swinging his weapon as he paces around the catapult.

Prince pulls Leon close to him and whispers his plan into his ear. Leon nods in understanding.

Working together, Prince grabs the sword by the handle and Leon gingerly grabs it by the blade. "Careful," he warns Prince. "If you move too fast, you'll cut off my fingers."

In unison, both boys maneuver the blade toward the wall where the chandelier is anchored. "We've got to do it at the same time or it won't work," Prince stresses.

"Yeh've got to do it at the same time!" Sir Maverick mocks. "Neither of yeh can lift a sword, let alone a shield. Ha! Both yeh come closer and test yer blade against mah spike. Yeh wee, pissy lads!"

The knight watches as the boys reel the sword back. "Oh sure, take a few practice swipes." The boys heave the sword against the wall, severing the rope. Sir Maverick's eyes trace the rope's source just in time to see the iron chandelier descend upon him. He releases the ball and chain and jumps out of the path of the crushing iron. The weapon swings across the table and narrowly misses Leon before it smashes into the wall and ricochets to the floor.

A deafening boom erupts when the hulking chandelier crashes down. Sir Maverick lies face down several feet from the chandelier. He struggles to get up, slowly rising to his knees. He lifts the face shield of his helmet and sees a mass of pasty white skin. Leon jumps from the war table with his shirt lifted, exposing his pallid, wiggly tummy.

Before he can even lift his hand, Sir Maverick's face is enveloped by Leon's blubbery lard. The force of the collision knocks Sir Maverick on his back. Lying on top of the knight, Leon shifts his body so that his stomach completely covers Sir Maverick's mouth.

"Choke on that, you pig's anus!" Leon screams victoriously.

Prince, following Leon's lead, flies across the room and jumps on Leon's back, pressing the soft tummy even deeper into the knight's face. He bounces off of Leon and lands near a thick curtained window. Jumping to his feet he snatches a braided cord that holds the curtain back.

Leon suddenly screams in agony. His girlish shrieks pierce Prince's ears.

"You bit me," Leon yells, pushing off the knight.

"Yeh taste like piggy!" Sir Maverick says, lying on the floor and gasping for air.

Leon looks down, grabbing two handfuls of his stomach. A slimy red blotch marks his skin. In a fit of rage, he runs back over to the fallen knight and begins stomping the knight's face. Sir Maverick moves to cover himself but Prince quickly jumps on the knight and grabs his arms. Using the curtain cord, he binds the battered knight's hands together while Leon unleashes a brutal, two-fisted assault. Blood pools out of Sir Maverick's mouth and nose.

"Well done, boys. Now enough of me. Finish yer task," Sir Maverick congratulates them with a blood-drenched smile. Leon looks around bewildered and distraught.

The boys slide the catapult out from under the wreckage and lift the heavy replica free from the debris. Before they leave, Sir Maverick chomps his teeth at Leon one last time. Leon thumbs his nose at the fallen knight.

✕✕✕

On the roof, Faye recounts her part in the scheme. " ... then, I lit the kitchen on fire and all the servants ran out!"

King Henry's smile droops to a frown. "Fire?" His eyebrows worriedly press together.

"Well, then I locked them out and we put out the flames, just before fetching all these eggs." She gestures grandly, smiles, and awaits his approval. Behind her, the other children set down the buckets of eggs and quickly retreat back into the castle.

"You lit the kitchen on fire?" the king repeats. "This cannot be," he thinks aloud, trying to piece together what his innocent little daughter is reporting.

Prince and Leon emerge through the door behind Faye. The sun peeks through a patch of fluffy white clouds and illuminates their exhausted features.

"We've done it, Sire!" announces Leon, falling on one knee. "I have conquered the knight and fetched the catapult, and all this with little help from my good friend, Prince," Leon humbly reports.

Prince glares at Leon. "*Little* help? The whole thing was *my* idea!" he retorts.

"'Twas not!" Leon barks, shoving Prince.

Sir Harmon and Sir Cynric pry their boys apart. "Let us not argue over technicalities," Sir Harmon interjects.

"Isn't it enough that you've accomplished the task?" asks King Henry. "Now let us put this weapon to good use," he grins.

✕✕✕

Outside the castle walls, Priest impatiently paces amongst the busy market shoppers while he waits for the king. "Where is that royal buffoon?" he mumbles to himself and tidying his long robes. "What could be of more importance than teaching budding youth?"

He looks at the high sun, checking the time, when a sudden blow to his head disrupts his thoughts. "Ah!" he exclaims as he rubs his sore head. Feeling something sticky, he holds out his hand, examining a tacky yellow substance and bits of hard, white shell.

※※※

Atop the castle, the king employs the spyglass to stare at Father Hayden through one of the archer breaks. "Aha! Ha! Ha! Direct hit, my boy!" Inside the spyglass he sees the priest survey the crowd, confused, and then peer up at the castle. "He's seen us!" the king shouts as he dodges back behind the wall.

"Impossible, My Lord," Sir Harmon reassures.

The three men crouch beneath the covered wall. Sir Cynric, Sir Harmon, and King Henry glance at each other and erupt in laughter.

"Criticize me, will he?" the king mocks. He looks at the boys and orders, "Send another volley."

Prince happily places another egg in the catapult while Leon gleefully cranks the wheel.

"Wait! Use more eggs," the king demands.

Prince eagerly fills the spoon-shaped catapult to the brim with eggs.

King Henry shuffles to a different archer break. Slowly, he pokes the scope over a corner.

"On my command," the king instructs.

Through the spyglass, the king watches Father Hayden contemplate whether he should leave the fountain.

"He can't make up his mind whether or not he should disobey his king," King Henry says between snickers. The knights erupt in laughter. "Oh, this is too cruel."

"I've never seen my father act this way," Leon says to Prince. The boys shrug and smile, enjoying the moment.

"Shift left," Sir Harmon says to the boys between chuckles.

Faye grows curious of the target. "Father, may I see?"

"Wait your turn, Daughter," King Henry scolds as he readjusts his position.

Faye puts her hands on her hips, squares her shoulders, and sighs dramatically.

"FIRE!" King Henry shouts.

✕✕✕

Near the fountain, Father Hayden makes out several white objects as they launch off the roof. He cocks his head to the side, transfixed on the curiosities. "Dear God!" he utters before three eggs strike him between his waist and head.

Several eggs also manage to hit a few innocent bystanders. Some run for cover while others cry out in surprise. One of the victims is a fear-mongering old zealot named Deborah Hardman.

"Ah! See, I told yous all!" she screams, wildly waving her arms. "The sky above is finally weary of its lofty perch! It's finally come, the day of judgment!"

A few of the wealthy merchants laugh while some of the more plainly-dressed onlookers appear worried. Another barrage of eggs pelts the crowd.

"The end is near!" several people begin shouting. Like a ripple moving through water, the panic spreads. The mob begins sprinting in every direction. Those who are unaware of the egg attack assume that the cry has been sounded for either a dragon or an ogre and begin fleeing for cover.

Father Hayden holds up his hands in an attempt to calm the panicked crowd. "'Tis not the sky falling, but a prank," he preaches.

The market becomes thick with people as they rush past him in every direction. Another egg hits him square on the head and drips down the side of his face, splashing into his horseshoe-shaped hairline. His eyes narrow as the people run and scream behind him.

When another round of eggs are launched into the air, a town drunk points at the unidentified objects and screams, "The clouds have lost their place; we're all doomed!"

✕✕✕

From atop the castle, King Henry's jolting laughter stops and he frowns.

"Now is it my turn, Father?" Faye asks with her hand outstretched.

Ignoring her, King Henry lowers the scope and observes Leon and Prince reloading the catapult. The scope drops from his hand and the king stands with a hint of despair in his eyes. "That'll be enough, boys. You're both squires. Congratulations."

Leon and Prince hug, slapping each other on the back. Faye watches them for a moment, feeling left out of the revelry. Dejected, she picks up the brown spyglass and looks down at the people scrambling about like ants. The chaotic scene excites her.

"Foolish people, this is why you need a king," she huffs.

"Sir Cynric, Sir Harmon, gather a few knights and restore order to the marketplace," King Henry orders, smoothing his beard nervously. "And, uh, speak to no one of this."

✕✕✕

Down in the market, Auntie picks up Princess and jumps into the horse cart, avoiding the panicked, pushing crowd.

"Lame brains!" Auntie shouts. "The sky is not falling; this is the work of either servants or squires."

The square filled with pandemonium. Winston tries desperately to stop people from stealing Auntie's produce, but too many hands pilfer what few goods remain. The cart is soon picked clean and Winston ducks beneath the cart's lip for his own protection. Behind him, he hears Merlin neigh and turns just in time to see the beast rear its head. The Clydesdale's agitated eyes roll around as the cart shifts back and forth from his jerking motions.

"Oh dear," Auntie mumbles.

Winston steps out from his shelter and yanks off his metal helmet. He runs over to Merlin and covers his eyes, then handles the reins and reels the horse in. "Stay calm!" he shouts at the horse. "Whoa boy, be calm."

The cart continues to rock as the excited horse tries to wriggle from Winston's grip.

"We should be getting out of—" Auntie stops and bites down on her lip. She sees people in front of the cart trample one another to get away from the market. "Never mind," she says, a hint of fear in her voice.

"Be still!" Winston commands the terrified, panting horse.

✕✕✕

Father Hayden stands on the fountain's edge, calling down to the people.

"BE CALM!" he bellows. "STOP! Just use your mind and *think*!"

In the crowd, he sees a raven-haired girl holding onto a woman who is lying face-down. He jumps down into the throng of people, pushing them aside, he claws his way toward the fallen woman. Bodies blur before him and he sees the little girl try to lift the woman's head, but a peasant steps on the back of her neck in the panic. A wave of people stomp on her in their haste to escape. Priest searches for the traumatized child, but can only hear her screams. The holy man lifts his bulky, leather-bound Bible and smashes into the panicked people. The hard book performs its job well, as Priest plows through the mob.

Once he finally reaches the woman, he faces the people charging her and holds the book high above his head like Moses raising the tablets. The golden cross on the book's leather surface glints in the sun. He shouts, "Part like the sea!"

In the frenzy, the people closest to him skirt around his frame while he swats at the others. With great effort, he manages to shield the woman from the tumultuous masses.

A bugle blast from the castle momentarily commands everyone's attention. A drawbridge lowers across the moat and Sir Harmon, dressed in black armor and mounted on an ebony horse, leads Sir Cynric and six other mounted knights across the wooden entryway toward the market. Looters quickly stuff their bags with what goods they can snatch up before the knights establish martial law.

Priest lowers his Bible and helps the dazed, sobbing woman to her feet. "Are you well, Madam?"

Gashes and scuffs litter her arms and face. Nodding, she lifts up her child and inspects the little girl for injury.

"Merchants, you are hereby ordered to pack your belongings and disperse!" Sir Harmon commands.

Auntie and Princess peer out from inside of the cart. Princess and Sir Harmon lock eyes. Though her eyes are wide and her hands tremble, she dutifully remembers what Auntie taught her. She unsteadily gets to her feet and curtsies.

With his sword drawn, Sir Harmon raises his facemask and lowers his blade in admiration of the child's bravery. His horse stands on its hind legs and cycles its front hooves, neighing.

At the top of the castle, Faye hands Leon the spyglass. "And you were worried about a little fire," Faye chides.

Prince surveys the crowd in dismay. "I don't feel so good about being a squire now."

"Why? 'Tis your noble right," Faye retorts. "These peasants will go on about their business and this day will continue as it was before, but you and I are on a path to greatness and 'tis all because of me," she boasts.

Prince glances over at her pretty, arrogant face with a frown.

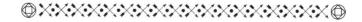

CHAPTER X

RUMORS & WOES

Eventually, the market clears out and the sun sets over the empty grassy field. In the dark, candles illuminate the homes and torches light the streets. A slight breeze travels through the empty avenues, tickling the flames and causing them to cast strange, dancing shadows.

In the King's Tower, the highest of the three columns, King Henry tells his wife Tessa the dramatic tale.

"I thought it all in good fun," he explains, "but I have seen things today from both the people and our daughter that make me question the sanity of our kingdom."

Upon hearing the words "our daughter," the beautiful queen perks up. She moves over to her graying husband and sits by his side on the bed. The stark contrast in their ages becomes more evident with each passing fortnight. She looks at King Henry with mesmerizing emerald eyes and says, "Darling, our daughter showed initiative today." She drags her delicate finger across his stubbly cheek as satin blonde hair falls perfectly around her flawless face. Lost in her enchanting gaze, King Henry relaxes. She clasps both hands around his face and finishes, "'Tis the duty of the crown to lead, not to be led."

"Yes, my dear Tessa, but my heart aches for those injured. 'Twas all my doing," he complains, lifting his hands and plopping them down on his lap.

Tessa adjusts her white gown and slips one leg over his. She takes his head and presses it against her chest. "There, there, my good and noble king; we all make mistakes," she comforts, stroking the top of his gray hair.

He sighs and looks down, where he notices a book at his wife's feet. "Reading has caught your fancy, has it?" He reaches for the book. The cover is metal and has an intricate pattern skillfully etched into the surface. The king stares at the pattern and is reminded of serpents weaving in and out, creating an innumerable tangle of knots. He runs his fingers over the fascinating design, then opens the book and begins to thumb through it.

"'Tis not just a book," Tessa counters.

King Henry looks up at her, eyebrows raised.

"'Tis a doorway to great power," she explains.

"What great power?"

"The kind that will elevate Tremble Nemble above all kingdoms," she answers with a sly smile.

"Above all kingdoms?" he mumbles, not comprehending. "Where did you get it?"

She snatches the book from his hands. "Sir Harmon traded for it and brought it as a gift from the Turks. According to this last passage, great power exists in summoning an unseen force by way of a mirror and three chants."

"Hmm," the king considers. "If that were possible, why haven't I heard of this book's power?"

Tessa presses her finger to his lips. "'Tis a secret. But I assure you, my king, you will be the most powerful man in all this land and the world. And I will be by your side, a great and eternal queen."

The king puts his head back on her chest. "'Tis good to be great, but that kind of power seems ill-conceived."

Tessa strokes his hair and puts down the book. She kisses him on top of his head. "Tomorrow, we shall see if this power is tale or task," she murmurs, her green eyes gazing upon the book.

✵✵✵

The next morning, King Henry wakes with a start. Unable to recall what had woken him, he sits up, stretches, and then sleepily looks around the spacious bedchamber. *Tessa's already up*, he thinks to himself, glancing at the empty space next to him. *'Tis unusually early for her*, he muses, noticing that the sun is not yet up. The king feels Tessa's spot and finds that it is still warm. *Hasn't been up long*, he realizes.

He removes the down comforter and slides his legs off the bed. His bladder is uncomfortably full and he heads for an adjoining room. He waddles over the cold tile to a cement bench with a hole in the center that connects to a drain, which runs the length of the castle column and into the circulating moat.

"Ahhh," he groans, his back facing the room. As he relieves himself, he notices an unusual dark shape on one of the decorative wall tiles. He leans forward to better examine it in the early-morning gloom. The figure has the shape of a man, but all of its details are blackened out, including the face, giving it the appearance of a dark shadow or silhouette. The king furrows his brow in confusion, certain that he has never before laid eyes on the peculiar figure. He shrugs and goes back to his business.

The king returns to his room and heads toward an extravagant cedar dresser with a swiveling mirror attached. The large rectangular mirror is set in a beautiful wood- and gold-leaf frame. Early morning light now streams into the room, lighting up golden knobs on the dark wood.

Making his way toward the dresser, the king bumps into a chair. He grunts, feeling the fuzzy grit of morning breath. He stumbles around the chair and reaches the dresser, where a large silver bowl of fruit awaits him. He looks next to it at his herbal, mouth-cleansing paste and decides instead on a ripe apple. Looking in the wide mirror, he rubs his red eyes and then bites into the firm fruit. Unsatisfied with his morning appearance, he puts down the apple, picks up a large pair of silver scissors, and starts trimming his beard.

A small crack in the mirror catches his attention. He tilts the mirror forward and runs his finger along the fracture. "Curious," he mumbles.

Adjusting the mirror forward, he catches a glimpse of something small and fleshy sticking out from beneath the foot of his bed. He smiles to himself. *Sneaking under the bed again*, he chuckles. Slowly, he moves over to the large, wool-stuffed bed. He carefully bends, lifting the cotton skirt to better see two petite feet. "I recognize these feet, you silly, little sneak," he says, tapping them with his finger. "Come on, Daughter, I'm in no mood for games," he says, moving to tickle Faye's miniature toes.

After grazing her frosty foot with his fingers, his voice changes from joking to serious. "Come out at once, Daughter!" he orders.

Faye's legs stay eerily still.

"I'm not playing," he reaffirms. Frustrated, he grabs her by the ankle. His eyes widen in shock when he feels how chillingly cold she is. Still, Faye refuses to move.

Finally, the king forcefully drags his mischievous daughter out to hip-level from beneath the bed. She remains stiff as ever. Her strange behavior fills the king with apprehension. He grabs her by her sides and pulls her out completely.

The king reels back in shock. Faye lies rigid and cold. Her skin is ashen gray and odd purple veins branch out all over her exposed face, arms, and legs like a pernicious ivy. The king's hand flies to his mouth and his eyes widen with terror when he sees his beautiful daughter's sallow, pale skin. "She's dead!" he says in shock. He looks down at his shaking hand, confused. "Tessa!" he screams.

At her father's yell, Faye jerks. No longer still and lifeless, Faye goes into violent convulsions. Her head twitches back and forth, causing her hair to thrash around in a knotted mess. Her blue fingernails claw at the air and she arches her back like a cat in pain. As she shakes, the king jumps into action. He grabs her by her shoulders, props her up, and tries to abate her violent thrashing. *She's alive!* he thinks as relief washes over him. However, the relief is quickly replaced by helplessness as he watches his young daughter writhe in agony.

"TESSA!" he roars again in alarm.

Faye makes one final convulsion and suddenly stops. Her eyes open for the first time and she looks directly into her father's eyes. For a moment, the king feels as though he cannot breathe. His throat tightens and he feels chills of fear course over him. His daughter's eyes are completely bloodshot; every bit of white is now turned red. The king screams.

Faye shakes her head emphatically as if awakening for the first time. A single blood tear leaks down her porcelain cheek, leaving a trail of red liquid red on the pale white surface. Dark blue circles form beneath her eyes, giving her a gaunt and battered look. Once again, her head thrashes violently back and forth against the floor.

"Wife, where are you?" shouts the terrified king.

Without warning, Faye's small, cold hand firmly seizes her father's wrist and she bolts into an upright position. "No! Don't call her!" she screams. She clutches onto her father with a death-like grip and begins to sob.

"What happened to you?" the king utters in alarm. Faye continues to sob, bloody tears streaking down her cheeks. The king strokes her hair. *Where is Tessa?* he wonders.

After they both begin to calm down, he pulls up her face so that it is level with his own. "Now," he says, "Tell me how you came to be this way."

Faye looks back at him, but her gaze instantly moves beyond him. Her eyes expand and she points a ghostly finger at the mirror while releasing a bloodcurdling shriek. The king turns around just in time to see the fracture in the mirror spread across the entire frame.

King Henry's heart pounds in his ears. He gently separates from Faye and stands. His knees knock and his hands tremble. "There is nothing there," he tries to assure both himself and Faye. He moves closer to examine the widened crack. For a split second, he thinks he sees the mirror bulge and retract. He blinks, unsure of what he saw.

Hyperventilating, Faye scoots herself back against the side of the bed. "He'll come for me!" Faye wails through muffled hands.

"What?" exclaims the king.

"He'll come for me! He came for Mum; he'll come for me!"

The king moves quickly to her side. "Who will come for you?" King Henry demands. Faye sits up and hugs her father's neck so tightly it begins to choke him. Her blood-soaked eyes remain fixed shut. Blood smears on her cheeks as she rubs her face against her father's neck.

"*It*," she breathes.

He rubs her icy little back. "You aren't making sense, Faye. Who is '*it*'?" he prods, uncertain if he wants to hear the answer.

"The man in the mirror who took Mother after she called his name."

King Henry moves his daughter so that he can see whether there is truth in her eyes. He gently rests her down so that she is eye-level with him. Her eyes open again.

Using his sleeve, King Henry dabs the beads of sweat from his brow. Terrified to his core, he takes a moment to calm his nerves. He wraps his arms around his daughter and lifts her onto the bed. Then, in a berserk, frenzied reaction, he picks up the chair next to his bed and throws it at the mirror, shattering it. Faye rolls off the bed and crawls back under it, as her father collapses to the ground.

✕✕✕

Months later, Faye sits next to Priest in a wide pew. Her eyes scan the interior of the beautiful edifice, from its ornately-carved oak railings to the majestic marble pillars that line the hall. Her gaze rises to the stained-glass Bible scenes and finally rest on the vaulted ceilings.

"I never noticed how the high arches look like acorns," she observes.

Priest smiles uncomfortably. "Can you now disclose what you witnessed?" he asks. He holds a vial of holy water in one hand and a thick golden cross in the other.

Faye sighs. On the exterior, she seems normal. The dark circles under her eyes have disappeared and the red veins in her eyes have receded. Her flowing blonde hair, and emerald eyes sparkle in the flickering candlelight.

"Who *can* tell?" she responds, then looks at the priest sternly.

"Can you say what it was you saw?" he repeats.

She leans in closer and whispers, "For your safety and mine, Father Hayden, I dare not utter its name, lest you are fully prepared to use your holy weapons." Her eyebrows lower, giving her face a somber expression.

Priest swallows and examines the holy tools in his hands.

King Henry sits behind his daughter in a gold brocade surcoat, listening intently.

"Do you at least have a name for it?" the priest asks.

Faye nods.

"Will you pronounce it?"

She scoots closer to him. He leans over and feels her warm breath tickling his ear.

"To protect you, I will never tell you its name, but I will tell you one thing: it enters through the mirror."

Priest's eyebrows lift and twitch but his eyes remain calm. Had it not been for a slight quiver in his lip, Faye would have assumed Priest knew no fear.

"Call it a 'no-see', if you must, for you can no more see it than comprehend it."

"How can one not comprehend what one's eyes have seen?"

"How can one comprehend and explain wrath?" She slowly retracts from his ear, as the bench creaks.

"Wrath? A 'no-see'? I'm afraid you are not making much sense."

The king sits up, putting his hand on the priest's shoulder. He vigorously shakes his head back and forth, signaling Father Hayden not to say it again.

"Very well. I will respect your wishes, m'lady, and I will do everything in my power to ensure your safety." Priest hands her the cross. "This will protect you in your every hour of need." He places a silver beaded rosary around her neck and hugs her gently. "I'm terribly sorry for your loss, my dear."

✕✕✕

Sir Cynric sits down to dinner with his wife, Odessa, and son, Prince. Steaming meat, green peas, and chopped potatoes are arranged on a silver plate before them. At a glance, Sir Cynric's family chambers on the fourth floor of the Baron's Tower appear modest compared to the king's, but their accommodations are much nicer than the homes of the citizens in town.

Odessa flips her silky black hair over her shoulder. Her hazel eyes nearly glow in the candlelight. She looks over at Prince, who is idly poking at the beef on his plate.

"Don't play with your food, son," she gently corrects.

Prince stares up at her with gloom in his eyes. Now a squire, he displays the gold eagle crest on the shoulder of his silver- and white-checkered tunic.

Divining the cause of his worry, she extends her hand and cups his cheek. "'Tis hearsay. People don't just disappear. Most suspect she ran away with the gypsies," she explains warmly.

Sir Cynric silences his wife with a firm gaze.

Odessa adjusts her brown dress.

"Faye told me something I'm not supposed to tell anyone," Prince confesses, looking down at his food.

Odessa leans in. "You can tell Mum," she assures him.

Sir Cynric listens with curiosity, hoping to hear a rational explanation to counter the rumors running through the kingdom.

"I promised I wouldn't tell." the boy mumbles.

Sir Cynric chimes in, "Son, I am a knight and I know how to keep a secret. You are a squire; you are not required to keep secrets, especially ones that could put the king's heart at ease."

Prince looks down and nods, wiping a single tear from his eye with the back of his hand.

"She told me her mother was torn to pieces and thrown into the mirror."

Odessa's mouth drops open in shock.

Sir Cynric swallows slowly.

After a lengthy silence, Odessa's frightened wide-eyes soften to her normal peacefulness. "They're just rumors and woes. The gypsy caravan seems more probable."

CHAPTER XI

PROTECTING & PROTECTED

Faye's eyes shift wildly beneath her closed eyelids. She awakens with a start and shivers from the nightmare. More than a year has passed since her mother's disappearance; it had been months since her last nightmare. As tears well up in her eyes, she shakes her head in an attempt to forget.

She throws back the covers and leaves her room. She wanders down through the cold, shadowy tower to the well-lit part of the castle: the kitchen. The warm fireplace softly illuminates the room and several candles flicker on the countertops.

Faye walks past the only blemish in the entire spotless kitchen - a scorched black line permanently marking the spot where she had lit the fire. On the counter, she spots two hand mirrors and immediately looks down, evading her own reflection. Continuing to avert her gaze, she cautiously feels for the mirrors and closes them inside a utensil drawer.

Feeling safer, she dashes down the adjoining servants' corridor and into Sue's small bedchamber. She softly taps on Sue's shoulder until the cook's eyelashes flutter open.

"Another bad dream?" Sue rasps. Faye nods, wiping tears from her eyes anew. The matronly lady sits up and wraps an arm around the girl's shoulders. "Well, at least they are coming less frequently. Let's warm you up, then." She eases onto her swollen, aching feet.

The woman's carrot-colored hair sprouts in all directions under her nightcap as she wanders into the kitchen. Wiping her hands on her cotton gown, she searches the cabinets. "Oh my," she says in disappointment. "Thomas forgot to harvest the last of the chamomile root from the garden."

Faye sniffles pitifully.

"No problem, my dear, no problem," Sue reassures as she reaches for the cape hanging on a hook next to the door. "The herb is only a few strides from the door. 'Tisn't any trouble, really," she understates, looking through the snow-crusted window.

Sue slips on worn leather boots and thinks back to the night she had found Faye huddled in the kitchen, shortly after her mother had vanished. She had awoken to soft whimpering and discovered Faye sitting on the countertop with her arms wrapped around her quivering knees. Although the scorched black mark on Sue's impeccable kitchen floor stung the cook's pride, she soon forgave the troubled child and the two became fast friends.

Sue opens the door to the garden and scurries out. Faye swiftly shuts it behind her. Now alone in the kitchen, Faye drags a chair over to the window and stands on it, trying desperately to watch Sue. She sees a set of tracks in the deep snow.

Outside in the wind and darkness, Sue gasps and exhales a thick vapor. "Oh, the things I d-do," she mutters through chattering teeth. She walks down a narrow set of stone steps and plunges into the knee-high snow.

"Thomas is going to get an earful, come dawn," she threatens through clenched teeth, opening and closing her fist for warmth. "Now, where is that good-for-nothing chamomile bush?" Arriving at the garden between the castle and the moat, she bends over to search through the snow-blanketed bushes.

After dusting the powdery flakes off several bulging plants, she finds it. Shivering, she reaches for the base of a dried plant. After several strong tugs, the plant pulls free from the frozen earth. Sue shakes the remaining dirt and frost from the withered roots and places it in the pocket of her cape.

Between the moat and the city walls lies a small and gloomy grove of trees. A thick gray fog hangs low on the ground and surrounds the trees, complementing their haunting, dark silhouettes. Within the black patch of forest, a pair of golden eyes stalks Sue's every move.

The kitchen worker kneels down and pulls out a few more branches from the stubborn bush. A bitter, whipping wind picks up and just beneath the noise, a whining howl echoes in the distance. Whipping around, she checks for the source. Closer now, the illuminated eyes glare across the wide, frozen moat. Sue sees only darkness and dismisses the sound.

Must be the wind. Yes, the wind, she shivers and wrings her collar closer. *Me ears are playing tricks,* she thinks. She breathes deeply and exhales a plume of vapor into the large snowflakes tumbling around her.

Completing her task, she pulls herself to her feet and hobbles back to the kitchen. Halfway to the door, a violent gust of wind churns up the fallen snow, causing the storming blizzard to assail her from all directions. Sue pulls her cloak close and shuffles forward.

The blustery weather lulls briefly, allowing her to hear the distinct, high-pitched bay of a wolf. She freezes in her tracks. Her breath exhales in short, shallow bursts. Ever so slowly, she turns to look behind her. Again, all she finds is darkness. "Is anyone out there?" she calls.

A slow breeze and a soft howl are all the answers she receives.

Fear overtakes her and she rushes to the door. When she gets close, Sue orders Faye with a wave of her hand, "Come on now, open up!"

Faye barely cracks the heavy door open when Sue pushes past and slams the door, latching it behind her.

The kitchen matron's chest rises and falls as she tries to catch her breath. Grateful for the warm shelter, she unties her cape and hangs it, looking back through the frosted window. Shadowy trees shift ominously in the wind. The woman takes a deep, calming breath but can't dispel the gnawing feeling that something was watching her. She stares at the frosted pane for a moment, assigning her fear to some sketchy potatoes and the castle's lively rumor mill playing on her imagination. As the cook turns back toward the kitchen, two gleaming eyes appear in the window behind her.

"Aaaggghhh!" Faye points at the window and screams.

Turning around, Sue screams and clutches her chest. The elderly woman exhales sharply, steaming up the window, and catches a glimpse of a golden flash that swiftly disappears into the night.

"Something is out there!" Sue gasps, checking the sliding lock to ensure it's secure.

She blinks, clears the window with her sleeve and squints for a better view.

Behind Sue, Faye nervously twists her nightgown with her hands and tearfully asks, "Has he come for me?"

"Has who come for you?" Sue stands on tippy toes, finding nothing but the empty stone landing below. Her head fills the window frame, searching left and right in the dark, chilly night. "I can't see anything," Sue finally determines, as she turns from the moonlit window.

A hulking silhouette dashes across the snowy field, leaps over the wide moat, and disappears into the dark woods. Its tracks quickly fill with fresh snow flakes.

Sue lifts the lid off the kettle and discovers a half-full pot of tea. "Will you look at that," she says in surprise. She sighs and mounts the kettle over the smoldering fire. She throws two more logs into the fireplace, which quickly catch ablaze.

As soon as Sue sits down at the staff's table, Faye climbs into her arms and buries her face in the crook of the cook's neck. "I miss my mommy," she whimpers.

Sue rocks the child back and forth, gently patting her back. "I know. As do I." Her eyes drift over the fireplace to a portrait of the king and queen in front of the castle. "As do we all."

✕✕✕

The next morning, Faye dresses in a golden silk gown. Her sleek bangs fall to the side of her face. A beautiful maidservant, named Katherine, wraps the bulk of her hair in a bun and weaves in a silver ribbon. Katherine's hair brushes against Faye's face. The little girl pinches a strand of the blonde fibers and giggles when the soft hair slips through her fingers.

"Will my hair ever be feathery like yours?"

Katherine pauses and moves in front of Faye. "How do you mean, m'lady?"

"You hair is soft like feathers," Faye says, leaning forward and dragging her hand down the woman's hair.

"Yours will be softer and you will be the envy of every eligible bachelor in the kingdom."

Faye shrugs and smiles brightly.

"Would you like them all in?" the maidservant asks, holding up silver hair combs studded with diamonds.

Faye nods. "Certainly!"

Katherine strategically places the sparkling combs on Faye's head. She finishes by placing tiny bluebells here and there.

"The blue will complement your beautiful eyes," Katherine soothes.

"Am I complete?" Faye asks, curious to know how she looks but not wanting to use a mirror.

Katherine nods and pats Faye on the back. The royal child leaps to her feet and swooshes her dress over to a wavy windowpane. As she spots her distorted image, she leans in closer, which causes her nose to bulge.

"Ahh—" Faye gasps, pinching her nose to ensure that it isn't as bulbous as it seems.

"I have a hand mirror," she offers Faye, pulling one from her dress pocket.

Faye gasps and reels back. "Get that away from me!"

"Forgive me, m'lady. I forgot," Katherine says with a quick, nervous curtsy. She tucks the mirror out of sight and scurries away. She reaches the thick door and pulls it open. Nervously, she looks over her shoulder and sees trepidation in Faye's eyes. The servant pauses, unsure of whether she should comfort the king's daughter or escape her presence. She vacillates but finally caves to her fears and exits.

After several deep breaths, Faye returns to calm. She turns back to the window and examines her disproportionate features.

"I'm utterly disgusting," she says with a huff. Patting her updo, she walks over to her dresser and grabs a leather-bound book. She tucks it beneath a slender arm and heads to the library for morning classes.

Faye intentionally thumps her leather slippers on the library's marble tile to announce her presence.

Matthew and Gregor greet her with a bow. Faye politely reciprocates with a curtsy, but notices the two boys exchange a devious look. She wants nothing more than to lash out at the fools before her, but her manners restrain her fury. Instead, she gently locks her delicate hands together and rests them on her puffy dress.

Faye tilts her nose heavenward and strolls past the boys. She quickly scans the room and sheepishly smiles as she spots Prince sitting in a circle of children.

Prince glances up and spots Faye on the other end of the library. With a wave and a smile, the squire welcomes the king's daughter.

She looks better today, he thinks with a grin.

Princess sweeps across the floor toward the class gathering.

A flicker of motion catches Prince's attention. Crouched behind Faye, Matthew and Gregor sneak up behind her.

What are those two up to? Prince wonders. He glances over at Priest, who is completely entrenched in his lesson. Not wanting to incur Father Hayden's wrath, Prince swallows his curiosity and focuses back on the lesson.

Matthew moves next to Gregor, a hungry glint in his eye. Just a year ago, Faye had dealt a blow to his ego when she stomped on his foot in front of the other students. Matthew had wanted immediate revenge, but Gregor had convinced him to wait until Faye had changed out of her black mourning gown. Matthew grudgingly agreed, but with the condition that Gregor would play an active role in the plot for vengeance when the time came.

Gregor was not sure that Faye really deserved Matthew's retaliation, but he had enjoyed conspiring with Matthew and laughing about how the escapade would unfold.

Now that the moment of Matthew's revenge had arrived, however, Gregor wasn't sure he wanted any part in the dirty deed. "Perhaps we are being too rash," Gregor whispers to Matthew.

Matthew reaches for the back of Faye's dress. *Justice at last,* he revels as he lifts a green toad up by its leathery leg. His face splits into a broad smile.

"Play your part," Matthew whispers, noting Gregor's hesitation.

Matthew slinks closer and pulls back the top hem of Faye's dress. Faye gasps at the sudden jerk. Matthew unexpectedly hands Gregor the toad, Sir Bumps. Taken aback by the sudden change in plans, Gregor caves to Matthew's gaze and slips Sir Bumps down the back of Faye's dress. As he does, he is puzzled to see Matthew holding up a hand mirror.

"That's not the plan!" Gregor hisses.

The toad's slimy skin slithers against Faye. Shrieking, she squirms as she turns around to confront her attackers and is shocked to see her own reflection staring back.

"Aaaahhhhh!" She whips around to hide her face.

Across the room, a small boy named Carson watches the entire scene. He leaps to his feet, points at Faye, and shouts, "Faye's dancing with toads!" His shrill laughter spreads like wildfire amongst the students. "She's as terrified of herself as I am of her!"

Matthew doubles over. "You should see your face!" he cackles, pointing a finger at Faye's terrified expression. He laughs so hard he has to clutch his aching sides.

Faye's face goes apple red as she lifts her chin toward the ceiling. "You'll pay for this!" she shouts, clawing at the back of her dress. "My father will lock you in the dungeon!"

Matthew lifts the mirror back to her face, which causes Faye to whip her head away as if she had been slapped. The children erupt in another wave of laughter.

Prince and Leon finally leap to their feet and rush to her aid.

"Stand back, filth!" Leon shouts.

"Be calm!" Priest yells, holding up his hands to regain control of his class.

Leon rushes to Faye's side and grabs at her arm. He spots the writhing bulge but hesitates to reach down her dress.

"My lady, I humbly request," Leon swallows nervously, "permission to reach down your dress."

"Ahhh!" Faye screams louder than when Matthew dropped the toad.

Trying to be more tactful than Leon, Prince pushes on the bulging toad in an attempt to lift it up the back of Faye's dress. Instead, he presses the toad against Faye's back.

"Stop! Stop! Stop!" Faye shrieks. She looks up at Prince, expecting him to be disgusted by her unsophisticated behavior. Instead, she finds his attention fully on Matthew. Prince's jaw flexes and he marches over to the prankster.

"You filthy git! I'll break your face!" Prince shouts.

Faye smiles but whimpers when she feels something warm trail down her back.

"Ewww!" Kenzie shrieks and points at Faye's moist dress. "'Tis watering her!"

"Warts will surely follow," says Mary, shaking her curly brown hair with disgust.

Faye unleashes a strangled cry and writhes in panicked fury, tugging at her dress. Finally, the toad is dislodged and falls to the ground. Faye heaves a sigh of relief. She looks back up just in time to see Prince smash his fist into Matthew's nose. The offender's nose bends at an obtuse angle and she grins, but the popping noise causes her to wince.

Misreading Faye's reaction, Leon quickly snatches her hand and gently pats it to comfort her. "Sh, sh, sh. All is well, Petals. Brave Leon is beside you."

Faye instinctively tries to jerk her hand away, but Leon's large, sweaty palm weighs her down. Oblivious to her repulsion, he continues to pet her hand.

Matthew stumbles back against a tall bookcase with his mouth gaping open. Blood streams down his nostrils and drips onto his clothes. Trying to assuage the blood flow, he looks toward the ceiling and gasps for air.

Prince grabs a fistful of Matthew's velvet shirt and pulls the older boy directly in front of his face. "By my royal oath, I swear I'll beat you within an inch of your life if you ever touch her again," he growls, shaking Matthew's head back and forth.

"Stop it!" Gregor shouts, trying to pull Prince off his friend.

"I'm a senior squire!" Matthew gurgles, trying to scramble to his feet.

"Rank means nothing!" Prince shouts, releasing Matthew.

The children leap to their feet, race across the checkered marble, and form a circle around the action. Each child eggs on the contention.

"Get up!"

"Hit him again!"

"Bash 'em with yer book!"

"Can I have the toad?" A wiry boy named Victor asks.

Priest slams his book and turns around just in time to see Leon shove his hand down the back of Faye's dress. The holy man storms over to the unfolding chaos. "ENOUGH!" he roars

The children freeze in place.

"You there," Priest points to Leon. "Retract your hand this instant!"

"Yeah, retract your hand!" Victor parrots.

Priest glares down beside him and raises the back of his hand to Victor.

"Ahh!" Victor squeaks, scurrying away from the furious holy man.

Leon guiltily retracts his hand. "I was just trying to help," he mumbles.

A gaggle of girls quickly encircle Faye and take her by the hand. Faye barely notices their comforting efforts, her heart still ablaze from Prince's courageous actions.

"What is this madness?" the holy man demands.

Victor appears back by Priest's side. "'Tis warts!" the gangly boy reports.

Priest looks down at Victor, squints, and sternly points across the library. "Go sit down at once!" he orders the entire class.

"Not without the toad!" Victor shouts.

Slowly, the other children return to their circle.

Priest points a narrow finger at Prince. "You! Come with me."

Faye, overwhelmed by the entire experience, plops down on the floor, landing directly on the forgotten toad.

"CROOACK!"

Matthew gasps. He points a warty finger at Faye and shouts, "You've killed Sir Bumps! Murderer!"

Prince cries out, but Priest clenches him by his arm, dragging him toward a dark part of the library. His eyes frantically dart from Priest's determined face to the surprising steel-like vice on his arm. *How can a man of God be so strong?* Looking down, he sees Priest's bony knees bulge in his brown robe as he walks. For a moment he's tempted to kick Priest in the shin, but the painful jerking of his arm makes him reconsider.

Priest pulls a chair from a dark corner at the end of the library. He lifts Prince and slams him onto the hard wooden seat. The jolt rattles Prince's jaw.

Priest turns around, lifts an inkbottle and pen off the shadowy table and slams them down in front of Prince.

"You shall write one hundred times, 'To live by the sword is to die by the sword.'"

Prince helplessly reaches for the white feather pen. He dips the hollow tip in the inkbottle and writes on the rough, yellowed paper. His shoulders slump in defeat and he feels his heart sink. "'Twould be better to fight Sir Maverick a thousand times than to write even one line of apology," he grumbles under his breath.

Observing the boy's scribbling pen, Priest relaxes his stern glare. "You shall remain here until your task is complete."

When Priest returns to the scene of the incident, he finds Faye on the floor, her face glazed over. "Are you well, m'lady?"

She looks up at him and slowly nods. He offers her a hand and helps her up.

When Faye stands, the class erupts in laughter and once again points at the back of her dress. When she feels the toad's slimy guts on the back of her dress, her face twists in disgust.

"Come now. Victor, dispose of this filth!" Priest says as he pinches Matthew's ear until Matthew is on his tippy toes and begins leading the gangly boy away.

"Owiee" Matthew whimpers, pinching his bloody nose.

Priest turns to Faye, "You may return to your quarters and freshen up before coming back to class."

Faye turns as Matthew is dragged past her and smears her sticky hand on his shirt. "Miserable buffoon," she hisses.

Matthew's jaw drops and he releases a squeal. More painful than his broken nose is the knowledge that his friend's entrails are smeared all over his clothes.

"Move along, piggy!" Victor orders Matthew, tugging him out the front door.

Priest dusts his hands in relief. "Rid of Victor at last," he sighs.

Across the room, Prince muses, *To be a squire 'tisn't so difficult. I'll be a knight in no time.* He smiles as he rubs the eagle patch on his shoulder.

CHAPTER XII

PARTINGS & PRINCIPLES

With spring comes life," Auntie explains, holding up a newborn lamb. She plunges her hands into a bucket of cold water and runs a bar of soap all the way up her arms. The water turns a rust color.

"Another inch taller and you'll be able to do this on your own, dearie," Auntie winks.

Princess tries to understand the connection between the pretty flowers of spring and the grotesque process of birth, but is left with a feeling of uneasy confusion. The violence of birth just seems so awful. *How could an animal so gentle and lovely be created through such a terrible process?* she ponders. From the mother ewe's cries to Auntie's barking orders, birthing leaves Princess overwhelmed. The slimy newborn lies at the feet of its exhausted mother.

Instinctively, Princess picks up a rag and starts wiping down the lamb. "I'm not your real Ma, but I can help clean you up," she coos.

Before arriving at Auntie's farm, Princess would never have imagined working with so many animals, nor would she have pictured herself in such a beautiful place. Now that the last of the frost has melted, green grass and pretty flowers are budding in the pastures and up the hillsides. The sweet scent of spring permeates the air. It is a scene Princess had never witnessed in the forest. The forest met spring with muted greens and occasional tufts of dainty flowers. In contrast, the flowers here abound in an explosion of colors, shapes, and sizes. Yellow dandelions, white daisies, and other flora cascade over the fields and hills.

Princess sighs. In the soft morning light, she listens to a symphony of birds welcoming the glorious day. Taxed by her work, the young lady can hardly wait for the chance to run off with Arthur and escape into a vast field of infinite dandelions.

Princess puts her hand in her pocket and pats her pearl. "Don't worry, Setchra. If Auntie will let me, I'll show you every flower I find!"

Princess feels a strong connection to the pearl, even stronger than her connection with Arthur. After several failed experiments, she had determined that Arthur could not hear her thoughts as Setchra could.

For instance, one day in the middle of winter, Auntie asked her to put Arthur outside in the freezing night. Despite Princess' whimpering pleas and tears, Auntie insisted that Arthur be put out in the harsh cold. As Princess was putting the dog outside under Auntie's watchful eye, she thought to him, *Meet me at my window after Auntie goes to bed and you can sleep with me in my warm room.* Smiling through the tears and staring into the dog's large brown eyes, she thought for certain that he had understood her secret message.

Later that night, when Princess opened her window, Arthur was nowhere to be found. The thought of him outside in the bitter cold made her heart ache. She crawled out of the small bedroom window and scaled the nearby apple tree. She strained her eyes in the darkness for Arthur, but to no avail. The overcast night sky created a blanket of darkness, making it impossible to see anything.

The icy wind blew in through Princess' open window, awaking Auntie. The tired caregiver had searched for the source and found Princess' room empty. Fear immediately gripped her that the girl had been snatched from her room by some unseen monster in the dead of night.

Auntie ventured into the freezing darkness only to discover her little girl sitting in a tree. The girl was standing on a low branch, scanning for that raggedy dog. Auntie did what any good parent would do and yelled, "You naughty little night owl!"

She then pulled Princess down from the tree and swatted her cold, little backside all the way inside the house and into her bedroom.

With the wind howling at her window, Princess felt awfully guilty and alone in her safe, warm room. Visualizing Arthur frozen in the cold, she tossed and turned half the night, wetting her pillow with tears. As her only comfort, she stared at the surface of the white pearl. She must have passed a thousand secret messages to Setchra that night, all of which she knew the pearl deciphered.

When morning finally dawned, Princess rushed into the kitchen and opened the back door. A burst of winter air rushed inside. Princess was shocked to encounter the happy mutt standing in the doorframe, safe as could be.

She squinted furiously at the panting dog. Arthur rolled onto his back, inviting Princess to come and rub his tummy.

Princess stared at the dog, thinking of how much she had hated Auntie the night before for both smacking her bottom and forcing her to make Arthur sleep out in the dreadful cold. All those wasted worries were for nothing. The dog was still there and was as happy as ever, staring at her with that dopey look on its fluffy face.

When Auntie wasn't watching, Princess spanked Arthur good and hard, the same way Auntie had spanked her. Of course, she felt bad about that afterwards. Although her childish swats hadn't hurt his puffy hide, Arthur's big brown eyes revealed puzzlement at the child's mild walloping.

Feeling the warm afternoon sun on her face, Princess sighs and shakes her head, dismissing those cold, winter memories. *Spring is here and it is time for a new start—that's what Auntie always says.*

Meanwhile, Arthur pants and watches Princess. He licks his black nose tilts his head one way and then the other.

Many mysteries might perplex the curious dog. For one, he may never understand why the little girl he loves so much had spanked him one day, or why Princess' squeaky voice has changed to a more mature tone. He sees the same little girl—slightly taller, perhaps, but still the same. He knows well her flowery scent and his sniffer assures him that Princess is, in fact, the same little girl, but his ears, he feels, have betrayed him. That sweet tone that had tickled his head when she talked, warmed his heart when she laughed, and made his ears stand tall when she called his name, had somehow changed. In its place, a softer, deeper tone had developed.

"Alright, dearie, that'll do," Auntie says. "How about you and Sir Arthur go and play?"

Princess feels the excitement bubbling inside her. A bright smile reveals her unrestrained happiness, an emotion she contagiously shares as she hugs Auntie.

"Oh, bless you, child!" Auntie rubs Princess' arms. "Now be sure to stay close to home. I don't want you wandering off or anything of the like."

Releasing Auntie, Princess says good-bye to the newborn lamb and gallops away from the smelly barn. She races across a newly-tilled field with Arthur, who happily barks at a family of yellow-breasted sparrows, sending them into flight.

Auntie leans against the barn's doorframe, easing some of the weight off her aching knee. She contentedly pauses to watch the happy pair cover the length of a field. Her corn blue eyes fill with happiness as she watches a single beam of sunlight blast through the overcast sky and illuminate the field where Princess prances. "Thank you," Auntie whispers, looking up at the heavens. "'Tis fortune to have such a token of joy!"

Auntie continues watching through the open barn door, checking to see that Princess has stopped safely before the edge of the field. She lifts up the lamb as though it were her own child, cradling it to her chest and then bouncing it lightly up and down.

"Now we shall unite you with your mother," the wise woman says, kissing the fleecy lamb on the nose. Auntie gently places the babe back with its mother, guiding its mouth to its mother's milk.

✕✕✕

On the south side of the castle library, the royal school children stand in a semi-circle around Priest. They casually chatter as they wait to be split into pairs to recite a new list of Latin verbs. Faye has discovered Priest's rotating pairing patterns and lines up accordingly. Leon steps between her and Prince, always looking to be close to Faye. Faye smiles knowingly.

Leon bites his lip and glances over at Faye, enthralled by her beauty. His determination to win her increases with each passing day. *She is the most beautiful girl in all of England.*

"One, two...." Priest counts, pointing his bony finger at Prince then at Leon.

And I am handsome, Leon raises an eyebrow at Faye.

"One, two...." Priest repeats, pointing at Faye on "one."

At least that's what my mum tells me, Leon considers, lowering his eyebrow. After a moment of philosophical debate, he deems his mum a reliable source in the matter. He looks at Faye and winks.

Faye looks ahead and ignores Leon's advances.

Priest finishes. "Evens pair with evens, odds pair with odds."

All of the students look around and begin pairing off, except for Leon, who continues to stare at Faye.

"Hurry along. This shouldn't take all day," Priest directs.

Prince looks around and turns to Faye. "Would you like to be my partner?"

Faye nods and casually replies, "Of course."

Leon's face falls as Faye smiles and walks away with Prince.

Faye puts her hand out in a lady-like manner. Prince takes it and escorts her past the study booths to the southern-most tip of the library where the king has his private Royal Study Chamber. They sit on rich mahogany benches with an ivory table between them.

Victor turns to Leon. "What are you waiting for, stupid?" he snivels.

Leon looks longingly at the Royal Study. He takes a deep breath, closes his eyes, and walks to the public study with the gangly boy.

In the cramped booth, Leon runs his hand over a carving in the wooden study table that reads "W.H. + T.S." He places his leather-bound book on the flat surface and plops onto the creaking bench.

"I've already memorized these words," Victor brags. He takes a seat next to Leon, forcing the stout boy into the corner of the booth. "I'm not wasting my time on Latin when" —he reaches inside a brown leather bag and whips out a pointy blue hat with yellow stars and a half moon on it— "I can practice magic!" From his sleeve he removes a silver wand and makes saliva-bursting *whooshing* noises at Leon, who remains less-than-impressed.

"I could change you into a..." he looks into Leon's face, "A stink bug!"

Staring down the point of Victor's silver wand, Leon groans and rolls his eyes. He snatches the silver stick away from Victor and bends it in front of the "wizard's" face.

"Ahh!" Victor squeals.

Leon tosses the wand over his shoulder and grabs Victor by his loose shirt, pulling him face-to-face.

"I'm a squire; you're a nobody! You'll do the lesson and you'll like it! Got it?" Leon commands, shaking Victor so hard that his hat slides to the side.

"I'm the king's nephew!" Victor screeches, adjusting his hat before it can fall. "And I don't have to do the lesson if I don't want to!" He cocks his thin arm back and cracks Leon across the face, exclaiming, "Tag, you're it!"

Leon's chubby cheek stings from the impact. He maintains his grip on the boy's shirt with one hand and swings back with the other.

Victor bends over, wiggling out of his shirt like a snake shedding its skin, and escapes just in time. He scoffs at Leon, who is left holding his empty shirt. The runt hastily scrambles for his vandalized wand and picks it up. He turns and points his wand at Leon, yelling "*Esse tu foetidum aeternum cimex!*" which translates to, "Be thou stinky forever, bug!"

Victor's shrills catch Priest's attention across the room. The holy man stands, slams his book shut, and strides over to the scrawny Victor, whose bare back is facing him. Priest snatches the lad by the ear.

"Ahh! Let go of me!" Victor shrieks, thrashing wildly as Priest drags him toward the library entryway.

Priest's footsteps smack the granite tiles and echo in the room, attracting the eyes of young spectators. The entire class turns their heads in unison, intent on watching Priest and Victor.

Priest wrenches open a library door and tosses Victor out on his backside. "Get dressed!" he orders.

Victor cups his hand to his throbbing ear, then holds his wand up at Priest and screeches, "I hate you, you ... you *diabolus!*"

"*Diabolus?*" Priest incredulously questions. "I'll show *you* a *diabolus!*" he shouts. Priest snatches him up, bends him over his knee, and swats him with Victor's own wand.

From their seats inside the library, the children snicker.

Faye and Prince peep around the corner of the Royal Study. Faye covers her mouth and laughs while Prince shakes his head in bewilderment.

Faye points and says, "Look, his spell has worked! Priest has turned into a devil." The kids laugh.

Prince sighs. "Poor Victor."

Faye looks up at him in disbelief. "Poor Victor? You must be jesting."

Prince sits back down and opens his book. "What about?"

"Though he is my cousin, he's an absolute pest!" Faye complains, rolling her eyes. She thinks back to the time Victor ruined her favorite white dress by pushing her into a mud puddle. "Oh, and he makes quite a stink at all our royal gatherings," she says, gritting her teeth while recalling the time he released a cage of agitated doves at church, dousing her perfect hair in excrement. "The little terror," she adds, shaking her head. She sits down and opens her book. "He is a complete bother!" she finishes.

"Well," Prince says defensively, "I feel bad for him."

"Why?"

"He doesn't seem to have any friends amongst us. Nor among his family, so it would seem."

"I think you would feel differently if you were related to him," Faye retorts.

"Do you know what *exemplo matrimonii* means?" Prince asks.

Faye looks perplexed while thinking over the phrase. "Precedent of Marriage?"

Prince nods.

"What does that have to do with Victor?"

"If your father doesn't have a son, you would have to follow a precedent of marriage."

"What does that mean?" she inquires, more interested in Prince than the topic.

"That you would have to marry your first cousin if your father has no son to pass the crown to."

Faye thinks for a moment, the realization growing on her face. "You mean I would have to marry that skinny little runt?"

Prince nods in affirmation.

"*That's* why he stares at me!" she hisses. Her eyes narrow as she shakes her head back and forth, her golden locks swinging from the momentum.

Prince bursts into laughter at Faye's expression.

"'Tis not funny, Prince," she says, relaxing her angry features. "What would you do if I had to marry that toad?" she tests.

"Oh I don't know, probably ride off into the sunset to slay dragons and kill ogres."

Faye leans on the table, cupping her chin in her hands, and bats her eyelashes. "Wouldn't you miss me?"

Prince stops laughing and takes her hand. "Terribly," he says sincerely.

Faye blushes.

"Prince!" Sir Cynric's voice echoes through the library, interrupting Faye's moment. As his father enters the room, Prince slides out of the study booth and renders a respectful salute.

Leon watches Prince mechanically salute his father with satisfaction. "He can be taught," Leon condescendingly mumbles, reflecting on the countless hours he spent drilling Prince.

"Yes, sir," Prince reports at the end of his salute.

Sir Cynric stands at the library's entrance, holding two objects of interest: a wooden bow and a leather quiver full of arrows. "Enough of this schooling nonsense!" he shouts. "'Tis time you learn what it takes to become a knight!"

Priest shifts in the seat at his desk, clearly offended by Sir Cynric's remarks.

Prince walks toward his father. When he passes Leon's booth, Leon quickly stands and renders a salute. "Sir Cynric of the brave Lion Brigade, I humbly request permission to join my good friend, Prince, on the quest toward knighthood!"

"Another time, lad; this is strictly father-and-son warcraft."

Disappointed, Leon respectfully nods and turns back to sit in his empty study. He looks up and catches a glimpse of Faye beckoning him over to her booth. He instantly livens up when he sees the object of his desire inviting *his* presence. He hurriedly gathers his things, then slides out of the booth and scrambles to the Royal Study.

When Sir Cynric and Prince leave the library, Faye whispers to Leon, "There's a secret passage by the fireplace, just over there." She points across the room.

Leon feels his heart speed up, dreaming that Faye wants to get him alone. "Okay!" he chirps.

Faye leans in close and explains how the secret passage works. Leon can hardly concentrate with her pleasant scent and perfect nose "so close to his face.

Faye parts a curtain and peers around the corner of the booth. Her eyes train on Priest, waiting for him to look away. She watches until the robed preacher sighs heavily, turns in his seat, and gazes tiredly out the window. She signals for Leon to get moving. He leaps toward the fireplace's secret passage. Faye stands, fingers clenched, hoping Priest won't detect the pudgy boy in the shadows. Her head pops back into the booth when Priest's watchful eye scans the corridor of study booths.

"Pssttt!" Leon hisses.

Faye pops out again, looking for the back of Priest's balding head. She dashes for the fireplace, barely making a sound as her soft slippers glide across the floor. Hiding behind the large pillar of the fireplace's frame, she steals one last look in the holy man's direction. She reaches her arm around the pillar, feeling for a small cement circle. As soon as her delicate fingers find it, she presses hard. The small circle releases a hidden lever within the wall and the wooden panel next to the fireplace quietly slides open.

Without another look back, the two children quickly slip into the passageway, closing the panel behind them.

✖✖✖

Below the library, Sir Cynric and his son walk past poorly lit rooms on the Commoners' Floor. Peasants sell goods to passing soldiers while castle blacksmiths pound away at shaping armor. Women in neutral dresses made from nubby, natural fibers, with warm woolen shawls wrapped around their shoulders, sell exotic oils while chickens scamper across the hay-littered floor.

Assaulted by the heavy smells of sweaty laborers and livestock, Prince looks at the scene with disgust. Conflicting emotions surge and swirls inside of him. *I'm the first of my age to be tested.*

He and Leon have tried guessing what the secret tests would entail. Although the young men are mandated to remain silent of all that happens during these royal rituals.

"Keep looking at them like they're trash, and they're likely to knock your teeth out of your head," Sir Cynric warns. "This you must know – you are no longer under royal protection."

Prince's father's words bring him back to the present, he stares straight ahead and replays his father's words. *What could he mean?*

"Things are different now, Son. You can't be spoiled anymore. You have to earn your keep now," Sir Cynric explains. "You're a squire and that means you're the lowest block in the castle."

"Lower than that block there?" Prince jests, pointing to the lowest gray square on the first floor wall.

"Much lower," Sir Cynric corrects. "You're in the foundation, or somewhere beneath the moat. That means that, though these citizens are not of royal lineage, any of them can discipline you for any infraction, at any time."

Discipline? Prince thinks.

Sir Cynric continues, "Pass by a woman who needs aid, and they'll whip your backside. Leave a pile of horse dung on the street, and you'll be beaten and covered in manure Show no mercy to the less-fortunate criminal, and they'll rob you blind. Treat them with disrespect, and they'll make you wish you never laid eyes on them."

Prince furrows his eyebrows, wondering how anyone, aside from his father or Priest, would be legally permitted to lay a hand on him.

"Do you understand what I'm saying to you, Son?" Sir Cynric asks as they reach the end of the castle, near the portcullis and drawbridge entrance.

"I guess not," Prince answers, confusion evident in his voice.

"I'm saying that you're a representative for all these people. They assume that one day you'll be like me, a royal knight. So, they test your teachings and tempt you to do wrong. When they catch you in an error, some will correct you until you represent their ideas of right and wrong. Some citizens will envy you; most will hate you. No squire has many friends outside his royal circle…," his voice trails off, as he realizes that his son doesn't quite follow what he is saying.

Sir Cynric bends down, places both hands on Prince's shoulders, and stares into his boy's eyes. "Son, these people are as important to the kingdom as our king. You must learn to develop a keen balance between what is right and what is wrong. You must also learn the difference between good and evil. I can nay help you with this task any longer. You must remember what you were taught, and prove your character."

Prince tries to find a logical balance in his father's conflicting advice. The only thing that seems to stick in his mind is that he could receive a beating for making a mistake. "You're saying not to make mistakes," he concludes. Sir Cynric shakes his head. "No, that's not all that I'm saying. I'm saying if you fail as a squire, you will be, at best, a blacksmith bound for this castle floor, or, at worst, a vagabond without protection from the crown."

Prince stares ahead blankly.

Behind Sir Cynric, Prince notices his mother walking toward them in a beautiful white gown. Her black hair frames her face, flowing from beneath a golden headpiece. She looks serene, but out of place in the filth. As she gets closer, Prince sees her dab her eyes with a white handkerchief.

Sir Cynric stares into his son's eyes, unaware of his approaching wife. "Every man must learn these lessons on his own, but this much I can tell you: your conscience is the scale by which you must measure everything you do or fail to do."

Odessa approaches and kneels down next to her husband, who looks at her in surprise. "Use your heart and your mind," she recites, a tremor in her voice. "Be wise, be brave, be noble." She holds up an olive branch, a custom of good journey and warm regards. "Hold fast to the principles we have taught you. Do you remember them?"

Prince nods slowly, confusion settling upon him. *Why is she upset?* Odessa reaches out and tucks the olive branch into his front breast pocket. He then recites from memory the oath his mother and father have taught him since he was a babe: "Do no harm. Take nothing that isn't yours. Obey your elders, except when asked to do that which is contrary to your conscience. Protect the weak, except when they can protect themselves. Fight for what is right…,"

Odessa nods and joins in on the last phrase, "… and remember who you are and where you come from." She hugs him and hands him the handkerchief.

"Is this my Indoctrination?" Prince nervously inquires.

Sir Cynric nods. "I've adjusted the draw on this bow. It should be lethal enough for you to use without wearing out your arm." He draws the strings back as if to demonstrate his point. Odessa stands up and puts her arms around her husband. Cynric looks sternly at Prince. "Shoot three pheasants through the heart. Don't come home until you do. Hit anywhere but the heart and you must leave the bird, for it will not count." Cynric removes a handful of arrows from the quiver. "Four arrows are all you will need. One for practice in case of breakage and three for hunting." He tosses the quiver to Prince.

Prince slings the bow across his chest and shoulders the quiver. "Yes, Sir! But, Sir…," an awkward pause ensues as he searches for the words. "You know that I do not have a sure aim!" he finally blurts. "I don't mean to be disrespectful or question your orders, Sir…but why must I do this?"

Sir Cynric furrows his brow and looks sternly into the young boy's eyes. "Son," he clears his throat, "To become a knight, every squire must go through trials. Part of being a man is learning to overcome your weaknesses. This is one of those trials. Do you understand?"

Prince nods.

Sir Cynric gives a curt nod and resumes a stiff standing position. "You have your standing orders, Squire. Now go out into the world and see for yourself what the kingdom is like!"

Odessa's shoulders slump at her husband's last command. She looks to him with sadness in her eyes and says, "Mercy," still hoping her husband might wait to send their young son amongst the commoners by himself.

Sir Cynric directs his stern gaze toward her. "We've gone over this before, Odessa. He must go. Mercy is for the weak."

Prince starts to perk up at the thought of exploring the town by himself. He imagines himself strutting back to his father in triumph, holding up a dozen fat pheasant with arrows through their hearts. His distant stare is suddenly brought back into focus by a sharp sob from his mother. Prince yearns to run up and comfort her, but he knows his father would not allow it.

"I shall make you both proud," he says, saluting his father.

Sir Cynric walks over to the rough stone wall and tugs on a long rope that hangs near the guard tower. A large bell at the top of the rope rings, startling Prince. The massive portcullis rises and the towering drawbridge begins to lower over the moat, letting bright sunlight through.

Chain links clank as the bridge lowers and Prince suddenly realizes that he's never walked across the drawbridge alone. He begins to understand what his father meant by no longer being protected.

When the drawbridge finally lowers, it slams against the ground on the other side of the moat, kicking up dust and booming from the impact.

As he crosses the plank, he is oblivious to the figures following him.

Faye and Leon trail Prince through the shadows of the common grounds. Faye swings a basket full of goodies from the kitchen. Leon shuts the iron face shield on his oversized black helmet and anxiously fingers a wooden sword hilt tucked in his belt.

Now on the cobblestone road that leads from the castle, through the townhouses, and into the surrounding farmlands of Tremble Nemble, Prince pauses, unsure whether it is okay for him to look back one last time. He becomes overwhelmed by surges of excitement, sadness, anticipation, and anxiety. He cannot help himself and turns around to wave. His mother waves back at him but his father has already left. Then he slowly turns away and enters the broad main street of Tremble Nemble. The bright morning sun blinds Prince for a moment. He lifts his hand up to shield his eyes as he looks out on the town. The smells and sounds from the marketplace assault his senses from every angle. Everything seems louder, bigger, and newer than usual.

Leon draws his wooden sword and shouts, "FOR GOD AND KING!"

With the bustling noise of the main street and the distraction of his own thoughts, Prince doesn't hear Leon coming from behind until it's too late.

Leon charges at Prince, cracking his wooden sword across the back of Prince's head and keeps running past him.

Prince reels from the blow, dropping to his knees. "Ouch!" Prince cries, rubbing the back of his head.

"I am the Great Dragon Slayer, Sir Leon!" the boy shouts, waving his wooden sword high above his head. Inside the helmet, his reverberating voice is much louder than the muffled sounds Prince hears.

"Wait for me!" Faye calls out, a good distance behind the boys. One hand grasps the basket of food, while her other hand grips the fabric of her dress, attempting to keep from tripping. Marketplace onlookers gaze at the group of boisterous children as they pass.

Prince feels something wet dripping from his now aching head. He tenderly touches the spot and looks at his fingers, revealing a blotch of blood.

Leon lowers his sword and charges Prince again. "Mercy is for the weak!" he yells in a girlish voice.

Prince leans down, grabs a rock, and takes aim at Leon's face shield. The clumsy squire can only see glimpses of Prince through his protective grate. With his vision of Prince jumping up and down through the narrow slit, he charges past Prince. Realizing his error, Leon turns about. "I am the Great Drag—"

Prince reels back and hurtles his large rock, cutting off Leon's charge. Leon's metal helmet vibrates from the impact.

The force of the stone spins the helmet backwards, trapping Leon inside the metal contraption. He drops his sword and reaches behind his head with both hands, prying at the metal grate. He manages to lift it halfway before it slips out of his chubby fingers and closes once more.

Leon yells, pushing on the base of the helmet.

He drops to the ground, rolling around and exposing his wiggling tummy in his efforts. Unsuccessful in his attempts to remove the helmet, he carefully rises to his feet. "I can't see!" he shouts, stretching his hands out and waving them blindly.

Faye ignores Leon's blundering as she runs toward Prince, smiling from ear to ear.

"In the name of the king, I order you to wait for me!" she calls, only partially joking.

Prince sighs and then grins.

"I'm coming with you," she pants, her eyes filled with excitement.

Behind Faye, Leon claws at the metal helmet while taking steps forward. Losing his balance, he runs into a tree trunk and falls over. "Help! I can't breathe!" Outside the helmet, his muffled pleas can barely be heard.

"No, you must stay at the castle," Prince informs Faye.

Faye frowns. "I must go with you."

Prince looks her up and down. "You're a girl," he snorts. He then turns around and starts off down the road again.

"But...," Faye protests. She stamps her foot and starts after Prince. "Squire, I insist I accompany you on your quest."

Prince turns around and meets Faye. He puts both hands on her shoulders and tries to use the same forceful tone as his father. "Your father is the king."

Faye eagerly smiles and nods.

"If any harm befalls you, he would hang me."

Disappointed, she sighs. "I can't go with you?"

He shakes his head.

Behind Faye, Leon rolls around on the ground, screaming, "Hey, I thought we were going to slay dragons!"

Prince half smiles and shakes his head at Leon.

To Faye, he says, "You must look after Leon until I return."

Faye wrinkles her nose as a tear drips down her cheek.

"We've had all winter together. 'Tis spring now and my father has given me a task." Prince leans in closer. "When I return, we'll sneak into the secret passage and prank Matthew and Gregor."

Faye sniffles and wipes the tear from her cheek. "I'll wait at the top of the castle until your return," she pledges.

Prince nods, slowly turns, and walks ahead, feeling a mixture of sorrow and excitement. Gradually, he disappears into the masses.

Faye throws her basket at Leon.

"Ouch!" Leon cries out.

Faye watches the distance grow between her and Prince. Though her eyes are puffy and red, they are filled with resolve. She clenches both hands together and sighs. *One day, Prince ... One day you and I shall wed.* Her emerald eyes sparkle with determination.

CHAPTER XIII

PRANKS & PURPOSES

An arrow fixed in his bow, Prince continuously scans the knee-high grass between the pointy pine Dragon Wall and the stony King's Wall. Having previously hunted pheasants with his father, he knows that they will practically let you step on them before taking flight.

"Patience," the squire whispers to himself, knowing the tendencies of the birds.

Prince thinks he hears a cooing bird a short distance in front of him, but the bird doesn't take flight. The grass seems to whisper and shift, convincing him that the clever bird is right in front of him, but he never sees it. He grows frustrated and charges through the brush to flush it into the air. Still nothing appears.

For hours, the squire stalks his prey, working his way around the edge of the isolated town. He returns to his starting point in front of the Dragon Gate. He groans in frustration.

Spotting Prince from the stone walkway above the King's Gate, an unshaven soldier with a lisp nudges the gatekeeper. "Hey Win*th*ton, lookie there."

Winston surveys the grassy space between the walls and grins when he recognizes the emblem of the squire on Prince's shoulder.

"A hunting we mutht go," the guard chants, causing Winston to break into a wider smile. The guards exchange a knowing look and Winston leans over the stone wall.

"Hunting for snipes, are we?" Winston shouts down at Prince.

When Prince sees the guards he snaps to attention and renders a salute. The two guardsmen look at each other with growing enthusiasm.

"Oh my," the guard says in morbid elation, "thith ith jutht too easy!"

"Watch this," Winston mutters to his lisping companion.

"I say there, have you had any luck?" Winston shouts to Prince.

"Pheasants won't fly!" Prince shouts back, wondering if he can lower his arm since the guards have not returned his salute.

"I, too, am a pheasant hunter," Winston says, nobly placing his hand on his chest. "Why, just the other day, I found me a flock right outside this here gate." He dramatically gestures.

"A flock?" Prince responds in admiration.

Winston leans over and whispers to the guard, "Open the gate."

Preston, the lisping guard, salutes with his tongue sticking out and his eyes crossed before scurrying down the stony steps. His gaping grin momentarily catches Prince's attention.

"You might be able to find a few yourself!" Winston shouts.

Prince holsters his arrow and slings his bow across his chest. He feels camaraderie with the soldiers, mistaking their jesting for benevolence.

"Thank you!" Prince shouts with a smile. *Father will be most pleased with me*, he thinks, feeling accomplishment for a task that has yet to be completed.

Preston pushes open the thick door of the King's Gate and ceremoniously bows to Prince. Enthused with the assistance of his new friends, Prince eagerly saunters outside the protection of both walls.

Maybe I can convince one of the soldiers to come down and shoot a few pheasants for me, Prince imagines. That would truly lighten my duty!

Prince becomes so entranced with his prospects that he hardly notices the massive King's Gate closing behind him. In his excitement, he realizes that he has forgotten to ask which way to go to find the abundant flock of pheasants. He abruptly turns around just as the gate shuts behind him.

"Good Sir," Prince shouts up at the guards' battlement.

Rather than finding the guards, Prince spots a shiny object hurtling from the top of the wall. Confused, Prince watches as the object free-falls onto his unprotected head. A loud *dong* rings in his ears and jars his body. The boy staggers backward and falls to the ground, momentarily blacking out. He lies there motionless while boisterous laughter erupts from the Guard Tower.

Prince gradually comes to. His vision is filled with the bright blue sky above. Prince sits up and feels as if his head is on fire. "Ouch." He reaches up and tenderly touches his head to find a bump already forming. The ringing in his head begins to subside and he hears a chorus of unruly laughter. A foul stench stings his nose and he begins to dry heave.

"Yuck!" the boy gags, scrambling to all fours. He searches for the source of the rancid smell and discovers a dented piss pot on the ground next to him.

Another pot clangs to his left when it slams against the cobblestone road, splashing its filthy contents over his hand.

"You missed, Preston!" roars one of the guards. Several guards cluster and laugh at the unfortunate squire.

Reality finally sinks in for Prince. A feeling of betrayal hits him as violently as the chamber pot had moments ago. Shame and bitterness wash over him as he feels the urine and slimy feces on his head, clothes, and arms.

He tries to slowly stand, then slips back into the foul mess. He looks down in disgust at the filth covering him. A third pot hits the squire's leg and Prince yelps.

"Got 'im!" yells Winston.

The boy flips over onto his side so he can rub his throbbing limb.

"Ha! Ha! Ha! Worthless squire scum!" Preston heckles.

With an aching body and ego, Prince desires nothing more than to crawl into a hole and hide. However, the image of Prince's father fills his head. *Get up!* Prince tells himself, feeling his face flush red with anger. He jumps to his feet and tries to shake the nasty sewage off his body. Tears of rage burn from the corners of his eyes and down his cheeks.

Furious and quaking, Prince cries shrilly, "You lied to me!"

He immediately regrets opening his mouth. The vile stench fills his mouth until he feels like he can nearly taste it. His stomach churns dangerously in protest.

Winston and the guards laugh. "All in good fun!" they jest.

"Feeling noble now, Thquire?" Preston clamors, clapping his hands together.

Prince draws a deep breath to shout profanities at the guards, but relents to the sickening odor. He doubles over and vomits.

The guards, standing at the tower's edge, howl with laughter once more. Preston imitates Prince and pretends to vomit, while Winston rubs his eyes with his hands and mocks Prince for crying.

The furious boy gives into his rage and reaches for his bow. He moves swiftly, unslinging his bow and nocks an arrow.

"I'll show you!" Prince seethes.

When he looks up to take aim at Winston, he finds six archers manning the solid wall, their bows drawn and pointed directly at him.

"Do it!" the toothless Preston taunts.

Winston holds up his hand, trying to hush the imbecile.

The sharp screech of the King's Gate interrupts the growing tension. Slowly, the huge entry cracks open, drawing everyone's attention. Prince turns and trains his arrow on the opening door, ready to fire. A large hand sticks through the opening, followed by another. The two palms open to him as a sign of peace. A huge head pokes through the space and a man steps through. The looming figure of a giant guard emerges.

"That's right," the guard says in a thick Scottish accent. "Keep that piece trained on ol' Charles."

Confused, Prince obeys and aims for the pupil of the guard's eye.

"See, they're waitin' for yeh to do something stupid," Charles explains, pointing a thick finger up toward Winston and Preston, "so's they can embarrass yeh even more."

Unsure of what to do, Prince draws a deep breath and feels his lungs burn, all the while keeping his weapon trained on the large Scot before him.

"They won't kill yeh for fear of bein' hung, but they can hit yeh in the leg or arm and blame it on yeh for firing first," Charles drawls. He slowly and calmly closes the distance to Prince, one step at a time. "They can maim yeh for sure, lad."

Prince takes a quick glance around him and steps back, intimidated by Charles' disfigured face. Although covered in scars, his face reminds Prince of Sir Maverick's. Prince stumbles back a few steps but keeps the taut bow trained on the massive man.

"I think yeh've had yer fun, boys!" Charles bellows up to the guards, who release the tension on their bows.

From his high position, Winston stares intently at the boy. A flash of shame washes over his face and the humor of the situation suddenly dissipates. "Archers, stand down," he orders. The guards disperse back to their posts.

"See, no one's going to hurt yeh, lad," Charles says, adjusting his belt and shifting his bulging belly.

Prince finally relaxes the tension on his bow. He begins to tremble from the ordeal.

Only Preston still finds humor in the scene. He bites his thumb and growls, taunting Prince one last time. "Go on about your day, pissant!" the guard chides.

Charles ignores the antagonist. "Let's go an' get yeh cleaned up a bit," he says, plugging his nose as he comes closer. "I know just the place."

Prince wipes tears from his face with his sleeve, smearing sludge on his cheek. He looks at the Guard Tower and scowls at Winston.

Winston shrugs, acknowledging his guilt but offering no apology. *Just a bit of fun for me and the men and a wee hazin for the squire.* Winston thinks humorously. He fails to realize that this experience is being burned into the boy's mind.

A short walk from the exterior gate, a river flows into the castle moat from the towering mountains and then courses east to the chilly North Sea. The hulking guard leads Prince to the grassy bank of the water.

"Get in there and soak yer clothes and body," Charles advises the reeking boy, adopting a fatherly tone.

Prince slowly inches toward the riverbank. The boy looks at the man suspiciously. The clear, running water looks harmless, but he is still wary of becoming the butt of yet another humiliating prank. Although he wants more than anything to wash off the stinking filth, his father's warning now echoes in his mind.

"How can I trust you?"

"Ah, for Pete's sake lad, it's just water. Yeh can see that fer yerself, can't yeh?" 'Sides, yeh needn't be getting yer nose all bent outta shape for the likes of those oafs. I been pissin' in their drinkin' cups fer well over a year now," he says with a straight face. The squire finally laughs and sets down his bow.

On the bank, Charles removes one of Auntie's white bars of soap from his leather pouch. "Use this, I gawt plenty," he says, tossing it to the filthy lad. Prince catches the soap and looks at it with surprise. The smell of lavender fills his nostrils and he sighs contentedly. Seeing a familiar comfort of home reminds him of his departure from Leon and Faye that morning. He feels a pang of guilt for not letting them come with him, but then looks down at the filth covering him. *'Twould have been more awful if this excrement had touched either of my friends,* he tells himself.

"I'm gonna leave yeh to it, boy," Charles calls over his shoulder as he walks away.

A good while of scrubbing, lathering, and soaking finally washes the disgusting scent away and replaces it with a fresh, lavender fragrance. Prince sighs and looks up at the leafy trees. The sun pokes through various openings in the foliage and casts scattered light spots on the water.

I've got to get back to my father's task, Prince suddenly realizes. A growl from his rumbling stomach interrupts his thoughts. He pats his belly and jumps out of the water, sliding his pants back on and cinching his rope belt.

Near the road leading back to the city walls, Charles sits on a boulder stripping the bark and moss off a nearly-straight stick. He puts a curved blade at the top of the stalk and pushes away with his fingers, shaving the dark bark down to the white pine. Thin strips of curled wood shavings pile at his feet.

"What are you doing?" Prince asks, surprised to see the giant still around.

Charles gnaws on a piece of straw hanging out of his mouth. "I noticed yeh only had four arrows," he replies.

Prince nods.

"I've gawt some extra arrowheads. Yeh can use strips of bark to seat 'em." He reaches for Prince's bow. "May I see yer bow?" Charles asks.

Prince reluctantly surrenders his bow, realizing the brute could seize it anyway.

"Now, yeh see the problem here," Charles says, bending the bow and plucking at the string, "is that yer bow isn't a weapon," he clenches the bow and draws back an arrow, closing one eye, "unless yer aim is dead on!" Charles releases the arrow and shields his eyes from the sun to better watch the spiraling feather.

Prince's head whips around to follow the arrow.

"I've only got a few arrows!" Prince complains.

"Well, go fetch it boy!"

"I'm not a dog!" Prince folds his arms.

"C'mon, boy! I'm trying to teach yeh a valuable lesson!"

Prince stands with his arms crossed, still refusing to move.

"Ah, I'll go with yeh then," Charles lowers his hand and snatches Prince by the arm.

"I'm not—Ow!" Prince says as Charles tugs him along like an empty garment.

Charles drags him across the grassy field. He looks right and left for the elusive arrow.

"Sometimes, yeh gotta go farther than yeh thought you had to," Charles says, continuing to pull Prince along.

"Let go, you're hurting me!" Prince shouts, trying to pull his arm free from the iron grasp.

Charles lets go without warning and Prince falls. The boy leaps back to his feet in a huff.

"There it is!" Charles exclaims, placing his hand on Prince's neck and turning his head.

"I see nothing," Prince heaves.

"Right there!" Charles repeats, pointing at a grassy space with the tip of his bow.

Prince squints and sees his arrow buried in the grass.

"Now, go get it!" Charles orders.

Prince snatches his bow out of Charles' hand and stumbles forward. He picks up the arrow and is shocked to find a small, brown bird dead at its tip. He turns around and looks past Charles, measuring the distance from where Charles took the shot.

"'Twas luck!" Prince dissents, after examining the great length that the arrow flew.

"'Twasn't luck, boy!" Charles growls. The mighty man stomps toward the youth and smiles triumphantly. "'Twas aim!"

Prince holds up the arrow and notices that it does not pass through the bird; instead, it stops about halfway, keeping the fowl firmly fixed to the arrow's tip.

"An' now yeh have yer fletching." Charles holds up one of Prince's arrows and points at the dead sparrow.

"Will you teach me how to make those?" Prince asks, shielding his eyes from the bright sun.

"Aye!" Charles nods. He and the boy walk back toward the road. Coming to a small patch of trees, Charles hands Prince a small hook-shaped blade.

"Yeh gotta find the straightest stick yeh can," Charles says, walking over to a low-hanging branch. Lifting it, Charles scans thoroughly. Prince watches the burly man's cool blue eyes shift back and forth.

"It's gotta to be smooth, too." Charles explains, licking his lips. "Yeh don't want a bunch of knots in yer arrow."

Prince's attention wanders. He examines Charles' hook-shaped blade. Speckles of rust litter the blade and the wooden handle seems to be handmade.

"Are yeh payin' attention, boy?"

"Yes, sir!" Prince snaps his focus back to Charles.

"Good," Charles says with a wink. "Now, go ahead and use the knife to cut that stick off, right there!"

Charles points.

"This one?" Prince asks.

"No, the one next to it."

"This one?"

"No boy, are yeh blind? I'm pointin' right at it!"

"This one?"

"Fer Pete's sake boy, it's this one right here!" Charles stomps over to the branch in question. "Now, cut it at the base and be done with it! Findin' a stick should never take so long!"

Prince chops at the base of the stick and frees it from the branch.

"Go find several more!" Charles barks.

Prince scans the branch and measures his stick up against similar branches, eventually getting a feel for the type of stick needed. "Not too bent, and not too knotted," he recalls.

"That's good advice when yeh court a woman!" Charles winks.

Prince doesn't understand the joke, but smiles anyway. The two walk over to a moss-covered log and take a seat.

"Now yeh gotta strip the bark with the blade." Charles takes the knife out of Prince's hand. "Strip the bark away from yeh like this," Charles motions, moving the blade away from himself, "else yer gonna slice yerself up real bad like this." The burly man holds up his hand and drags a finger down a long straight scar.

Once Prince strips all the sticks, Charles shows him how to split the tips and seat an arrowhead.

"Fix it in place with strips of bark and a bit of sap." Charles goes back to the tree and finds dripping sap. He rolls the arrow in it, and then wraps the curled strips of bark around the arrowhead.

"Finally, yeh gotta tie it off with an over, under, back, and forth." Charles slowly shows Prince how to tie the arrowhead in place. Next, he plucks the feathers out of the sparrow's wings.

"Sap is a wonderful tool," Charles says. "Yeh can make wine, fix yer beard," he pinches a little sap and drags his fingers along his beard, which smoothes the curled hairs, "and build arrows." Charles begins humming, as he dabs the feathers in sap, then fixes them to the back of the arrow.

"Strips of bark fix it in place when you go round and round, tuck through and ... yer done!" Charles says with a swirling motion so quick that Prince misses the demonstration.

"Do it again!" Prince orders.

"Sure. You go round and round, tuck through and yer done!"

He hands Prince the arrow. Charles' arrows seem much heavier than the ones his father had given him. He sniffs the freshly cut wood and feels a sense of pride. His fingers trace the smooth stick and cold arrowhead. After carving and wrapping several more arrows, Prince sets down the last arrow in the pile by his side.

"Now, cut a nock in them and I'll teach yeh how to shoot that thing," Charles says, handing Prince the bow.

"You can teach me how to shoot better?" Prince asks excitedly.

"If yeh wanna shoot at a bird like me, aim just below the beak."

"That's it?"

"Well, have yeh been taught to stabilize yer shot?" Charles places his hand on Prince's stomach. "Exhale, inhale, and hold it—right?"

Prince nods.

"Well, all yeh need to know from there is that yeh aim just below yer target and let it go fuzzy a bit.

Once yeh see the point of yer arrow come into focus, hold yer breath and release. Yeh'll hit every time!"

Prince visualizes the concept. Charles' instructions are much simpler than that of the royal instructors who bombarded him with techniques and complicated principles.

"I'll go hack some hay for a target then," Charles says, walking away.

Prince finishes cutting notches into the bottom of the sticks. He looks down at the spotted bird with the long arrow gruesomely protruding from its body. A moment of remorse for the creature passes before he picks up the little bird and scrapes its lifeless body off the arrow.

Charles returns with a bundle of straw. He kneels down in the damp field, scoops a mighty handful of mud, and then rubs it on the center of the bushel, staining it a reddish-brown.

"Look at that," Charles says, pointing to Prince's stack of arrows. "Yeh done good boy! Yeh cut yer grooves just fine," he compliments, thoroughly inspecting the notches Prince made. "Well done, lad!"

Prince smiles, feeling a rush of pride.

"Why are yeh helping me?" Prince asks, inadvertently imitating bits of Charles' accent.

"I was squire once too, yeh know," Charles explains. "Didn't pan out, though. So, now I see yeh down there getting a right good hazin' and it reminds me of m'self." He smiles, nudging Prince with the back of his hairy, red hand. "And yeh know what that young me says to the old me?"

"What?"

"Do unto that wee lad as yeh'd have had done unto yerself."

"Oh...," Prince answers, confused.

"So, I opened the gate, and there yeh smelly were! Ha! Ha!"

Prince laughs too, still confused, but happy all the same.

"Now, I'll set this in the field and yeh can go practice a good distance from the castle, before yeh find yerself in more trouble."

"Thank you!" He wraps his arms around Charles' large hips and hugs him tightly.

"Ahh, 'twasn't much," Charles answers, rubbing the boy's head with his enormous hand. "Yeh'll find pheasants aplenty in the field, so mind yer task and get back to the castle."

Prince smiles, feeling a sense of security return that was stripped from him a short while ago.

"I'll be standin' at the top of the King's Gate waitin' fer yeh. Be back before dark, yeh hear?"

Someone will be watching for me, Prince thinks gratefully.

Charles pats Prince on the back.

"Get to it, boy!"

Prince waves and watches the gentle giant stroll away, then holsters his new arrows.

CHAPTER XIV

PREPARING & PLANTING

With the sun high in the sky, Prince is grateful his clothes are dry and free of the awful odor. At the same time, a fierce hatred ignites his heart at the thought of what the guards did to him. He glares in the direction of the wall.

Determining to move even farther from the loathsome guards, Prince heaves the hay target onto his shoulder. He walks down the stone path for quite some time and gradually notices that the dense forest almost touches the road in some places. As he passes the thick trees, he remembers his father telling him to stay out of the shadowy forest. *In the Dark Forest lies great danger!*

Prince has never been so close to the Dark Forest without his father. He stands immobile for a moment, inspecting the shadows blanketing the trees. With the sun high in the noon sky, he's glad to see a few patches of light penetrate the murky darkness. Several unfamiliar noises frighten him and he takes off running past the still trees. A safe distance from the eerie forest, Prince finds a grassy field with freshly cut hay encircled by yellow rolling hills.

'Tis as good a spot as any, Prince determines. He steps out into the field a good distance from the road. Near the base of a hill, he sets up the hay target, eager to master his skills.

"Elude me no more," Prince says to the cooing pheasants he hears all around. Trying to remember everything Charles taught him, the squire fires a few shots. Only one hits the target.

"Aim below the target," he repeats, letting the red circle blur as the pointed arrow comes into focus. A bead of sweat dangles from Prince's eyebrow just as he's about to shoot. He releases the string and fires the arrow into the ground.

"Drat!" he curses. Resetting the arrow, he draws his string back and holds his breath. He releases and watches one of his handmade arrows miss the bundle completely.

Focus. Hold your breath, he thinks. *What am I doing wrong?* He aims below the red dot and recites the Lion Brigade's pillars. "Strength," he whispers, holding his breath. He releases the arrow and hits the target dead center.

"Yes!" he shouts, throwing his hands in the air. His arrows spill out of his leather quiver. He quickly picks them up. Overwhelmed with excitement, he carefully strings another arrow, draws back, and closes one eye, picturing Winston's smug face.

"Honor," he exhales, holding his breath for one second before releasing the arrow. Just as Charles had said, the tip of the arrow covers the red target. The spiraling fletching soars across the field and strikes inches away from his first shot.

Prince stares at the arrows in the center of the target in disbelief. Slowly, he looks down at the bow. "I dub thee—" Prince kneels and taps both of his shoulders with his bow, "Sir Prince. Now, rise a knight!" Nobly, he stands and looks out over the horizon. "I will guard these lands with life and limb!" Prince pledges, waving his hand over everything but the Dark Forest.

The boy practices for another hour. In the process, he manages to turn his arm bright red from releasing the taut string too close to his tender forearm.

"One last try," he mumbles, aiming his best arrow at the target. *I do not want to be stuck out here all night,* he thinks, taking careful aim with one eye closed.

His tired, sore arm wobbles. Waiting too long for the perfect moment to release, his aim drifts. When he thinks he finally has the shot, he straightens both fingers and releases the arrow.

The string vibrates and Prince watches the white feathers soar well above his target and over the hill.

"Ahh, buggar!" he shouts.

He runs to his target and gathers his remaining arrows, then begins his search for the stray.

✶✶✶

Princess is thrilled! Auntie relented and finally allowed her to wear her beautiful, white hand-me-down dress outside to welcome spring. Now that Princess is properly dressed for it, she can really pretend to be the "Fairy of Spring and Good Smelling Flowers." Princess skips through Auntie's flower garden, which is nestled between the hills a short walk from the farm.

She crosses her legs and sits carefully on the ground, holding Setchra up to a white daisy.

"It's got a yellow bulb," she says in a raspy voice.

"Yes, I know, Setchra," Princess answers in a normal, pleasant voice. "That's where Auntie says they put all the pollen."

"What's pollen?" Setchra asks.

"I don't know," Princess answers. "Stop asking stupid questions!"

Princess slowly traces Setchra along the white petals and down the green stem. Once she determines that Setchra has had a good look, she leans in and sniffs the daisy herself.

"Mmmhh...."

"What's it smell like?" Setchra asks.

"See for yourself." Princess holds up the pearl and makes a sniffing noise.

"Smells good," Setchra answers. "What about those?"

Princess looks up and appraises the flower-speckled meadow before her. She stands up from the moist grass and dusts herself off, taking a deep breath of the fragrant air. Thousands of green stems prop up white daisies. To Princess, the flower field looks like a great white ocean. Bustling bumblebees fly from flower to flower, their movements causing the sea of flowers to wave like water.

Princess shields her eyes with her hands and looks up at the patchy blue sky. "It's so beautiful today, don't you think?" she chirps to a panting Arthur.

A silvery-blue butterfly flies past Princess' face and alights right on Arthur's nose.

"Halt!" Princess orders her new friend.

Arthur, thinking that Princess is talking to him, stops as well. Though every part of him wants to snap at the blue-winged insect tickling his nose, he obeys his young master.

"You, I shall name Obedience, for staying where I told you!" she says, pointing at the still butterfly. Arthur raises his furry paw to swipe at the tickling insect, but a gust of wind pushes it off Arthur's nose and sends it back into flight.

"Arthur, you scared away Obedience!"

Arthur sneezes, then fiercely paws at his nose.

Princess sighs and looks at the field again. Sporadically intermingled beneath the daisies are tiny purple flowers that lean over like bells. Millions of tiny red and light blue wild flowers mix in with the array of flora. Their buds unwrap in perfect clover twists that burst out of green pods. Large, white stargazer lilies with purple cores seem to explode out of the ground and stand above the lush plain. Among the lilies are rows of red and pink rose bushes Auntie planted to complement the wild flowers.

Princess closes her eyes and inhales deeply once more, trying to capture the mixed aroma. "'Tis Auntie's flower garden," she says to Setchra, swaying her dress back and forth. "Let's go fetch Obedience."

Arthur barks and follows after Princess.

She gallops up a short hill and down into the next valley, giggling as she goes.

Her hair bounces freely and her pretty white dress trails behind as she runs. She beams with delight, leaping and playing among the flowers.

The butterfly soars out of reach. Princess flops down by a cluster of lilies, closes her eyes, and inhales the sweet scent. She holds her breath, hoping that the fragrance will last forever. When her lungs begin to burn, she exhales slowly, opening her eyes halfway. Through the narrow slits of her eyes, she observes the shifting wheat stalks on the edge of the valley glowing against the bright sunlight.

✲✲✲

Prince parts the tall straw and scans for his missing arrow. He breaks off a stalk of wild wheat and puts it into his dry mouth. He salivates and realizes why Charles put the straw in his mouth.

Prince keeps his bow at the ready. *If the other side of the hill looks like this, my arrow will be lost forever*, he thinks. He shuffles the stem of wheat in his mouth and bites down hard. It crunches and releases a musky taste. "Mmm...," he sighs, gnawing on it as he walks. His stomach grumbles again. Rather than ignore it, the boy grinds the stalk until it is mushy, then swallows. He grabs a fistful of the stalks and chews them as before to squelch his hunger.

He feels the earth incline beneath his feet and leans slightly forward to maintain balance. A gentle, welcoming breeze brushes the sea of stalks left and right, covering the hill in a golden blanket.

Now at the top of the hill, Prince looks down on the world below. Tall wheat covers the opposite side of the hill and several adjoining hills. He grabs a fistful of stalks and rips them from the ground in frustration. "This is pointless," he gripes, throwing the stalks on the ground. He examines the ridgeline and the grassy, speckled valley lying below him. It parallels the Dark Forest on the north and some farmland with crops on the south and west. *Surely there are pheasants along the edge.* He ventures forward to get a better view of the lower plain.

Prince watches the wheat ripple and sway. His attention is drawn to a small figure in a valley on the other side of the hill. Curious, he moves forward and realizes that it is a young girl squatted down in a proper English garden.

Concealed by the thick, golden stalks bordering the east side of the garden, Prince watches the girl snap a single lily by its stem and spin it around. Soft, golden light passes through her illuminated hazelnut hair. She gathers more lilies and makes a bouquet as she hums a soft, pleasant tune. Prince continues to watch as she tosses all of the flowers over her shoulder but one. She holds a lone lily up to her face.

"Your name shall be Hope," she says, her voice traveling up the hill to Prince. Intrigued, Prince drops to the ground and crawls through the wheat toward the garden, not wanting to disturb the scene.

The girl smells the flower, inhaling its natural perfume. "Hope is divine!" she proclaims. Pressing the flower to her nose, she begins twirling.

"Hope makes you act funny!" she says in a raspy tone.

Prince reaches the edge of the garden and parts the wheat to watch the display before him.

A smile spreads across his face at the antics of the strange, alluring girl. On a whim, he leaps to his feet and calmly says, "My lady."

Engaged in dizzying twirls, Princess is startled by the sudden voice. She cries out and falls to the ground, dropping her lily.

Idiot! Prince scolds himself.

"Who's there?" Princess demands, squinting into the bright sun.

Say something! Prince thinks, but can't seem to speak.

Princess shields her eyes from the sunlit stalks, hoping to get a better view. Prince's shadowy figure steps out of the glowing field and into her sight.

Princess gets ready to chide the stranger for scaring her, but sees his kind face and is immediately pacified.

Stepping forward to make sure the girl is unharmed, Prince notices the lily, Hope. He leans down and picks it up, then holds it to his nose, eager to see what it smells like. He inhales and smiles.

As he approaches Princess, he lowers his hand to offer his assistance. She takes it and notices the eagle emblem embroidered on his shoulder. When she stands, she promptly curtsies.

Prince stares as the girl bows before him. Caught off-guard by her cordial manner, he freezes.

"I apologize, Sir. I didn't notice your royal title," she says, tilting her head in deference. "I assure you, I meant no rudeness; 'twas only a blunder."

A few moments pass before he realizes that he hasn't responded.

"A blunder." Prince blushes. "Ah … you needn't be stately. My father is a royal knight, but I am just a lowly squire."

Princess smiles at Prince's humble response.

She had expected him to be more rigid, more formal, more ... *royal.*

Unsure of what to do next, Prince looks down at the lily in his hand and tries to mask his embarrassment by showing extreme confidence.

"Hope is pretty, but I've seen prettier," he remarks.

Princess' face immediately falls. She raises one scrutinizing eyebrow and puckers her lips to the side of her mouth.

Again, Prince's mind shouts, *Idiot!*

"I've never been inside the castle, so Hope is the best I have," she says curtly. The girl reaches out to take back Hope, a hurt expression on her face. Her fingertips brush Prince's hand and their eyes lock for a moment.

"I didn't mean to insult Hope," Prince manages to say.

Princess presses the flower to her nose. "All is well," she forgives him. Her lips part once more into a smile as the sun sets between their illuminated silhouettes.

CHAPTER XV

DISTRESSED & DISTRAUGHT

Prince rubs the back of his neck nervously. Unable to collect his jumbled thoughts, he absent-mindedly grinds the tips of his toes into the ground.

"Well," Princess finally says in a sheepish voice, "'tis getting late." She smiles shyly. Although intrigued by the boy's appearance, she does not want Auntie to worry. Besides, she feels a little uncomfortable under Prince's gaze. Princess curtsies and extends her flower. "Pleasure to have met you."

"Yes, 'twas...," Prince mumbles. He leans forward and reciprocates with a bow. As Prince rises again, he's startled to see a great black shadow cover the ground all around them. He jerks up and looks to the sky. "Wait a moment!"

"Well, perhaps I could stay a bit longer," Princess answers, lost in her own world.

High in the amber sky, a black dragon flaps its enormous wings. A cold shiver runs down Prince's spine and dread fills his palpitating heart. The enormous creature's black scales reflect the setting sun's purple light.

Princess observes the sudden change in Prince's demeanor and assumes she has done something to insult him. "Have I offended you in some way, sir?"

Prince continues to gape at the terrifying beast circling above.

The dragon scans for any sign of prey. The setting sun blinds him, shielding the children from imminent death. The reptilian monster unknowingly sails over them, continuing his circular flight pattern.

Prince finally jerks into action. "Follow me!" he shouts, though he has no clear idea of where to go.

"What?" Princess asks.

Prince extends his hand urgently. She instinctively takes it as she looks over her shoulder to see what was holding Prince's gaze. When she spots the black swirling dragon, images of her parents cloud her mind. She freezes and clenches Prince's hand so hard that she pops his knuckles.

"Come on!" Prince orders and tugs her violently from her frozen position.

"Aaaahhhh!" Princess screams.

There's no use, Prince thinks, pulling the girl along. *We are as good as dead!*

As they scurry away, Prince pictures the massive monster descending on them to scorch their flesh with its fiery breath. His pounding heart makes his ears throb. Prince quickly peeks over his shoulder and sees the goliath circling high in the sky. He holds his breath as he sees it turning and flying over the farm to the south.

The children run through the tall grass as fast as their legs will carry them.

Why is it circling? Prince wonders.

The ferocious dragon flaps its dark wings in the colorful sunset sky. Its jet-black scales contrast sharply with the orange, pink, and purple streaks that cross the heavens. Its long, spiked snout sweeps side to side, detecting the faint scent of human flesh. It widens its circle and scours the field, but it is still unable to spot the fleeing children.

Prince realizes that he is running headlong for the ominous forest and slows his pace, looking for any other way to escape. Blinded by fear, Princess continues to sprint, preventing Prince from stopping or changing his direction. Prince's father's voice echoes in his mind, *The monsters live in the forest.*

"Wait!" Prince yells, trying to catch Princess' attention. "There are dark creatures in there!"

The last remnants of the sun finally fade below the horizon, allowing the dragon to see more clearly. Its glowing scarlet eyes are immediately attracted to the frantic motions of the children. As it recognizes its prey, the dragon curls back its scaly lips to reveal a row of razor-sharp teeth. The beast arches its sleek, armor-plated back and releases a deafening screech.

Near the edge of the woods, the terrified children look back to see the colossal dragon diving down upon them.

"Run!" Prince shrieks.

The dragon's sharp talons poise for a catch in its howling descent. The beast then flicks its forked tongue in and out of its mouth as it savors the children's scent.

"Don't look, just keep running!" Prince screams, holding onto his bow with one hand and crushing Princess' hand with the other. The two children dive into the dark forest as a blast of heat erupts behind them. Princess yelps in terror and the two get to their feet. Falling leaves and branches bombard the children as they run through the dense forest. Prince looks up and glimpses the faint outline of the dragon clawing the treetops from above.

"I can't see!" Princess whimpers.

Prince turns around, cups his hand over her mouth, and puts his finger to his lips. He pulls the girl near him and throws an arm up to protect her from the debris. "It's trying to discover our location—" he waits for another barrage of branches to cover his voice and continues, "—if it hears or sees us, we are finished." He drags his finger across his neck for morbid emphasis. The children huddle down in the brush together, trying to be as silent as moths.

Unable to flush the children out, the dragon pulls up from the tall trees. The beast whirls around and hovers near the border of the shadowy tree line. Its leathery wings create a powerful downward thrust that rattles the trees as though they were mere weeds. Slowly, the monster descends until its bulging belly suspends above the ground. Its hindquarters delicately touch down, while its smaller arms swipe at its snout. Its long tongue slides out of its mouth and into its cavernous nostrils, refreshing its sensory glands with the children's scent. Releasing a great bellow, the dragon attempts once again to scare its prey out of hiding.

Princess screams, too startled by the nearness and strength of the blast to stay silent.

Having located its prey, the dragon turns in the children's direction and peels back its monstrous lips. A bright, static blue light crackles at the very back of the dragon's throat. Suddenly, an orange blaze surges out of its mouth in a fiery explosion. The dragon sways its head back and forth, setting the woods ablaze in the direction of the children. Blistering heat waves over them and orange light illuminates their pale faces. Prince winces and shields his face with his hand, then hurriedly looks over at the girl.

Princess looks up at him, her hands pressed against her ears. Huge tears roll down her cheeks and her chest heaves up and down in sheer terror.

"What do we do now?" she stammers. Though the initial blast missed them, flames grow around them. Fear immobilizes the children as waves of heat radiate through the forest.

Prince looks at the shaking girl and realizes that he needs to be strong for her.

Knights smile in the face of danger, Prince hears his father's voice. Prince stretches his arm out toward Princess and declares, "Danger smiles in the face of knights!" He forces a smile.

His bumbled reassurance seems to work because Princess slowly lowers her hands from her ears. Although she didn't hear a word Prince said, his confident smile reassures her. She doesn't know where his courage came from, but she is glad that he is with her.

A crackling blue light glows through the trees behind Princess. *No!* Prince inwardly screams.

Without thinking, he whirls Princess around and thrusts her to the ground, shielding her with his own body.

Another stream of fiery breath blazes past them, but this time on their left side. Feeling as though he were in Hell's fiery furnace, Prince looks up to find that they are right in the middle of a giant firetrap. With the flames spreading throughout the brush on either side of them, there is nowhere to go but farther into the dreaded forest.

Overwhelmed and out of options, Prince makes the only decision he can. He leaps to his feet and pulls Princess' trembling body up with him. Grabbing her hand, he retreats into the Dark Forest.

Prince feels a powerful, roasting wind on his sweaty face. The fueled flames grow higher and wider with each gust and an overwhelming heat begins to scorch the children's skin. The fire races at an enormous speed as thick, thorny briar bushes ignite. He and Princess duck under branches and scurry through narrow openings to escape the raging inferno. Sharp thorns snag their clothes and stab at their flesh.

"Ouch!' Princess cries.

"Shh," Prince hisses, shuffling forward on all fours. Scratched and bleeding, the pair escapes the briar patch and scramble across the forest floor. Moist vapors created by the fire's intense heat rise from the damp ground and create a low-hanging fog.

⁂

A rabbit pops his head out of a hole and leaps into the fray. He begins thumping his foot on the forest floor.

A handsome fairy with short black hair and silver irises appears from inside a squirrel hole. Hugging an acorn, he flutters his long, translucent wings.

"Um ... Amble," he calls over his shoulder, scratching his silver pant leg with his pointy black boot.

"Yes, Cole," a squeaky female voice replies.

"There's a big nasty fire out here."

"Oh really?" Amble says, poking her head out of the little opening. A green stem dangles out of her mouth, perfectly matching her short lime-green hair. She flips her head to remove her long, fluttery bangs from her bronze eyes.

"Humph," Amble sighs. "I suppose that's what Hop was thumping about." She speaks out of the side of her mouth, the stem bouncing with each word. Amble spits the stem out and flips back around toward the hole. The fairy flaps her butterfly-like wings, fluttering in and out of her home. Each time she disappears into the dark orifice, she returns with her arms wrapped around a small acorn.

"Cole, take the sack!" Amble shouts, tossing Cole a white sack.

In her rush, Amble's wings brush against Cole's. "Ha! Ha! That tickles," he giggles, flapping his wings until he's hovering outside the hole. He zips around and gathers the acorns, tucking them into the sack as quickly as he can. A sparkling blue dust cloud cascades off him and slowly drifts toward the ground.

"That stings my lungs," Amble hacks, waving the smoke away from her face.

Across from the pair, a chubby brown-haired fairy bounces on a branch. His bulging tummy protrudes over a pair of too-small white fur shorts. "Uh ... which way do we go?" he squawks in a low voice. He hugs a half-eaten acorn with one arm and sniffles, rubbing first his silver-colored iris, then his copper-colored one.

"Go home, Bumble!" Cole yells to him.

Cole and Amble dart away, leaving glowing trails of pink and blue.

"Uh, alright!" Bumble mumbles. He takes a bite out of his acorn, packing his cheeks full. With a bounce, the tubby fairy springs from the branch and flaps his stubby wings. His face scrunches and turns red from the effort while his sputtering wings vibrate like a bustling bumblebee. The fat fairy hovers, exerting twice the effort of Cole or Amble. A sparkling purple cloud trails him as he flees the inferno.

✕✕✕

Prince sprints headlong into the forest and catches a glimpse of a rabbit thumping its foot, sounding the alarm for the woodland creatures. The forest comes alive with squirrels, chipmunks, groundhogs, foxes, and rabbits pressing deeper into the dark woods.

If 'tis safe for them, 'tis safe for us! Prince determines, pulling Princess along. Just then, a set of familiar, flapping wings catches Prince's attention. He whips his head over his shoulder and finds a flock of pheasants flying right past him. Consumed by the race to escape the dragon's fire, Prince fails to grasp the irony of the situation. Smoke fills the forest, pushing the children and the woodland creatures forward.

✕✕✕

On the outskirts of the forest, the dragon works expertly, moving back and forth to keep the two walls of fire burning strong. When he is satisfied with the initial stages of the trap, the monster lifts off the ground and flies over the fiery forest. His blood-red eyes make out its desired destination and he dives toward a small clearing in the middle of the forest. The two firewalls run on either side of the clearing, forcing anything within the trap to run into the open. The dragon swoops down until it comes to the clearing's far side. He reels back his horned head and parts his scaly lips. Flames lap at its nostrils just before the beast unleashes a stream of blazing orange, connecting the two glowing lanes of fire in a perfect triangle. His trap complete, the monster looms over the orange walls, watching for movement in the clearing.

✕✕✕

The children continue their reckless sprint. As they reach the edge of the clearing, Princess trips over a large root, falling headfirst into the dirt and dragging Prince down with her. Princess cries out and grabs a bloody knee.

"Come on! Get up! We have to cross the clearing," Prince shouts, tugging at Princess' hand.

A crackling noise sounds from the forest, barely audible over the rushing flames. Two deer stampede past the children and leap into the clearing. Within seconds, the dragon materializes out of the darkness and seizes the first doe with its steely talons. The fatal blow comes so swiftly that the severed deer doesn't even know it's dead. It tries to cycle its front legs, blinks twice, then goes into its death throes. The children shrink back in terror. The full severity of the situation weighs down on them as they watch the dragon disappear with his prize.

"We can't go into the clearing!" Princess whispers.

"It was waiting for us," Prince shudders.

The surviving doe whips around but loses its footing. It falls hard on its side, then frantically struggles to its feet. *Go, go, go!* Prince silently roots.

The animal covers a short distance before the snarling dragon appears once again out of the dark night. In one powerful swoop, the beast covers the distance and seizes the doe.

Princess watches the deer kick its legs in resistance before it is crushed. She covers her face in horror. *We're as good as dead!*

The shadowy dragon disappears once more.

"What do we do? What *can* we do?" Princess frantically begs, looking over to Prince for guidance.

Prince surveys the scene, searching for an escape route. The wall of fire surrounds them and the clearing, blocking every route of escape. *There's no way out,* he realizes. He looks down at Princess, defeat in his eyes. She wraps her arms around her legs.

Our eyes, our hearts, and our wits echoes in Princess' mind. She wipes the sweat off her brow. "I thought you were a squire," she says, looking at Prince. She pulls up her apron to cover her mouth and nose from the clouding smoke.

Prince forces a weak smile and nods. He follows Princess' example and lifts his tunic to cover his face. "I will stay by your side," he promises, his voice muffled by the cloth. He puts his head between his knees and struggles for air.

Through breaks in the forest, Princess can see the dragon stacking his kills. Moving with unfathomable speed, the dragon launches back and forth from air to ground, each time returning with a fresh kill.

As the flames grow, the children crawl toward the clearing little by little. The powerful blaze illuminates their surroundings. In the growing light even a small rabbit's body is visible, flopping in the dragon's red-stained fangs.

The winged demon lifts from the ground and flies above his triangle of death. His head shifts back and forth, painting the forest with even more flames, forcing woodland creatures into the clearing.

A feeling of numbness travels up her sweltering arm and she gasps for air. Princess reaches in her pocket and wraps her fingers around Setchra. A blanket of blackness overtakes her and she falls onto her side.

Won't be long now, Prince thinks, feeling fiery death lap at his skin. He reaches over to grasp the little girl's hand, but finds nothing beside him. He lifts up his head and struggles to open his eyes in the oppressive heat and smoke.

He looks at the ground beside him and finds it vacant. He slowly looks forward and discovers the girl in front of him, standing with one arm outstretched. Her head is cocked to the side and she makes a strange clicking noise with her tongue. He looks at her glistening face through the rippling heat waves and notices that her pupils have dilated drastically.

Prince's shock begins to dissipate as the little girl crouches down beside him, moving with the pearl out in front of her.

"Do you see a way out?" Prince shouts over the crackling trees. Fiery branches fall down behind him.

"Yes," Princess croaks in a raspy voice. She lies flat on her stomach and motions for Prince to follow. She begins scooting across the hazy forest floor, skirting the clearing and heading toward the wall of flame to their left.

Just as the smoke and heat become unbearable, Prince feels cool moisture saturate his clothes. He looks down and sees that the mucky forest ground has softened to marsh. Not wanting to lose sight of Princess in the hovering fog, Prince scoots faster to stay close to her side.

Princess gasps, stumbling face-first into a streambed. She quickly rises, coughing, and glances around blankly.

We're saved! Prince silently cheers. "What are you waiting for?" he asks. "Soak yourself!" The squire rolls around in the cool, muddy water.

Prince jerks his mother's handkerchief out of his pocket and covers Princess' mouth while he tucks his nose and mouth in his tunic.

"Keep this over your mouth," Prince instructs.

A giant, sparking fireball shoots to the ground and erupts on impact beside the streambed. The children barely have time to pull their heads beneath the steaming water before the ground explodes in flames all around them. Surfacing from the stream, the children cough from the pluming smoke.

Prince raises his head just above the water, protecting the rest of his body. The squire looks around and finds that the stream passes straight through the firewall and away from the clearing. Though Prince is frightened by the prospect of passing straight through the inferno, he realizes that this is their only avenue of escape. Taking Princess' hand, he pulls the girl along through the streambed.

"We'll burn alive!" Princess insists, pulling back from the direction of the flames.

"The stream will protect us," the boy reassures her.

Princess reluctantly nods and they begin inching their way forward through the shallow water. She wipes her stinging eyes as she and the boy move closer to the flames. She turns and peers over the streambed at the clearing one last time. Through the gloom, she sees the watchful dragon pounce on a wild boar, ripping it to shreds with its powerful mandible. She shudders and moves forward through the water.

"Hurry!" Prince chokes out, tugging Princess along with him. The stream gets deeper and Princess stops.

"I can't swim," she shouts.

Prince turns back toward her. "We're going to have to completely submerge to make it through," he says, trying to sound calm. "I'll hold onto you and pull you along." He looks into Princess' eyes and she nods slowly.

"On my count," Prince instructs. "One, two, three!" He pulls Princess under the water with him and swims forward. When he can stand it no longer, he surfaces, bringing her up with him.

"We made it!" he says, relieved, looking back at the firetrap behind them.

Overcome with emotion, Princess cries.

Prince pulls her forward until they are a safe distance away from the fiery fray. They exit the stream and find themselves deep in the forest.

"Why doesn't the dragon come after us?" Princess asks, while the pair wind through the Dark Forest away from the fire.

"Dragon wings are thin," Prince explains. "They would be punctured by the trees."

Prince motions with a nod for Princess to follow him. Wet, tired, and traumatized, they crouch down and venture into the unknown.

CHAPTER XVI

DEVISING & DEFENDING

Auntie grunts as she struggles to lift a scalding copper pot from her cobblestone fireplace. Using two metal pot hooks, the robust woman snares the deep, steaming pot through the iron rings on the sides. She leans forward and keeps her elbows high. Beads of sweat drip from her face into the hot stew.

The ginger-haired woman drops the bubbling pot on the wooden counter. Candles on the wall flicker from her labored motions and heavy breath.

"Whew." She dabs her brow with her forearm. "That's not as easy as it once was." Placing her hands on the coarse counter, Auntie takes a moment to catch her breath. She leans over the steamy vapors and inhales deeply.

Once she recovers, she uses a knife to cut strips of meat away from a bloody chicken thigh. She cuts until the bone is bare. She breaks the bone, gathers the feet and the head, and tosses it all into the pluming broth.

Where is that girl? 'Tis nearly nightfall, the middle-aged woman thinks, setting the knife down and adjusting her apron. "She's done it this time! If I've told her once, I've told her a thousand times—dinner is at twilight," she growls as she stomps over to the window. A foreboding red sliver rests just above the horizon, but is quickly swallowed up by darkness. She chews her lip nervously.

Auntie returns to the counter and picks up the knife. Cutting tops off carrots, she masterfully strips their skin. "She's never been this late before," she mutters, shaking her head while slicing the carrots into thin orange discs. When the pieces pile high enough, she tosses them into the pot, then cuts celery stalks.

Finished with the vegetables, she spins around and removes a long bread paddle from the wall. She uses her apron to undo the sliding latch on the stone oven built into the side of the fireplace. The iron door creaks down and the chains holding the door snap tight. Auntie stares into the red embers and licks her lips. She inhales the wholesome aroma of fresh bread and examines the two loaves rising to perfection in the little oven. "I'm going to eat it all m'self is what I'm going to do! And why not? I gathered, mixed, and baked!" she continues.

Auntie skillfully removes the bread pans from the oven and sets it down on the worn counter next to her simmering stew. She drapes a thin white rag over the steaming bread to keep it warm and deftly mule-kicks the oven door behind her, causing it to close with a raucous bang.

Well, I may as well sit down and rest a bit *while I wait for the girl*, she reasons, moving over to a chair at the kitchen table. She rests her head against the wall, blinks her heavy lids, and soon nods off to sleep.

Auntie jerks awake to the smell of something burning.

"The bread!" she exclaims, jumping to her feet and scurrying over to the small stove. She is about to open the little door, but glimpses at the loaves on the counter and remembers that she has already removed the bread. She pauses mid-step and sniffs the air.

"Well, somethin's burning," she detects.

A faint scratch at the door distracts her.

"Coming!" she shouts, thankful that Arthur and Princess have finally wandered back to the cottage. When she opens the cold, creaking door, Auntie's nostrils are assailed by the acrid smell of smoke.

"Wildfire!" Apprehension builds in her as she looks out into the darkness. She searches for Princess, but is disappointed to find only Arthur. The dog pivots immediately and begins running away and barking.

A wave of anxiety washes over Auntie and she takes a step back.

"What have you done with her, Arthur?" she scolds the unkempt dog.

Arthur sprints forward and barks with fervor.

"You awful, mangy mutt! Show me where she is this instant!"

Auntie steps out into the yard, hoping that the dog will lead her to Princess. Her eyes are drawn to a pale amber light, glowing beyond the barn, causing

Auntie to stop in her tracks. Her eyes widen with fear as she realizes that the glow is coming from the forest.

"Forest fire!" She gasps. She runs toward the barn to get a better look. Arthur continues barking and jumping around Auntie's feet in a frenzy, but stops before reaching the barn. His body grows rigid and he growls deep in his throat.

"Princess!" Auntie shouts, consumed with worry. "Princess, where are you?"

Merlin neighs from within the shadowy timber structure, sending brown and white chickens exploding from the barn's entry. Auntie jumps back in surprise and Arthur crouches low, whimpering.

"What in Tremble Nemble is going on?" Auntie exclaims. "Princess, is that you in there?"

A heavy wheezing answers from behind the barn.

Arthur trembles from the awful noise. Auntie freezes in place.

"What is it, boy?" she whispers haltingly, keeping her eyes on the now silent barn. She swallows nervously, trying to wet her dry mouth.

A loud hiss punctuates the night and tapers off into a gurgle.

Auntie musters the courage to edge over to the garden. She crouches down and hides behind the tall tomato plants.

A gust of air makes the blades of grass ripple around the sides of the barn.

Auntie's able fingers grasp a fistful of fresh mint leaves. With every sound coming from behind the barn, the certainty grows in Auntie's mind, along with her trepidation. She wets her lips, squints, and spits off to the side to ward off evil spirits.

"Arthur," Auntie whispers in a commanding voice, "stay here."

The trembling dog has no problem obeying his master.

The matron makes her way to the side of the barn and begins inching along its wooden wall. She gulps as the rumbling noise gets louder. When she finally reaches the back corner of the barn, she pauses to collect her nerves. She closes her eyes and grits her teeth, then forces herself to peek around the corner.

An enormous black dragon lies fast asleep in the hay. His scaly side expands as he breathes in, creating a sound like a blacksmith's bellows. Hot, putrid air washes over Auntie as the bloated creature exhales. She shudders as she observes its sleek black scales, razor-sharp talons, and pink forked tongue pulsing with every sleeping breath. Even in sleep there is no mistaking the deadliness of the ravenous reptile before her.

Thank heavens the beast sleeps, Auntie thinks to herself. *Goodness knows what I'd do if the dragon hadn't already worn himself out. He must have had some feast to sleep as it does.* She could not let the dragon continue to sleep—the longer it slept, the hungrier it would be when it finally woke from its slumber.

Auntie looks around and finds a small rock a short distance to her left. She quietly shuffles over to it and scoops it up with her free hand. Moving back to her post at the edge of the barn, she chances another look around the corner at the black demon.

Do it now, she tells herself, clenching her jaw and fidgeting with the rock in her hand.

With surprising precision, she chucks the stone at the monster's face, hitting it square in the snout. She crouches down by the barn, staying as still as she can. Upon impact, the dragon roars to life, emitting a short burst of flames. It claws at its snout and tries to orient itself. The scent of human flesh catches on its slithering tongue.

Auntie springs out of the darkness.

"That's it! Come and get me!" she cries.

The dragon rears back and slams its head against the barn wall.

Auntie grinds the fresh mint leaves in her hand and closes the distance to the dragon as it turns to meet her assault.

Spying the fearless old harridan, the monster prepares to destroy her with one swift blast. As it inhales a deep breath to fuel the fire, Auntie spots the blue, crackling sparks in the back of its massive throat. Lunging forward to close the distance, she hurls the mint leaves toward the beast's white, glowing teeth. The soft, fuzzy leaves swirl through the air and catch in the dragon's breath. The crushed mint flows right into its gaping maw as it prepares to blast Auntie to ash.

The leaves make contact with the soft fleshy inside of the dragon's mouth. The dragon's narrow snout snaps shut and a blast of orange fire explodes out of the sides of the demon's mouth and nostrils. Auntie turns around and sprints back to the side of the barn before a wave of heat overwhelms her.

Behind her, the dragon's lips part and its body shakes in fury. It tries to draw another deep breath, but it hacks and chokes on the pungent, minty odor permeating its mouth and throat. Whipping its head from side to side and coughing great plumes of smoke, the monster spreads its wings and prepares to launch into flight. The orange glow of firelight illuminates the thin, webby membrane of the dragon's veiny wings.

Auntie pops her head around the corner of the barn, careful to stay out of the path of the dragon's sporadic bursts of flame. She shudders at the enormity of the beast.

The massive reptile spots Auntie and tries to pounce, but sneezes violently, shooting its body backwards into the hay pile. Its crushing weight sends straw flying into the air in all directions. The dragon rocks back onto its feet, its fury rising. The monster postures menacingly, but is overtaken by yet another sneezing fit. The dragon snorts and sniffles, a coughing explosion bursting into a stream of flames. It thrashes its head violently, whipping its tail and crushing an apple tree near the barn. The scattered hay catches fire in several places on the ground.

"Serves you right!" Auntie scolds the predator. Hacking in a fit of rage, the dragon scrapes at its horned snout with its front claws. The fuming beast inhales deeply, its back arching from the exertion. It releases its breath in a string of sneezes, one following the next.

"Blast me now, you sniveling, over-sized lizard!" she dares the dragon, holding up her fist and shaking it once for emphasis.

Agitated by the growing effects of the mint leaves, the dragon slithers its forked tongue in and out of its mouth as it attempts to clear the passage. The moist saliva only spreads the cooling effects of the plant. The dragon emits a racking sneeze, causing it to discharge a ball of flames skyward. When the heat makes contact with its now sensitive teeth, it screeches in agony.

The creature bellows in frustration. Flapping its wings, it hovers just above the barn. It glares at Auntie through its cold eyes, then retreats into the dark, starlit night.

After a moment, she brushes her long, wispy red bangs out of her eyes and sighs. "One of these days, Tabatha Shepherd, dragons will be the end of you."

Returning to Arthur, she leans down and stares into the sheep dog's eyes. "Now, boy, tell me where the girl is."

He covers his eyes with two fluffy, trembling paws.

Auntie gives him a firm stare.

His nostrils flare and fill with the dragon's repulsive odor. His trembling body refuses to believe that the dragon has departed.

"Very well," Auntie says, pressing the nail of her middle finger to the pad of her thumb. She lowers the pressed digits toward Arthur's snout and flicks his wet nose. He yelps in pain. The thud tingles and makes him sneeze. Like smelling salts, the gesture brings him back to his senses. Arthur's big brown eyes shamefully shift left and right. The shaking subsides and he rises to his feet, his tail wagging low and cautiously. Arthur starts to walk to the field, his courage rising. The dog barks once and sprints toward the forest.

"Blast it all," she curses, pressing her open hand to her cheek. Dreading what she may find, she follows.

CHAPTER XVI

LEADING & LED

Far from the dragon's smoldering snare, Princess clutches Prince's hand. Darkness surrounds them, with only occasional moon rays seeping through the trees above them. A hooting owl triggers a raven's caw, which echoes distantly like a screaming child. The forest comes alive with strange noises. One distinct howling noise sends chills up Princess' spine.

The cry of a wolf rips through her mind and brings her mother's voice back from the grave. Wolves, Princess, are terrible creatures, her mother had told her. They hunt in packs and kill for pleasure. Because they thirst for a child's flesh, we must always stay close to father and his sharp axe!

A sound like a snapping branch causes Princess to jump and look behind her.

"We should go back," Princess whimpers, gripping Prince's arm with both shaking hands.

"Dragons are territorial," Prince informs her.

"If we go back, it will be waiting!"

"Wolves are territorial. They hunt in packs!" Princess counters.

"Wolves?" Prince wipes his sweaty forehead with his grimy sleeve. He makes every effort to stay calm for the girl's sake. He reaches out and pats her shoulder. "Wolves are the least of our worries. I've sharp enough arrows to ward off wolves!" Prince waves his hand as if dispelling her concerns. "'Tis dragons we've no defense against."

"You aren't afraid of wolves?" Princess feels her racing heart begin to slow.

"Not in the least!" Prince pronounces, but he is grateful that the darkness hides the worry in his eyes. "'Tis the fiery beasts in the sky that I fear."

Princess shudders at the thought of being killed and tossed on the pile of carcasses. *Killed by wolves, or killed by a dragon?* she ponders, weighing the grisly options in her mind.

"Killed is killed," she mumbles, unhappy with her present choices.

"We are *not* going to be killed," Prince assures her. "A squire always finds his way home!"

At the mention of home, Princess stops. "Auntie!" she gasps, swallowing a lump of fear as she realizes that her dear mentor could be in dreadful danger. She turns to Prince with wide eyes. "How will we return home?"

Although the boy is as anxious as Princess, he does his best to remain calm. "If we can find the edge of the forest, then we might be able to skirt around it, until it leads us to the castle. The dragon won't dare attack us there."

"Castle?" Princess' fear for Auntie is quickly replaced with excitement at the prospect of visiting the castle.

"Of course!" Prince boasts. "We must alert the Dragon Brigade that there is a dragon in the area."

Princess tugs on Prince's hand. "What are you waiting for? Lead on, squire! Lead on!"

"Well, that's the problem," Prince admits, glancing down at her fingers on his. "I don't know which way to go. I have no bearing and I can't navigate in these strange woods without stars to guide me."

Lost in the darkness? Princess' heart begins pounding again. She looks up and searches the vast night, praying for just one star to guide them. She realizes how futile it is to find her bearings in the dark. She feels fear erupt and spread down her shivering limbs.

"We must stay close to each other," she says, terrified of losing her sole companion in the oppressive darkness.

"Of course," Prince agrees. He looks around, trying to figure out what to do. "Let's keep pressing forward in the same direction," he finally suggests. "We'll be moving away from the dragon at least."

Princess agrees, though she doesn't like the idea of blindly wandering around in the spooky woods.

The children move forward again, making their way through the underbrush.

"Oww!" Prince exclaims, rubbing his shin.

"What is it?" Princess asks.

"Just a tree," he answers, sticking out his hand to inspect the object in front of him. He finds the sides of a tall, uprooted tree.

"It's huge!" Princess exclaims as she examines the outline hulking above her.

Prince places the toe of his boot on a branch and pushes himself up. He feels the rough bark poke his feet though his soft soles.

"We can climb over this. It's just lying on its side." He turns to Princess and reaches for her hand. "Maybe we can see something from up there!"

"Are you sure?" Princess asks, nervous to climb in the dark.

Prince ignores her question. "Hand," he calls out. Princess places her hand in his and waits for the boy to pull up her tired body. "Put your foot on the knot and push up," he instructs.

The squire pulls her up and stabilizes her against a branch, then turns and scales a few feet up.

"You climb like Guinevere," the girl declares, impressed.

"*Who*?" Prince spins around to help her again.

"My cat!" Princess smiles, reaching for Prince's outstretched hand.

"You named your cat 'Guinevere?'"

"Uh-huh." Princess nods.

"Sounds like a person and not a cat." He heaves her up the next branch, trying not to lean so far forward that his arrows slip from his holster.

"You're lucky you're a boy," Princess says between strained grunts.

"Why's that?"

The tip of Princess' toe finds something to press on. She wedges her bare foot in the dark mass, then pushes while Prince helps her up the enormous tree's curved side. Bark snags and pulls at her now-filthy dress.

"Omph!" She hangs over the edge of the tree rim. "Because," she grumbles, pressing both hands down on the rough bark and slowly standing, "you don't have to worry about a dress, or hair, or any of the sorts."

"True." Prince continues scaling up the branches. "But you don't have to fight in wars."

"You don't want to fight?"

"'Tisn't whether I want to fight or not," Prince firmly places his foot. "Father says, 'fools fight, heroes win.'"

"How can you win if you don't fight?"

"Good question," Prince says, pulling himself up. He continues to help Princess up despite the stinging scratches from the snagging bushes.

Once on top of the trunk, Princess dusts debris off her dress. Prince shakes his head, wondering why she bothers trying to clean the ruined fabric of her dress.

Princess combs her long hair out of her face. "Ladies must always be proper and presentable," she informs Prince in a mock-Auntie tone.

Prince raises an eyebrow.

"This would be less dreadful if my hair weren't constantly in my face!" she complains.

"Why don't you just tie it up?"

Princess stretches out her empty hands. "With *what?*"

Prince rips a piece of fabric from his shirt. "Here!" He hands it to her.

With one hand, Princess pulls her hair tightly back. With her other hand, she ties a bow around her ponytail. "Squires must be noble, ladies must be proper; so it goes and everyone knows," Princess continues, staring cross-eyed at a loose strand of hair dangling in front of her face. It rises and falls with the wind, tickling her nose. "If the labor of a squire is half as daunting as a lady's duties, you've much to endure!"

Prince is about to argue that squire labor is *much* more difficult than a lady's duties, but he is distracted by a faint glow in the distance. He squints and is able to make out a hazy blue trail glistening over the forest floor.

"Do you see that?" Prince shouts, pointing to the faint, soft glow.

"See what?"

"Follow me. I see a light!" Prince begins scrambling down the other side of the tree.

"Wait," Princess whimpers, inching her way down the scratchy bark. She reaches the forest floor and finds Prince impatiently waiting. The boy sets off in the direction of the glow, pushing through the clawing underbrush. He stops and reaches his hand out to the struggling girl.

Princess gratefully accepts his hand, and the squire leads the frightened girl onward. She clasps his palm so tightly that his fingers turn white.

Patiently, the squire helps Princess through the difficult terrain. Every step seems to be hindered by a branch, vine, or briar patch. All the while, he keeps an eye on the glowing trail, hoping that he's found a way out. With tremendous effort, the children fight their way along the overgrown trail. They continually stumble and fall until they are both bleeding and bruised. Once they reach a break in the underbrush, they can finally see the glowing trail more clearly.

"Stay here until I whistle for you, like this." Prince demonstrates the low whistle.

Princess nods and sniffles quietly. She tries to push away the fear that once Prince leaves her side, he will be lost forever, leaving her alone in the darkness.

Prince emerges from the dense thicket and approaches the dazzling blue mist. The strange luminous trail twinkles like the heavens and seems to beckon him closer. He smiles and his face glows blue with the peculiar floating vapors. In awe, he drags his dirty, scratched hands through the mist. The blue cloud instantly wraps around his fingers, causing his hand to glow with an eerie incandescence. The inquisitive boy holds his hand up to his face in wonder, examining the magic at work. An incredible warmth crawls up his arm. He closes his eyes and sighs.

"You simply *must* feel this!" he shouts back to Princess.

"I thought we were supposed to be quiet," Princess replies in a loud, harsh whisper.

Prince, too entranced to answer, begins to laugh as the mist travels up his arm and spreads to his neck and cheeks. Still wary, Princess watches the blue mist illuminate Prince's face, giving the odd appearance that his head and hand are floating in the thick darkness. Intrigued, she finally decides to leave the dense underbrush.

"You didn't whistle like you said you would," Princess pouts when she reaches the fairy trail.

"Come feel it!" Prince exclaims, waving his glowing hand to beckon the girl closer.

Princess' eyes widen. "Does it hurt?"

"Hurt?" Prince smiles widely, revealing luminescent blue teeth. He reaches out and bops Princess on the nose with a glowing finger. Princess gets ready to reprimand the boy when warmth ignites at the tip of her nose.

"Ooh!" she gasps, going cross-eyed to see what is happening. The warm glow softly spreads through her cheeks, her ears, and her face.

"Do you feel that?" Prince asks eagerly.

Princess nods, giggling at the sensation. "Why do I feel this way?"

Prince chuckles, "It must be fairy dust."

"Why?"

"Because it makes you laugh! At least that's what Victor says."

Prince extends his hand in invitation and Princess grasps it. He pulls her closer to the dust as her eyes widen in delight.

Slowly, she dips her hand into the fairy trail the way Prince had. She gazes in awe as the blue glow spreads across her fingers and up her wrist. She puts her hand on Prince's chest, leaving a blue handprint on his tunic. "Look!" she cries, pointing at the blue outline.

"Look at *this*!" Prince grins, grabbing a fist-full of fairy dust and rubbing it into Princess' hair before she can react.

"Never mess up a maiden's hair!" the girl exclaims. She moves away from Prince, summons her best pouty face, and folds her arms. Afraid that he has crossed the line, Prince moves closer to make amends.

"I'm sorry," he says, raising a hand to try to smooth her disheveled hair. He fails to notice the gleam in Princess' eyes until it's too late. The girl reaches out and pushes him into the glowing path.

She giggles as Prince falls backward into the blue haze.

"Whoa!" Prince exclaims. He grabs the giggling girl and pulls her into the warm glow. They both laugh until their sides hurt, rolling around in the intoxicating, luminous blue light.

Finally, Princess stands, glowing from head to foot.

"I suppose we should be getting on," she half-heartedly suggests.

"Agreed." Prince rises to his feet as well. He takes her hand and the pair moves along the twinkling path.

As they walk, Princess glances up occasionally at the boy's glowing face. "Promise you won't let go of my hand?" she asks.

"I promise," Prince replies, giving her hand a slight squeeze. Princess smiles, happy for the first time since encountering the dragon.

At the edge of the scorched forest, Auntie trudges around the fading fire.

Princess must have run in here, she reasons, a flicker of hope igniting in her heart. Auntie knows that the dragon would not be able to make its way through the dense underbrush without significant injury, giving Princess a chance of survival. She makes her way into the forest, following the blackened path made earlier in the night.

Small fires are still scattered throughout the forest and embers crackle in the quiet night. Auntie moves forward in the flickering light of the dying flames, her apprehension rising as she sees the extent of the damage.

"Princess?" she calls, hoping against hope that the girl will answer from somewhere in the shadows. When there is no answer, she continues forward, following the path of ash and smoldering embers into the Dark Forest. She quickens her pace as the heat from the ashes begins to seep through her thin shoes and into her feet.

"Princess!" she yells, growing more frantic as time passes. Suddenly, she stops in her tracks at the edge of a clearing. Her eyes go wide and her breath catches. She stares in horror at the carnage before her. Tears form at the corners of her eyes.

"No…," she whimpers, leaning against a scorched tree for support. Flames still linger at the edges of the clearing, lighting the morbid scene before her. Even in the poor lighting, Auntie can see that not a single area of the clearing remains unscathed. The entire ground is charred black. There is no bush, no grass, and no trace of anything living. The smell of charred flesh assails her nostrils and her gaze is drawn to the large mound of corpses at the opposite edge of the clearing. She blanches and grabs the tree tighter to stabilize herself.

"Why me?" she laments. "Why would you let her into me life just to take her away, Lord?" She takes a deep breath, steeling herself to enter the horrific scene. She steps tentatively into the clearing, making her way toward the animal carcasses. Dozens of charred animals and animal parts lie in a smoky heap. The pile comes up to her head and is nearly as wide as her cottage.

No child could stand against this, she thinks, feeling her hope shatter. She reaches the edge of the large pile and fights back the bile rising in her throat. A partially-charred deer head sticks out, its wide, glassy eyes lifeless and frozen in terror. Auntie feels sick, but is determined to know if Princess' scorched body lies somewhere in the pile. Slowly, painfully, she begins pulling down animal corpses, sorting through the ghastly pyre.

After working her way through about half the pile, Auntie can take it no more.

"Princess!" she screams, pounding her fist against her chest. "I should have told her about the mint!" she cries. "Why did I not tell her?"

Consumed by frustration and sorrow, she grabs a doe by its stiff hoof and wretches it from the pile. "Please!" she wails as tears drip down her dirty cheeks. "Please don't let her be in this place!" Her fears consume her and she breaks down, collapsing beside the dead.

Meanwhile, Arthur sniffs around the clearing. Approaching the edge, he finally catches the familiar scent of Princess. He begins barking wildly. Auntie pays him no mind. Her strong frame rattles between gasps as she mourns the loss of her child. Unfazed, Arthur barks again and turns toward the heart of the forest, aiming his nose in the direction of the scent. Absorbed in her grief, Auntie ignores the hound.

CHAPTER XVIII

OBLIVIOUS & OBLIGING

S hhh," Prince suddenly hisses, holding his finger up to his lips. He peers into the woods.

"What's wrong?" Princess asks.

Prince signals for her to stay low. Although he no longer walks in the blue haze, he still glows faintly. He presses his hands against a large boulder next to the fairy trail.

Princess watches the boy and awaits an explanation, her face scrunching with fear and impatience. Her heart beats rapidly as she scans her surroundings.

"Be still!" the boy calls out. He scurries up a rock for a better vantage point.

Princess nervously presses her lips together. She hesitates for a moment, then scrambles up the boulder behind him and grabs his arm.

"I told you to stay low," Prince scolds.

Princess ignores him. "The fairy trail's fading," she observes, looking down at it from her new perch.

"Do you hear that?" Prince asks, nodding into the distance.

"No."

"Listen," he whispers.

She tilts her head and strains to hear. She finally discerns faint, low-pitched wails. She starts to tremble.

189

"What do you think it is?" she asks.

Prince shakes his head, unsure.

Princess is suddenly hit with a strong desire to run and hide. She is about to slide down the large rock into the shadows, but instead moves closer to Prince.

There's nothing to fear, she tries to comfort herself. I have my eyes, my heart, and my wits.

The dull cries grow louder.

Princess shuffles her feet even closer to Prince, then slides her hand into his, locking her fingers tightly with the boy's.

"I can't see anything ahead," Prince whispers.

"Sounds closer," Princess whispers back. "I hope 'tisn't bats." She wrinkles her nose. "I *hate* bats!"

Prince glances at Princess, amused that she would be so scared of bats after all they had been through. In a pale sliver of moonlight, he catches the look of disgust on her dirty face, and despite her disheveled hair and tattered dress, he's impressed with how pretty she still is.

"Skraw!" A harsh, grating cry pierces the night above the children, rattling them both and interrupting Prince's thoughts.

The little girl screams at the top of her lungs.

Prince releases her hand, unstraps his bow, and reaches for an arrow.

"Skraw!"

"Die, beast!" Prince shouts, wildly shooting his arrow in the direction of the frightful sound. The string vibrates in Prince's fingers and a black, shiny bird lands on a branch overhead.

"'Tis a raven!" Prince exclaims, reaching for another arrow.

"Skraw!"

A second bird squawks right beside Princess, causing her to jump backwards.

"Two ravens!" Princess shouts, scrambling back to Prince.

"Skraw!"

"Skraw!"

Several more black ravens caw as they gather in the surrounding branches. Though nearly invisible in the dark, their flapping wings trigger dreadful memories of the griffin for Princess. The poor girl panics. "There are too many!" she shouts as Prince removes another arrow from his quiver.

Princess grabs the boy's arm and yanks. He loses his balance and is forced to run down the boulder after his frantic companion. Incited by the chaos, the ravens begin swooping down at the heads of the children.

"Run!" Princess screams, pulling Prince down the fading fairy trail. Loose, hanging branches snap across the children's faces as they run. The fleeing pair swat as a black whirlwind of beaks and claws reaches them.

The shrieking scavengers do their best to alert predators of an easy meal on the run. A lone raven darts in front of the children, then swoops back toward the treetops. A second follows suit.

"They must be silenced!" Prince shouts. "Now every monster in the forest knows where we are!"

He pulls up and forces Princess to stop. He takes his bow and nocks an arrow, aiming up at the birds once more. Right as he is about to release, however, the clustering birds fly off, cawing as they go.

Prince lowers his bow and shakes his head. Oddly, the fierce forest grows silent. He releases a deep breath and turns to Princess. "This way," he says softly, resuming his walk along the fairy trail.

"Aren't you scared?" Princess asks, reaching in her pocket to wrap her fingers around her pearl for comfort.

"I'm a squire; I fear nothing," he fibs, trying to calm his pounding heart. The boy steps over a log and onto a springy cord as thick as the castle's curtain ropes.

Princess starts, "But you said—"

"Wait," Prince interrupts. Feeling the bouncing cable beneath his feet, he presses on it a few times. "There's something wrong with this branch."

"Oh, what is the matter now?" Princess stresses, still recovering from the encounter with ravens.

"I don't know," he mutters, "but it—" He stomps his feet on the unusual fiber. Unbeknownst to Prince, the cord begins to vibrate across an enormous web, spanning a great distance of the forest.

"'Tis what?" Princess sighs impatiently.

"'Tis sticky!" Prince curiously observes as he wraps his hand around the thick thread. He strains his eyes to see it in the darkness. The line is nearly invisible but appears to shimmer in the waning moonlight.

"What is sticky?" Princess whispers.

"What *is* this?" he frowns as he struggles to remove his hand.

Princess looks down. "I can't see it, but it smells like a peat bog."

Above the unsuspecting children, the ravens wait eagerly, inching closer as Prince tampers with the sticky trap.

"Come on," Prince invites Princess with an outstretched hand, bouncing on the springy cord.

High in the treetops, pale eyelids pop open, revealing two silver irises. A black, hairy spider's leg slowly slips out of the darkness and presses against the web, having detected the subtle vibrations.

Down at the forest floor, Princess reluctantly eases over the log and down onto the ground, barely missing the spider's silk.

"The trail goes this way," Prince points.

"Are you certain?"

"Of course," he hesitantly responds.

Detecting uncertainty, Princess prods, "*Now* are you scared?"

"Certainly not."

"Not of anything?"

"Not of most things."

"What about ogres, trolls, and werewolves? You're afraid of werewolves, aren't you?"

Prince reaches back to help Princess. They begin climbing up a steep, wooded hill. "Werewolves aren't real," Prince answers, turning his back on a scampering shadow high above him.

Princess cocks her head to the side. "That's not what my ma said."

A stunning, shapely woman rises over a leafy branch in the top of the forest. Her eyes dilate as she grimaces and reveals two sharp fangs.

Concealed by the dark woodland, an arachne descends to the forest floor by a glistening string. Her torso, head, and arms seem human, her lower half is that of a black widow spider. All eight spider-legs are outstretched while she leans back and holds onto the silk rope with her pale human-like hands. When she hits the forest floor, she sets her front legs on the ground and her silver hair shifts against her shoulders from the movement.

She places the silky strand in her mouth and severs it with a quick snip of her pointed incisors. She puts her hairy spider-leg on a brittle branch and shuffles her weight. The branch snaps.

Prince stops, twirls around, and listens. He tightens his grip on the bow.

The arachne watches the boy freeze in place a dozen yards in front of her and impatiently holds her position while eyeing the bow and arrow in the boy's hands.

Prince squints, but can barely make out anything. His eyes dart hastily, desperate to find the source of the broken twig.

"What's the matter?" Princess whispers.

"Nothing," the squire replies, not wanting to falsely upset her. Finding no danger, he ignores his rising fear and turns to follow the trail.

Gently, the arachne takes another step forward. Pale fairy light glistens off her half-human, half-spider exoskeleton as she proceeds to stalk the children.

"Your ma is wrong about werewolves," Prince declares, re-sparking their conversation.

"Is not!" Princess refutes.

"Have you ever seen one?" Prince asks.

"Well ... no," she admits.

Creeping after her prey, the arachne eagerly cycles her insect legs and reveals a red hourglass-shaped mark on the center of her abdomen. Her mouth waters at the thought of blood. Venom drips down her bottom lip from her protruding, pointed teeth in anticipation of her meal.

"What about griffins?" Princess challenges.

"Fake!" He pauses, unable to shake a foreboding feeling. He turns around and inspects the black, indistinguishable woodlands.

The creature quietly leaps off the trail and into the shadows.

Princess stops in her tracks and puts her hands on her hips. "Griffins are *not* fake!" she shouts angrily.

Quickly, the arachne creeps forward, her eight legs moving while her arms remain free and ready. She pauses beside a fallen tree. A low, rapid clicking noise escapes her lips. She growls; her fingers curl with excitement.

"Have you ever seen one?" Prince asks, reaching the top of the hill.

At the recollection, Princess struggles to fight back tears, then answers in Setchra's deep, raspy voice, "Yesss!"

A short distance behind her, the arachne easily surmounts the large log, rubs the hairy bottoms of her legs against it, and tastes the bark with her pointy feet. When she discovers the children's scent, she licks her lips and swallows as though she can already taste their rich, warm blood.

Children, she detects, wiping black saliva from the corner of her mouth. *Haven't had one in ages.* Behind Princess, the arachne scurries silently toward the little girl with lightning speed. Her legs cycle mechanically, clawing over forest debris and closing the distance. Her torso rocks back and forth, maneuvering around branches.

Prince looks at Princess in surprise. "You *have?*" he asks incredulously.

"I don't want to talk about it," Princess sniffles, wiping her nose. She folds her arms close to her chest and hugs herself, suddenly feeling the chill of the night air.

As the arachne scuttles up the incline, she leans forward, prepared to skewer a warm dinner. Her oval abdomen pulsates with excitement.

Prince ducks under a thick branch and pulls it back for Princess.

When the arachne gets close to the unsuspecting girl, she lunges for Princess.

Prince releases the branch. The hardwood birch smashes into the woman's teeth with so much force that it fractures one of her pearly fangs on impact. The blood-sucking stalker tumbles down the hill, snapping her delicate legs as she goes. She lands in a peat bog at the bottom, rendered unconscious from the fall. Her hairy, tangled legs spasm as her body begins to sink into the marsh.

The ravens squawk, sharing exciting news. Not one bird remains idle when there is wounded meat in sight. They descend from the trees in a black flurry, attacking the incapacitated creature.

Startled by the cracking underbrush, Princess whips around just as the branch swings back at her. The branch narrowly misses, but almond-shaped leaves slap her face. She inhales sharply.

"Are you well?" Prince tries to simultaneously search the darkness for the source of the commotion and check on his companion.

More shocked than injured, Princess nods. "Are the ravens back? We should go!"

"Skraw, skraw, skraw!"

"Nothing there but those blasted birds," he says, turning back to the girl. He examines her faintly glowing face and sees that she is uninjured. He removes leaves from her hair. His fingers brush against her cheek, causing Princess to blush.

"*Tinksel*," she says.

"'Tinksel?'" Prince tilts his head and presses his eyebrows together questioningly.

Princess nods. "'Tis thanks," she explains, then nervously looks away. "Everyone says 'thanks,'" she continues, "I say '*tinksel*.'"

"Oh," Prince responds, amused and puzzled.

Behind the oblivious children, the ravens frantically peck at the arachne's soft belly, opening her up. Their beaks stab incessantly, awakening the creature. She snatches a raven and bites down hard, while its brothers persist in attacking her soft belly. The bog holds fast and the woman is unable to escape. Her fatigued body goes limp and her appendages lie flaccid at her side, as her green innards spill into the muddy bog.

The children start moving again. Princess asks, "Are you afraid of *anything*?"

Prince becomes somber and thinks for a bit.

"Truthfully, I'm only afraid of no-sees," he finally admits.

Princess puts her hands on her hips. "Wait, you said you were afraid of dragons!"

"Well, I mean," Prince fumbles for the right words, "dragons can be killed, but no-sees cannot."

"I've never heard of a no-see."

Prince waits for a moment, then wipes sweat from his brow. "No-sees are monsters so treacherous no one has ever lived to utter a description," he whispers.

Princess thinks for a moment. "Then how does anyone know they exist?"

"Well," he says, adjusting his bow, "someone I know was taken by one."

Princess shivers. "Taken?"

Prince frowns. "Yes, taken," he confirms. "Her daughter is a friend of mine. She heard her mother's last screams."

Princess gulps and scoots closer to Prince as they walk.

"She says she saw her mum torn to pieces and tossed inside a mirror by some dark force. She will describe the monster to no one, not even me."

Princess' eyelids flutter wildly as she tries to imagine the dark force. Crickets chirp and fill a moment of silence. Though she does not know the girl, she feels an immense sorrow for her. "Your poor friend," she murmurs.

"'Tis a sad tale," Prince nods.

"These stories are scaring me." Princess shudders, thinking back to the horror of watching her own parents die.

Princess' somber tone makes Prince regret telling such an awful story. "There's nothing to fear," he comforts, "for I am a squire!" He pounds his chest with pride. "And soon to be a knight," he exaggerates, not mentioning that the arduous road to knighthood takes years and years. The boy looks back at Princess, expecting her to be impressed. Instead, the girl gasps and points past him.

"Look!" she cries.

Prince whips around, instinctively reaching for an arrow. "What is it?" he exclaims, quickly scanning the surroundings for a new evil.

"There's another one!" Princess shouts, jumping up and down in excitement. In front of them a purple fairy trail shimmers faintly in the distance. She bounds down the nearly-faded blue trail toward the twinkling light.

"Wait!" Prince cries, running after her.

When they reach the new fairy trail, Princess leaps from the blue path onto the brighter purple stream.

"Do you smell apples?" she asks, twirling in the magical mist. The purple vapor spirals around her as she spins.

"Apples?" Prince asks, panting as he reaches the new trail.

"I thought I caught a whiff of apples!" Princess giggles.

The boy watches Princess spin in dizzying circles as he catches his breath. He notices that her hair takes on a shining luster. "Look at your hair!" he exclaims.

Princess pauses and pulls her ponytail over her shoulder to find the fibers shimmering with an almost metallic reflection. The strands pulsate with a mesmerizing, violet light.

The purple magical dust fills her with ease and makes her feel giddy. "I feel as though I could fly!" she shouts, leaping in front of Prince with her arms outstretched. Her small frame floats momentarily between each bouncing step in the magic dust.

Prince watches her bob along like a light feather caught in the wind.

Behind Princess, Prince sees a pink fairy dust trail ignite and light up the darkness. He strains to see the fairy, but can only discern the lingering, brilliant path.

"There's a pink one!" Prince shouts, but Princess is too entranced to hear him. She continues to marvel at the tickling sensation coursing through her dust-covered body.

Prince walks off the faint blue trail and steps into the pink path. Instantly, he feels a happiness swell inside him. The two children laugh as they bounce up and down in the dark forest.

"You can fly, too!" Princess shouts with delight. Her voice echoes off the tall tree trunks.

"Ha! I feel like I can fly!" Prince bellows as the highlights in his brown hair begin to shine.

"Your hair!" Princess says in awe. "'Tis amazing!"

"There's even more!" Prince points to innumerable blazing fairy trails of every color. The children's eyes light up at the splendid array of bright hues weaving through the trees. The exploding paths ignite in front of them with incredible speed and head into the distance.

"Oh my," Princess gapes as the sparkling fairy trails illuminate the forest.

The gathering trails all seem to travel in the same direction, leaving smoldering, glittering glory in their wake. The trees look like they are on fire, burning pink, purple, red, blue, and green. The radiance emanating from the combined trails gives off a hazy, dream-like mist.

"Where are they going?" Prince wonders.

Princess jumps off the purple trail and seems to disappear into the darkness. "Let's follow the pink one!" she squeals, merging onto the pink glow.

"Wait for me!" Prince calls.

Princess gallops in the pink mist, her skin taking on an even more magnificent glow. "This one smells like tulips!" she cries out, laughing at the new tickling sensation running along her sides.

"My tongue feels tingly," Prince suddenly announces, scraping his tongue on his front teeth.

"I want to feel all of them!" Princess yelps, hardly containing her glee.

Prince presses his fingertips on his tingling tongue. "'Twould be divine," he replies.

The children follow the pink path a short distance, forgetting their fears in the sweet, cool air. With each bounding step, gravity seems to weaken. The powerful dust overflows their hearts with joy as they glide along.

"What is that?" Princess asks. In front of them, a faint light illuminates the treetops.

When Prince observes the strange luminous effect, he halts and grabs onto Princess' hand.

"Ow, you're hurting me!" Princess tries to wiggle her hand free.

"Shhh!" the squire hisses noisily. "It may be the dragon." He chuckles and presses his hands to his belly.

Princess giggles. "The dragon?" she whispers.

Prince nods, placing his index finger to his lips and smiling mischievously.

"Why would the fairies fly toward the *dragon*?" she croons, vainly attempting to suppress her laughter.

"I think we should push forward a bit more and make sure 'tisn't the dragon," Prince whispers.

Too giddy from fairy dust to seriously consider the situation, the children edge their way forward. As they progress, the strange pale light grows stronger, illuminating more of the forest around them. It shoots out from the looming trees at odd angles, lighting the green upper leaves of the treetops before them. As they get closer, little glowing specks float aimlessly in the rays of light, reminding Prince of dust particles.

"I don't think that's a dragon," Princess whispers. She looks around and notices that the pixie trails all seem to converge on the strange luminescence.

"What 'tis it, then?" Prince asks.

"'Tis a fallen star—'tis so bright white!" Princess speculates.

"Why would all the fairies fly toward a fallen star?" Prince challenges.

"Perhaps they draw their power from it?" Princess shrugs.

"Well, let's find out," the boy replies, nudging Princess forward.

"Don't push me!" she reprimands.

"Well, how do you suppose I should tell you to move forward?"

Princess thinks of something Auntie might say. "Press on," she announces.

Prince chuckles. "Press on," he says, rendering a mock salute.

Princess sighs in frustration. "That's still wrong." She turns her back on him.

Prince tilts his head questioningly.

"It should be said like this"—Princess takes a deep breath—"PRESS ON!" She holds her hands up as if holding leather reins and gallops away toward the strange light.

Trying to stay close behind Princess, Prince unslings his bow. "I'll lead, you follow!" he commands.

"No! I will lead; you will follow!" The defiant little girl waves him off as she increases her pace.

Prince relents. "I'll gallop beside you."

Between the spaces in the trees, the galloping girl notices that the illustrious glow has the same powerful color as white lightning. She begins to wonder if a bolt of lightning didn't somehow get stuck in the forest, rather than a shooting star; the air seems to be humming with power. As they draw closer, their skin begins to prickle and buzz like the shock that the metal latch of a door can sometimes give. The feeling is not unpleasant, but fills them with energy.

Moving through the now-bright forest, Prince can see every detail of the rough bark on the trees. He looks up and notices that the light now resembles a nebulous dome that seems to project a constant brilliant light over the towering trees. Prince's curiosity flares and irresistibly draws him to what seems to be the ending point of the fairy trails.

Princess slows her pace as she spots the dome. She and Prince stare like two dusty moths mesmerized by the glow.

"You wanted the lead," Prince teases her, coming to her side. "PRESS ON."

"I, ah...." Princess stammers. "I think it best if you lead on." She steps back. "After all," she hides behind him, "you have the bow."

Smirking, Prince takes the lead. He gathers his courage and shouts, "PRESS ON!" valiantly holding his bow above his head.

His bold blast reassures the girl and, snatching her hand, he leads her into the glowing mist.

CHAPTER XIX

DISCOVERING & DISCOVERED

As the children charge into the glowing mist, they discover that the fog refracts the light, making the dome appear closer than it actually is. The children's feet disturb the vapors, which swirl around them in cloudy plumes.

Exhausted and thirsty, Princess swallows dryly. "Please," she gasps, "let us slow our pace."

"But we are almost there," Prince counters.

"I'm thirsty."

Prince stops and appraises his weary companion. Seeing her fatigue makes him realize that he is tired as well.

"Think of it," he says, ignoring the discomfort of his own dry mouth. "What wonders must lie at the end of the fairy trails?"

Princess raises her head and grins. The anticipation of their magical destination creeps into her exhausted legs and arms, giving her newfound energy. She lifts a hand and reaches in her pocket to remove the pearl.

"Look, Setchra!" She extends her pearl over Prince's shoulder to give it an unobstructed view of the glowing dome.

"Looks like a fallen star," Princess croaks in Setchra's voice.

"I thought so, too," Princess agrees, giggling.

Prince looks at the girl curiously. "Does it please you to pretend?"

"I'm not pretending." Her face scrunches.

"You aren't pretending to be the pearl?" Prince prods.

"Setchra is the pearl; I'm me."

"Well," Prince sighs, "From where I'm standing, you and Setchra are one and the same." He smirks and starts moving toward the illuminated dome again.

Princess gives an angry *humph* and crosses her arms.

"You had better follow along," Prince calls over his shoulder, croaking in a Setchra-like voice.

Princess flips her hair and stomps after Prince.

As the children travel deeper into the fog, it increases in thickness, swirling around them. Princess shivers from a drop in temperature.

"Setchra was right," Prince suddenly announces. "'Tis like a star fell from heaven and landed in the forest."

"Precisely," Princess nods, pleased that Prince concurs with Setchra.

As the children move forward, the darkness fades in the presence of the powerful light. The smoldering haze ebbs and flows around their bodies and illuminates the trees. The strange effect makes the green leaves sparkle like jewels in the midst of the mist.

Princess looks up at the sky, but nothing is visible through the fog and trees. "Maybe the star fell from the heavens when it grew old and now fairies live in its glow!"

As they finally draw near the source of the powerful luster, Prince pauses at the dome's outer edge to examine the sprawling cloud above them. The dome looms over the children, bathing them in light. A spectrum of sparkling colors pulsates within the hazy mass. "I think something dwells in there," he whispers.

"'Tis the fairies!" Princess declares, pressing her fingers against her cheeks in excitement. "And if fairies go there, 'tis safe for us!"

Prince pauses and sifts through his memories, recalling historical paintings in the library. In every image he can recall, the pixies seem magical, kind, and alluring; never menacing or dangerous. "Agreed," he answers. He continues to gaze at the solid wall of glowing haze before them.

"Why must we wait?" Princess asks. "We simply must enter that fallen star!"

Prince smiles, takes her hand, and plunges through the final wall of mist.

"I can hardly see!" Princess yelps.

The boy squeezes her hand. "Stay close!" he orders.

He leads her through the haze confidently, even though he has no earthly idea where he is going. A white light emanates from within the fog, radiating brighter and brighter as they move farther into the core. Small, crackling currents sporadically jump between colored clouds like a miniature lightning storm caught in a rainbow.

"Do you smell that?" Princess asks. "Smells like honey and sugar and fresh cream." She sniffs. "And something else."

Prince halts and begins sniffing, as well. "Cakes and pastries!"

The boy follows his nose, leading on with a growling stomach.

The mist glows brighter than ever before as the children follow the scent. Princess looks up and spies thousands of sparkling, golden orbs of light floating in the haze.

"Oh, what wondrous magic!" she declares. Her smile shimmers from the glow. "They're like shining stars!" She giggles, trying to catch the gleaming sparkles in her cupped hands.

Prince tries to grab the twinkling orbs but repeatedly misses. He opens his pressed hands to find only air.

Princess laughs as she moves through the sparkles. The twinkling lights enter her open mouth and she gasps. "They're delicious!" she exclaims. She promptly opens her mouth, sticks out her tongue, and chases after the shimmers as though they were snowflakes.

"Wait for me!" Prince shouts, trying not to lose the girl in the dense fog. He opens his mouth and catches some sparkles. Each twinkle bursts on his tongue, tasting the distinct flavors of vanilla, honey, and cinnamon.

The children dash deeper into the opaque shroud, mouths open to chase the array of scrumptious flavors. Abruptly, the thick wall of fog ends, opening up to the source of the brilliant light.

"Oh my," Princess gasps, reaching the center of the dome first. She halts, awestruck.

"What is it?" Prince calls, trotting to catch up with the girl. He reaches her side and freezes, awestruck by the sight before him. In the center of the fog spreads an immense meadow. Green and lush, the meadow surrounds a garden containing an exquisite array of flowers. The cornucopia of scents, shapes, sizes, and colors overwhelms the children. Moss and grass encircle the flowers, creating a green ring between the misty forest and the spectacular garden. A miniature crystal castle rises up from the center of the garden, complete with pointed spires. Within the castle, a celestial glow pulsates through the translucent, crystal walls. Sparkling pixie trails of every color crisscross the small valley.

"That is the tiniest castle I have ever seen!" Princess gapes, staring in awe at the sparkling structure.

Prince scans the round garden. "'Tis segmented by color," he notices. Completely surrounding the pulsating castle, the garden is carefully divided into slices of pink, white, red, yellow, blue, purple, green, and orange flowers.

"'Tis a flowery rainbow!" Princess titters, clapping her hands in delight.

To Prince's left, amidst the pink flower section, a begonia's petals part. He watches a male fairy explode out of the begonia and zip across the garden. Pink pixie dust trails the fairy's path. Prince looks back at the pink segment. Spiral petals shift back and forth as fairies move from flower to flower.

Princess, unable to contain herself, steps across the green perimeter to the glorious garden before her. "Hello there," she says, kneeling eye-level with a sun-shaped dahlia. A slender fairy with long brown hair lies in the center of the flower. Princess pokes the fairy, which causes the tiny pixie to reach up and paw the tip of the girl's finger.

"Shh ... sleeping," the fairy lady says, rolling over on her side. A faint rumbling snore emanates from the fairy, causing Princess to squeal softly. She stands up and looks again at the magnificent scene, watching as the entire garden seems to shift and move. Her eyes widen when she realizes that she is seeing thousands of glittering fairies swarm around majestic flowers, fluttering their translucent wings and spreading their powdery luster over the variegated garden. Fairies pop above the tall flowers, hover, and dive below the soft petal horizon.

"All of the fairies match the color of the flowers they work in!" She spots a pink fairy disappear back inside a begonias of the same color. Princess watches in amazement as fairies leap off petals and hop from flower to flower around her. She reaches inside her pocket and slowly removes the smooth pearl. "Look at them," she says in wonder, holding Setchra out in front of her. The smooth, creamy surface looks like an eye without an iris, reflecting the brilliant scene before it.

Princess giggles and walks over to the white wedge of the garden and into a cluster of waist-high calla lilies. She kneels down and drags her finger along an elegant conical rim that sweeps outward into the shape of an upside-down bell. In the flower's core, a glowing yellow spadix extends from the center of the bell.

"'Tis the most beautiful flower I ever saw!" she sighs rapturously.

Prince continues to taste-test the array of sparkling sun drops floating around him. He smacks his lips, tasting a new flavor each time.

"Honey!" he guesses at one. Prince closes his eyes and enjoys the potent aroma. Lost in a serene, savory bliss, his euphoric state is interrupted by the girl.

"Have you ever seen flowers such as these?" she asks.

Prince shakes his head. "Not even in the castle."

Princess' enjoyment escalates with the knowledge that not even the castle dwellers have seen the beauty of this garden. Feeling like a queen, she tilts her head back and spins in dizzying circles.

Prince kneels down to observe a winged fairy lady. The exquisite creature has red hair held in a petite up-do and adorned with several baby's breath blossoms. The slender nymph dotes on her garden with a sprinkle from a tiny gold watering can. A bead of water lands on an ivory gardenia that rests beneath the calla lilies.

As the red-haired fairy floats around, her white dust trail sparkles with flashes of silver particles.

"A sprinkle here, a touch there, and everything blossoms in its way," the fairy squeaks.

"Why don't they notice us?" Princess asks, moving behind Prince to observe. The fluttering fairy adjusts the white petals of her dress, oblivious to the children's hovering faces.

Another pretty pixie bursts onto the scene. A glittering lime-green dust cloud plumes around her. The new arrival has brown, shoulder-length hair and copper eyes. Princess lifts up her pearl to see the majestic ladies.

Holding a bronze watering can and rapidly flapping her opaque, dragonfly-like wings, the green fairy sings, "A little more here and a little more there and everything will blossom in its own way." The brunette fairy smiles at the red-haired fairy in white, who seems taken aback by the intrusion.

"No," replies the red-head. "See, it is a little *sprinkle* here," she sets down her watering can on a flower. "A little *touch* there...." All at once, she raises her hand high above her head. Spheres of blue lightning glow and crackle at the tips of her fingers. "And a little *touch* over *there!*" she shouts, throwing her arm forward and releasing the glowing orb. The tiny blue lightening crackles off her tiny fingertips and leaps through the air. It hits the brown-haired fairy with a shocking *snap*, sending her tumbling over the white lilies.

"Ahh!" the brunette screams as she flies backwards through the air. She lands in a sprawling heap on the ground, her singed hair now standing on end. Blinking violently, she pushes herself up as her body convulses several times.

The lightening not only jolts the brown-haired fairy but also an adjacent daffodil, causing its petals to instantly grow and its buds to blossom. The daffodil's yellow center illuminates like a firefly and its petals seem to soften like satin. The stem glows and takes on a magnificent emerald color.

A handsome male fairy appears through the jungle of grass wearing a mint leaf for a loincloth. A dark blue glitter trail follows him. "Jubilee!" he scolds, shaking a finger at the red-headed fairy. "Lightning is only for growing!"

Jubilee smirks as she playfully flutters her wings.

"I *was* growing," she purrs with a seductive smile, tickling under the man's chin with an index finger. She turns around and slowly bends over, picking up her gold watering can as if nothing had happened.

"Er … ahh … yeah," the fairy man mumbles, his cheeks blushing a deep rose.

Ponther!" the scorched fairy shouts, flying over and slapping the handsome fairy across the face. "This is how you defend me?" She sniffles and wipes her nose on her charred forearm. She spins around just as Jubilee turns to glare at her. Without warning, " the brown-haired fairy draws back and punches Jubilee in the face. Jubilee lets out a painful squeak before tumbling over a calla lily and disappearing beneath the gardenias. The brown-haired fairy zips off in a tiff, leaving a glowing green dust cloud behind her.

"Elza, wait!" the male fairy hollers after her. He looks at Jubilee and shrugs, then flies after his insulted wife.

"Why can't I keep a man?" Jubilee sobs as she pulls herself on top of a gardenia blossom.

"Wow," Prince exclaims, thoroughly confused by the whole interaction. His soft exclamation attracts the attention of the sobbing Jubilee. She gasps in fear and zips away.

Quicker than Prince can blink, a gorgeous blonde fairy appears and slaps him across the face. The impact from the fairy's miniscule hand wrenches his head to the right.

"Shame on you!" Tillie shouts.

"Ouch!" Prince gasps, pressing a hand to his smarting cheek.

"Oh, I'm sorry," the pretty fairy exclaims. "I just turned four hundred and eighty-nine and I sometimes forget my own strength," she says, squeezing her tiny bicep. She tilts her head sharply and pops her neck. Ready for action again, she hovers in front of Prince's face. "Are you a foey-foe, or a friendly-friend?"

Rubbing his cheek, Prince quickly responds, "Friendly-friend!"

"Good!" Tillie exclaims. Her mood rapidly shifting, she flies up to Prince's face and presses her cool hands against his cheeks.

"My name is Tillie. And you are...?" She releases his cheek and peeks over his shoulder at Princess, who is moving the pearl in for a closer look.

"My name is Setchra. Stop hitting my friend," Princess says in the pearl's low, creaky voice.

"Oh my!" Tillie cries out, staring at her reflection in the pearl and primping her hair. She then zips away, leaving a gold dust trail in her wake.

Before Princess can finish blinking, Tillie returns with a plump older fairy with curly gray hair, shining silver irises, and a beautifully woven dress made of purple and white flowers. A high, curled collar extends from the top of the dress past her ears.

"Guests, Mother," Tillie exclaims. "We've guests!" She flies in front of Princess' face, examining every detail of the girl's appearance. "And she's so pretty, Mother. May I keep her?"

"No!" Princess creaks in Setchra's voice.

Tillie shakes her head back and forth. "Names? You simply must have names!" She shakes a finger at the children and bursts out, "You are entirely too cute not to have names!"

She crosses her legs as she hovers over Prince.

Before Princess can answer the exhausting fairy, Tillie taps her foot on thin air and claps her hands.

"Come now, tell me your names this instant!" she orders, her long ponytail swooshing behind her.

"I am Princess, from the Kingdom of Tremble Nemble," Princess announces with a curtsy.

Astonished that her name is similar to his, Prince excitedly blurts out, "Hey! My name is—"

"Did you see that, Mother?" Tillie's jaw drops and her eyes flash with excitement. "She curtsied. I want to curtsy. Can I curtsy, Mother?"

Without an answer, Tillie reciprocates Princess' curtsy and then giggles. The laughter overtakes her body, shifting her wings back and forth. Without warning, she flies in circles around the children, exploding gold dust all over them. The sweet smell of sugar and vanilla reaches Prince's nose, making him salivate. Tillie's dust lands on the children, causing a light glow to rise off their skin.

Princess laughs at Tillie's hasty, fluctuating responses.

Tillie curtsies again. "Oh, I did it again," she says, clasping her hands to her mouth. Zipping around the children and her mother, she curtsies at least a dozen times.

Suddenly, she flies up to Princess and belatedly gasps, "Tremble Nemble? You are dangerously far from home!"

The old fairy flies over to Prince and hovers in front of his nose. "I am Queen Ilda," she introduces.

Her silver hair and metallic eyes catch his attention. "Madam, your eyes are metal," he stammers.

"Mother, can you believe it? We've guests!" Tillie interrupts.

Both Prince and Queen Ilda turn their attention to the spastic fairy. Tillie runs her fingers through her hair and pats down her skirt. "I simply can't believe it!" she clamors, kicking her feet in exhilaration.

"Do you get very many guests?" Prince asks.

"This is my kingdom. I'll be asking the questions," Queen Ilda says. "Now tell me your name."

"I am Prince, son of Sir Cynric, and I, too, am from Tremble Nemble."

Queen Ilda flutters closer to Prince's eye. Little puffs of wind tickle the side of his nose.

"Have you come for our magic?" the wise ruler asks, her face stern and unflinching.

As if on cue, dozens of fairies line up on either side of the hovering Queen , flexing their muscles and making menacing faces. Remembering Tillie's slap, Prince nervously blurts out, "No!"

The fairies relax their stances but continue to stare through narrowed eyes. Prince views the small army of fairies stretching out before him and continues his explanation. "We were chased into the forest by a dragon."

A collective gasp echoes through the crowd as the fairies scatter and hide behind the nearest flowers. Terrified, they make the flowers shake. Murmuring to each other from behind their hiding places, they create the illusion of whispering blossoms.

Queen Ilda holds up her hands to silence her subjects.

"Dragon, you say?" Queen Ilda asks, raising an eyebrow. Prince and Princess nod their heads in unison.

Tillie appears over her mother's shoulder. "Mother, they aren't guests—they're *refugees*! Oh, this is awful, just awful! So young, and delicate, and...." She sighs and disappears again.

Queen Ilda rolls her eyes. "Your parents must be very worried," the fairy queen politely states. She clucks her tongue and presses her wrinkled lips together. "Tillie!" she summons.

In an instant, the lively Tillie pops up, bobbing her head with excitement.

"Oh, yes, there you are," Queen Ilda says, pointing her finger at her. "Summon your sisters."

Tillie zips off in a golden shimmer and almost immediately returns with five fairies trailing behind her. Red, pink, green, blue, and purple dust trails combine with her own. Their powdery colors mesh and blend like a sparkling, misty rainbow.

"My daughters – Millie, Nillie, Jillie, Lillie, Billie, and Tillie – will provide you with sustenance, provisions, and anything else you need to ensure your safe return to Tremble Nemble," Queen Ilda assures Prince and Princess.

Prince renders a salute to Queen Ilda, which causes her daughters to giggle and bat their eyelashes.

"We will be forever in your debt, Queen Ilda."

As the children stand before the queen, the ground subtly parts between Prince and Princess with a crack no longer than a finger length. No one seems to notice as bits of earth trickle into the break and a green stem rises out of the dark dirt. The curled stalk slowly unwinds and bulges into a white-tipped rose bud. Within seconds, the stem straightens. Tiny green thorns punctuate its stalk and red veins branch through the petals and gradually turn the blossom red.

Only Tillie's erratic eyes notice the unusual rose. For once she is motionless, curiously watching the strange plant burst between the children. The pointed pod at the tip of the stem peels back, petal by petal, to expose a crowning red bud.

Tillie zips over to her mother and clasps her hands against the old woman's weathered face. Flabbergasted, Queen Ilda, turns to discipline her cheeky daughter. Tillie points to the ground at the small, protruding rose bud.

"Extraordinary," the queen mutters, averting her attention from her spirited daughter. The other fairies gather around, sitting on top of flowers and holding onto the stems of plants as they watch the budding rose grow.

Princess follows the gaze of the fairies and discovers the flower unfolding at her feet. Intrigued, she watches the lime green thorns turn dark green and then harden into brown.

The glowing petals burst open, launching a glittering gold cloud out of the flower's core. The center of the flower unwraps in a twisting motion, displaying a breath-taking crimson rose in full bloom. A thin stream of shimmering gold flows around the edges of each petal.

Tillie's eyes widen and her wings vibrate with excitement. "Mother," she whispers, mesmerized by the rose's enchanting beauty, "what is it?"

Prince impulsively reaches for the crimson petals but retracts his hand at the last moment, fearing retribution from the spectating fairies. Irresistible warmth pulsates from the rose.

Queen Ilda stares in silence, stunned by the exquisiteness of the flower. Enchanted, she glides over to the glorious blossom.

Prince and Princess look to Queen Ilda for an explanation. The rose's glowing, gold-tipped petals illuminate the old Queen's face, reflecting its image in her shining silver eyes.

She folds her arms and inspects the alluring petals. "This is the rare Akaycia rose," she announces with veneration.

The crowd of watchful fairies *ooh* and *aah*.

※※※

On the outskirts of the meadow, a large, rust-colored eye gleams in the shadows of the Dark Forest.

CHAPTER XX

HUNTED & HUNTING

W hat's so special about an Akaycia flower?" Prince asks, studying the magnificent bloom.

"Rose, my dear boy. An Akaycia *rose*," Queen Ilda corrects, shaking her gray locks. "What makes this rose so special is that it only blooms in the presence of *true love*." She looks at the children with an all-knowing smile and sighs. "It has been so long...." She trails off, her eyes glazing over as she recalls ancient memories.

Princess blushes while Prince inches away.

"Love? Yuck! Squires want not for love," Prince protests. "Courage and honor are what I yearn for!"

"Who's in love?" Princess asks, her cheeks blushing an even brighter crimson. She grasps Setchra in her clenched fist.

"You, child," Queen Ilda answers, flying directly in front of the little girl's perplexed face.

Silver dust illuminates Princess' eyes as Queen Ilda peers into them, searching for confirmation. "Ah...." she says, fluttering down to Princess' heart, "there it is." The old fairy smiles broadly, lifting the wrinkles in her cheeks. "It warms, but does not yet burn."

The perspicacious queen turns and flutters over to Prince.

Prince bites his bottom lip. His heart pounds and his eyes drift to the side under the queen's scrutiny.

"What is it you search for?" the squire asks, shifting his weight.

"Embers," Queen Ilda answers, searching his blue irises.

"Can I see, Mother?" Tillie asks, flying next to the queen. She presses both of her hands against Prince's lower eyelid and peers into his eye as though she were gazing into a window.

"Ouch!" Prince cries out. The squire jerks back and rubs his irritated eye.

"Hmm," Queen Ilda murmurs, hovering to his chest. She presses her ear against his pounding heart. "Aha!" she says, pulling back.

"I want to hear!" Tillie declares. The queen waves her hand, beckoning Tillie forward.

Tillie presses her ear against Prince's chest. Gold dust emits in plumes as her wings flutter.

"Stop that!" Prince says, swatting at the golden fairy.

"Oh, his heart beats with the rose!" Tille exclaims.

"It does not!" Prince growls.

"The flame is lit, and soon his love will
spread." She looks at Princess and winks.

"What do we know of love?" Prince asks, blushing. "We're only children! I hardly even know this girl," he continues, his face twists in frustration under the scrutiny. "In fact, I didn't even know her name until she told *you!*" Prince turns away from Princess and folds his arms defiantly.

Princess gasps at the squire's insulting behavior and turns her back to him, feeling humiliated.

"I wouldn't love him if he were the last boy on earth!" she counters.

Fairies gather closer around the children.

"Kick him!" Elza shouts.

"Yeah!" Bumble chimes in. He flutters up to Prince's face, mimicking a kicking motion with such fervor that he tumbles through the air.

Jubilee flutters up to Prince's ear. "If *she* doesn't love you—" The beautiful fairy blushes and struggles to finish her sentence as a fit of giggling overtakes her.

"It matters not how you feel now," Queen Ilda interjects, silencing her subjects. "Before your arrival, there was no Akaycia rose." The Queen's eyes change from their liquid silver pools into hard, bright white rings. "Then you arrive and there is the Akaycia rose." She grins omnisciently, gesturing to the pulsating rose. "What to do, what to do," she ponders in a singsong voice. She rests her hand on her chin, wriggling her wrinkled cheeks each time she clucks her tongue.

A whistling sound rips through the air, interrupting their conversation. A lengthy arrow whizzes past Prince's ear and dismembers several fairies before it disappears into the fog. Colors of fairy dust mix and then fade as the fairies' eviscerated bodies disappear.

One fairy tears off a damaged, bloody wing and hides below the flowery garden. The broken wing puffs like a dying breath and disintegrates into a pile of dust.

Princess screams.

Prince's eyes stretch wide and his mouth drops open. He looks around wildly, unsure of where the danger is coming from. He grabs Princess' arm and pulls her through the flowers toward the misty trees and the security he hopes they offer. Princess stumbles and falls to the ground.

"Get to your feet!" Prince shouts.

Princess feels as though she is being pulled through a mud bog. She begins to shake and can't seem to stand up. She reflexively covers her head with her arms, as though to shield herself from another attack.

"Get up!" Prince shouts again, tugging on her, but Princess continues to cower on the ground. The boy manages to pull her up and push her toward the tree line.

On the other side of the meadow, a muscular cyclops leaps out of a briar patch. He flexes his naked torso and blinks a leathery eyelid as he bends at the waist, animal-hide pants stretched across his backside. His wide eye dilates as he inhales fairies through his gaping mouth, chomping them as quickly as he can.

Feeling the earth tremble, Princess turns and glimpses the approaching danger. The giant cyclops spots the child and takes aim just before she is about to vanish into the fog.

"Gahhh!" Princess screams in agony as a long arrow penetrates through the back of her shoulder blade and slams her face-first into a tree. She feels the rough bark smash against her cheek before searing pain overpowers her and she passes out.

Prince gasps as Princess is jerked from his grip and pinned to a large oak tree. He yelps as a circle of blood expands and trails down her back.

Dumbfounded by the inexplicable chaos, he stares at the impaled girl in shock. His eyes begin to burn with tears and fury begins to build inside of him.

"Children!" the cyclops grins, grinding fairies with his boulder-like teeth. "My favorite meat!" Swallowing the tasty fairies, he beams wickedly. Shredded wings and fairy parts stick between his teeth. The giant lifts a massive hand to wipe fairy powder from his mouth.

Glitter trails ignite in a blur. Fairies turn into a protective orb and encircle Queen Ilda. They blaze into the fog wall, abandoning their garden. In one quick blink, Prince is left alone to face the horrific beast. He runs to Princess as the cyclops grins at his pinned prize.

When Prince reaches the girl, he hears her whimper faintly. Blood trickles down her arm and back. Prince's entire body shakes in shock. A surge of anger ignites within him when he hears the cyclops chuckle across the garden. Slowly, the squire turns around. He spots the hideous monster as it removes another arrow from the holster attached to his leg.

The cyclops tilts his massive crossbow down, positions his foot on a wide notch in the bow, and grips a bowstring the length of both children. His massive biceps bulge and his neck muscles flex as he pulls back the thick cord with a sonorous grunt.

"Scream!" the giant mocks Prince. "It's always better when you scream." Lifting his arms, the monster readies his crossbow. Fear overtakes Prince and he freezes, waiting for the deathblow to come.

"I said, scream!" roars the cyclops.

Prince remembers that he, too, has a bow.

"Very well, then," the cyclops growls, placing his finger on the silver trigger.

Numb and bewildered, Prince glances up at Princess. He watches as her limp fingers uncurl and drop her beloved pearl. The blood-stained gemstone drops at the squire's feet. Knowing how much the pearl meant to her, he somehow unfreezes and bends down to pick it up.

As he turns the pearl over in his fingers, he hears a long, low whistling and feels a breeze ruffle his shirt, followed by a loud cracking noise. Looking up, he sees the cyclops' arrow vibrating in the tree exactly where his head had been.

"Hold steady!" the giant thunders.

Prince drops to the ground and covers his head with his hands. After a short pause, the boy slowly lifts his head from the earth to see the monster in the same place. The enormous cyclops blinks and locks its eye on Prince.

"Don't worry," the monster shouts. "I have more."

Prince covers his ears, trying to block out the cyclops' voice.

The muscular giant locks his bow back and loads another arrow.

"Stand up so I can end this quickly!" he orders Prince.

"No!" Prince pipes, uncovering his ears.

"All right then, I'll come for you!" The cyclops lowers his cross bow and stomps his hefty feet.

Prince watches helplessly as the giant closes in on him.

"Aha! Now I can see you better." The cyclops takes a deep breath and holds it, preparing to loose his deadly arrow. Time seems to slow as the giant releases the arrow, sending it flying with a reverberated spring.

The boy darts to the side like a scared rabbit. When he stops, he sees the lengthy arrow sticking out of the earth at the edge of the flower garden.

The cyclops lets out a frustrated snarl and restrings his crossbow.

Prince glances up at Princess. Oddly, he focuses on the dress Princess tried so hard to keep clean.

The one-eyed monster clutches its abdomen, shaking with laughter at the boy's misery. "I would rather you run," he hollers, slapping his knee.

Peering into the fog wall, Prince wonders if he can outrun the monster. He readies to sprint into the mist, but looks at his bloody fingers. A burning ache fills his heart and instantly calms his stomach. The rabbit turns into a little lion. He hears his father's roaring voice command, *Stand strong!*

The terrified squire stands up and wipes away the tears trickling down his face. He slides his hand through the top of his bow and twists the weapon from his shaking body in one fluid movement.

The cyclops takes a thunderous step toward Prince and laughs at the dramatic gesture. "Your bones will rattle against my teeth, boy!" he roars.

Though Prince's fingers tingle and his arms feel like lead weights, he raises his shivering arm behind his back and reaches for an arrow. *I can't leave her alone.* He looks at Princess once more for strength, fumbling through the quiver on his back, he pulls out a white, swan-feather arrow his father had given him.

"Ha, ha, ha!" the cyclops mocks, moving closer to the boy.

Prince's clammy hand places the arrow against the tightly woven string. He exhales and glares up at the gigantic creature, valor shining in his tear-stung eyes.

"I'm going to skin you alive and eat your flesh to the melody of your wails!" the monster growls. Moving through the garden's center, he closes the distance on Prince. The monster takes a booming step into white daises and Prince feels his arms go numb. The boy's heart thumps so loud that it echoes in his ears. His arm shakes, yet he somehow manages to nock his arrow.

"You think that *toy* can hurt me?" the cyclops scoffs.

Prince bites his lip and stretches the string back as far as it will go.

Humored by the boy's feeble efforts, the goliath pauses and flexes his broad chest. "Take your best shot!" he challenges, thumping his fist to his carved pectorals.

Shutting out the stinging insults, Prince closes one eye and exhales. He steadies himself and mentally recites, *Strength, honor...* Holding the last bit of his breath, he aims slightly above the cyclops' chin and whispers, "Courage," letting the taut cord go.

CHAPTER XXI

FIGHT & FLIGHT

Bong! The boy's arrow snaps into flight. White feathers rotate over the flowers and sink deep into the cyclops' wide eye, piercing the pupil like the center of a target.

"Ahh!" the monster wails, dropping his weapon and falling to his knees.

Prince takes a step forward and shakes his fist with newfound confidence. "Die, monster!" he screams furiously.

The blinded giant thrashes his head, covering his wounded eye with his hand. A few tortured grunts escape his lips as he grabs the protruding arrow and pulls it out with a jerk. "Argh!" the monster bellows, his deafening howls shaking the leaves on the trees.

Dark blood oozes down the cyclops' broad nose and spilling over his cheeks. He feverishly rubs his wound, hoping to alleviate the scorching pain. "You will die, boy!" he roars.

Quickly, Prince draws another arrow and aims for the cyclops' face. He feels the string vibrate with the release and watches the spiraling feathers cover the short distance.

"Ugh," the cyclops grunts, feeling the arrow penetrate his cheek. He pulls it out with ease and throws it away, leaving hardly a nick in his leathery skin.

"Nothing you have can destroy me, boy," the cyclops snarls. "You may have blinded me, but I have other senses."

Prince panics and fumbles at his quiver for another arrow.

The cyclops begins to crawl forward, patting the ground before him, in search of the boy. "Just make a sound," the cyclops seethes, "and I will crush your body between my bare hands!"

Prince freezes, terrified to shoot another arrow for fear that the twang of the bow will draw the cyclops to him. He places one leather boot on the ground and then another, silently moving back from the giant beast.

As Prince creeps backward, Tillie materializes next to him, making the boy jump.

"You must train his own weapon on him," she whispers. Prince nods in understanding and scans the garden for the cyclops' crossbow. He spots it directly behind the monster, who continues to move toward him on his knees. Prince draws in a deep breath, gathering his courage.

Brains beat brawn, the boy mouths to himself, then launches into a sprint. In his peripheral vision, Prince sees Tillie rush off in a burst of gold.

The giant hears the rustle of feet and feels a gust of wind brush past him. "There you are!" he yells. He lunges toward the movement and clips the boy's heel with his blood-covered hand.

Prince stumbles and falls as the monster frantically searches the ground for the boy's body. Prince rolls out of the cyclops' reach.

"I smell your fear," the cyclops laughs. His nostrils flare open as he sniffs and snorts.

The squire leaps to his feet and dashes for the crossbow.

"Graww!" the cyclops lunges for the boy again, but narrowly misses. He falls forward and props himself up on all fours.

The boy tugs on the crossbow, willing it to move. His small muscles strain in valiant effort, but fail to lift the weapon. Hearing the boy struggle, the cyclops turns in his direction.

"Why do you remain here?" the cyclops demands.

Prince ignores him and continues to grapple with the bow.

"Does the girl keep you here?" he asks, a wicked grin spreading over his face. Prince stiffens, but remains silent.

"Very well," the monster continues. "Rather than chasing you, you shall watch me devour the girl." The cyclops laughs. Coldness grips Prince's heart as the monster use his keen sense of smell to pick up the scent of Princess' blood. Tugging and heaving with all of his might, Prince desperately tries to budge the weapon. Hopelessness grips him as the cyclops crawl closer to her. Prince finally gives up on trying to lift the giant weapon and grabs his own bow, sending an arrow streaking toward the monster.

The cyclops grunts. He pulls the arrow out from the back of his thigh. "I'm getting closer, aren't I?" he taunts, as he continues to crawl forward.

"Leave her alone!" the squire shouts.

"Shall I eat her first, or you?"

Prince looks at the monster, unsure of what to do.

Streaks of glowing light abruptly blaze through the small clearing as dozens of fairies stream into the meadow. Working as one, they pick up the crossbow and maneuver it.

"Psst," Tillie whispers, reappearing at Prince's side. She points to the positioned crossbow.

Prince clenches his fist and feels the flames of hope reignite in his heart. "I said, leave her alone!"

The blind creature stands and raises himself to his full height.

"You shall watch me eat her raw!" he roars.

"All brawn and no brain," Prince shouts, "leaves you slain!" At the last word he kicks the silver trigger. The bow fires.

The arrow careens through the air and strikes the cyclops in the torso. A loud *thud* reverberates as it passes through his chest cavity. The fatal blow brings the monster to his knees. His leathery eyelid blinks as he falls face-first to the ground. The cyclops lies motionless, his tongue drooping out the side of his gaping mouth.

Prince gazes at the still monster as waves of relief and regret wash over him. Although glad that the cyclops cannot inflict more damage, Prince feels sick at the gruesome sight. Taking a deep breath, the squire moves forward to examine the twitching body.

Behind him, Princess cries softly as she returns to consciousness. Whimpering, she presses her numb fingers against the rough bark.

"Argh!" the little girl shrieks.

Prince's head whips in her direction. He collects his thoughts and shouts, "I'm coming!" The lad dashes across the fairy garden.

Princess feels a warm hand on her wounded shoulder and hears her mother's voice. *Princess.*

Sheer pain snaps Princess back to reality. The little girl tries to lean back but cannot. Realizing that she's pinned, she panics and claws at the tree.

Prince reaches the girl and grasps the arrow's end. Interlocking his fingers around the shaft, he leans back and pulls with all his strength.

"Stop!" Princess wails, her bottom lip quivering.

"I have to get the arrow out!" Prince insists, putting his foot on the tree for more leverage.

"No, don't!" Princess begs. "Just let me be."

"No! I'm pulling it out!" Prince exclaims, trying again. Princess screams in agony. Her breath begins to shudder as her limbs start to lose feeling.

Tillie arrives on the scene and quickly surveys the damage.

"Death lingers on her lips, foolish one!" the fairy warns, holding up her hands to stop Prince. "I need my mother," she decides and then vanishes in an explosion of gold dust.

"Ma...," Princess moans.

"Don't die," Prince whispers. He wraps his arms around the girl's cold trembling body, trying to comfort her.

Prince thinks of that first moment when he had spotted her in the field of flowers. The squire feels a crushing guilt for bringing her into the forest. He feels the girl's body go limp.

"Princess!" he exclaims. "Princess, wake up!" He looks at the girl's pale face but sees no sign of life. A loud sob escapes his lips. He trembles from grief and hugs her tighter.

CHAPTER XXII

TRAILS & TREASURES

Queen Ilda appears in the meadow with a legion of fairies. Prince looks up mournfully, exposing his tear-stained face.

"You may have the courage of a lion, but you've the sense of a lamb," the queen barks. "Removing the arrow with the head still attached would most certainly cause her death. If it hasn't already...."

The queen snaps her fingers and a group of fairies appears by her side. "Carefully remove the little girl's body. Fly underneath her arms and support her limbs," Queen Ilda commands.

Elza flies behind Princess' motionless body and arches her hand. Blue sparks ignite at her finger tips, sending a bolt of lightning that severs the back of the arrow. The other fairies hold onto the girl, keeping her from collapsing to the ground.

"Heave!" Tillie shouts. Together, the fairies lift the child and slide her body off the splintered shaft. Prince cringes when he sees the long arrow stained with her blood.

"Oh my," Tillie murmurs. Stretching out her delicate fingers, she summons a yellow bolt of lightning and skillfully cauterizes the wound. A puff of smoke escapes as she finishes with a flick of her finger.

"Ho!" Tillie shouts while the group of fairies eases the child to the ground.

Tillie flies up to Princess' face and lifts her eyelids. "Dark, dark, dark!" she laments. She moves to the girl's chest to examine the wound.

"Is she dead?" Prince brings himself to ask.

"Hard to say," Tillie says, tapping her finger to her chin. She looks up at the pale boy and feels a twinge of sorrow for him.

Queen Ilda flutters over and presses an ear to Princess' heart. "Faint," she concludes, "but still beating."

A wave of relief washes over Prince.

The queen nods and her subjects toss tiny armloads of peat moss on the girl's wound. They spit on the moss and stomp it into a paste.

The queen gasps. "The rose," she mutters, zipping across the garden in a silvery flash. She stops at the Akaycia rose. "If anything has the power to revive her fading heart, why not the object of true love?" With a swipe of her hand, Queen Ilda releases a powerful blast of white lightning. The bolt severs the stem with a noise like breaking glass. Grabbing the rose with one hand, the queen flies back to the group, victoriously displaying the magnificent flower.

Tillie reaches for the glowing petals.

"Tillie!" Queen Ilda scolds. "This is not a toy!" The queen pulls the radiant rose close to her chest, protecting it from her curious daughter.

"We are not without gratitude," Queen Ilda turns to Prince, "but I've no time to properly thank you. Your scent brought the cyclops, and the girl's blood will draw monsters far worse."

The queen flicks her hand, sending a troop of fairies toward the cyclops' body. The sprightly creatures grab the monster by his arms and legs and drag his body from the clearing. They throw him into the briar patch where he had first surveyed the garden.

Prince looks back and forth between the queen and the disappearing cyclops. With a resounding thud, the monster's body vanishes into the prickly bushes. Fairies swarm the thorny brush and ignite it with dozens of tiny lightning bolts. An energetic dance ensues as the fairies fan the growing flames around the corpse with their fluttering wings.

"These herbs will cover your trail," Queen Ilda continues. On cue, two fairies quickly sew mint and garlic onto the edges of Prince's tunic. The boy watches with wonder at the swift work.

"And now, you must leave," the queen announces with a sorrowful sigh.

"Princess is about to die!" the boy exclaims.

"My dear boy, we will take care of that here and now." Queen Ilda motions for her daughter.

"Up, up, up!" Tillie shouts at the fairies, clapping her hands. "You must stand the girl up! Mother says the children must flee this instant!"

With uncanny strength, the fairies lift the unconscious child off the ground. Her head tilts forward and her hair covers her pale face.

"Come on! Lift her up!" Tillie prods.

The wise queen flies up to the girl's pallid face. As she approaches, the incandescent Akacyia rose grows brighter in Queen Ilda's hand. "We haven't much time," the queen mutters.

She gently plucks a single rose petal and recites, "Moss of peat, magic rose, heal this girl from head to toe. Still no more, death take flight; part the distance, find the light. Of life, of warmth your blood retain; stand your own, regain, *regain!*"

The fairy queen reels back and throws the silky petal at Princess' face. The gold edges of the petal burst, showering Princess with shimmering sparks. The fiery particles cascade and swirl around the young girl's frame. The petal settles on Princess' lips, immediately transforming them from blue to fleshy pink.

Prince watches in amazement as Princess suddenly gasps and opens her eyes.

The girl moans. A soft light fills her body and outlines her frame. The fairies set the revived girl on her feet and release her when they see that she has the strength to stand on her own.

"Am I in heaven?" Princess asks, examining her glowing hands with awe.

"You're alive!" Prince shouts, pouncing on the girl and wrapping his arms around her neck.

Prince's sudden embrace shocks Princess, but she hugs him back and squeezes her eyes shut. Fragmented images of the horrible cyclops flash in her memory. When she opens her eyes, she glances down and sees her blood-flecked pearl partially covered by a leaf. Princess releases Prince, leans down, and picks up her prized possession.

"I'm sorry, I didn't mean to drop you!" she says, cradling the pearl in her hands.

"It's okay," Setchra croaks. "Are you better now?"

"Was I hurt?"

"Yes," Setchra's raspy voice break. "Very badly."

"I don't feel hurt—"

"Your eyes have changed!" Prince interjects. He reaches out to touch her face but Princess pushes his hand away.

"No they haven't!" Princess refutes, pulling away in surprise. "Setchra, are my eyes different?" she asks, holding the pearl up to her face.

"All fairy flowers create changes in mortals," the fairy queen explains. "Let me see your eyes, child." Queen Ilda hovers in front of Princess' face. "Ah, yes, the crystals in your eyes have solidified and sparkle like jewels. The amber sparks give your skin a soft golden glow and your hair a luster almost as compelling as the petal."

Princess examines her arms and lifts her hair in wonder, wishing she could see her own eyes.

"Once touched by the rose, anything goes," Queen Ilda chuckles quietly. She flutters in front of the children. "Take the rose, dear children. After all, you are the rightful owners." With a flourish, the fairy queen benevolently bestows the bloom upon the bright-eyed girl.

"However," Queen Ilda adds, raising a finger, "Be warned, for the petals are magic and shall do the holder's will."

Queen Ilda and Princess lock eyes. The girl watches the queen's eyes transform from metallic silver to brilliant white rings.

"If your will is good, then moral acts shall follow," Queen Ilda continues, "But if your will is bad, then evil will never falter. Either way, know that what you reap comes from what you sow."

"For me?" the girl asks quietly. Princess takes the rose from the queen's outstretched hand. As soon as her fingers touch the stem, a surge of warmth courses through her veins.

The queen smiles and begins rhythmically flapping her wings to create a low buzz. In response to the queen's rumbling call, the fairies rise from the garden and hover above the flowers. Sparkling dust billows from their chests, blanketing the entire garden and mingling with the foggy wall.

Princess clutches the flower close to her chest.

As if connected to the rose, each pixie begins humming its own individual tune that blends into a pleasant melody and unites them like a choir, adding a surreal touch to the passing of the rose.

Sensing that this is some kind of sacred ceremony, the children watch reverently.

Princess draws a deep breath at the magical scene unfolding around her. The luminous blossom pulsates in her hand. Syncing to the rhythmic throb of Princess' heart, the rose's light brightens and dims with each beat.

Prince reaches for the flower and grasps the stem. Both children hold the rose and a glow passes over them. As Prince tightens his grip, the stem grows bright green and the petals brighten and stretch. A single sphere of golden pollen ejects from the center of the rose like a miniature sun.

Queen Ilda's quick eyes catch the tiny flare of pollen and she catches it midair. She closes her eyes and inhales as if she has received a cup of nectar from the heavens. The intoxicated fairy queen opens her eyes, completely spellbound by the pollen. She shakes herself from her reverie and flutters back to the children.

"Pluck a petal," she teaches Princess, "cast it north and rhyme a spell. That is how you harness the rose's power."

The children nod solemnly, holding the flower like joint torchbearers.

Queen Ilda presses her lips together and nods in approval.

"You've been paid—now go! Return here nevermore."

Tillie appears next to the children in a flash of color. "We will illuminate your path home," she announces. Her five sisters emerge behind her, creating a rainbow of dust around them.

"Follow our trail," Nillie says, pushing on Tillie's shoulders.

"Don't worry if it zigs and zags," Millie adds with a wink, propping herself on top of Nillie.

"We won't lead you astray!" Jillie continues, piling on top of Millie.

"You will be back in Tremble Nemble in no time," Billie says, landing on Jillie's head.

"Come sisters, we depart!" Lillie waves.

Stacked on top of each other, the royal fairy daughters flap their wings in sync.

"Bye-bye!" Tillie grins wildly. She and her sisters abruptly disappear in an explosion of fairy dust. Their translucent trails shoot past the foggy wall that surrounds the clearing and enter the Dark Forest.

Another group of fairies fly up to the children carrying a wrapped bundle.

"Honeycomb, nectar, nuts, and berries for your long journey home," the fairy Cole explains, handing Princess the bundle.

"Put it in your pocket!" Amble orders.

All around the children, fairies rise from the garden to say farewell. Sparkling glitter showers the area as they ascend into the sky.

A tiny fairy child shimmies up a lime green stem, eager to observe the excitement. She pauses once she discovers Queen Ilda resting on the ivory lily above her.

"Come," Queen Ilda invites, patting the silky petal.

The sheepish child giggles and pulls herself onto the lap of the plump fairy queen.

Princess watches in amazement, gripping the Akaycia rose tightly in her hand and beaming.

"Have you ever seen anything so marvelous?" she asks Prince, gesturing to the sparkling garden before them.

Prince shakes his head. "Not in all my years at the castle," he admits.

Reluctant to disrupt the moment but eager to send the children on their way, Queen Ilda sets the fairy child down beside her.

"Go, now. Follow the narrow path home."

In unison, the fairies drop to the ground, kneeling before the children in farewell. Sensing the grandness of the moment, Prince takes Princess' hand and raises the splendid rose high above their heads. The fairies clap their tiny hands and cheer as the children turn around to follow the fairy trail home.

Basking in happiness, the squire turns one last time to wave to the fairies, feeling for a moment as though he were a knight with humble, doting subjects.

Before the children exit the garden, specks of yellow pollen burst from the Akaycia rose as a parting gift to the fairies. The fairies descend on the glowing pollen in a flurry, gathering the specks in their arms.

"Mine," Bumble shouts, using every ounce of energy to flap his tiny wings. He manages to lift off the ground, but the other fairies move more quickly and snatch up the floating pollen.

"Aw…," Bumble grumbles in disappointment.

Hovering behind the Akaycia rose, he is suddenly hit on the nose by a particle of falling pollen.

"Oh!" he croons, going cross-eyed. With a loud slurp he sucks the pollen into his mouth. "Yum!" he smacks as the pollen glows through his chubby cheeks. The fat fairy hovers behind the children and collects an armful of falling pollen.

Meanwhile, the other fairies rush the pollen back to their respective flowerbeds and feverishly stomp the glowing bits into the ground. As the pollen sinks into the earth, the garden comes to life with a sunlit aura. One by one, hundreds of flowers begin to bloom where the pollen has touched the earth.

"Must we depart?" Prince asks, reaching the edge of the haze. The boy glances over his shoulder, wondering if he should petition Queen Ilda for permanent residence.

Catching a glimpse of her molten silver eyes, Prince decides against it.

Raising the flower above their heads one last time, the children step together into the hazy mist and disappear from the magical garden.

"Farewell," Princess whispers as the vapors conceal the magnificent secret dwelling.

Walking in the fairy trail, the children feel weightless and giddy as they did before. The gray morning light sporadically breaks through the thick canopy of trees and touches the fairy trail, making it disappear.

"We had better hurry!" Prince says to Princess.

"Why?" Princess muses, fixated on the rose.

"Look!" Prince points to the break in the line of glittering dust. "The fairy trails fade in sunlight."

"But it's still so dark," Princess says stroking the rose petals and glancing over her shoulder at the thick shadows.

Both continue to hold the flower, neither one wanting to release the magical object. Princess jerks the flower, tugging Prince toward a tree trunk. The powerful Akaycia rose glows brightly between them, illuminating the tree's bark and exposing several large mushrooms that wind around the base like a staircase.

"I can see everything now!" Princess exclaims, enjoying the lighted forest. Her eyes travel up the towering trees, where the rose's light brightens the branches and leaves.

"Wait," Prince says, stopping in his tracks.

"We can't carry it around like this."

"You can let go any time you want," Princess replies, eagerly tugging the flower her way.

"No, I mean we can't walk through the forest with this light," Prince explains, tightening his grip on the flower.

"Why?"

Prince looks all around in the light of the glowing rose. "Because everything can see us now! It will draw everything to us like a beacon."

"But it's so pretty," Princess says in Setchra's voice, holding the pearl between her fingers. She uses the pearl eye to scan the stem and blossom, ensuring that Setchra gets a good look.

"True, but every wicked beast within the forest will be drawn by its constant light." Prince looks firmly into Princess' eyes until the girl finally relents. She sighs and lets go of the flower. As soon as she releases it, the flower dims.

Prince ignores the girl's sour expression and unshoulders his quiver. "It'll be safe in here," he informs her.

Seeing the fate of the beautiful flower, Princess instinctively snatches the rose back from Prince and shields it.

"Mine!" Setchra's voice creaks.

Prince sighs in exasperation. "The fairy queen said there were beasts far worse than the cyclops. Do you want to face something worse than that one-eyed monster?"

Princess' eyes widen in fear.

"It'll be okay, Setchra," she reassures. "He will keep the rose safe." With a sheepish grin, she penitently hands the rose to Prince.

Carefully, the squire lowers the marvelous flower into his quiver, tucking the leaves and petals in as delicately as he can. He holds up the quiver to examine his work, but the rose's glow continues to seep through the material.

"Now it can be a torch to light our way home!" Princess exclaims.

"No, it cannot," Prince answers, pulling his mother's handkerchief from his pocket and stuffing it into the quiver's opening to veil the flower's light.

"Careful!" Princess warns. "I don't want it crumpled when I show Auntie."

"Who says you get to keep it?" Prince asks.

Princess purses her lips. "Queen Ilda gave it to me."

"Yes, but King Henry should inspect and inventory it."

Princess shakes her head in disbelief. "Absolutely not!"

Prince opens his mouth to argue but decides to refrain when he sees the girl's pouty lip and welling eyes.

"All right then, I'll let you take charge of it until I talk to my father. He'll know what to do."

Princess nods and they continue on their way home along the fairy trails.

"Stay close," Prince orders. Following the intertwined pixie paths, Prince bravely leads the way. Queen Ilda's warning echoes in his mind.

What else could be in this forest? he wonders. A slight twinge of anxiety makes him long for his mother's comforting touch. Prince takes a deep breath to calm his nerves.

As he walks, he realizes that hiding the flower is hardly enough to mask them. The fairy dust not only lights a trail but also illuminates their every move.

"We should walk off the path," he suggests.

"Why?"

"Same reason as the rose; everything can see us in this light."

"But we walked in the fairy path on our way to the garden," Princess counters.

"That was probably foolish," Prince replies. "And that was before we saw the cyclops."

At the mention of the cyclops, Princess gulps and moves off the path, where she feels the full weight of her body once again.

As they continue walking off the trail, Prince notices that the fairy dust still clings to Princess' face. A faint glow lightens her cheeks, forehead, and chin, making her features even more striking than they already were.

The children walk through a patch of fading light and Prince catches a glimpse of the wound on Princess' shoulder. Noticing a rim of pink scar tissue through the dried peat moss, Prince reaches out and touches the crusted mud.

"Ouch!" Princess gasps, jerking from Prince's prod.

Half of the mud patch breaks off and confirms Prince's suspicions. Princess' wound is mended, except for the pink scar, which is no wider than a clam.

"You're healed!"

"Then why does that hurt?" Princess asks, poking Prince back.

As she does so, she feels her stomach emit a deep, gurgling noise.

"I'm famished!" Princess says, clasping her hands to her belly. She feels around in her pocket and removes the parting gift from the fairies. Unwrapping the small bundle, she pops a strawberry into her mouth. "These taste marvelous!" she exclaims.

Prince unravels more of Princess' stash. "It should taste better with honey." Prince smears some of the dripping honeycomb on his berry.

"Ooh!" Princess shivers. "'Tis getting cold."

Prince searches the canopy, finding a break in the trees, he views the sky. "'Tis only the early afternoon, but 'tis already so dark," he observes, searching around the forest.

The children continue to walk beside the fairy trail, enjoying honey on their berries and nuts. They drink nectar out of a miniature flask and feel surprisingly satiated by the small meal.

Princess licks her sticky fingers. She belches loudly and immediately glances over at Prince in mortification.

Prince chuckles. His laughter eases Princess' embarrassment and she shrugs, sheepishly grins, and presses her hands to her mouth.

"Excuse me," she croaks in Setchra's voice.

"No need," Prince says, waving it off. "I've never thought much of Setchra's manners."

Princess giggles through her cupped mouth. "Setchra should be more lady-like in the presence of a knight!" she scolds the accused pearl.

"I am not a knight, but a lowly squire," Prince corrects.

"Yes, but surely you will be knighted as soon as we make it back to Tremble Nemble," Princess proclaims. "After all the times you rescued me!"

Prince thinks for a moment and bites his lip. "I wish you were right," the boy says. "But I am afraid I will never become a knight now that I have failed my father's charge."

Princess looks at him questioningly. "What charge?"

"I was to shoot pheasants and bring them back to my father promptly."

"Oh," Princess stops. "But instead, you saved me from the dragon"—her voice cracking—"you led me through the Dark Forest, you protected me from the cyclops… and now you will not be knighted because of it!" Her chest begins to heave with emotion.

Prince places a hand on the girl's shoulder, touched by her concern. "Perhaps you can plead for me on my behalf," he smiles sweetly.

The girl sniffles and wipes her face with the back of her hand. One tear dribbles down her cheek and lingers on her jaw. Prince curiously squints at the droplet. He reaches for it just as it begins to fall to the ground. Rather than dispersing in the boy's hand, the tear hardens and crystallizes, like water turning into ice. Prince cups his hand and peers at the strange, rock-like object.

"You may think yourself a squire," Princess continues, placing her hand on Prince's cupped hands, "but I see you as a knight."

The distracted boy nods and moves his hands out from underneath Princess' to look closer at the tiny object. Light from the fairy trails reflects in the facets of a perfectly formed diamond in his palm.

"Look!" Prince exclaims, presenting the sparkling stone to Princess.

"Were you listening to anything I said?" Princess asks in exasperation, waving her hands and nearly knocking the precious stone out of Prince's grasp.

Scrambling, the boy secures the jostling stone before it can plunge to the ground.

"Careful!" he admonishes, hugging the precious diamond close to his chest and shooting Princess a stern look.

"Silly squire," the girl huffs. "I have a pearl; I have no need for a diamond!" She turns around and stomps down the path toward home.

Prince shakes his head and looks down to examine the diamond in his hand again.

A high scream splits the air.

Prince looks up, panicked, he fears the worst. He spots Princess crouched down near the path pointing to something in the distance. "It's a ghost!" Princess cries, covering her eyes with her hand.

Beyond her, a white light pulses from the depths of the forest.

CHAPTER XXIII

PATHS & PERSUASIONS

P rince rushes to Princess' side, eyeing the mysterious white light in the distance.

"There's no such thing as ghosts," the boy declares. "Did we circle back to the garden?"

"No, there's no dome. It's a ghost come to eat us!"

"Maybe it's a new fairy. Do you think there's another fairy garden here?"

Princess perks up at the idea of another garden, but ducks behind the boy when she spots the bright light again.

"How do you know it's not a ghost?" she inquires, peeking over Prince's shoulder.

"A ghost wouldn't let us see it from afar," Prince explains.

"But you said they weren't real!"

"They're aren't!" the boy concludes.

Princess bites her lip, unsure if she feels better or worse. Though Prince's confidence is comforting, she cannot help but imagine ghosts sneaking up behind her.

"We should go see what it is." Prince proclaims. His curiosity gets the better of him and he begins moving off the path.

"Don't leave me!" Princess gulps, scrambling after the determined squire.

Walk with a light step when pursing your prey, son. Prince remembers his father's instruction. He lifts his foot quietly and uses the tip of his boot to sweep dry twigs from his path before taking his next step. He sneaks steadily toward the mysterious light.

Princess looks back at the pixie path and tugs on Prince's shirt. "We're an awful long distance from the trail," she frets.

Prince looks over his shoulder. "With the forest as dark as it is, we should be able to see our way back to the path," he assures her.

"But must we drift so far from the trail?"

Prince ignores her question. "If it's another fairy garden, think of all the flowers we could take back home!" he declares, his face filled with excitement

Princess perks up at the thought of more flowers. She squints in the darkness, trying to tell if the squire is teasing or being truthful. "Well, maybe we can find more Akaycia roses," she concedes.

"Precisely; stay low and keep quiet! Follow my lead."

He begins to stalk like his father had taught him. She mimics every move. The darkness begins to press on Princess. She flinches every time a leaf or stick brushes against her skin, imagining some new monster.

"I want to go back to the path," Princess murmurs, feeling a touch of remorse.

"Very well, you wait here and I'll come back for you."

"You can't leave me all by myself!"

Prince shakes his head. "Fine, then come with me!"

Princess nods, tentatively accepting the squire's terms.

Prince unslings his bow and places one of the homemade arrows in the string as he and Princess press on.

"See anything?" Princess asks after a few minutes, gripping the boy's shoulder.

"A bright light," Prince responds flatly.

"Anything dangerous?"

"Yes," he responds. Instantly, he feels Princess' hand tighten on his shoulder.

"What is it?" she hisses, digging her fingers into his shoulder and pulling him to a stop.

"Me," Prince answers in a hushed voice. He gives her a wry smile.

Princess releases her grip and hits the back of Prince's head. "I meant monsters, you silly, foolish boy!"

Prince chuckles and relaxes the tension on his arrow.

As the children skirt a clump of undergrowth, the pulsating light flashes, nearly blinding Prince. He leaps to his right to take cover behind a fallen tree, blinking his eyes to restore his vision. In his haste, he leaves Princess behind, her arms outstretched and searching for him in a panic.

"Where did you go?" she whispers.

"Behind a tree," Prince whispers back.

"Don't leave me alone!"

"Stay where you are!"

"What if it's a cyclops?"

"Then it would have smelled us by now. It would already be hunting us."

"Hunting us?" Princess squeaks. A rush of fear sends Princess scurrying toward Prince, but the frightened girl miscalculates the distance and bumps into him. The sudden push almost causes Prince to release his arrow.

"Be careful," he hisses.

Princess crouches beside him. "Let's go back to the path now," she implores. Prince ignores her.

"Prince, be a good squire and lead us back to the path."

"I am," Prince says. He sneaks up to a moss-covered log. "I just have to see what this is first."

Princess screws her face up and huffs noisily.

Peering over the log, Prince finds a large, round boulder obstructing his view of the pulsing light. The rough edge of the boulder is illuminated as though the light source were directly behind it.

Princess scampers over to the boy and pulls on his sleeve. "If we go back now," she whispers, "I'll give you a...." She pauses, thinking what a boy might want. "I'll give you a kiss!"

Prince tilts his head and considers the offer. After a moment of hesitation, he leans in and whispers, "If we kiss, then we violate the bans and are wed in clandestine. Are you prepared to be my bride?"

He leans back, unsure of what he wants the girl's answer to be. His heartbeat quickens.

Princess purses her lips, then whispers, "Yes." She leans in and closes her eyes. "If I can take care of Arthur, I can take care of you."

"Who's Arthur?" Prince asks, a hint of jealousy in his voice.

Princess opens her eyes. "He's my dog," she explains, then puckers her lips again.

"Your dog! I'm not a dog, I'm a squire."

Princess relaxes her lips and shakes her head at the fickle boy. "Let's go back to the fairy trail. Prince, we have been lost for nearly an entire day! 'Tis getting darker and I don't want to be in these woods when the sun goes back down."

"If I am to be a brave knight one day, I must never retreat!" he argues, hungry to satisfy his curiosity.

"Don't go," she begs.

Prince rises and pulls the bow's string tight. He presses forward, ready to fire at the first sign of trouble.

"Prince!" Princess whispers before slumping down at the base of the log. She pulls Setchra out of her pocket and begins nervously petting her.

"What should I do?" she asks.

"Go with him," the pearl croaks.

"But I'm scared!"

"Then stay here with me where it's safe."

"I think that's a good idea," Princess agrees. After a brief pause, she whimpers, "How do you know 'tis safe here?"

"I don't."

"Then why are you telling me to stay here?"

"I'm not," Setchra grumbles.

"I'm confused!" Princess moans. She takes a deep breath, then leaps to her feet and pushes herself over the log. "Wait for me!" she huffs, scrambling to catch up with Prince.

When he reaches the edge of the boulder, Prince eases around the towering rock. Princess catches up to the boy and stops behind him, keeping a wary eye on the light.

The squire recalls his father's training on how to maintain night vision and presses forward with one eye shut and his arrow aimed at the light. He waits for the light to dim, then opens his closed eye and shuts his open eye. He takes a deep breath and moves around the boulder.

As he clears the rock's edge, he sees the end of a stubby white snout. His heart pounding with excitement and trepidation, Prince waits for the brilliant light to dim again before taking another step. The light fades; Prince opens his protected eye and pops out from behind the boulder.

Tucked within a clearing and surrounded by boulders, a winged unicorn colt rests on the ground. At the sight of the stranger it hops to its feet. Its horn glows with a lightning-white luminescence. Prince gasps and stumbles backward, stunned by the majesty of the creature before him.

On the other side of the boulder, Princess gasps as Prince is seemingly consumed by a brilliant glow. The girl closes her eyes and screams, "I warned you!"

She blindly scurries backward and hears the twang of his bow. She stumbles on a large tree root and crashes on her bottom. Placing her head in her hands, she begins to hyperventilate. She rocks back and forth in a daze, considering Prince as good as dead.

When the dazzling light fades, Princess opens her eyes and summons the courage to ask, "Are you dead?"

When Prince doesn't respond, she scrambles to her feet and holds out Setchra.

"I need you to peek around the corner and tell me if he's still there," she whispers.

"Very well," Setchra grumbles.

Fully expecting to find Prince vaporized by the powerful light, Princess gives a start when Setchra responds, "He's still there!"

"Come see this!" Prince shouts.

"I don't want to; I'm scared!"

"You won't believe what it is!"

Gulping, Princess inches toward the boulder's edge. As she prepares to peek around the corner, she jerks back.

"I don't want to!"

"Don't be silly." He moves to grab the girl and drag her around the boulder.

Princess hears flapping wings and a high-pitched neigh.

"It doesn't sound like fairies!" Princess says, her hands pressed tightly over her eyes.

"'Cause it is not fairies!"

Princess slowly relaxes her hands and then cracks open her eyes. "Well, what is it?"

"A pegasus-unicorn!" Prince explains.

"A what?" Princess asks, leaping to her feet. She scurries around the corner and squeals as the white colt shuffles its wings and whinnies. Princess claps her hands and giggles. "It has wings!"

Prince spots his arrow in front of the unharmed creature.

"Thank goodness," he mumbles. "I thought I aimed for its head."

"You aimed for its head!" Princess swats Prince. "How could you?"

Prince winces and shrugs sheepishly as Princess turns back to the colt.

"Hello, there!" she croons. The colt's ears stand straight up at the sound of her voice.

Prince reaches down to pick up his arrow but immediately jerks his hand back. "Ouch!" he cries out.

"Oh, what's the matter now?" Princess asks.

Prince puts his fingers in his mouth. "My arrow's so cold, it burns!" he explains, dropping his bow.

"Stop being childish," Princess sighs, turning back to the colt. She extends her hands, looking over the creature. It tries to step toward her, but its rear leg rattles a chain.

"What's the matter, unicorn-pegasus?" Princess asks. "Don't you want to be friends?"

"It's a pegasus-unicorn," Prince corrects.

"Same thing," Princess huffs. Her voice goes sweet again, "Come here! Come here!" she beckons.

The colt steps forward again, revealing a metal clamp clenched on its hoof.

"Prince!" she shouts.

Prince moves to Princess' side and spots the clamp.

"We have to help him," she pleads.

Prince nods and moves toward the trapped colt. It steps back and spreads its wings.

"Whoa, whoa!"

"You're scaring it!" Princess scolds.

"I'm trying to help!"

"Then help it, don't scare it!"

The colt jumps into the air and begins flapping its wings. The chain snaps tight and brings the creature crashing back to the earth in a painful collision. Loose feathers drift around them.

"It won't let me help it!" Prince shouts. He jumps back as the colt shakes its head.

"Stop!" Princess cries out. "Maybe we could use something to pry off the trap," she suggests, scouring the ground for a stick.

A loud thud shakes the earth behind the children.

Sensing the danger, the colt frantically cycles its hooves. Releasing a neigh, it tries to fly away. Once again, the winged creature crashes to the ground.

Prince searches the ground for his weapon, but finds a large brown hoof pressing his bow into the forest floor. The boy watches helplessly as his only defense snaps beneath the crushing weight of the muscular, hooved appendage. The tight string loosens and twists into tangled knots.

"No!" Prince shouts, his heart sinking.

The dark, looming figure approaches the children. A flash of bright light from the colt's horn illuminates a half-horse, half-man towering over them. The brawny beast holds a pair of silver shears in one hand and a large bow in the other. He stares intently at Prince and Princess, his long hair draping over his burly shoulders. Two pointed horse ears protrude from the sides of his head and part his shiny hair.

"Thieves!" he accuses, his copper eyes blaze.

His voice is unnaturally deep and loud, like a roll of thunder.

The terrified children freeze in place.

Behind Prince and Princess, the colt darts right and left, jolting the chain and neighing in its futile attempts to escape.

"Were you attempting to steal my meal? Answer me, mortals!"

"We are not thieves," Prince finally musters the courage to respond.

"Then what are you?" the centaur asks, folding his arms.

"We are lost children," Princess pipes up, "who were chased into the Dark Forest, shot by a cyclops, and protected by fairies."

The centaur's harsh features soften. "The fairies protected you?" he asks.

"Yes! And now we are being bothered by a big, ugly, stinky horse-man!"

Taken aback by the little girl's high-pitched barrage, the centaur raises an eyebrow.

"I apologize for any inconvenience," the centaur says. "Are you hungry?"

Surprised, Prince looks at Princess, who nods.

"You must have wanted the delicious meat for yourself," the centaur concludes.

Confused, the children look at each other.

"I think he's talking about eating the pegasus-unicorn," Prince whispers to Princess.

"We don't eat unicorn-*pegasus-es*!" Princess shouts, putting her hands on her hips.

Furrowing his brow, the centaur scrutinizes the girl. "Do you mean the alicorn?"

"Ali-what?" Princess says, perplexed.

"Their meat is tasty and tender," the centaur calmly responds. "Especially when they are young."

"Monster!" Princess gasps.

"Monster?" The centaur looks at Princess quizzically. "I am no monster. If I were, you would both be in my belly."

"But you're going to eat the unicorn-pegasus-alicorn!" Princess huffs.

"Will you trade us for the alicorn?" Prince asks, hoping to calm Princess before she pushes the centaur too far.

"For what?" the centaur questions.

"Yes! We'll trade anything!" Princess exclaims.

Prince shoots an exasperated glance at the young girl, but Princess ignores him.

The centaur relaxes his concentrated expression and closes his shears.

"What have you to offer?"

Princess hesitates, then reaches into her pocket and pulls out her pearl. "This!" she declares, holding out her beloved possession.

The centaur steps forward, his black tail swaying. "Put your items before me so that I may gauge their worth."

Princess steps forward and places Setchra in front of the centaur's massive hoof. Prince places the sparkling diamond tear beside the pearl.

The centaur leans over and carefully examines the delicate pearl. "Tainted," he comments, spotting the flecks of blood.

Instinctively, the little girl's hand presses against her freshly-formed scar.

"And what is this?" he asks, lifting Prince's diamond. Thumbing the precious stone with care, the centaur rises and returns the diamond to Prince. "I've no need for jewels. Have you anything else to offer?"

"We are only lost children," Prince says. "What have we to offer you?"

"If nothing else," the horse-man says, "then we've no trade." He steps forward, prepared to claim his trapped prize.

"Wait!" Princess shouts, desperate to save the defenseless alicorn. She grabs Prince by the shoulders and spins him around. "Don't let him hurt Peggy!"

She reaches into Prince's holster and removes the effulgent rose. "What about this?" she asks, certain a deal can be struck.

The soft aura of the rose lightens the forest and reveals the centaur's sharp jawline and high cheekbones. Princess patiently awaits his response.

"I've no need for fairy flowers," the centaur says, deflating her hope. Turning his wide body around, he whips his tail and hits the children in their faces.

Princess squeals and rubs her stinging cheeks.

"We should go," Prince says, placing the rose back in the quiver.

Princess gasps as the centaur seizes the chain and jerks the alicorn closer.

The colt neighs, stomps, and makes every attempt to escape.

Princess watches in disbelief, too stunned to look away. Her mind keeps flashing back to the recent attack on the fairies, and the thought of another beautiful creature being slaughtered is too much for her to bear.

With each tug, the alicorn screeches and discharges white feathers in its struggle. Foam drips from its mouth as it begs for aid.

"This will soon be over," the centaur says, opening the razor-sharp shears. His slim eyebrows converge in concentration and his jaw muscles tighten. Princess whimpers as the centaur reels in the last bit of clanking slack and lifts the colt up by its hindquarters. Hanging upside-down, the terrified alicorn beats its wings against the centaur's chest as he deliberately slides the shears near the colt's neck.

Princess has no doubt as to what will happen next. Living at Auntie's farm, she had seen plenty of headless chickens flap their wings before their bodies went limp.

"Stop!" Princess screams. She runs up to the centaur and falls on her knees at his hooves. "How could you be so cruel?" she asks, clenching both fists and beginning to cry.

The centaur shrugs and looks down curiously at the child.

"What is the colt to you?"

"He's my friend!" Princess sobs.

Reluctantly, Prince interjects. "Is there *anything* we could offer in exchange for the colt's life?"

Eyeing the youngsters, the horse-man lowers his shears. "Have you a dragon?" he asks.

Caught off-guard by the preposterous request, Prince bursts out in laughter. "I don't keep dragons; I kill them!"

Unfazed by the boy's disrespectful laughter, the centaur shrugs. "I don't keep an alicorn; I eat it," he counters, pointing the shears at Prince. Flexing his long fingers, he opens the blades again and prepares for a quick snip at the alicorn's exposed neck.

Dangling between the razor-sharp shears, the colt neighs one last time in heart-wrenching despair.

Panged by the struggling foal's neighs, Prince promptly shouts, "Can we offer a service, sir?"

Delaying the execution, the centaur holds the shears poised.

"If you will but spare the colt's life," Prince barters.

"Yes," Princess adds. "Prince will do anything you ask!" Unbeknownst to her, teardrops trickle down her cheeks and crystallize into tiny diamonds, littering the forest floor.

"Don't make offers we can't keep!" Prince quietly scolds Princess.

"How tall are you?" the centaur asks, interrupting the squabbling children. "I could be persuaded to trade service for dinner."

"What service can I offer you?" Prince hesitantly asks, wary of the eager look on the centaur's face.

"Your frame might be small enough to squeeze through a rabbit's hole," the horse-man states, lowering the shears. The centaur smiles, absent-mindedly shaking the distressed colt.

"What would you do with a rabbit?" Prince asks.

"The animal itself is useless. But the entry to its home signals a nearby dragon den." An ominous grin steals over the centaur's face.

"He'll do anything!" Princess exclaims, not noticing that the boy is shaking his head in the negative.

"The boy signals he will not," the centaur observes, "But the girl says yes. Which is it: yes or no?"

Princess turns her fluttering eyelids to Prince, silently begging him to comply.

The boy sighs. "Yes."

"Excellent! Then we have a deal."

Wrapping his rear hoof around the end of the anchored chain, the centaur pulls on it tightly and snaps the links with ease. The alicorn squirms, but the muscular man manages to wrap the chain around its neck and fix it in place. "This will hold him fast." He lowers the colt to the ground and turns to Prince. "I've been searching for an alternate route into the dragon's chamber, but I've been unsuccessful," he says.

"What must I do?" Prince asks, wishing he hadn't relented.

"Stay alive!" the centaur proclaims with a slight smile.

CHAPTER XXIV

DANGERS & DEALS

Why did I agree to this? Prince shifts uncomfortably atop the centaur as the horse-man trots deeper into the Dark Forest. The boy fights the impulse to grab the centaur's mane and force him to take them back to the fairy trail. Instead, he keeps his hands on the centaur's bulging sides for balance.

To his right, Princess rides the alicorn, which is led by a chained leash to keep it from flying away. The centaur holds the end of the chain and tugs the winged colt through the forest.

Prince glances at the back of the centaur's head and notices a red, green, and blue braid woven into its hair. *I wonder how he earned his colors,* the squire thinks, remembering the distinguished knights who earned their colors in battle.

"What's your name?" Prince inquires.

The centaur takes a deep breath and Prince feels the horse-man's ribcage expand beneath him.

"My name is Brutus."

Princess perks up and joins the conversation. "Are you a brute, Brutus?"

Brutus ignores her and releases a long, heavy sigh.

Looking over his shoulder, the squire watches the fairy trail fade in the distance and feels a pang of regret for striking such a ridiculous deal.

"You needn't look behind you," Brutus says, as though reading Prince's thoughts. "The past will only bring a storm of remorse."

"You speak as one familiar with remorse," Prince counters.

"Ha!" The centaur flips his mane. "I am familiar enough with bargaining to know that the obligator of any deal often feels remorse after committing."

"And what does the executer feel?"

Brutus thoughtfully taps his chin. "Suspense that the obligator will fail, I suppose."

The centaur's calm tone and logical argument surprise Prince. "And what if the obligator fails?" Prince asks.

"If the obligator fails, then I will be the least of his troubles."

"Why is that?"

"Because he will not be alive to witness my disappointment."

A lump forms in Prince's throat. "So ... you intend to kill me if I fail?" he manages to ask. A few beads of sweat trail down his face.

"Don't be ridiculous," Brutus responds. "I am no murderer."

Prince looks back at an oblivious Princess, who smiles at him and beams with sheer delight.

"Look," she whispers, "he's prancing." Giddy, she holds onto the alicorn as it gambols forward.

Prince shudders and looks back at the centaur. "Then who will kill me?" he inquires.

"The dragon, if you summon him!"

Prince gulps and looks back at Princess, wondering if she is listening to the centaur.

"You keep prancing, Peggy. You've had a terrible time, haven't you?" the little girl croons, stroking the colt's mane. "Prince will protect you," she continues.

Even though it is the winged unicorn that is bound by metal links, Prince feels like the prisoner. As Prince watches Princess dote on the colt while she ignores his impending doom, the squire feels a surge of jealousy replace his anxiety.

"I don't understand," Prince says. "A while ago, you were thanking me for all of my sacrifices. Now, you want me to make more sacrifices—for a colt?" His voice cracks with emotion.

Princess smiles. "He's not just a colt. He's a colt-unicorn-pegasus-alicorn!"

The squire huffs and mockingly mouths, *colt-unicorn-pegasus-alicorn.*

"Besides," the girl continues, "you were the one who insisted on leaving the path. *I* wanted to stay by the fairy trail. If you hadn't wandered away, we never would have found Peggy in the first place. It's practically your duty to protect him now. Are you going to finish what you've begun, squire?"

"Quiet!" the centaur orders, halting abruptly. "Do you want to summon the dragon?" He points to a narrow, hissing hole in the ground that blows steam.

Prince swallows down the retort he had prepared for Princess. He eyes the ground, holds his breath, and climbs off the centaur's back to examine the hole. "That's not a rabbit's hole!" Prince shouts.

"It was once."

Prince hovers over the opening, his face illuminated by a faint orange glow emanating from its depths. A strong, musky smell assails Prince's nose and he leans away, turning back to Brutus.

"You honestly believe a dragon could fly out of that little hole?" Prince asks, hoping that the centaur is joking about the entire ordeal.

"No," Brutus responds, leaning down eye-level with Prince. "But they could break the earth out from under us and bury us alive." He clomps on the hollow-sounding ground for emphasis.

Prince nervously bites his lip, detecting no emotion in the centaur's copper eyes.

"What is it you require of me?" Prince asks.

"I shall lower you through the narrow entry," Brutus says, turning around and pulling a long rope out of a hollow tree trunk.

"You will get the dragon's egg, tie it to the rope, and tug on the line." The centaur demonstrates, jerking on the line of rope. "I will pull the egg out and you will climb back up."

Remembering how his mother once haggled for bread in the market and got double her order for the same sum of gold, Prince decides to test the limits of the centaur's demands.

"You didn't say I'd have to climb," the boy states.

Brutus shakes his head. "You can't climb?" he asks, scratching his broad chest.

"Was I obligated to climb?" Prince asks.

"You should have inquired about the terms of your obligation before committing, squire."

Princess looks up from petting the alicorn. "Prince really is a fantastic climber," she explains, smiling broadly.

"Princess!" the boy hisses.

"*Most* squires can climb," the centaur continues, pinching the royal emblem on Prince's tunic.

"I *can* climb!" Prince defends, swiping the centaur's hand away. "But that wasn't part of the deal."

Narrowing his eyes, the centaur rubs his chin inquisitively. When his arms fold, his biceps bulge.

"In your mind, what were the stipulations of our deal?"

Prince walks over to the centaur and examines the bow slung across his chest. "It has become clear to me that you are entirely too large to squeeze into that little hole," Prince explains, placing one finger on the bow, "or you would have already gone down there on your own."

The centaur's eyes flash as he focuses on Prince.

"It has also become clear to me that you want that dragon egg more than you are willing to admit."

Brutus watches Prince's fingers move up and down the tightly-twined bowstring. "I'm willing to bet it's worth a hefty sum—"

"Get to the point," the centaur interrupts.

Prince jostles the bow, making sure he can

handle the lengthy weapon. When he feels how light it is, he folds his arms and assumes the same thinking position as the centaur.

"For your bow, the arrows, the colt, and a guide back to the fairy trails, I will retrieve your dragon egg. And I don't climb; you pull me up."

Too distracted to pay any attention to the negotiation, Princess strokes the colt's small snout and moves Setchra along its feathered wings. "Soft," she croaks, giving her pearl a complete tour.

"I should have killed you both back at the hollow," the centaur says quietly, testing Prince's nerve.

"But you didn't," the squire answers firmly, feeling his legs wobble from hidden fright. He watches the centaur's face as he contemplates the deal. The centaur's front hoof digs at the ground while his human fingers drum on his arm.

"Done," Brutus finally concedes.

Prince spits in the palm of his hand and stretches it out to a disgusted recipient.

"Your word is enough, squire," the centaur confirms.

Prince awkwardly retracts his hand and wipes it on his filthy tunic.

"Lift your arms," the centaur instructs, slipping the rope around Prince's small waist. "Hold this," he commands after wrapping excess slack around the tight line. "When your feet hit the ground, unwind this end," the horse-man explains. "That will set you free."

Prince nods nervously and steals one last glance at Princess.

She looks up from braiding the alicorn's mane and waves at him. "See you soon!"

"You'll find the eggs near the fire river," Brutus informs the boy, pulling him over to the small opening. Hot, hissing air causes Prince's skin to prickle.

"Wait!" Prince resists, digging his heels into the soft earth.

"The terms have been set," the centaur reminds the squirming lad. "If you are not back by dawn, the deal is off!" With that, he lifts the boy up into the air and drops him feet-first into the hole.

Prince claws at the surface to keep his head above the rocky fissure. "Isn't there any other way?"

Prince's troubled voice causes Princess to leap to her feet and abandon the alicorn. "Stop, you're hurting him!"

Prince locks eyes with Princess briefly and wonders what will become of her if he does not return. A swelling heat rises over his legs. The full weight of what he has committed to presses down on him.

The centaur leans over and pushes on Prince's forehead with his front hoof. "You *will* do this!"

Stuffed into the natural vent, the squire feels the confined pressure of the soil ease just below his waist. His body scrapes against the gritty earth while his cycling feet search for ground that isn't there. Hot, sulfuric air makes his eyes sting and causes his nose to run.

"I can't breathe!" he shouts, fighting for air. His body slips completely through the vent and into a steaming, cavernous hell.

At least a hundred feet above a narrow magma stream, Prince spreads his arms in panic and waves them wildly like a windmill.

The rope swings Prince straight into a jagged mineral cone dangling from the ceiling. His ribs smash hard against the stalactite and crack on impact. "Ahhh," Prince cries out. His body slowly spins as he reaches above his head, grasping the rope to stabilize himself. The centaur slackens the rope.

The boy catches fragmented glimpses of the fiery stream beneath him in his swirling descent. *'Tis a flowing river of dragon's breath.*

The oblivious centaur continues to lower Prince closer to the molten rock. Reeling from the pain in his throbbing ribs, he instinctively folds his arms. Suspended in midair, his balled-up frame sways like a pendulum. An overwhelming heat causes beads of sweat to form on the boy's face, neck, and chest.

Prince looks around the enormous cavern while he dangles above the river of fire. The underground dwelling is lit by the glow of liquidized basalt flowing beneath him.

He looks up at the broken ceiling of stalactites and shouts, "Hold the line, Brutus!"

✳✳✳

Back on the surface, Princess watches the centaur's back muscles ripple as he lowers the rope hand over hand. His wiry tail whips left and right.

"Don't worry," she says to the alicorn, stroking its body. "You'll never be like that awful, terrible man ... horse." She wrinkles her face at the centaur's back.

Ignoring the little girl's chatter, Brutus clucks his tongue. At his call, five tiny men slide down his colored braid and over his shoulder.

The horse-man holds out his hand as five brownies dressed in mouse-fur pants rush into his palm and form a straight line respective to their age. The tiny savages adjust their beetle-shell breastplates and ready themselves for action. Each bearded man holds a different tool. The oldest of the bunch grips a miniature rock hammer. Another clasps a shovel with half an almond shell for the blade. The youngest clutches a small metal pick, while the two middle men trade each other a pair of pliers for a pitchfork.

"Labor, Lord?" squeaks the oldest, holding his hammer above his head.

"Help the boy find the egg," Brutus orders them.

"Aye, Sire," the senior shouts and runs down the rope, followed by his four loyal brothers.

✳✳✳

Prince squints into the darker reaches of the cavern, but finds it difficult to see through the wavy walls of heat that rise from below. Scanning the pointy cones on the cavern's charcoaled floor, he wonders why the minerals twinkle like fairy dust.

The rope slowly lowers until Prince's body hangs over the blistering magma. Prince realizes that he will have to reach the banks of the blazing river if he is to survive. Fighting against the pain in his side, he stretches out a leg and tries to swing closer to the black edge of the river's perimeter. He pumps his legs, attempting to gain momentum and reach the shelf, but is unable to make the distance. Prince's world begins to unravel when he realizes he will not reach it.

His breathing quickens, his lungs burning and his ribs aching.

When he feels something tugging on his shoe, he immediately flinches, flicking his foot. As he feels his body being pulled through the air, a new wave of panic wells up and threatens to break through. Tears brim in his eyes, just as he feels solid ground beneath his foot.

"Thank you, Lord!" he whispers a quick prayer on the acidic air. Gratitude and relief wash over him as he rubs his burning eyes.

With a little effort, Prince is able to set down his other foot and pull himself to safety. "Thank you," he mutters again, releasing the rope, which sways back over the molten river.

"Be quiet, stupid!" he hears a man's shrill voice shout in his ear.

The terrified boy blinks wildly and looks around for the source of the voice. "Who's there?"

"Who do you think?" a different voice asks.

"I don't know; that's why I'm asking!"

"You ask too many questions! You should just know!"

"How would I know?"

The voices go silent.

"Have I gone mad?" he mutters. Prince inspects the cavern all around him; it appears completely deserted. Slowly, he creeps closer to the sparkling mineral walls.

"You're not mad, you're stupid," a new high-pitched voice sounds.

"It *was* stupid to make a deal with Brutus!" Prince admits. "If you are anything more than a voice, show yourself!" he shouts.

"He's definitely stupid," a final high-pitched voice shouts in his other ear.

Shaking his head back and forth violently, Prince shouts, "I am not stupid!"

His voice echoes off the dark walls and travels down the winding cavern.

"Grawr!" a dull echo responds.

"You're definitely stupid," two voices simultaneously squeak in his ears.

"I am not," he protests softly, searching for the growl's source.

"Prove it!"

"How?" His eyes blink wildly as he stares into the unknown.

"Hide!" the five brownies shout in unison.

Prince stumbles back, falls, and watches the magma rise as though something were traveling beneath its surface. When the ripple reaches the seemingly solid riverbank, it starts to split. A giant crack in the floor opens and fills with molten earth. The crack branches out and races toward Prince.

"Not that way, stupid," a voice shouts, "turn around!"

A different voice chimes in, "he's not going to make it."

Another voice responds, "silence!"

Prince gets to his feet and shakes his head, trying to wake up from this terrible dream.

"Behind you!" one competing voice shouts. Disoriented, Prince looks behind him at the cavern wall.

"Not that way, turn around!" another little voice screams, causing the boy to whip back around.

Prince is horrified to find the rippling magma traveling right for him. He follows the voice's advice and spins around. Along the cavern wall, he spots several tall, stalagmites rising from the floor. He makes a mad dash for the mineral peaks.

"Well, well, maybe you aren't stupid!" a voice praises Prince.

Looking over his shoulder, he sees the black crust break apart and a bright orange wake emerges. He clutches his ribs in pain as he wedges himself between two gigantic stalagmites.

"Are you trying to crush me to death?" one of the five men shouts as Prince presses himself further into the shadows of the narrow space.

"Voice, you have a body?" Prince asks.

"Of course I have a body!"

Prince feels a tickle on his cheek, like an insect crawling on him.

"Then show yourself!" Prince whispers.

As the boy reaches to scratch the itch, he feels the tickle spread across his cheek and scurry up the ridge of his nose. He sees a tiny, bearded man, no taller than his thumbnail.

"Hide yourself!" a high-pitched voice answers.

"His skeleton's going to be stone!" another voice chirps.

"Quick!" a different voice shouts, "Pick up ash and rub it on your arms and face! It will conceal your scent!"

"Oh, they're going to find him! He's as good as dead. We should run for the shadows!"

Prince quickly leans down and breaks off a piece of black crust. He crumbles it in his hands and rubs it on his face and arms.

"He listens! Maybe we do stand a chance."

The ripple swells into the wide cave and splashes magma along the bank and on the walls across from Prince. It stops and the magma swirls, forming an ashy shell on its surface as though it had never been disturbed. A black, forked tongue pops and slowly flips back and forth.

"He's in there," a voice squeaks.

Prince inches to the edge of the mineral cone and peeks around. "I see nothing," he whispers.

As if on cue, a silver dragon lunges out of the burning liquid and beaches itself on the opposite bank. Its tongue slithers in and out of its mouth, detecting faint hints of an odor that it can't quite trace.

"Friend, show yourself," the horned reptile whispers in a soft, eerily human voice.

Prince shrinks behind the mineral cone as sheer terror courses through his veins.

The slender dragon is much smaller than the one that chased Prince and Princess into the Dark Forest, but more terrifying for its ability to communicate. Heat waves radiate off its shiny, metallic skin. The beast inhales deeply and begins to hack. Magma oozes out of the corners of its mouth. It swallows and scans the shadowy cavern with its glowing silver eyes.

"Down here," the beast says calmly, "we are all of us friends. You may call me 'Lazim.'"

The dragon hacks again, sending an amber glob down its mouth and onto its long black claws.

"Don't believe him!" warns the eldest brownie.

The dragon's coughing fit is followed by a long silence. Prince listens closely, but only hears bubbling from the molten river and an occasional hiss of escaping steam.

"My patience is short. If you won't show yourself, I will summon my sister!" the beast roars, deafening Prince. Pointy stalactites break free from the ceiling and crash to the ground, shattering like icicles. Prince huddles in the shadows, praying he will not be discovered or skewered.

A bulging ripple sails past Lazim and bursts out of the blazing river. A chrome dragon, slightly smaller than Lazim, lands on the bank and looks up with burning red eyes.

Trembling, Prince gathers enough courage to peek around the corner.

Feeling something poke his ankle, the boy swipes at the annoying jab and peers around the cone.

The new dragon peels back its lips, revealing pointed black teeth. Its tail hits the centaur's rope dangling over the magma river.

"We're doomed!" a helium voice whines.

Startled by the rope, the monster regurgitates a blazing blob across the dark cave. The sailing, red ooze illuminates the shadows and splashes against the cavern wall.

"Grawt!" the chrome dragon roars. The sound reverberates off the cavernous walls and brings more stalactites crashing down.

"Izel is his sister. Her sight is better than his, but she can't speak," a tiny voice informs Prince.

"I never knew dragons could talk," Prince whispers to the unseen voice.

"They aren't much different than you and I," a brownie whispers.

"Well, they look different."

"Looks are deceiving. It's what's inside them that you should fear."

"How can you tell what's inside them?"

"When their eyes blaze red, they lose their wit and become completely carnal."

"Who *are* you?" Prince whispers, curious how the voices knows so much.

"Friends."

The boy keeps his gaze fixed on the dragons.

"Perhaps a deal can be struck," Lazim calls out in a kind tone, taunting the darkness with a charming invitation.

"He never honors his bargains," a brownie warns Prince.

Prince shifts his weight and feels another sharp jab at his ankle. He strains his eyes to see what irritates him and discovers a human skeleton finger. His eyes widen and he jolts. He sees five white fingers cemented in place and looking as though they are reaching out of the igneous rock. He wiggles his fingers, and realizes what the voices meant about his skeleton becoming stone. Comparing his hand to the bony fingers, Prince notices that their length is roughly the same size as his own. He swallows and shrinks farther back into the shadows, careful not to make a sound.

"My sister and I will be merciful," Lazim says as his sister scans the shadows.

"Don't listen to them; they lie!" the oldest brownie squeaks.

"I believe you," Prince whispers. "But what do I do?" His arms and legs quiver uncontrollably.

"Be as still as the stone!" whispers one of the tiny voices. "If they could locate you, we'd be dead already."

"You think they'll drop any eggs?" interrupts one of the little men.

"Watch the sister," a different voice responds.

Prince cautiously scoots back. Staying to the shadows, he keeps a careful eye on Izel. He can't decide if he is more frightened by a talking dragon or a silent one.

The silent dragon stands still, though her head shifts as she slowly scans the cavern. Her brother seems to have lost interest and releases a nostril of steam.

"'Tis nothing, sister. Let us return to our chamber and tend to our children."

Lazim turns back to the fiery stream and eases his way into the magma. Izel lingers, searching the cavern one last time before she finally turns. As she spins around, she thrusts her hooked shaped claws into the basalt and breaks off pieces as she flicks her foot.

"Why is she doing that?"

"Just watch!" a little voice whispers.

Inhaling rapidly, the dragon's scaly sides flex. She spins around several times. Pushing her tail down on the crust, she arches her back and lifts her head. Her rib cage contracts and pushes out a sparkling egg. The egg tumbles along the crust and teeters near the stream.

"Oh no!" Prince gasps.

"Grawt!" the mother stomps toward the torrent and presses down hard on the bank. Parts of the shelf break away. Prince watches the egg drift off, floating on top of the fiery magma.

Her pointed talons scratch against the hardened crust, breaking it apart.

Izel arches her long neck, screeches, and drops several more eggs. One egg rolls across the embankment and finally rests in a nook near the wall.

"Spontaneous cycle," a brownie comments.

"You don't know anything," one of the five brothers huffs.

"They have to lay frequently because they hardly ever hatch," another unseen brownie asserts.

"This whole cavern is covered in shell fragments," one of the men admits.

"Brutus should free our wives after this," the oldest of the men informs his brothers.

Finished laying her eggs, the chrome beast eases back into the burning liquid. Before completely submerging, a translucent lens blinks over her eye, protecting her vision. Metallic, scale-like plates seal her nostrils and allow her to immerse herself. Her forked tongue sticks out in one last attempt.

"She's testing you," the eldest brother informs Prince.

"Now we know for certain they can't smell you."

"Wait 'til you see her swim away," another voice squeaks.

As the crust begins to harden, Izel's tongue slowly retracts beneath the surface, then disappears completely.

A rippling current trails as she swims away.

Prince breathes in deeply, calming his racing heart.

"Let's go!" one of the men shouts, leaping from Prince's shoulder and sliding down his shirt and pant leg.

Prince watches the five miniature men scurry out of the shadows and into the light. Whooping and hollering, the five brothers run toward the closest egg. They surround it and begin dancing like savages. "Our wives will be freed! Our wives will be freed!" they chant in their high-pitched squeak.

Hoisting the egg up on their shoulders, they each shout directions as the egg tilts one way and then another.

"Forward!"

"No, backward!"

"Left!"

"Whoa!"

Struggling, they carry the egg over to the dangling rope.

"Pipe down," the oldest brother growls, dragging the rope's slack over to the egg as far as it will stretch.

Prince carefully lifts the sparkling object and examines it in awe. Discovering a metallic shell beneath the crystal surface. He pats the glittering surface and detects a radiating warmth.

"Stand on top of it," the oldest man instructs, "Or he'll leave you down here like the last one." The bearded man nudges his head in the direction of the cemented skeleton's hand.

"Won't I crack the egg?" the boy asks.

"Ha!" a whiny voice mocks. "You wouldn't crack it without a lightning bolt."

"Yeah!" another voice adds. "That's why it takes a fairy to crack the egg. Bet you didn't know that, did you?"

Prince shakes his head and follows the little man's advice, stepping on top of the egg. He clasps the rope and jerks on it four times as he was shown. Gradually, the rope pulls tight and lifts him, the egg, and the tiny men out of the vast cavern.

CHAPTER XXV

RETURNING & RETURNED

B rutus lifts up the rope, his massive body leaning back from the exertion. His front hooves dig into the soil, piling up small mounds of dirt.

Princess watches the centaur's arms flex and ripple. *So strong,* she thinks, standing up. She approaches the hissing fissure and cranes her neck to peer inside. *Please be all right,* she silently prays.

As if in answer, Prince's fingers appear over the rim of the fissure.

"Pull harder!" Princess orders the centaur, clapping her hands in excitement.

Brutus heaves, pulling Prince's dusty head above the surface. His hair, clothing, and skin are all covered in ashes as though he has been rolling around in a fireplace. He gasps for air, still clutching the rope.

"Keep pulling, keep pulling!" Princess shouts.

The centaur gives one last heave and the boy explodes out of the earth, landing on his injured side.

His cracked ribs crunch painfully. *Stop!* the boy wants to scream, but his injured ribs and the smoke in his lungs impede his ability to breathe. All that escapes the boy is a small wail.

"Prince! Are you well?" Princess asks, rushing to the filthy squire.

"No," he groans, spitting out dirt.

"I knew you would make it out!" she exclaims, smothering the boy with a hug.

"Ahh!" Prince grunts. "Get off me!"

The girl releases the boy and sits up. "Sorry," she murmurs. "Did I hurt you?"

The centaur trots over to the egg, which landed a few feet from Prince and rolled against a mulberry bush.

"Finally," the horse-man exults. He picks up the sparkling dragon egg and examines it. Light from the vent reflects off the egg and dances across his jubilant features.

"Excuse me, Sir," the oldest brownie interrupts. Behind him, his four brothers press together in solidarity. "Can we, um...," He clears his throat and scratches his whiskers, "can we get our wives back now?"

Brutus examines the egg for fractures. "What about *my* wife?"

"We can get her, too."

The centaur nods firmly, his copper eyes glinting. "After I repay the children, we shall take the egg to Vanderbolt and retrieve our wives together."

"Vanderbolt...." The smallest brownie shudders.

Brutus turns to Prince. "Can you walk?"

"I believe so." The squire winces and pulls himself up to a sitting position.,

"You sure are brave," Princess croaks in Setchra's voice.

"Yeah, you sure are brave," a small voice sounds in her left ear.

Princess furrows her brow and looks around in confusion. Slowly, she holds her pearl to eye level. "Setchra?" she whispers.

"Hello," another high-pitched voice affirms in her right ear.

"You are finally using your own voice!" Princess laughs.

"What is so funny?" Prince asks, wondering if the girl is laughing at his discomfort. He starts to rise but stops and grasps his ribs.

"Don't tell him anything! He's stupid!" a squeaky voice shouts.

"Setchra, how dare you. He is not stupid!" Princess rebuffs, holding up her pearl.

Hearing Princess talking to herself and saying "stupid," Prince halfheartedly smiles, fighting to ignore the stabbing pain in his side.

Brutus walks up beside Prince and leans down. "Brace yourself," he warns the boy.

The centaur carefully lifts Prince and places him on his feet. "How does that feel?" the horse-man asks.

Prince takes a step forward and winces.

"Like an arrow in my side," the boy answers.

"Does it hurt to breathe?"

"Yes."

The centaur nods. "You've cracked your ribs. Do you want a ride?"

The boy nods. The centaur gently picks him up and twists around to place Prince on his back.

Meanwhile, Princess continues to argue with the little men, thinking that their voices come from Setchra.

"Prince is not stupid!" she shouts at her pearl.

"Is so!" a whiny voice shouts back.

"Oh, you make me so mad, Setchra!" Princess raises her voice, her hands clenched in frustration.

The centaur laughs and leans close to the irritated girl. "Watch closely," he tells her, clucking his tongue. Instantly, a little man leaps from Princess' shoulder and into the centaur's outstretched hand. Princess gasps, watching as three more tiny men leap into the horse-man's palm. Her eyes widen as she hears a tiny voice in her left ear shout, "Must we leave, Joshua?"

The oldest brother turns and beckons for his hesitating brother. "Come down, Johnny!" he shouts.

"Very well." The last and youngest man bounds onto the centaur's long finger.

"She was so much more pleasant than the stupid one," Johnny says.

The centaur looks up at Princess and winks.

"They're so dramatic," the girl mumbles, eyeing the five men.

The centaur moves the men closer to his hair, where they climb up the lengthy strands and disappear into its tangles.

"All the more reason for a protector," the centaur responds.

"And what do they offer in return?" Princess asks.

"Counsel and comfort."

"Comfort…," she repeats. She looks at the alicorn longingly, then back at Prince. She sighs heavily and says, "I should comfort him, shouldn't I?" She stretches out her arms. "Will you help me up?"

A muffled shriek from the fissure diverts the group's attention.

The centaur tucks the dragon egg under his arm. "It is time to go," he declares. He reaches down, scoops up the little girl, and swiftly puts her on his back. He hastily unties the alicorn's chain from the tree and jerks it forward.

Brutus turns and begins trotting through the Dark Forest, nimbly jumping over logs and roots. Princess wraps her slender arms around the centaur's waist, squeezing tightly. Hearing Prince moan from the impact, she removes one arm and reaches behind her to hold the injured boy in place. Prince inhales sharply every time the centaur leaps.

Looking behind him, Brutus sees a slosh of lava spew out of the hissing hole.

"Hold on tight!" he shouts, charging into a fierce gallop.

"Faster, Brutus!" Princess shouts, thrilled at the exhilarating charge. Her hair whips wildly. She glances over her shoulder to check on Prince just in time to see fire erupt from the clearing. The centaur runs furiously, putting distance between them and the lava gushes from the dragon's lair. The alicorn neighs and keeps pace with the centaur, vigorously flapping its wings each time they jump over an obstacle.

The wind rushes by as Brutus masterfully navigates through the dark surroundings, keeping the dragon egg safe in his powerful arms.

"Are you thirsty?" Princess asks the heaving centaur.

"No," Brutus huffs, finally satisfied with the distance between them and the dragon lair. He slows his pace to a steady trot.

Princess lets go of the centaur and turns to look at Prince.

"Are you well?" she asks.

Prince grimaces and nods, keeping his hand firmly pressed to his side.

She leans down and whispers in his ear, "I could use the rose to heal you. Shall I?"

Prince raises a finger and holds it in front of his lips, shaking his head back and forth. "No," he whispers, pointing at the centaur. "He may not know of its power."

Princess nods in understanding and gently pats his hand. "You must be in an awful lot of pain."

Prince nods. Catching a flicker of light out of the corner of his eye, he forces himself up. "Look!" he shouts.

The centaur whips around, removing his bow and arrow with incredible deftness and speed. "What is it?" he asks, pivoting to shoot whatever danger might present itself.

Shocked by the centaur's agility and precision, Prince responds, "It's the fairy trail."

"Just a fairy trail?" Brutus asks. He cautiously lowers his weapon.

"*Just* a fairy trail?" Princess jumps in. "That's how we get home, stupid!"

The centaur blinks in surprise and twists his body to face the little girl.

"Stupid?" he says.

"Yes," the indignant girl huffs. "Ever since we met you, you have been nothing but dreadful! You are a very bad man-horse!"

"What have I done to merit such an insult?" the horse-man snorts, twitching his ears.

"What have you done?" Princess exclaims. "What have you *not* done? First, you trapped a poor innocent unicorn-pegasus-alicorn behind a rock. Next, you were going to *eat* him. What kind of awful monster eats a sweet little unicorn like Peggy? Next, you made Prince fetch a dragon egg out of a fire hole because you weren't brave enough to do it yourself! And then you didn't even know that the fairy trail was our path home!"

"You keep a good tally," he mutters. "I never wanted this."

"Then why do it?" Princess asks.

"My hand was forced. That is all you need to know." His copper eyes blaze. The centaur folds his arms as he moves along the fairy path.

"Psst," Johnny hisses from the back of the centaur's hair, trying to catch the girl's attention.

Princess sees the man motioning with his tiny hand and leans closer. "I can't hear you," she whispers, watching him shake his head in frustration and motion for her to come even closer. She pulls her hair back and presses her ear against the centaur's tickling mane.

"Can you hear me?" he asks.

Princess nods slowly.

"That boy behind you." The little man points behind Princess. She looks over her shoulder at Prince, who is resting his head on the centaur's back. "His wits are not really all there, now, are they?"

Princess pulls back, pressing her lips together in disdain. She squints vehemently at the little man.

"His wits are *too* there!" She shakes her finger at the horse-man's mane.

Johnny squeaks, still looking at Princess and laughing at the plucky girl. He beckons for Princess and finally convinces her to lean in close again.

Johnny's little eyes travel up and down Princess' giant frame. Her swooshing hair and sparkling eyes mesmerize him. "You and me, we aren't stupid – 'cause we belong together!" He winks at Princess.

Princess wrinkles her face in disgust.

"Never in all my years!" Princess says, sounding more like Auntie than herself.

"I can't help it!" Johnny chirps. "I loved you from the moment I first laid eyes upon you, you giant, wonderful girl!"

Revolted by Johnny's advances, Princess uses her thumb to press his little body back into the centaur's hair.

"Hey!" he pipes. "This isn't how you treat love! You're supposed to pucker up and—" His voice muffles as she pushes him farther into the hair.

Princess pulls out Setchra and croaks, "Bugs don't know what love is!'

"I'm no bug! And yes, I *do* know what love is," the little voice howls as he pops back out. "I already got one wife." He proudly puffs his chest out.

"Johnny, behave!" Joshua shouts from above. "What about Judith?"

"Oh, I love her, too." Johnny grins. "But I got a lot of love and that woman might be big enough to contain it!" As he hangs onto one of the centaur's locks, he leans his bearded face toward the little girl. He simpers and bats his eyes at Princess' beautiful face.

"Yuck!" Princess gags. "*Behave,* little whisperers."

Brutus laughs and his long brown hair shakes, tickling Princess' face. She laughs as well. The mood becomes infectious and Prince begins to chuckle.

"Ha, ha—ahhh." He clutches his ribs and tries to hold back the painful laughter. Releasing a sigh, the squire marvels at the pleasant mood that now pervades the Dark Forest. Never in his wildest imagination had he thought an adventure would have so many ups and downs. He glances over at the alicorn and clicks at it. The white colt runs up beside him and brushes its snout against his hand.

He likes me, Prince thinks. *The king will think him a far better prize than the rose.* His eyelids grow heavy as he rubs the colt's nose. He nods, then falls asleep atop the centaur.

Princess watches the early light of dawn peek through the trees and feels a surge of happiness. The air seems warmer now and she closes her eyes, savoring the moment. The stench of the forest's damp, rotting wood is beginning to be replaced by the sweet smell of grass and wild flowers.

"Dawn brings peace," she murmurs.

"Day light blinds creatures of the dark forest," the centaur explains.

Princess cocks her head. "Blinds them?"

Brutus nods. "Metallic eyes deflect sunlight."

Princess thinks back to the mermaid, Setchra, and remembers her silver irises.

"Where do you get metallic eyes?"

"Where do you get your blue eyes?" the centaur responds.

"My mother, I suppose."

Princess' heart tightens for a moment as she reflects on her mother's last words: *Our eyes, our hearts, and our wits.*

"As far I as can remember," the centaur looks skyward and taps his chin, "I got mine from the fairies."

Princess thinks of Queen Ilda and realizes her eyes were silver, just like Setchra's. "How did the fairies give you your eyes?"

The centaur shrugs. "I do not recall."

"Strange that you wouldn't remember."

The centaur nods and continues along the fairy trail.

The trees begin to thin out as the entourage reaches the edge of the forest. Huge, towering boulders begin to replace the lofty timber. Princess sees the fairy trail zip up and over the soaring rocky heights, though the trails have nearly disappeared in the bright sunlight.

Brutus moves carefully around the gigantic rocks, but he still stumbles from time to time over the hard, uneven surfaces. A steady waterfall cascades from the mountain and snakes down into a clear stream.

"I'm so thirsty, I could drink it dry!" Princess exclaims. "Press on, centaur, take me to the water's edge!"

"This is as far as I go," the centaur announces, stopping abruptly.

"Why?"

"Because I am blind in this light and cannot traverse these cursed boulders."

The rising sun glints off the mystic falls. Princess smiles at the blue sky and takes comfort knowing that monsters with metallic eyes cannot see during the daylight. She twists around to wake Prince, but hesitates when she sees his peaceful face.

Brutus feels no such reluctance.

"Wake up." Brutus shakes the boy by his arms.

Prince's eyes twitch and crack open.

"What? No!" Prince mumbles, still dreaming. He slumps down again and begins snoring.

"Don't do that," Princess says, pushing away the centaur's hand. "Prince," she delicately taps him on the shoulder. "'Tis time to wake."

"Are we home yet?"

Princess shakes her head.

"Of course not," Prince grimaces, slowly sitting up.

The centaur lifts Princess and sets her on the ground.

"The deal was an escort home," Prince grumbles.

"He's blind in daylight," Princess explains. "And he can't walk on the river rocks."

"River rocks?" Prince looks around and sees that the terrain has transformed. A gray riverbed, which parts the forest and leads up to a mountain, trickles nearby.

The horse-man lifts Prince off his back and gently sets him next to Princess on the ground.

"There is a trail at the canyon mouth," the centaur explains.

Prince nods and tries to stifle a yawn.

"Listen well," Brutus continues, removing his bow. "You have upheld your end of the bargain." He hands the bow and holster to Prince. "You have earned this. Never sell it and never surrender it."

"I won't," the boy promises, feeling the lightweight weapon with awe. He traces intricate carvings on its surface with his finger. "How far to our home?"

"I have no idea how to get to your home," the centaur confesses, "but I was willing to follow the fairy trail as far as I could. Had the trail been dirt or cobblestone, I could have helped you to our bargain's end. But I cannot be expected to take you where I cannot go."

The boy looks down at the bow and arrows, then back up at the centaur. "You had no intention of upholding your end of the bargain, did you?"

The centaur presses his lips together in frustration. "What more could I do?"

"Is there any other route around the mountain?"

"None that are safe for children."

Prince grunts, folds his arms, and looks away. He unslings his holster and hands the concealed rose to Princess.

"Perhaps," the girl interjects, "We should exercise a great market principle."

The two look at her blankly.

"Forgiveness!" she bursts with a smile and open arms.

Prince sighs while Brutus folds his arms and rubs his chin pensively.

"That's easy for you to say," Prince answers. "My side aches terribly, and who knows how we will find our way home."

"The trail will take us home," Princess confirms. "I saw the fairy trail wind up the mountain top."

After a brief moment, Prince stretches out his hand to the centaur. "So long as you know that if our paths cross again, you are in my debt."

"I accept your terms," the centaur smiles in gratitude, oblivious to Prince's outstretched hand. "Should our paths cross again, I will remember your courage and fairness."

The centaur turns and reaches forward with his hands, blindly feeling his way into the shadowy forest.

With his hand still outstretched, Prince clumsily shifts from a handshake to a wave. "Farewell, Brutus!"

"Now, release Peggy!" Princess exclaims gleefully.

Brutus chuckles and pulls the alicorn's chain close until it is directly in front of him. Following the links of the chain, the centaur reaches the manacle around the unicorn's neck and releases it.

Princess squeals in delight and runs forward to give Peggy a big hug.

"I love you so much!" she croons, kissing its soft neck. The colt neighs loudly in response.

Johnny, seeing his chance, stealthily slides down the centaur's braid and leaps onto the colt's feathery wings. He makes his way to its mane and snuggles in.

"Hey there, you look like you could use a friend," Johnny squeaks.

The colt's ears rise and twitch, piqued by the high-pitched chirp of Johnny's voice.

Princess releases the alicorn and lets it prance freely in the clearing. It shakes its mane, nearly casting Johnny off his perch.

Watching the half-horse, half-man disappear into the woods, Prince sighs and turns in time to see Princess chasing after the alicorn. He smiles, wondering if she will be willing to trade the rose for the colt. The colt suddenly spread its wings and flies away. He sighs and wishes he had chosen the rose.

"Come back here, Peggy!" the girl shouts. "You are coming home with me and Auntie is going to love you as much as she loves me!"

CHAPTER XXVI

NAVIGATING & NAMING

Princess pouts and turns to Prince. "Peggy will come back, right?"

Not wanting to upset her further, the squire nods. "Of course he will."

Her mood lightens considerably.

The bright morning sunlight streaks across Prince's face as he slings the bow across his chest. *The bow is meant for someone much taller than me*, he muses as it clacks against the river rocks at his feet and threatens to trip him.

"I can't wait to get home!" the boy moans, grasping his aching side. He unslings the bow and lifts his tattered shirt to examine his ribs. Behind him, Princess clasps her hands to her mouth when she sees the black and blue bruises across his side.

"I can't carry the bow like this," Prince says, lowering his shirt. Holding the weapon like a walking stick, he hobbles down the riverbank and scans the water for a shallow pass.

Princess hesitates. "What should I do, Setchra? He's been terribly wounded!" She looks expectantly at the pearl in her hand and waits for counsel. Hearing no response, she frowns.

"Come on!" Prince beckons. "We can cross here!" The boy dips the bow in the river, showing ankle-high depth.

"He seems well enough," Princess says, tucking Setchra away and rushing to join the boy by the river.

Not wanting to get wet, the little girl hops from rock to rock. She stops and pats her dress out of habit. In the early morning light, she can finally see how filthy it is.

"Prince, I'm bleeding!" she screams when she sees the dry trail of blood covering the front of her dress.

"'Tis on your back, as well."

She panics and twists herself around. "I'm dying!"

Prince sighs. "No, you're not!"

"Farewell, Setchra!" Princess holds her pearl up.

"Bye," Setchra croaks.

Princess plops down on the ground. "I feel faint. I can hardly breathe. 'Tis the end of me." She lays flat on her back.

Prince watches Princess' entertaining theatrics until he can stand it no more.

"The fairies healed you, remember?"

She bolts upright. "That may be, but Auntie is going to kill me when she sees my dress."

"Let's press on." Prince extends the bow. She grabs it and he struggles to help her up. When she's back on her feet, she looks up and wonders how the wounded squire will manage on the steep trail. Halfway up the mountainside, the granite cliffs flatten and sprout patches of green grass.

"Look up there!" Princess points.

Prince scours the mountain pass, noticing the cracks, jags, and shadows. Struck by the awkward protrusion of a single pine tree high on a craggy cliff.

"Strange place to make a home," he says, impressed with the pine's ability to grow in such a harsh environment. He wonders how the spruce took root in the first place. *With no soil, it seems impossible that it would grow.* He pauses for a moment and taps his finger to his chin like the centaur had. "I suppose, where there is a desire, there is a possibility."

Upstream, Princess leaps onto larger and larger rocks, stopping on a boulder as tall as she is. "Come on, Prince," she shouts. She leaps onto a particularly jagged rock and her toes teeter on the edge. Rotating her arms in wide circles, Princess manages to regain her balance. "Whew, that was close, Setchra."

Prince enjoys watching the girl frolic. Her dress plumes at each bursting jump, reminding him of a jellyfish swimming.

Princess crosses the river and continues leaping across the rocks that lead to the mountain pass. As she progresses, she finds that the gaps separating boulders grow wider. *Do it*, she dares herself, looking across a particularly tricky gap.

Working up her nerve, the little girl bites her lip and raises her dress above her ankles. She steps to the back of the boulder and takes a deep breath.

Now! she urges. Running across the boulder, she leaps across the gap. She extends her leg midair, hoping it will fall on the flat side of the boulder. Her toe catches on the boulder's edge just before the top. Her knee hits the solid surface and she scrapes the bottom of her outstretched arms. She begins to slide down the rock's side, but manages to hold on to the edge before sliding off.

"Help!" Princess whimpers, wondering if she will fall to her death if she cannot hold on.

Prince laughs as Princess' feet dangle only inches above the ground.

"Don't laugh!" she shouts, embarrassed.

"Mind the gap!" Prince chuckles, holding onto his painful ribs.

Grunting, Princess begins to pull with all her strength. Her small arms wobble, while her feet paw at the angular boulder, searching for footholds. She manages to pull herself up. She proudly stands and shouts, "Victory!" She raises her arms above her head like a conquering gladiator.

"Victory?" Prince teases. "I would not be so proud of that pebble."

Princess gasps.

"Be kind," she grumbles in Setchra's voice. "He is hurt."

Working his way into the canyon, Prince turns and whistles, calling for the alicorn. The colt is nowhere in sight.

The boy sighs in disappointment. "All that labor for a loss."

"What was lost?" Princess asks, slightly ahead of the boy.

"The alicorn."

"Peggy will be back," she says. "You said so, remember?"

The alicorn neighs high up on a grassy cliff. The sparkling horn is visible, even from a distance.

"Up there!" she excitedly points.

"How did he get up there?"

"He flew, of course!"

Free to roam the dangerous heights, the alicorn celebrates its liberty. The majestic colt sniffs the grass with its pink and white nose and begins nibbling on the blades.

"Look at her!" Princess croons. "She's smiling at us." The alicorn spreads its wings and stretches them with soft flaps.

"How do you know it's a 'she'?"

"Peggy has to be a girl."

"Why?"

"Because no boy would fly up to eat grass on a cliff."

"What would a *boy* 'Peggy' do?"

"Eat the grass down here."

Up on the cliffs, Johnny stomps his foot on the colt's mane.

"Hey, stupid! You're going to be the end of me!" He holds desperately to the animal's mane as it whips him back and forth.

The alicorn looks around while it continues to feast, searching for the voice that mysteriously rings in its ears.

"Do you think she'll follow us all the way home?" Princess asks, scanning the cliffs above.

"I hope so," Prince answers. "Father would be pleased with me if I brought home an alicorn. That's far better than pheasants."

The children travel toward a thin waterfall that spills down the mountain.

"'Tis so lovely," the little girl says. When she reaches the pool's edge, she kneels down and slurps handfuls of crisp water into her dry mouth. "'Tis the freshest water I've ever tasted," she gurgles. She plunges her head into the pool. "Brrr!" she sputters, whipping her hair back. "'Tis *cold!*"

Prince smiles at the girl as she splashes water his way. "Ha!" the boy laughs, flinching from the cold water.

The alicorn's flapping wings interrupt his thoughts as it glides down from the cliffs above. The colt plops its hooves down at the edge of the crystal blue pool. It promptly lowers its head and drinks.

"Hello, Peggy," Princess says, reaching for the colt's neck. The creature jerks its head back and trots away. "Very well," she splashes at it. "I'll clean up before I pet you." Princess washes her hands and face. "Come, clean up!" she shouts to Prince.

The boy moves closer to the pond and Princess splashes him again.

"Stop that," he cries.

"We could use the magic on you," Princess offers Prince his quiver, seeing the boy clutch his bruised side.

Prince looks down and nods in agreement. Carefully, he removes the rose. Its glow brightens the shadows beneath the waterfall.

Princess' eyes light up as Prince presses his fingers against a soft petal. He feels the pulsating warmth course through his fingers.

"Do it!" Princess encourages, clapping her hands together.

Prince hesitates, remembering what the fairy queen said about bad reaping bad and good reaping good.

"How do we know if this is good?" he asks.

"Just do it and then we will know."

Prince sighs and releases the petal. "If it's the wrong thing to do, I could jeopardize my knighthood."

Princess throws her hands up in the air. "Just do it!" she insists.

With a heavy sigh, Prince replaces the rose in his quiver. "I cannot partake of that which may be good or may be bad. If I am going to be a knight, my father said I must know for certain what is good and what is evil."

"Isn't the pain unbearable?" Princess asks sympathetically.

"Excruciating."

"If the magic was good for me, then why not you?"

Prince ponders this for a moment. "I'm not near death," he concludes.

Suddenly, he spits in his hand and reaches for Princess. "Spit in your palm," he orders.

Her mouth falls open in disgust. "Never!"

Rolling his eyes, Prince grabs her by the wrist, leans down, and spits into the palm of her hand.

"Eww!" she shrieks.

He mashes his hand into hers and firmly stares into her eyes. "Swear that you will use this magic like medicine – rarely, if ever!" he charges.

Princess looks back at him in disgust, eager to release his grip. "If you spit on me again—"

"For our safety and that of our families, swear it," he presses.

An image of Auntie flashes in Princess' mind. The thought of anything happening to the rugged woman is more than her little heart can bear. "I swear to use it rarely, if ever!" she repeats, shaking his hand.

Prince smiles. "And swear you will keep it a secret," he adds.

"I swear! Now, *let go of my hand!*"

Satisfied, Prince releases her hand. Princess crouches down and thrusts her hands into the freezing water, scrubbing her palm with her fingers. "I simply cannot believe he spit on me! Has this rodent no manners?" she mutters to herself.

Prince skirts the water's edge, moving toward the mountain's base by the waterfall. Leaning against a rock, he opens his mouth and catches stray droplets from the cascade. He winces at the pain from the awkward movement.

"Why don't you kneel down and drink from the pool?" Princess inquires.

Prince leans his head into the waterfall's spray and motions for her to come closer.

She shuffles over to him. Prince shakes his head and wipes the water from his face. He leans in close enough to whisper in her ear. "Squires kneel only to their king," he says, then pushes her into the pool.

The little girl yelps before landing in the rippling water.

Laughing, Prince holds his aching side. Her wet hair droops over her face and part of her dress floats on the surface around her. She stands and shouts, "'Tis cold!" She gasps, her lungs quaking from the biting water. "You cruel, wretched, awful, beast of a boy!"

Prince sets down the bow and quiver and eases his way into the freezing water.

"That's not nearly enough!" Princess shouts, splashing him in the face.

Prince's mouth opens wide. "Oh, stop, 'tis freezing!" he stutters. Submitting to the cold, Prince takes a few steps into the water until he is neck deep. "'Tis not so bad. In fact, it helps the ache in my side," he says through chattering teeth.

The alicorn trots back and forth at the water's edge, unsure of what to do.

"Don't jump in there, you dumb beast!" Johnny shouts. "I can't swim."

※※※

Back in the Dark Forest from whence the children came, a grumbling snore vibrates off the lips of a large black wolf. As the children's laughter echoes through the canyon, the snoring ceases. Black lids crack open, revealing yellow eyes.

The sounds of children splashing and playing are well received by two pointy ears that shift back and forth. The wolf rolls to his feet and stands. He stretches his wide, powerful limbs, arching his back and exposing long, black claws. The beast yawns, revealing jagged fangs.

Sensing nearby foreign voices, the wolf stands and shakes vigorously. Bone fragments fly from his thick fur coat. The black creature would perfectly blend in with the shadows if not for the tip of his bushy tail, which looks as though dipped in silver paint. The wolf leans back for one final stretch and then stands perfectly still. He licks his nose, activating his sharp sense of smell, before pointing his snout skyward and sniffing. The wolf recognizes the strong odor of humans. His grizzly mane stands on end, completing the wolf's transition from waking to hunting.

CHAPTER XXVII

COMINGS & GOINGS

P rince clambers out of the water. The alicorn gallops up and nestles its warm body against the shivering boy.

The bright sun shines on the children through a sparse scattering of clouds. Invigorated by the chilly swim, Princess exits the water. Her dress and undergarments are heavy with water. She wrings water out of her stained dress and eyes the narrow dirt trail that coils and winds up the rocky mountain. "Shall we continue on the path?" she asks, motioning to the trail.

Prince grabs the arrow holster and slides the band over his head.

"Unless you want to stay here."

The children start making their way up the steep incline. Prince soon falls behind. "Wait," he huffs. "I can't move that quickly."

Princess stops. While waiting, she spins her dress back and forth to dry it.

"We are on our way home!" she chirps.

While Princess waits for the boy to catch up, she spots the alicorn stomping the dirt path in search of roots. "He's digging!" she laughs. She peeks around the next curve in the trail. "Prince, look!" she shouts. "The path is taking us *behind* the waterfall!" She moves to a ledge behind the waterfall and watches the clear water cascade down in sheets. Muted light enters the wall of water and dances on the dark mossy rock beside her.

When Prince fails to answer, she leans against the wet cliff wall. Moss grows on the rocks behind the waterfall, along with peculiar little yellow flowers. Princess leans in and draws a deep breath. "Yuck, you stink!" she exclaims, smelling nothing but the musky moss.

Rounding the bend behind the girl, Prince sniffs himself. "I know; a proper bath is long overdue."

"How far do you think we are from Tremble Nemble?" Princess asks, peering down at the terrain through the waving sheets of water.

Prince leans on his bow. "I wish I knew. Maybe a sunset, maybe a day, maybe longer."

"I hope less than a week," Princess blurts out. "I miss Auntie. And I don't want Peggy to tire out before we get back."

"I must confess," Prince says. "You are absolutely terrible at coming up with names."

Princess scoffs, "I like Peggy!"

"What if Peggy is a boy?" Prince asks, plucking the string on the bow and noting that the high-pitched tune differs from that of his old bow.

"Then I would call him Peg."

Prince points the half-drawn bow at the girl, ignoring the pain in his side. "My point exactly," he releases an imaginary arrow accompanied by a loud *twang*.

"Auntie didn't think I was good at naming things, either," Princess admits. She sticks out her bottom lip.

"Why don't you practice by naming that?" Prince asks, pointing to the rippling pool beneath them.

"Can you name a pool?"

"You can name the pool, the waterfall, the mountains, the forest—though I think Dark Forest suits it well."

Princess closes her eyes and inhales, trying to find inspiration for the pool's name.

Stinky Musk, she thinks. *No, Prince'll probably laugh at that.* Opening her eyes, she combines the evergreen smell with the water mist.

"Misty Green," she mumbles as Prince hobbles up the path. "No, that won't do, either." She scurries after the boy. "I know – Heavenly Tears!"

Surprised that Princess came up with a good name, Prince nods in agreement. "You named the pool, so I will name the colt." He smiles.

"That's not fair! You tricked me!" Bunching up her dress, the ruffled girl charges up the trail. "You scoundrel!"

⁂

Down beside the riverbed, the black wolf scans left and right, straining to detect his prey's whereabouts. Though the children's faint scent lingers everywhere, the waterfall's mist masks their exact location. The wolf runs its tongue along its fangs.

High above the wolf, blurred objects move behind the translucent waterfall and tromp up the path. The children climb the steep mountain trail, feeling confident that they have left danger behind. Their experience in the Dark Forest had taught them that monsters rule the night, but humans govern the day. However, while monsters' vision confines them to darkness, other predators have no such restrictions.

Legendary among both villagers and farmers, the wolf used to descend upon young shepherd boys who worked in the fields. Though he would also eat men and women, children were the easiest kills. He hardly had to exert much energy for the kill and most children were easy to carry off. On more than one occasion, the wolf had ripped through a herd, slaying sheep, not to consume the meat, but to draw the young shepherds to their flocks. To him, setting the stage was only half the killing game. Once the herdsmen saw the carnage, the wolf pounced and played with his victims like a cat, prolonging their death to revel in their torture. The fear he sensed from his victims' pounding hearts brought him vicious pleasure.

Though the wolf enjoyed hunting shepherds, he knew it was only a matter of time before the territory was littered with traps. So, as cunning wolves do, he wandered in search of more favorable hunting grounds, never returning to the same place twice. The wolf eventually found he had more success sneaking into farm homes under the cover of darkness and gently pressing his ivory fangs against the necks of sleeping children. When the frightened babes awoke, they would inadvertently press their necks into his terrible jaws. The wolf would euphorically clench down, ever so slowly, and drag them away.

Though the wolf was clever, not all of his hunts went without mishap. One time, a child had enough air to release a cry, which awoke a pack of loyal farm dogs. Awakened by the din outside, a mother came forth with a lit candle in time to get a terrifying glimpse of the wolf dragging her dead child out the window. This incident earned him the title 'Quick Silver', because all that the mother saw before her child was gone were the terrible yellow eyes and a flash of silver.

Farms like Auntie's were an opportunity the wolf could seldom resist. He had, in fact, ventured past Auntie's farm years prior and made off with a few chickens and a lamb. Though he preferred the flesh of children, the wolf was similar to the tax collector: once on a farm, he was not going to leave empty handed.

The wolf leans down and drinks from the stream. As he drinks, he tastes the children in the tainted water. Unable to control his quivering hunger, the predator stalks about, inspecting the water for his prey.

✕✕✕

Near the top of the granite pass, Princess leads the way. As she stomps up the narrow path, she vacillates between talking about her dog and elaborating on the great, loving woman who adopted her, Auntie.

"She's tougher than any knight I know," Princess asserts.

"How many knights do you know?" Prince inquires.

Princess stops and puts her finger to her chin. "None," she shrugs. "But nonetheless, I'm certain she is!"

Prince chuckles at her sweet ignorance. "Well, if you're certain, it must be so."

Behind the children, the daring alicorn stands near the edge of the cliff and stomps its hooves.

Why is it drawn to the edge? Prince wonders.

Without even a whimper, the little horse dives off the jagged rock face.

Prince gasps, feeling as though he has suffered a great loss.

The horse falls with its snout tilted down and its ears bent back. The rushing wind presses against its face, sending a thrill through its body. With its feet and wings tucked in, it descends at an astonishing speed. Only a short distance from the fatal earth, the colt tilts back its head, pops open its wings, and glides down to the mouth of the canyon. The alicorn drifts in great circles, as graceful as any bird in the sky.

Below the alicorn, the wolf's black head emerges from the streambed and spots the happy colt. It growls in anticipation.

"Did you hear something?" Johnny whimpers, detecting the faint sound.

Flapping its majestic wings, the alicorn masterfully slides through the narrow canyon and circles back up the path. He lands at the pool where the children had bathed. Behind the alicorn, a black shadow slinks out of the stream toward the winding trail and the waterfall.

Oblivious of the alicorn and the wolf, Princess continues singing Auntie's praises. " ... She works real hard, too," she chatters.

Prince nods distractedly and peers over the edge of the cliff, wishing he could freefall like the alicorn.

"From sun up to sun down, she works, work, works," Princess rambles.

Down by the pond, the colt leans forward and gulps down the cool water. Behind it, the patient predator follows the scent of the alicorn through the canyon pass until it comes to the pool beneath the waterfall. The wolf crouches on its haunches, preparing to leap forward in one robust bound.

The alicorn, having satisfied its thirst, raises its powerful wings and springs into flight. The wolf lowers its ears and watches the unsuspecting colt spiral upward.

"But I do get to play with Arthur," Princess continues. She stops, shuffles her bare feet, and sniffles to herself. "Which is why I'm in this mess in the first place." Frowning, she contemplates either flicking the dog's nose when she returns home or hugging him with every ounce of strength she has. Undecided, she flips her nearly dry hair and sighs, "I miss my home." Her shoulders slump.

"Don't you think Prince misses home?" Princess grumbles in Setchra's voice.

"I suppose," she answers, looking down in her pocket.

"Then offer comfort to him who needs comforting," Setchra croaks.

The wolf patrols the path until he reaches the bend behind the waterfall. There, he finally discovers the children's trail. He tilts back his head and howls, "Arwooo!"

A distance up the mountain, the wolf's howl is lost in the rushing water and whistling wind.

Ascending toward the mountaintop, the alicorn ignores Johnny's wails. "No more! No more falling! No more!" The little bearded man screams and clutches the alicorn's mane, turning the color of split pea soup.

The colt twitches its ears and flies to the edge of the cliff.

"Land!" Johnny orders, flipping his body over like a flailing fish. He wraps his tiny arms around the colt's fluffy ear. "Please land! Can't you hear me! I'm begging you! Land!"

The alicorn twitches its head and releases a loud neigh.

"Oh, no!" the little man gurgles as the colt flattens its ears, tilts its head forward, and prepares to freefall once more. The granite walls of the cliff blur. "Ahh!" Johnny screeches all the way down the mountain.

At the last moment, the alicorn pulls up, but closer to the earth than before. It circles the mouth of the canyon, flies back up the jagged walls, and repeats the process again and again.

Prince watches the colt fly up and down and shakes his head in disbelief. "You see that?" he asks Princess. "If you tried to ride him and fell, you would die!"

The wolf pants from the uphill sprint, his pink tongue hanging out. He stops and sniffs the air. Inhaling deep breaths of the children's odor, he froths at the mouth and lets out an excited yelp. Adrenaline courses through his body and he takes off again.

Flying to the top of the mountain, the alicorn hears the yelp and scans for the source. It looks over the side of the ledge and spots the wolf in aggressive pursuit of the children, running only one switchback behind them.

Nearing the top of the mountain, Princess' good mood gradually dissolves until her homesickness overtakes her and she begins to cry. Prince hobbles over to his companion.

"Prince, I just want to go home," she sniffles, looking at him with wide, blue eyes.

"There, there," he says. "All will be well."

The little girl shrugs and wipes her nose on her sleeve. "Will we really return?" A fat tear runs down her cheek and falls to the ground as a large diamond.

"Whatever it takes, I'll get you home," Prince pledges.

"What if we don't make it?" she sobs, and wraps her arms around Prince who grimaces in pain.

"I will do everything in my power to return you safely home to your Auntie," he cries out, "but only if you release me! Your grip is hurting my side!"

"Oh—" Princess relaxes her hold.

Prince gasps for air and presses his hand to his side.

"I'm sorry!"

Descending quickly, the alicorn flaps its wings and watches the wolf closing in on the children. As the colt cycles its hooves, the tip of its horn begins to glow the color of lightning. Nearing the mountain, the little colt lowers its slender snout, flattens its wings, and aims for the wolf.

Princess spies the alicorn streaking through the sky behind Prince. Beginning to feel better, she turns around to once again take the lead.

"Lancelot is, of course, the one I miss the least," she prattles, back to her usual cheerfulness.

The colt flies only a few feet above the wolf, staying out of reach. The wolf growls at the winged colt but continues his headlong run at the children.

Princess proceeds, "But Auntie has been very good to us, hasn't she, Setchra?"

Holding up her pearl, she answers in a low raspy voice, "Yes, I like what she cooks; 'tis very yummy."

"You must be mad!" Princess rolls her eyes. "You don't even have a mouth!"

Prince shakes his head at the silly girl. "Then how does Setchra talk to you?"

Princess looks at her pearl, perplexed. "How *do* you talk to me?"

Had the children looked behind them, they would have witnessed a spectacular and terrifying sight. The alicorn flies over the wolf, kicking at the creature's snarling snout. The wolf takes several swipes at the flying horse with his long claws. Determined to protect its rescuers, the alicorn rears its head, its horn strobing like a twinkling beacon. Startled by the light, the wolf shirks away, growling.

The alicorn flies in a figure eight above the predator. Quickly diving down, it closes the short distance to the wolf's rear and touches his bushy tail with its pulsating horn.

Feeling a brief touch, Quick Silver turns around and snaps his jaws, but the colt is already out of reach. An excruciating chill courses through the wolf as the colt pulls back and flies higher. The wolf yelps, his hindquarters falling clumsily to the ground.

"What was that?" Prince asks, coming to a halt.

"What was what?" Princess counters, continuing to push forward.

"I thought I heard something."

"'Twould be nice if it were Arthur. Oh, how I miss that mutt."

Prince looks around for a moment, but seeing nothing out of the ordinary, follows Princess again.

Unable to lift his rear legs, the wolf drags his hindquarters in a feeble effort to stop the freezing burn creeping up his spine. Transparent ice shards climb the wolf like a deadly cocoon. Before the wolf can release a last wailing howl, the magical frost consumes his lungs and locks his torso in place. The alicorn's magic overcomes him, transforming him into a glistening statue of ice. The frozen figure releases one last breath of fog that rises into the air.

"Wow!" Johnny shouts, taken aback by the alicorn's power. The colt flies over the mountain pass and lands between the two children.

"Where did you come from, Peggy?" Princess asks, delighted that the colt has returned.

"His name is not Peggy!" Prince dissents.

"What would you call him, if it's even a boy?"

"Pegasus, of course."

"But it's a unicorn-pegasus-alicorn."

"You got to name the water."

Frustrated, Princess stomps her foot.

Prince pets the alicorn's white coat.

"Pegasus will have to do," he says, stroking the colt's nose.

"That's an awful name!" Johnny whines. "I'd go with White Death."

Unable to hear the tiny man, Prince turns, raises his hand, and announces, "I present to you, Pegasus! The most fearless winged colt you'll ever lay eyes upon!"

Princess curtsies. "Pleased to meet you," she says, holding her hand to her mouth and giggling.

"What?" Prince inquires.

"Why's he doing that?"

Behind Prince, the alicorn parts its lips, exposing its large horse teeth in an apparent grin. Pegasus neighs in a high-pitched whinny and lifts its head up and down, whipping strands of its fleece-like mane.

"Whoa, boy," Prince says, stroking its snout.

"You can't just call it a boy!" Princess says, walking past Prince and getting behind the radiant colt.

Without ceremony, she lifts its tail and leans down to inspect the colt. She lifts her head up triumphantly. "'Tis not a he, but a she!"

"You can't tell by looking at it," Prince smirks.

"Of course you can. Auntie showed me how on Merlin."

"Well," Prince clears his throat, "Unicorns don't show until they're eight, so alicorns must be the same," he counters.

"Oh." Embarrassed, Princess slowly lowers the tail. "Well, we should be getting along then."

"It's because alicorns are the most innocent of animals," Prince informs her.

Nonchalantly, Princess strides past the know-it-all boy. "'Tis time I get home," she huffs. "My Auntie will be very upset not knowing my whereabouts, and I'm tired of being wrong."

As she stomps up the last few feet of the summit, Prince shouts, "Wait!"

"Oh, what now?"

"Well, over this crest there may be a valley, an ogre, or a hostile village. We cannot know for sure."

"And?" she rebuffs, feeling her knees go weak at the word "ogre."

"I was taught that you are never to just pop over a hill. You're supposed to tactically creep up and sneakily peek over."

She folds her arms. "Your ways are quite complex, squire."

"Your silhouette will be seen for miles if you just stomp your way up and stand upright."

"Well then, what are you waiting for? Show me how to be a sneaky," Princess mocks.

Prince nods and reaches for an arrow. His fingers fumble through his holster and fail to latch onto the feathers he's used to finding with ease. The centaur's arrows are quite a bit longer, so he keeps reaching higher and higher but cannot seem to feel the feathered end. He winces at the pain in his side.

"Oh, give it a rest," Princess scolds him. "You're putting on a terrible show." She walks behind him and removes an arrow for him.

"Thank you," the boy says.

Princess follows Prince's lead as he crouches down, even though she feels that the boy is being silly. Wrapping his index finger around the arrow to hold it in place, he turns around and lifts his finger up to his mouth. "Shh," he whispers.

"I'm not making any noise."

"I know, but I thought I would warn you before you do make noise."

"You can only *shh* me if I'm making noise!"

"Well now you *are* making noise, so *shh*!"

Upset that Prince had pulled her into a "shushing" trap, Princess wrinkles her nose and teeters on losing her temper again.

Prince turns and tries to crawl with military tact, but a searing pain freezes him in place. He curls up in a ball and moans in agony.

"What are you doing?" Princess asks.

"Being tactical."

"Is your tact working?"

Prince frowns at her.

"Press on!" Princess bellows, running past the squire and storming up the last few feet of the incline.

Exasperated, Prince grunts.

"Oh my!" Princess gasps.

Prince hobbles to the top of the mountain and discovers his home, Tremble Nemble.

High above the kingdom, the two children bask in the moment, their figures ignited by the golden afternoon light. A wave of relief sweeps over

Prince. To his left, he watches tears well up in Princess' eyes.

"I wasn't sure we would make it home," she sniffs happily.

Looking over the kingdom, Princess sees the castle in a whole new light. Below them at the edge of the mountain range, the towering castle radiates in magnificent splendor. She can see the long, pearly columns rise out of the rectangular structure like glimmering white spears, and that the pointed blue roofs are actually made up of hundreds of individual shingles. Its giant walls and tall pillars cause all other structures to look like miniscule specks of sand in its glorious presence. The white stone walls reflect the sunlight, making the structure sparkle and shimmer like crystal.

She gazes down at men that look like ants as they circle the rooftop, wearing their blue uniforms and shiny helmets that gleam in the light. Townhomes hug the base of the castle in countless rows, while cobblestone roads spread across the vast kingdom like spider webs. On the west side of the kingdom, the bright green farmlands begin at the town wall and end at the Dark Forest, traveling south as far as her eyes can see. Following the main cobblestone road, Princess thinks she can pick out Auntie's farm.

The alicorn joins the children.

"Let me see!" Johnny howls. He clambers out of the alicorn's hair and perches atop its head. "Wow, that looks like a place I could spread my wings."

Just then, the alicorn shoots its wings open, shakes its head, and gallops down the hill.

"No, wait!" Johnny holds onto the alicorn's ear. "I didn't mean it! Not again!"

Leaping off the ground, the alicorn flies away with Johnny screeching in its ear.

Princess feels an ache in her heart when the alicorn soars away. Worried about the magnificent creature, she bounces on her tippy toes.

"Oh, that foolish little beast!" she shouts, shaking her fist at it. "I'd planned on keeping you as well!"

"You had, had you?" Prince says, folding his arms.

"What would you do with Peggy?"

"What would you do with the rose?"

"Everything," Princess sighs. "You have knights to protect you. I need the rose to protect Auntie and Arthur."

Prince rolls his eyes. "And Setchra, and Lancelot, and Guinevere, and Merlin, and all your flowers. Fine. The rose is yours."

Prince sees the winged pony glide past the castle. "I hope he returns."

"I hope *it* returns," Princess corrects him.

"Precisely."

Princess sighs and starts down the mountain. Prince leans down, feeling the throbbing ache of his ribs in full force. He picks up the bow.

"Wait for me!" he shouts.

"Come on, Prince! We're almost home!" Princess says, skipping down the path with the heroic squire hobbling behind her.

CHAPTER XXVIII

FRIENDSHIPS & FAREWELLS

The children wind down the mountain path and end up on the east side of the kingdom. Approaching the large outer wall, Prince pauses.

"There's only one gate, and it's on the south side," he grumbles.

"Aren't you excited to get home?" Princess bubbles. "Let's go before it gets dark."

Searching the skies, Prince looks for the alicorn. "Foolish, feral colt. 'Twas all for nothing," the squire sighs, his shoulders slouching.

"No, squire," Princess intervenes. "We've the rose, a diamond, and a centaur's bow!" She beams brightly.

"Yes," Prince's mood lightens. "I suppose I do have that. But an alicorn would come in handy right now." He eyes the tall outer walls.

The little girl nods emphatically and walks beside the towering wall, dragging her fingers on the smooth stone as they circle to the south.

When they are closer to the entrance gate, Prince moves into the tall grass.

"What are you doing?" Princess asks.

Prince scrambles for an excuse, more willing to go into another dragon's lair than face the guards who humiliated him. "I—I have not yet completed my task," he sputters. "I still need three pheasants."

"After all that has happened?" Princess asks in surprise. "Well, then, I shall leave you to your task and return home."

"No, no, I shall first escort you home," Prince quickly offers, thinking that it would be easier to sneak her past the guards in the tall grass and return under the cover of darkness. *If they throw waste on her, I would have to kill them*, he thinks. He clenches the centaur's bow in anger.

"You there! Halt!" a guard shouts from above.

"Run!" Prince yelps, scurrying deeper into the tall grass.

"Why?" Princess asks, holding a yellow daisy to her nose and pausing mid-skip to gaze up at the voice coming from the wall.

"What have you there?" the guard asks, looking down at Princess.

Princess holds up the flower.

"Daisies, Sir," she mimics his authoritative tone.

"Run," Prince hisses, crouching in the field.

"Who's that with you?"

"Him?" the girl asks, pointing at Prince.

"Don't tell him my name!" Prince pleads.

"State your names and purpose!" the guard bellows.

Prince whispers loudly, "Don't tell him who I am!"

"I am Princess," the little girl curtsies, "and this … is my brother. He's a little slow."

Prince wrinkles his nose in disgust, but stays quiet to avoid the attention of the guard.

"'Slow' stupid? Or 'slow' crippled?" the guard asks.

Princess covers her smile. "Both!" she shouts.

Prince seethes but presses his tongue against his teeth. He can feel the blood rising to his face in anger and embarrassment.

"Pick a daisy for me then, will you?" the guard asks with a toothy smile, waving her on.

Prince clenches his fist. "'*Pick one for me*,'" he mimics. "That's not what he means. He means pick one for me and I'll throw my piss pot down on you."

"I shall! And one for my brother, too!"

Prince turns to convince Princess to hide, only to see her turning the corner toward the front gate.

"Wait!" he shouts, hobbling after the girl.

At the front gate, Princess finds the cobblestone road. "Oh, Auntie, I'm coming!" she sings, skipping down the path.

Prince scurries through the tall grass. "Shh!" he tries to hush her.

"Why so secretive? Are you really a thief and not a squire?" she asks, twirling her dress and smelling her daisy. "Pick one for Prince," she says, pinching one petal and dropping it.

"Pick one for Setchra," she says in the pearl's voice, plucking another petal.

"Pick one for *Prince*!" she shouts, looking back at the guard tower as she pronounces the boy's name.

"Don't be unkind," Prince pleads, worried that the guards will recognize him at any moment.

When they have moved far enough away from the walls, Prince emerges from the tall grass. He grunts and holds his ribs as he moves down the hard road. Thinking of ways to minimize the impact, he uses the long bow as a walking stick.

Princess promptly scurries off the path toward a clump of trees.

"Where are you going?" Prince moans, irritated by hunger, sleep deprivation, and the fact that Princess just called him her *slow brother*.

Princess returns with a broken branch. "Use this," she says, "and give me the centaur's bow."

"Why?" Prince asks, holding fast to his prize.

"You don't want to wear down your trophy, do you?" Princess takes his bow, slings it across her chest and skips away, pressing the daisy to her nose. When she hops too high, the bow clacks against the sunbaked road and receives damage than when the boy had used it as a walking stick.

Prince sighs and shakes his head, but can't help smiling at the girl's buoyant spirit.

As the children progress along the cobblestone road, Princess sings a song that Auntie had taught her. "Flap your wings good and fast, you good, good, strong birdy," she trills. "Fly up high among the clouds, you good, good, strong birdy." She then launches into the chorus line, singing, "Good, good, strong birdy," over and over.

"Is that the whole song?" Prince finally asks.

Halting, Princess looks at the squire in surprise. The little girl reaches inside her pocket and removes Setchra. "Yes, don't you like it?"

Prince removes his diamond and mocks her raspy Setchra voice, "Yes, but there has to be more to the song than 'good, good, strong birdy.'"

"Well, there isn't," Princess responds. She squeezes her pearl, wondering if Prince's diamond can talk to him the way Setchra talks to her.

"'Good, good, strong birdy' really are the lyrics?" Prince asks.

Princess scrunches her face. "What are 'lyrics?'"

"The lines in a song."

"I thought that was 'singing.'"

"Yes, but on a scroll, the singing goes in lines and is called lyrics," Prince informs her.

"Oh," she rolls her eyes and hops away again. "I can't read anyway, so I'll just call the *lilacs* 'singing.'"

"'Lyrics,'" Prince corrects, watching her skip onward.

With the sun still high in the sky, the pair moves along. Princess prances and sings while Prince limps forward, until Princess comes to an abrupt halt.

"That's it!" she exclaims, pointing to Auntie's cottage. Relief and excitement course through her veins as she spots the farm.

Prince sighs. "We had to arrive sooner or later." Removing his quiver, Prince passes the rose to Princess.

"Are you sure?" she asks.

He nods. "The diamond will be more than enough for me."

"You truly are noble," she says, taking the rose and handing Prince the centaur's bow.

"I don't know about noble," he shrugs off her compliment.

"Don't you want to meet Auntie?" Princess asks, stepping toward the cottage.

"No, I just want to get back home," Prince admits, rubbing the back of his neck.

"Farewell, then," Princess says.

"Farewell," Prince responds.

The two children stand for a moment, unsure of what to do. Finally, Prince turns to walk away. Before he can take a step, Princess grabs his arm, leans in, and plants a kiss on his cheek. Prince presses his hand to his face in shock, turning a bright shade of red.

"Silly squire," Princess laughs. She waves and runs toward Auntie's cottage.

Prince waves in return. "Farewell," he falters, then limps away with a boyish grin.

Hobbling down the path, Prince sees the alicorn appear over the treetops of the Dark Forest and fly toward him.

"For the love of everything good on this earth, please land!" Johnny protests.

"You came back!" Prince shouts.

"You noticed," Johnny responds, unheard by the boy.

The alicorn releases a boisterous whinny and lowers itself to the ground. It folds its feathery wings to its side and trots over to Prince.

"I'm so glad you came back," Prince exclaims, stroking the horse's snout.

"I'm glad you finally landed," Johnny gasps, collapsing in the alicorn's mane.

"I could use a little help," Prince admits, walking side by side with the colt. "That is, if you will permit me."

The winged colt stops and sniffs Prince.

Prince tentatively lifts his leg and attempts to mount the alicorn. The colt skirts away, snorting.

"Oh, come, now," Prince says in frustration. "I don't think I can walk one more step. Are you going to stand there and let me suffer?" The boy snaps his fingers and whistles for the horse to come back.

Rearing its head, the alicorn circles around Prince and stops right in front of him.

"That's more like it! A little gratitude never hurt anyone." Prince grabs a mane-full of hair and prepares to sling his legs over the alicorn. As soon as his thigh touches the colt's back, the alicorn neighs and trots off again. Prince stumbles over, grasping his side.

"Oh, forget it, you stupid horse! I should have let the centaur eat you!"

※※※

Outside the cottage, Arthur barks wildly.

"I heard you, Arthur," Auntie scowls at the door, wiping tears off her cheeks. She searches the countertop for something to throw at the obnoxious hound. Skipping over a lengthy kitchen knife, she settles on a squishy apple.

"Just one more bark and I will let you have it good and well."

"Arthur!" Princess cries. She blazes across the green grass toward the kitchen entrance.

Excited by her voice, Arthur barks louder, trying to alert his master.

From inside, Auntie shouts, "Have you gone mad, Arthur? Can't you let me alone with my grief? Cease barking this instant!" She comes to the door, flings it open. "Heckle me, will you?" Auntie charges. She hurls the apple just as Arthur lays down and covers his eyes with his paws.

"Oof!" The apple pegs Princess in the face, knocking her down.

"Ahh!" Auntie screams, slamming the door shut. "Phantom!" Auntie screeches. She shudders and begins wringing her hands. "You've summoned her ghost, you idiot," she curses Arthur.

Princess rubs her cheek and pulls away a sticky hand. "How could you hurt me? I love you!" Princess says. Shocked by Auntie's harsh reception, she begins to pout, holding her hand to her face.

Inside the cottage, Auntie presses firmly against the door and tries to slow her rapid breaths. *Could it really be her?* she wonders. She shakes her head in disbelief. "No child could survive a dragon attack. Be gone, phantom!"

"Phantoms are monsters, and monsters can't be in daylight!" Princess shouts back.

Auntie peeks through a crack in the door. "But your dress is covered in blood! Prove that you are who you say you are!"

"Well ... phantoms can't feel pain, and my face hurts!"

Auntie slowly opens the door. She scans Princess' face and sees a welt on her fleshy cheeks.

"It is you!" she comes to life and flings the door wide open with so much force that the door swings back and smacks her in the back of the head, knocking her down the steps.

"Oh, Auntie!" Princess leaps to her feet. She stretches out her hand and rubs Auntie's head. "You have to rub it!"

"Yes, you do!" Auntie answers, then laughs with tears in her eyes. "Rub it good and hard."

Auntie wraps her plump arms around Princess. "Thank you, Lord! Thank you so much! Princess, you've come home to Auntie," she sobs.

Auntie cups Princess' cheeks with her hands. When the sweet child looks her in the eye, Auntie discovers her irises sparkle with an unusual luster. Princess wipes a tear from her eye as another one breaks free from her cheek. Squinting curiously, Auntie watches the murky liquid fall from the little girl's jaw and transform into a diamond. When it falls to the ground, Auntie picks it up and holds it to her eye. Unable to believe what she sees, she looks Princess up and down. Spooked, Auntie grabs Princess' little hand and spits in it.

"Yuck! Why did you do that?"

"To ward off evil spirits! What happened to your eyes?"

"The fairy rose makes me cry diamonds," Princess explains, fresh diamond tears drop from her face as she presents the quiver to Auntie.

Auntie bends down and scoops up the gems with a wrinkled hand. She presses the diamonds between her fingers and looks up in awe. "Child, what has become of you?"

�

Prince hobbles along the trail singing, "Good, good, strong birdy, flap your wings high and...," he pauses and tries to remember the lyrics. Unable to recall the words, he shrugs and continues, "good, good, strong birdy."

With the sun now low in the sky, Prince works his way back to the castle, wishing he were already home. The squire hears the familiar sound of pheasants cooing. He struggles with an overwhelming desire to return home, but decides to complete his father's task. "Filthy fowl!"

He crouches slowly, trying to ignore the stabbing in his side. Pausing for a moment, he glimpses a pheasant in the waving grass. Removing an arrow from the centaur's quiver, he nocks it in the tight bow. He hunches over and waits for the pheasant to show itself. When the bird emerges, the boy struggles with the string, finding it much more difficult to pull back while squatting.

"I can't return empty-handed," he strains, tugging on the string. "I must honor my father!"

When his shaky arms align, he releases and watches the long arrow wobble toward the pheasant. It falls short, ricochets off the cobblestone road, then glances off the bird's plump chest. The pheasant tumbles over and lands on its back with its feet propped up in the air.

"Yes!" Prince celebrates. He hobbles over to the limp bird. "One is better than none!"

As he reaches down for his well-deserved trophy, the bird leaps to its feet and cocks its brown head to the side. Shocked, Prince jumps back. The bird lets out a high-pitched squawk, signaling several other pheasants to emerge from the grassy stalks. Without warning, the infuriated birds charge at Prince.

The squire yelps, turns on his heels, and runs as fast as he can.

The flock of pheasants closes on the boy's hobbling legs. They flap their wings and claw at his backside. The quills on their heads wave wildly as they land and peck at his ankles.

"Leave me alone!" Prince shouts, turning around and swinging his bow. He misses and tumbles to the ground. The pheasants converge on the top of his head and peck him repeatedly. He covers his face with his arms, but the birds move to his exposed side and nip at his ribs. The boy moves his arms to his sides and the birds seize the opportunity to leap in the air and claw furiously at his face. Waving his hands wildly, he backhands the leader and sends it flying. The flock follow their leader back into the grass, making a ruckus as they go.

"Be gone with you!" the boy screams. He pants and wipes beads of sweat from his forehead.

"I killed a cyclops, but I can't kill a bird!" he sniffles. The overwrought squire shifts to his knees and sobs. Burning shame courses through him and flows out in large tears.

"All I want to do," he heaves, "is make my father proud." He takes big gulps of air, gradually regaining his composure.

"Stupid bow." He glares at the bow and hurls it over his shoulder in disgust. He grips his side and struggles to get up, wiping burning tears from his eyes. He stands defeated, looking down at his empty hands. With a sigh, he turns around to retrieve his useless weapon.

Scanning the ground, a glint catches his attention. He looks up and shields his eyes. A short distance in front of him, a knight approaches in chrome armor that reflects the setting sun. The mounted knight wields a lengthy lance. His armor-plated horse stomps and lowers its head, revealing a golden lion's emblem on the knight's breast plate. The warrior presses his metal gauntlet to his pointed helmet and flips up the face shield, unmasking his identity.

"Oh no," Prince panics. "'Tis exactly as I feared." He starts to tremble, terrified to see his father in full battle dress.

Sir Cynric tosses his lance. The lengthy weapon rattles against the road.

Prince flinches and debates fleeing.

With a swift flick of his leg, the baron dismounts from his Clydesdale.

Prince shrinks back as his father steps forward, his metallic boots grinding on the cobblestone. A fierce look locks Prince in place. Cowering under his father's gaze, the boy hangs his head in shame.

"Forgive me father, but—" Prince holds up his arms, bracing for a beating, "I tried my best."

Cynric scoops up the wounded boy and presses him against his cold metal breastplate. Tears well in his eyes.

"Thank God you are alive!"

Prince finally allows himself to break down and melts into his father's embrace. Although still outside the stone castle, Prince is home.

※※※

The stillness of night casts a reverent peace over the kingdom. Torches flicker in the darkness, pulled and prodded by a subtle breeze. A half moon reflects ivory light. Protected by the castle walls, Prince rests in a soft feather bed. He nestles into the down and exhales in his sleep. Safe in Auntie's cottage, Princess shuffles on a straw mat and dreams of fairies and alicorns. It would be hard to imagine that the two children had escaped the horrors of the Dark Forest.

Behind the castle, near the royal garden, a pair of glowing yellow eyes look down at hairy hands covered in blood.

"What have I done?" a specter sneers, and frantically wipes away the crimson stickiness. The desperate creature stands to its towering height, leans back, and howls, "GOD FORGIVE ME, I'VE KILLED AGAIN!"

✖ -THE END- ✖

✕ ABOUT THE AUTHOR ✕

Henry Ranger (preferred name) is a wanderer and seeker of truth. An eclectic author, Henry chooses to live off the land as much as possible, and uses America's great rivers navigate and fish. Henry has lived an exceptional life with a diverse array of experiences that he, along with his friends, Pablo and Moonshine, share on his blog. As avid fishermen, the three travel together and enjoy adventures across the country. These journeys inspire and influence his writing.

Henry deeply appreciates your readership and welcomes any questions you may have. Feel free to contact him at: HRSeekerofTruth [at] gmail [dot] com

Made in the USA
Charleston, SC
01 November 2015